AN UNNAMED PRESS BOOK

Copyright © 2021 Keenan Norris

www.unnamedpress.com

Unnamed Press, and the colophon, are registered trademarks of Unnamed
Media LLC.

ISBN: 978-1-951213-25-1
eISBN: 978-1-951213-27-5

Library of Congress Control Number: 2021933983

Designed and Typeset by Jaya Nicely

Manufactured in the United States of America by Sheridan, Inc.

Distributed by Publishers Group West

First Edition

THE CONFESSION OF COPELAND CANE

A NOVEL

KEENAN NORRIS

The Unnamed Press
Los Angeles, CA

THE CONFESSION
OF COPELAND CANE

Jacqueline

Don't worry about who I am. Like Copeland would say, don't vex, or do it on your own time and about yourself. Don't vex me. I have enough to worry about all by myself. I stayed up all night last night with my thoughts, and on this sleepless morning they are still with me. Maybe I should say yes, yes, I'll make this recording and risk my reputation and possibly my freedom in the process, or maybe I should tell him to turn himself in, make sure to text it to him, put it in writing so that law enforcement doesn't go getting its black people confused.

Who am I? I could say more about myself, but it would only reveal my methods of misdirection. The real tell is what I decide to do with this dilemma that that boy has decided to drop into my voicemail like an orphan child onto my doorstep. If I put my student journalist suit on, there's no way I can say no to the wailing child. Not when his story has all but knocked on my door and asked me to tell it. Not when his story could make my career before I've even made it out of college—and all I have to do is hit record. That's a question, not a statement—that's all I have to do?

I have no idea what to do, let alone what comes next, only that Cope's got to talk to someone, got to tell his story to someone (to everyone?). After all, law enforcement via Soclear* has wasted no time telling theirs:

> Early reports indicate that the remaining fugitive is a male between ages fifteen and twenty-five. African American. Athletic build. Has a history of criminal behavior as a juvenile. Investigators are reviewing his records.

A second bulletin states that if he does not turn himself in before their next scheduled briefing in two days' time that they will bring charges. They might charge a single individual or multiple persons, maybe with one crime, maybe with multiple crimes. The public wants answers, so apparently everything is on the table. The timetable is even on the table; charges might come sooner.

---

* Soclear Broadcasting: America. Politics. Business. Alert Desks.

One part of me doesn't want to involve myself in this. Another tells me that I'm already involved, that there's no way not to be involved. Maybe being black means there is no means of escape. I'm always implicated, even when I have no connection to the crime, even when it's only my heart that keeps me here thinking, questioning, fighting myself over freedom.

Like, I know what the Fourth of July wasn't to the slave, but what's freedom to me? I think Cope is probably freer than I am. At least he's not scared of the surveillance state. Even if his fearlessness is all from ignorance, it's still more than I can say for myself. Confession: I've never participated in a proper street protest. In justifying this terrible apathy, I excuse myself by saying the same things that most people say, which is that even if I had picked up a sign and marched somewhere in a crowd of like-minded, angry people, there would probably be more police than protestors once we got where we were going, and, another excuse, that large crowds hive contagion, and, to top it off, that the merger of certain major media with the surveillance state simply isn't worth messing with. Oh, and that it isn't 2020 anymore, that everything is so different now—even though so many things are the same. (I mean, in fairness, there have been some changes. The city within a city that I once called home did go private. Its public school turned private, making Piedmontagne even more exclusive than it already was. Then the private police showed up. At first you would see one here, one there, in some weird uniform, standing guard in front of the custom courtyard gating of a mansion. Then the compounds went up, neighboring the mansions, and I started to see more and more cops in private security colors, usually a menacing corporate insignia flush upon black fabric, but other times nothing, no identification at all.)

At college, my Media Studies professors tell me that the merger of network news with national security has been so subtle and so slow that now that it's happened, now that it's in place, its omnipresence escapes notice. One ancient professor whose name is on a textbook tells us that everything in America is the will of the people. That our capitalist system, its outcomes, is the decentralized voice of all 375 million of us. That we actually desire this new COINTELPRO or we wouldn't be liking and hearting and clicking on all this crap. I took that argument in, and at first, I thought the woman most likely needed to retire, but then I thought how simple yet fathomless her thesis was, how much it implicated me and everyone else, and then my brain started decentralizing, flying apart like a Frisbee fracturing as it's flung across the campus lawn. I came to the next morning, my face planted in the book that the professor has her name on, which we were studying for her class, of course. I felt painfully out of my depth or above my pay grade or whatever cop-out makes most sense, and I still feel that way—like I'm copping out out of ignorance, like all I know are the questions that I have wandered into. So why's Cope calling me?

That boy. He's out there, phoning me like fear of arrest doesn't factor into his equation. Like fear is foreign to him, which I know it's not. Maybe he knows something I don't and has figured out how to evade the police and the news, but I doubt it. As for me, I'm careful beyond careful not to state whether I'm contemplating my innocence in a studio apartment, or a small condo, or a town home, or a student hostel. And my city shall remain undisclosed, thank you. I police myself better than the police ever could. Here, how about I play detective on myself, interrogate my own imagination. Where might I be? How about an unaccounted-for New York City cellar? Underground, literally. Like Cope's phone, I'm old school: I testify under penalty of perjury that I am me and the Pharcyde is on the phonograph. I'm smoking the finest California Kush, so good they might recriminalize it. Meanwhile I've strung LED lights across the perimeter of the ceiling to illumine me to myself.

That story makes more sense than the other one repeating itself in my thoughts. That story is the one where I tell Copeland to play it safe, turn himself in, and prove his innocence in court. As soon as that story starts to take hold and I make my mind up to call him back and tell him what to do, I hear laughter, loud, deep laughter. I'm laughing, but it's not my laugh, not my tenor at all that I'm hearing; it's something from the insides of the city instead, a boy laughing through the streets and my body so loudly that all I can hear is him, and his laughing becomes crying and crying becomes testifying, and he calls out through me to me: *Ain't shit safe, girl!*

Cope

They already arrested Keisha, Free, and DeMichael, snatched them up easy cuz Soclear done searched out they location. And then law enforcement did that criminal contact-tracing thing, followed them from they phones and whatnot, bagged them up. Long as we're talkin' technology, boss, you might as well know my audio comes to you unencrypted in this bootleg ol' Pre-sage voice app, the most off-brand, unheard-of cell phone app you will ever encounter. It calls itself the Cayman Islands of apps. Don't ask how I got this mess on my phone, but it's all yours truly gots to work with right now, so you might have to trust me on this one, even if you're not trying to trust this technology.

Real talk, Jacq: I only ask that the people hear me all the way out. It won't jeopardize y'all no kinda way, except maybe in y'all's feelings. I cain't tell you about your heart, Jacq. But I'ma tell you what's in mines. Nobody wanna hear why shit hit such a swerve and went so left, but the fact is it was all kinda facts done built up to the one big fact—excuse me, edit that—the one pivotal incident that everybody and they momma cares so much about: the crime in question, the weed that worked its way up from spoilt soil to choke the chief gardener.

Now I'm giving testimony the only way I know how without having Mr. Miranda's rights read to me. I'm making a real record right now not just of how that man got got, but about everything that got me here, Copeland Cane, the alleged accomplice, the fugitive, the ghost, the rabbit, the radiated, the remediated, medicated, incarcerated, the child who fell outta Colored People Time and into America, the whole deal, to go against the apex predator they steady creating me into on the news feed every five minutes.

And fair warning, I tend to tell three stories to tell one and get sidetracked sometimes, but I'ma try and not do that shit.

*

Since they wanna go and air me out for everything I done did since I done crawled out the crib, here's some back in the day: I'm Copeland Cane V, but it's probably more'n five of me in our history, we just don't have the records on all that. They say the name comes from a plantation, the Copeland plantation in Louisiana, and that after slavery ended my people came with that given name to Oklahoma, Greenwood, and, yes, my folks' folks' folks' folks' folks did get torched up out that mug when the white people went and burnt up Black Wall Street, murdering three hundred some people of the sun. At least that's why I believe they left. I know for a fact the fam fled out that bitch on account of somethin' mean June 1921—them and all of Oakland's Oklahoma ancestors done came out west, no turn backs, not one piddlin' pillar of salt left behind, as Daddy would say.

But now that old man does look back, and he blames hisself like my predicament can be put down to his parenting. But, real spiel Curt Flood Field, deep in the heart of East Oakland that old man's always been around for me, which is more'n most kids can count on from they father, even if, truth be told, mines was too much around for me. Yes, back in the day, Daddy had me surrounded. He was everything to me, even if, by the accounting of the government, he barely existed, having no employment, no property, no credit, just a Social Security number and a name. When it came to work, he stayed unemployed, or he stayed employing hisself, mostly unsuccessfully, which ain't much different, am I right?

Now, don't get it twisted, the old man was a hard worker. Had him his tools, his parts and pieces, plots and plans drawn up and scribbled down on Post-it notes and loose sheets of paper that was scattered round the apartment like so many surprises. He was an inventor, you dig. His mind never rested, and never let me rest neither. On God, Jacq, any hour I wadn't in school had me on work detail. Inventors need laborers, after all, so I served as Daddy's workforce no matter the project. Sweep that porch. Go pass out these flyers. Knock on them doors. Haul this water. Run tell that to him/her/them/the man on the telephone/the customer over there/the icy motherfucker with the permits and the mad on 'bout any and everything east of downtown. And while you're at it, dodge a hungry stray dog or two. Wadn't no money in it neither. Once in a blue, the old man would throw me a couple cowry shells: *Here, just so you don't go hollerin' to yo' teacher or momma about no slavery; don't go askin' for no salary, though, that food on yo' plate, clothes on yo' back, and roof over yo' head is CEO money, damn near. Focus, boy,* he would say, *we tryna make somethin' of ourselves.*

From this young sahab's perspective, my old man's vo-cation made about as much sense as Arabic. Wadn't nobody else's father trying to invent anything when the post office was hiring and shit. But with time and experience, now I see his inventions as the natural response to an East Oakland existence, what with all the tests and experiments and other mess we done had ran on us—what else could a man do but start experimenting his own self? If the old man had a problem, it wadn't his career choice, it was that he wanted to make more of hisself'n the world would allow: Daddy dreamt of uplifting our neighborhood and overcoming it all at once, making millions off a code-switching app, a black business magnet, and anything else you couldn't think of but he could. But selling dreams to broke folks who ain't seen inside they eyelids in who knows how long—well, suffice it to say, Daddy's dreams was always a little outside his reach.

Meanwhile, Rockwood remained well within our grasp: the Rock, that towering old East Oakland apartment complex, which, like Daddy, didn't fit the description. Understand, Rockwood was not *the hood*. Not in the 2010s, it wadn't. That whole line about our buildings being Oakland's last housing project, which they sold us all the way to the wrecking balls, that woulda been news to us residents back in the day when I was knee-high to a Nike shoe. To the contrary, the Rock was actually tranquilo.

Come to think of it, I'm not sure if we was even all that poor, or if the city just got too damn expensive, but most folks had lost jobs in '20, found worse ones in '21, and ain't really recover since. Those losses alone labeled our neighborhood. But it wadn't a homeless camp on every corner back in the day. And wadn't all these compounds for rich folk just flaunting they wealth right in front of us. The wealthy was strictly segregated to downtown back then. And with it being less of the extremes in the streets, it wadn't so common for folks to covet the next man's bag, let alone for them to gank it at gunpoint. We lived in an apartment complex, not a housing project; a neighborhood, not a quarantine zone. It was only as I got older and the housing projects nearby, buck-wild Ravenscourt and the rest, was razed that the place where we lived was deemed guilty by its disassociation from the future of the city, from this future state that don't even wanna include us. But it wadn't always like this. In the beginning, Oakland was rough, sho nuff, but Soclear and that thing y'all call America was a million miles away. As long as we played it close, life and death felt safe on the Rock.

---

*Insurgency Alert Desk, Third Bureau: In keeping with the public trust bestowed upon it, Soclear Broadcasting is compelled to issue the equivalent of a community charter to the citizens of the country that it serves. Amid the political and environmental shocks of the previous decade, members of the American armed forces and government surveillance systems experts teamed with Soclear Corporation to establish the Insurgency Alert Desk to more effectively communicate information about domestic terrorist threats by providing timely, detailed information to the American public about the dangers that must be combatted.

The journalists of the Insurgency Alert Desk are only one part of Soclear Broadcasting's print, online, social media, and televisual universe. We deliver to a greater degree than any other news organization in world history all the news of consequence fit and unfit for print, from government communiqués to breaking bulletins to deeply embedded reporting on politics and business. The most influential network and media empire in American history, Soclear has been without peer in viewership and online traffic in the decade since the upheavals of 2020. According to a 2028 Brand Keys Influencer report, Soclear ranked as the brand most instrumental in shaping American public opinion. The research and analysis company also named Soclear as the top brand in the country for morning and evening political commentary in its Consumer Loyalty Engagement Index, while a 2029 Hoover Institution poll found Soclear to be the most trusted source nationally for political coverage. Owned by Soclear Corporation, Soclear Broadcasting has risen above the rest in an era of crisis to dominate the American news and opinion landscape.

+Urban Dictionary: Soclear: 1) Having come to national prominence in the wake of the White House insurrection with the express purpose of providing far right–wing journalism on terrorist and insurgency threats, Soclear has expanded into a comprehensive American news and entertainment media organization valued at upward of $30 billion; 2) Founded by Stephen Miller and having come to national prominence in the wake of the *8:46 protests and riots, Soclear is a multilayered media and security organization that exploits factional conflicts in the American government and municipal police departments to advance its authoritarian, racist, xenophobic agenda; 3) Sieg Heil.

Rockwood didn't have no elementary school, though, so when the quarantine came down and schools opened back up, we were sent away: each morning seen us sent several blocks off to a below-code campus where we learnt numbers, cut up the King's English, and forgot what innocence was.

The day stands out, unforgettable even if I was tryna get it out my memory: there I was, minding my own damn business, a child small and skinny and sentenced to the shadows. You see, for a second grade grasshopper like myself, being big and strong, but slow, woulda been just fine. Everyone would know not to test me, or if they did, they woulda social distanced while they did it—outta arm's reach at the very least. Small, slim, and fast would work, too—I'da been good at the games kids play by juking dodge balls, two-hand-touch tacklers, and queer smeerers. What does not work is small and skinny and slow, especially if you done been moved ahead one grade class because of some test you took 'fore you knew how to read. That's what I was, a child ahead of his time, a kid cursed with lankiness and littleness and so dead on my feet that I couldn't catch a cold butt-neked at the wharf after dark. So I was always picked in that last pocket of losers.

That's why on that fateful day, the day my life began, I wadn't doing no more'n my usual, playin' the background, avoidin' competition like my existence depended on it. But the great DeMichael Quantavius Chesnutt Bradley, who was in my same grade but wouldn't so much as glare in my di-rection most days, was having none of it.

"Aiiiyo," DeMichael, who was almost the size of a grown man, commanded, "you in the race now."

Put a question mark on the end of that if you feel like it, just know it ain't always the tone of the voice, let alone the words being said; sometimes it's the size of the speaker and whether that boy has a reputation for puttin' paws on people that's the issue. DeMichael had that rep and he was actually twice my size, a great big, broad-shouldered child with frying pans for hands. Word was he had already been held back a grade, but a year's growth in no way explained young Black Hercules. You see, I grew up pulling up old clips from the Cartoon Network where house pets killed whole families, kids committed war crimes, and whatnot. So it was easy to imagine

DeMichael as the Complected Hercules who might actually tear my head from my torso if I told him, *Nah, nigga, I don't wanna run, I'ma just be chillin' right here in a private meeting with myself.*

"Get in on this, family," DeMichael encouraged, or threatened.

The other runners, Keisha, Free, Trey, Miguel—these wadn't regular schoolchildren, now. Keish was tall than a mug and had the longest stride I had ever seen. I was pretty sure she could outrun me just by stretching. Free was half her height and half Egyptian, but everything else about them was one and the same. They loved the same music, kept the same crushes, got sent home the same day for wearing the same bloodstained *8:46 shirts to school and shit. Trey was tall and athletic, too, but he was the opposite of both them girls as soon as recess ended; bruh didn't care about none of that back-in-the-day stuff, no politics, history, or anything else had to do with a book. And then there was Miguel, whose daddy got deported and still cain't get back in the country. They mighta came up in chaos, but somethin' good had got in they water, cuz these kids was no less than the future stars of every sport. Keisha and Free could run, Trey could run and hoop. Miguel seemed to be good at everything. Each of them was destined for domination. They would doubtless leave your boy in the dust, dust up to my eyeballs. I pictured my body post-race, a dusty, old mummy cast in last place forever like the people at Pompeii cased up in ash.

I stared at them from my shade tree. The handball wall where they was gettin' ready was flush white with smogless sunlight. They stood out black and tan, tall and short, boys and girls. But they all had wings for feet. It had rained the day before and there was still dew in the dark places, under trees and in the shadows cast by everything above us. I liked to play those spaces anyway, but the seldom few days of rain and the day right after the rain when everything was still shadowy and cool I loved even more. I didn't understand athletes, the way they let the sun beat on them, how they wailed away at they own bodies with invented torments.

Of course lookin' back now, I realize that we ran for a reason. Yeah, every game requires running, but it went well beyond that. We was still supposed to be staying seven feet apart back then, and the simplest game kids can play without touching, tackling, or smearing each other is to race, so running was encouraged by our institutions. But it was what the institutions didn't give a thought to that really had us on the run. With the hard times and low funds, the school district had sold off all its yellow school buses, which meant we sometimes took the public transit, when it wadn't running late or was so crowded grown-ass men body blocked us back to the street. Shameful as shit and frequent as the morning sun, we was forced to make a run for it. We booked it along boulevards under billboards that advertised all the things our families couldn't dream to afford, sprinted through vacant lots and warehouse back alleys, hopped fences and trespassed private properties, and played the angles between the front and back bumpers of cars gridlocked in traffic. Our teachers understood why they pupils was always late, but that didn't stop them from marking us down by the minute for our tardiness, so we ran to stay enrolled, and naturally necessity became the way we played, which made sense since all our games was really just a way to get ready for the world.

I was fittin' to face the world hecka slow-footed and complected, a bad combination when you consider all the scrapes we people of the sun find ourselves in.

"Time to run," DeMichael ordered.

I moped over to the wall and watched as the others knelt like ready predators, bodies planked perpendicular above drawbridge lever arms. I watched as shoulder muscles children ain't even supposed to have flexed with weightless waiting, each hand shaped an empty pyramid against the gravel, and sneakers beat battle drums against the concrete wall.

I copied. Kneeling, I imagined I was a character, not in a cartoon clip but in one of them video games I couldn't afford, was too scared to steal, and anyway would never have Daddy's blessing to play. "ON YOUR MARKS," DeMichael called from where he knelt, ready to race as well, the fifth predator, and I was just prey in the game, a peasant 'bout to be pillaged in *Assassin's Creed: DeMichael de' Medici*, a prostitute fittin' to get iced in *Grand Theft Auto: International Boulevard*. "GET SET," he said, even though I was still just figuring out what to do with my feet. "GO!"

I stood straight up, and like always everyone was two steps clear of me 'fore I even started moving. Trey took the lead. Miguel, who was beautiful, flew right behind him, and Keisha, taller'n all of us, taller'n a teacher or two, Usain Bolt–ed right after them. Free was short and small, but her legs rapidly disappeared into a whirling rainbow of green and orange and purple shorts and socks and shoes. The color wheel fled ahead and I gave up as usual, and then I caught an image of some interest from the corner of my eye—big, slow-ass DeMichael was lookin' at me and I was lookin' at him, and we was tied stride for stride, and then I was giving myself the beginnings of whiplash from trying to hold his gaze as he fell back from my pace. And now I was striding, knees up and out, proper form, and Miguel, who gave up winning the race and relaxed into less than a sprint, was coming back to me, too. I was close enough to him to see sweat sparkling the braided rope of brown hair that swung behind him. Keisha and Trey and Free flew away, and the dirt and grass and ants and bees that they shoveled up with each back kick freckled my face. I closed my eyes and imagined Miguel's Rapunzel braid flying away and his toy head buckin' back and forth. I thought how I had broke every toy my parents had ever bought me. Not outta anger, just experiments—how far could my plastic superhero fly when I threw dude? How fast could the toy car go when I revved it hecka hard? Whatever happened to that one with the wings and—never mind.

Keisha won, like always. Trey finished second, outrun at the very end once again. Free spun into third. And Miguel finished fourth. I was a fabulous fifth, but way ahead of DeMichael, who admitted afterward that he only made me run cuz he didn't feel like finishing last. He didn't expect that I would outrun him.

After the race, he pulled me by the arm so hard I thought I would come completely apart. It woulda been some shit. Boy succeeds for the first time ever at anything his daddy didn't make him do, next minute he goes and gets hisself killed by a mutant ten-year-old: "Youngblood Stomped Out Just for Living."

"You gotsta make one of, ya know, the other kids race," he campaigned. "One of them slow friends you got."

With my free hand, I wiped the crap off my face. I couldn't make nobody do nothin'. I was thrilled I was faster'n DeMichael and scared of what he might still do with my arm. Keisha was walking back toward the tree balancing pebbles on the fingertips of her left hand and flicking them at Free with her free hand. Free ducked the pebbles like Muhammad Ali—no nerdy awkward slaps, no scared squinting eyes, just calm, cool fakes and feints—and she somehow kept talkin' trash the whole time, too, tellin' Keish how she was just tall and lucky to be that fast for a giraffe. I wanted to be that kind of cool.

Meanwhile, DeMichael hadn't let go of my arm.

"I cain't make nobody race if they don't want to," I whined, no Ali in me.

"Yes, you can."

"No, I cain't."

He stared at me. This was going nowhere.

"Nah. How?"

"Family, just tell 'em I'ma kill 'em if they don't. Ain't hard." If Free was Ali, DeMichael Quantavius Chesnutt Bradley was Mike Tyson crossed with a Glock.

He let go of my arm, and then he balled his fists kinda playfully and circled me and threw a couple jabs my way. They thudded painless, playful against my stiff shoulders, the light in his eyes surprising. He was just playin'. It dawned on me then that DeMichael had no intentions on hurting me.

*

I had running buddies after that—not in the sense of a kid with a crew of dudes who squad out wherever the leader orders them to go. Copeland Cane's never been enough of a boss to snap my fingers and have disciples at my beck and call like that. I literally mean these jokers found it in they hearts to run with me. At recess. Around Rockwood. On the few and far between occasions when Daddy allowed me outside for somethin' other'n unpaid labor. Now when we ran to and from school, I wadn't running in my lane alone. We ran together, clowned, dozened, zigzagged into each other's paths, figured out how fast we could fly by foot while talkin' each other up at the same time. They had much more to say than I did. Where my siblings was all step-kids in Inglewood, they had the wisdom of eleven- and twelve-year-old elders at home to school them on knockin' boots without making babies, ancient medicine marijuana, black god math and religion, and what it's like when your fish start to swim or, for Keisha and Free, when you get your first cycle, not to mention breasts, butts, and bras.

Keisha had a coin that her orisha cousin gave to her as a birthday gift. It was silver colored, and on the front was a shield partway encircled by a wreath of leaves. On the back was a star, and the words that surrounded the star said some stuff in Spanish about freedom or somethin', but Keisha insisted it was an ancient Swahili token from the lands of Timbuktu. Free said that that couldn't be cuz Timbuktu is in a whole 'nother part of Africa from the Swahili lands and, besides, ain't no Spanish spoken in Africa. To which Keisha came back that Free was always frontin' like a know-it-all cuz she was light-bright and almost Arab. To which Free conceded, OK, it probably was from Timbuktu Swahili if Keisha would let each of us hold it for one en-tire school day. That convinced Keisha of the greatness of her possession. So the following week each of us—Free, Miguel, Trey, even DeMichael, even me—got to hold the coin the whole school day and only returned it to Keish after we ran home to the Rock.

*

One of them days after recess raced away with us and the bell to go back to class rang, we dipped back into the little classroom, everyone except for Free, who stayed outside to say her prayers, and DeMichael, who I figured was praying to the ditch day gods cuz he was nowhere to be seen as soon as I left him in the dust during our daily race. I did my own thing: sat in the back of the room, last row, Jim Crow, just so I wouldn't appear too eager to be taught. Stupid, I know, but I'm giving you true details, not no dreamt up story shaded a certain way to make me look like somethin' I'm not. Two rows in front of me, Trey fell asleep as soon as his butt hit his chair, his head angling down into the bony pillow of his shoulder. Keisha sat up front in the middle seat. Even sitting down, she sat up straight and was a full head higher'n all us boys. Miguel, meanwhile, sat in the middle row, where three lovestruck girls tended to his braids. They giggled as the teacher talked. Free's praying shadow rose from the ground and her actual body walked back inside and sat down in the seat next to Keisha. Her posture was perfect, just like Keisha's. The teacher told the girls behind Miguel they needed to stop all that giggling or go outside. And then, without no warning, a woman burst into class in shrieks and hollers. She bug-eyed the room. Them eyes of hers terrified me, as did the tat on her throat that looked like a stenciled scar. Her Baghdad blowout hair shot straight up from her scalp. She paced around the front of the class mumbling to herself, and wadn't no one trying to talk to her or touch her, cuz not only was she talkin' to herself, she was bigger'n everyone in class, including our teacher, Ms. MacDonald, who was this small, extension-cord-thin, squirrelly-lookin' lady with all the traits you'd expect of a second grade teacher: young, female, so white she probably thought mayonnaise was spicy. She even wore her mask perfectly and at all times, where the other teachers took theirs off as soon as the classroom door was closed.

Ms. MacDonald woulda been altogether too nice and too square for Oakland, except for them three tats she sported: one read NAMASTE in looping green letters, the second was an elephant in lotus position, and the third said ANARCHY. Ain't nobody in the town a full four-sided square, not even the teachers. Half the class had practically dropped out the school during the shutdowns, when everything went online except for the kids who didn't have no one tellin' them to stay in they books. Now those kids were having a hard time with reading, writing, and wanting to be back in school. The other half of the class was like me, playing along like we hated school, too, meantime loving it on the low. But nobody, no matter how far they had fell behind, had a problem with Ms. MacDonald. So when the troubled woman made a straight line for her at the head of the class, being heroes and whatnot, we kids just froze like it was winter in a cold world.

The woman stopped mumbling and pacing and faced Ms. MacDonald. She got real quiet, and then she lunged and snatched the mask right off of Ms. MacDonald's face. She struck at our teacher and both women went flying against the wall. The next thing I remember is a gang of flailing, open-handed scratching and smacking. Blood studded the whiteboard, slurring the spelling lesson that had just started. We stared like we was hypnotized. The women fell this way and that. Ms. MacDonald was the one screaming now, not to mention fighting for her life just as much as the crazy woman was trying to end it, or whatever it was she wanted to do. What the woman wanted no one knew, but the fight rolled on, bouncing off the front wall with the whiteboard to the walls on each side, like three-dimensional ping-pong. They battled back to the head of the class, where Ms. MacDonald stood when she taught us, but now the big woman had took hold of Ms. MacDonald's bird neck and was going to town strangling the shit outta her. We, the students, finally came to. Somebody threw a book at the attacker. It missed.

"Punch her, Ms. MacDonald!" someone yelled. "In the stomach!"

Ms. MacDonald couldn't do that. Her hands went limp and fell open at her sides, and her face turnt paler'n it knew it could get.

"Kill the bitch!" someone cried, and for a second it wadn't clear whose side they was on. Then Keisha threw her old, eaten-up textbook and it caught the assailant in the ribs, which loosened her hold on Ms. MacDonald's neck. Ms. MacDonald began fighting back again. She elbowed the crazy woman somewhere sensitive and the woman wailed, "It's ants on me! Help me! It's ants in my skin! Cain't you help me? Why cain't you help?!"

Her cry activated me and I jumped up and jetted for the door. I could hear others following me. I raced ahead and other feet followed. We became one big, bootleg relay team racing for the principal's office. It was a short distance, maybe two hundred meters, maybe three hundred. Keisha and Trey caught up to me, but I was really running now and not even they could pass me. We burst thru Principal Morgan's double doors all at once.

"HELLLLLP!"

"Ms. MacDonald is getting strangled!"

"Gettin' killt!"

"Killed?" Principal Morgan peered over his mask at us.

I looked around the unorganized office space, gangs of files in folders on the floor, papers stacked like decks of cards about to be shuffled, and the boy serving out detention in the corner. DeMichael sat there, his body tilted against the wall in a cynical gangster lean. He looked up curious at the crowd that had formed. "Killed?" he parroted Principal Morgan.

"Killt!"

"You should come," I said di-rectly to DeMichael. Kinda blurted it out like I ain't know how to ask politely for things. Then I caught myself. I had never ordered nobody to do nothin' 'fore that day, and here I was tellin' DeMichael of all people what to do. I braced for somethin' bad to happen, but all big homie did was nod his head and look to Principal Morgan.

"Can I?" DeMichael asked.

Principal Morgan lowered his mask and breathed heavy. Adults always seemed to know what was what. Even if they couldn't fix it, they understood what the problems were and why the situation was hopeless. But not Principal Morgan. I could tell by his pancake face that he understood way less about what was going on than we did and it might take too long to get him up to speed. He looked over at DeMichael, then back at us. "Yes, DeMichael," he decided, "you should come help."

So we dashed back to the classroom. My lungs burnt with the taste of hot pennies and trampled dust. I leapt thru the open classroom door and was the first to try to jump on the woman, which meant I was the first to realize that tusslin' with a dope fiend ain't easy. She backhanded me to the ground and the left side of my face smacked the cold tile floor. I rolled over onto my side, curled up to protect myself, and watched the drama unfold from a fetal position. Big Keisha and little Free took they turns wrestling the woman and did a little better, probably on account of not being newborns. But they still was just kids, so she banked them both back into infancy as Principal Morgan, who was still in the womb, hung back like a bitch. Finally, after Trey was chucked aside, DeMichael moved in. The woman hesitated as he approached; she wadn't counting on no full-grown man confronting her. Before she could defend herself, DeMichael threw a right cross that started in San Francisco, crossed the bridge, and made contact with a quaking bone-on-bone crack—a terrifying frozen moment in time. The woman jerked back and went to bed 'fore she hit the floor. Everyone just sorta went still wherever we stood, or in my case curled up, except for Ms. MacDonald, who was gasping back to life and returning to her European complexion. Then old dead-leg Principal Morgan made the next move. Old man got on his cell phone and called the po-lice cuz I think that was the only thing he knew how to do, call in the authorities. "Multiple assaults. Children and adults in danger," he rattled off, eager than a muhfucka for the cops to arrive, which is sorta suspect for a black man, just my opinion.

Meanwhile, the assailant lay motionless, limbs lying at wrong angles and whatnot, like a Macy's mannequin dropped from the fifth floor. Keisha and Free got up slow, dusting theyselves off, making sure they bodies still worked. I stayed laid out at eye level with the woman, watching her for signs of life. I heard a low gargle and then the sound of wind pressed thru too tight a space. She was snoring.

I think we was still staring slack-jawed when the po-lice showed up. They hustled into the classroom, five or six of them cats. From my front row seat on the floor, I seen DeMichael slide off into a corner of the classroom. He kept patting at the hand he hit the lady with like it was broke or scuffed or somethin'. The cops cuffed up homegirl even though she was slept dead away from that punch. Threw her body around like she was some dumpster trash, like she wadn't still alive and snoring even though her snores reverberated the walls of the classroom. Then one of the mofos asked Morgan who had did the damage, and Morgan looked up and down and around till he seen DeMichael. I was expecting them to give him a hero's welcome, maybe place a badge on him and promise him a job in some Hollywood, magical-ending type of stuff. But this was the hood, not Hollywood, so them niggas walked up on him with batons drawn, had him turn and face the wall and put his hands behind his back and shit, and then they cuffed cousin no different'n they cuffed the criminal, and later when I found it in me to stand up and look out the window as they left, I seen them put both of them in the same squad car. It was so shady, blood.

We ended up leaving school late and missing the bus back to Rockwood.

Wadn't no big deal, we was late for everything. We just did what we always did when the city forgot about us: me and my friends, if I could call them that, jetted thru our alleyways, jumped over our fences, ran underneath billboards and in between gridlocked cars. There was just no DeMichael following behind us now.

Rumors flew around about what happened to big bruh, rumors that the po-lice actually charged DeMichael with a crime, sent him to juvie behind saving Ms. MacDonald's life, rumors which, lookin' back on it now, I take to be true because the boy did disappear on us for quite a time after the incident. I was a kid, so it all kinda washed over me back-day. But knowing what I know now about the way the world works, I suspect DeMichael really did catch a case that day. The perils of Young Black Hercules, I suppose. The moral of the story is: being a hero idn't the way to go, let the lady die. Keep your cape in the closet. Don't try that Luke Cage shit in real life. It might just cost you a chunk out your childhood.

In them early days, we bore witness, never testified, lived and learnt and forgot the lessons. The crackhead came and went. Ms. MacDonald took a week off to heal from her injuries and then she returned, same as ever, still our favorite teacher despite her weird white girl ways. Business returned to usual. Even DeMichael would be back around eventually, bigger and badder'n before, and quieter and less playful, too. But I never did spend time thinkin' about it, not back then. The world was simple, as was Copeland Cane. The po-lice and our principal were bad. And so was crack. And to mess with Black Hercules was to mess with your very life.

---

*Insurgency Alert Desk, Third Bureau: Soclear Broadcasting exercises tremendous tact when considering what we put on our airwaves, keeping first and foremost the prerogatives of our nation's security organizations and the health, safety, and security of the American people. As a result, the Insurgency Alert Desk has as its policy that we do not release what law enforcement deems excessively detailed reports of heinous crimes. In our mission to serve the American people, we report that information which is necessary to the public welfare. We do not release information that

We were not a family of street protestors. No *8:46 marches for us back in the day. No, ma'am. When them streets started talkin', we hushed up. Daddy's notion of safety meant our family stayed our butts at home whenever protests about anything sparked off anywhere in town. Which might be why my worldview was so simple—I stayed home.

In that small apartment home where I was sheltered, the old man never missed a chance to go dark mode on me and Momma. The same po-lice who had welcomed white terrorists into the White House and the Capitol Building on live TV would shoot black people dead for talkin' outta turn to them, or staying silent when told to speak, or standing still in a suburb, or moving too much while being beat down. Wadn't none of these protests finna change none of that.

"The same old bullshit," he would declare. "Y'all don't know how it go. But I do. I'm older'n the both of you combined."

Which wadn't quite true, he wadn't *that* old. But we would nod our heads nevertheless, just so he would feel like he had proved his point. But the only thing that proves anything is time. Look at me now, got

---

glamorizes those individuals who commit mass shootings, extremists who commit acts of political terror or insurgency, or those who foment dissent against the United States of America. While striving behind the scenes to uncover the truth through all the considerable means at our disposal, we do not and will not publicly interview their friends and family for the purposes of show and spectacle. We do not publish their baby and graduation pictures. We will not risk personalizing and romanticizing these individuals simply to drive ratings.

Once their mobile devices have been tracked and their contacts have been traced and the individual has been brought to justice, there will never again be the imperative to identify them. Soclear Broadcasting refrains from referring to them by name but instead simply says that they are "the accused" or "the assailant," except on occasions when the individual is brought to court, is being indicted on criminal charges, or is standing trial for their crimes. Their name will effectively disappear from these airwaves. Soclear Broadcasting and the Insurgency Alert Desk pledge to the American security apparatus and to the American people to never personalize any individual who is suspected of committing criminal acts against the state or who is suspected of organizing protest actions against the state.

+Insurgency Alert Desk, Third Bureau: Copeland Cane V was first entered into the California Gang Member Database on his first birthday. He was subsequently removed from the database at the age of five due to an algorithm error. It appears that he was reentered into the database only after he became criminally involved as a teenager.

these fools wanting me dead or in jail, and they'a tell you to your face it ain't personal, it's the law—the old man got that one right.

But back in the day, his declarations had us headed for the door any ex-cuse we could find. Like when my hairline slanted even slightly offline and Daddy went on a tear, Momma would use my grooming as her reason to hustle me exit stage out the apartment and off the Rock and over to the old Nation of Islam barbershop on MacArthur and Eighty-Third. I swear, that barbershop and the swap meet became our little hideout from the hopeless politics of our people.

'Fore I go any further, please understand that visiting the Nation barbershop had nothin' to do with religion. Do not get it twisted, Momma was no more a Muslim than she was the president. A Bible and hella pessimism is all that lady got faith in far as I can tell. But she admired the Muslims' ways, they black suits, clean white undershirts, red bow ties, red, black, and green face masks, and the fact that rain or shine they was always on time. No funny business with the Muslims, they ain't try and push up and flirt with her or leave for ten minutes halfway thru a cut to smoke a blunt or bet the Sunday football games. They could be counted on to be neat and clean and punctual with they stuff. They abided all the governor's safety protocols. The most law-abiding folks you would ever wanna meet. But then the Nation barbershop closed. The brothers who ran it wadn't much for social media—they only posted quotations from *Message to the Blackman in America* on they IG—so we had to find out they had shuttered by Momma deciding she was tired of my naps, taking off work early to walk me over there, and finding out that the Muslims had been swapped out for a burrito joint. It was things like that, when he got wind of it, practically sent Daddy into convulsions: "See what I been tellin' you, Sherelle? My best bet is to get me a conk and rename myself Raul if I wanna get hired out here." Not that he was ever interested in having any job that someone would have to hire him for. But that didn't stop him from railing 'bout how black folks was the first to lose work in the shutdowns, the first to come up short on rent, the first to be evicted. The American Black Man had got shafted for hundreds of years by all kinda newcomers: Europeans, Mexicans, Asians, Africans—forget *build that wall*, Daddy wanted land walls, seawalls, sound walls, nets, quotas, and a big ol' money order to Mexico to keep them jokers at home.

Didn't help that our fellow peoples of color wadn't exactly Martin Luther King they damn selves, especially the ones who loved hip-hop so much they couldn't help but put a "nigga" in every sentence they spoke as we sat one row behind them at the aid office or waited in line next to them at the taco truck. Daddy would politely ask these Asian and Mexican and Middle Eastern boys to upgrade they vocabulary: "Y'all need to shut the hell up. Aye'body wanna be a nigga, and then the cops come and ain't a one of y'all black."

"Yo, calm down, my nigga," would come the response.

"I. Said. Don't. Say. That. Mess," Daddy would say. And you'll notice outta respect to that di-rect heritage yours truly don't say that word to this day, unless the niggas ain't black.

But them niggas had no need to heed our heritage, which meant things was bound to get heated: they "niggas" would turn to "niggers," and our requests would turn to threats, and then security would have to show up and me and the old man would have to get gone 'fore the cops came. An interesting cat, Daddy was.

Me and Momma walked down MacArthur to a storefront with a metal plaque hanged out front that read BARBERS and a dim light that glowed behind a curtained window, the type of place that didn't follow no health codes, didn't have no masks, and turnt out the lights soon as the po-lice came up the street. If you think everybody obeyed them restrictions it's only cuz you wadn't in the hood, where you can die a hundred different ways and folks is used to taking heaven-and-hell chances scrambling to make a living. Momma tried to turn the knob, but it was locked. I watched the solitary light rock back and forth, a weak old bulb suspended from the ceiling by a single dirty white string. A man unlocked and opened the door, and we walked into what was not a barbershop but a simple room, an SRO really, with that one lightbulb hanging from the ceiling like a lonely moon and a barbershop chair right beneath it, and a medicine cabinet nailed to the wall behind the chair, and a second chair—wooden, rickety, narrow-assed—posted opposite the barbershop chair. Momma, who always masks up in close quarters outside her home, went and sat in the wood chair while the man who had opened the door, a tall, wiry-thin brother built like Daddy but with dollar signs tatted above both eyebrows and teardrops engraved along both his cheekbones, one of them cats who looks like he just climbed out an Oakland pothole, this man of all men was to put his razor to my head and neck.

The strange man went about gettin' his blades and things together, and then he asked over his shoulder if Momma wanted me to have the usual low-cut, faded and tapered in the back, the hairstyle of 95 percent of all black males in America and on earth. And then, interestingly, after she answered, "Yes, ain't nothin' new in East Oakland," he asked me, "What about you, sir? That what you want?"

I wadn't nobody but my momma's child. She had the money so she had the say-so, so it never ever occurred to a young grasshopper that his opinion mattered much. I wadn't at the speakin'-my-mind stage of development just yet. Which is why I just nodded my assent, a word I hadn't read to know back then.

I looked at Momma, whose unmasked eyes stared at the man, who, I assume, kept his eyes on my head. "You got a good head of hair," the man said. Back then, my hair had an evenness to it even when it grew too long that barbers appreciated out loud: *Boy, you tellin' me you ain't took nothin' to this jungle and it's never flat on one side?* And: *It stay like that even when you run around and tussle at recess and be a full-fledged boy?*

Tufts of thick black hair started to fall like snow from a smoke-filled sky. My body went rigid as his blade slid just above the lobes of my brain. He ticked it along my jugular and the lightbulb flickered and I realized my life was his. I worried the strange man was fittin' to slice me on accident, that unsanitized instrument of his transmitting ghetto gangrene into my bloodstream. It was bad enough we had to worry about the flu snatchin' us dead without going and courting other unknown diseases. I watched Momma watching the man. Her eyes was hard and ready—I figured she was focused on "if this goes down, then what do I gotta do next?" type strategies. She worked as a hospital orderly but she coulda made good in the military, that woman. She turnt them hard eyes toward me. I knew if I flinched and showed my fear, she'd slap me rigid right there, and once we got home I would have more to fear from her'n from blood with the mean tats and the razor.

He buzzed along both my temples, pinpointing my line not once, not twice, but thrice; hecka detailed, this dude. Then somethin' funny happened: the strange man finished with my line and then he did my fade, and then instead of dabbin' that stuff that burns the bacteria off, he lathered my whole head with this soothing stuff. It went from wet to warm, from warm to cool. Then he shampooed my scalp and took my head in his hands all delicate, like I was somethin' too fine to damage, and massaged my lobes, my temples, my whole head. As he worked, he hummed a song about a diamond in the back and a sunroof top, and Momma started to nod along to his rhythm. I nodded my head in his grasp and I realized just how unpredictable this life would be, and I closed my eyes and slept off completely and didn't come to till he was finished.

I never did see brother man or his barbershop again. We moved on. The ghetto flu burnt itself out, things opened back up, folks took off they masks, and we began to explore the changes that had came to East Oakland. We began to frequent a newly opened barbershop on Seventy-Ninth next to an auto repair place underneath a billboard that advertised football tickets in football season, and basketball tickets in basketball season, and European vacations couldn't no one below the sign afford the rest of the year. (It wadn't till real recently that I realized that all that signage is meant for the people on the freeway that fly past us.) This shop had a lot more going for it'n two chairs and a lightbulb, but the people that came with the furniture left much to be desired. The barbers, all men, was constantly carrying on, trying to get Momma's number and talkin' loose about they own women, calling them "broads," "jump-offs," "gold diggers," and "dream killers," filling my young impressionable mind with all the dog food that dudes like this gobble up. On top of it, not a single one of them fools wore a mask, and some of them even went on about how the health and safety stuff was just a white devil plot to track and control complected people.

Miguel from school was a regular there, too, since his hair required much care. Maybe we bonded in that barbershop, I cain't call it. It was a different kinda education, that's for sure. Them dudes schooled us in things that textbooks won't tell you: they knew the address of every black-owned barbecue and side-door catfish spot and underground nightclub and weed gate and ho stroll, every back road where the white and black and brown devil cops took the girls who refused jail. And they offered that knowledge freely. Me and Miguel just listened and took hood notes, him maybe more studious about it than me.

To hear the barbers tell it, the cops had STDs from the streets and loyal wives at home in they sheets. The barbers didn't seem like saints they own selves. The old head who cut my hair was the type to brag how he had been faithful to the same two broads for the past five years. He'd talk about his girlfriends to me when I was in the chair, how they complemented each other and what he called "the relative merits of monogamy versus two at a time," till Momma would get tired of it and speak up from behind her mask that he needed to shut the hell up and stop corrupting her son and to take his ass to church or a mosque or a Buddhist temple cuz he needed Jesus in his life. That didn't make much sense, especially seeing as her tongue idn't exactly a prayer book, but everybody understood what she meant. The barbers stopped talkin' about women altogether and took up the wholesome subject of sports gambling.

Momma truly hated that place. When one morning Rockwood awoke to the industrial-grade odor of barbecued hot combs, razor metal, and Sulfur8, I think she was happy. We went and stood outside in the courtyard where we could see the flames lick up over East Oakland in orange spirals that turnt to ink-black smoke as they flew, drawing a Muslimina's veil over the morning sun. Folks broadcasted live and di-rect every theory they could think of for the fire, and some fool from across the way in Ravenscourt set off one of them cherry bomb fireworks that trembles the ce-ment like God's heartbeat.

"Maybe it's an act of God," I said. It was a term I had heard in the news when a tornado tore up houses in faraway places like Arkansas and Georgia.

"Cope," Daddy said, "if it's a Lord above, He don't have time for what's going down in Oakland."

Neither did the media. I know cuz I checked the next day and it was a story about the ongoing violent unrest from Far Right and Far Left political whatnot and this and that, and it was a story about the stock market or stock exchange or somethin' breakin' hella records, and it was a story flexin' a new genius phone that was still in production at the time that would do everything faster and better and more trackable. And it was like the fire never even happened. Wadn't nothin local 'bout our news, which is why I never paid it attention till it started paying attention to me.

When it came to the news, God, and anything else that told him how to think, Daddy wadn't having it. "Prayer won't get you nowhere," he liked to say. Matter fact, I remember him saying it that very morning right after he said the bit about God and Oakland. It rhymed, which meant it stayed with you when he said it, which is why Momma held on to it and turnt it around on him a month later when it still wadn't no operating barbershops and my dome was turning fully funkdafied.

"Prayer won't get us nowhere," Momma chided. "We cain't find a decent barbershop within walking distance. Look at him! Boy looks like a young Michael Jackson on crack. How you plan to handle this, old man?"

I knew for a fact Daddy couldn't care less about my hair. He had lost his back when dinosaurs and Dru Down was roaming Oakland, so what kinda fur coat covered his boy's head just wadn't his concern. But Momma pressed: "You see somethin's wrong, Copeland Cane, you gotta change it. We cain't let another generation go untended to. Ain't that what you always tellin' this child of yours? Don't make yourself a hypocrite now."

She had him boxed in by his own mandate, and Daddy paused for a long uncomfortable time. Then he spoke: "Sherelle Rowland, there's somethin' 'bout you, ol' girl, I cain't stand 'bout myself. It's like you in my head. I need to start cuttin' hair again."

"You fittin' to cut my hair?" I asked. Remember, the man's totally bald. Not a hair follicle graces that dome. I questioned his experience, let alone his skill.

"Hush," he chided. "Don't go doubtin' me now, Cope. Done forgot more 'bout cuttin' heads'n yo' young butt ever gon' know."

I looked at him, not trusting. "But you're bald," I said.

"You don't have to touch the flame to know it burns, boy. Now have some damn faith."

Apparently, the old man had took care not only of his hair-challenged head but the heads of many a brother on the Rock back in the day in the '80s and '90s. All of that experience blessed his razor. Back at school, Keisha and Free asked who new was handling my hair. Them two can put anything, don't matter what it is, on social media in the morning and it'll have five hundred followers 'fore lunch is served, na'mean?

So one girl told another and another till the news found somebody's mother, and easy as gossip Daddy had messed around and found hisself the barber not just to his boy, but to a whole curious clientele that was, all counted, me and several short-haired women deep. Whenever we really was down to the sugar water and shutdown rations, he would put his inventioneering on hold and focus solely on the cuttin' of heads. His clientele was women who wanted they heads shaved close, but ain't feel like puttin' up with the smart remarks from they sisters at the salon, not to mention the #metoo moments that men's shops trafficked in. They never had to worry about that with the old man. Daddy didn't play those games, and the absence of any men besides hisself and yours truly, whose fish had yet to swim, made our home a place a woman wouldn't mind gettin' her hair cut.

Daddy's barbershop was the back porch of our apartment. The ladies would bop on in in they basketball shorts and puffy jackets, some old scarf thrown across they face, and give Momma a nod, dap me up, and sit down in the dinner table chair—"Come on wit' it, dreamer. Keep this head right." The straight girls came clanging in in they high heels and designer masks, with a momma's switch in they hips, and they would sigh and sit down and say, "OK, dreamer, gimme that Toni Braxton, gimme that blond Goapele one mo' 'gin."

Lookin' back, it was special. Now, if you wadn't lookin' back but was in that time and place and it was your job, like some old-timey Charles Dickens street child, to scurry the floor sweepin' up the loose locks, fetchin' the barber his different razors, and whatnot, then it was simple hard labor that would have you tight for life—or at least till you find someone to take your frustration out on.

*

The year I turnt thirteen, this white family decided to rent space close enough to Rockwood that they son, this blue-eyed boy pale than the moon, ended up zoned to our school. The system was not working for those white folks. Not that it was the school system's fault that, unbeknownst to it, that mug harbored a menace and that menace was me.

We was in the same year, me and this boy, so we ended up in the same classes. For no good reason (unless you count stupidity), I perpetrated my first offenses against him, made it my personal mission to drive the little blond invader out the hood. Hand on any holy book you wanna give me, I confess it had somewhat to do with what his race symbolized to me and a whole lot more to do with hurting a child who showed up soft as wet bread, even softer'n yours truly. I turnt into a verbal DeMichael on his ass with none of DeMichael's redeeming qualities.

When he first arrived I asked his name. From behind his food-stained mask, he twisted his tongue around somethin' with, like, fifteen letters and one vowel. "Huh?" I responded. "Krzyzewski?" even though "Krzyzewski" wadn't even close to what he had said. "Krzyzewski" was just the one name with a bunch of consonants that couldn't cosign each other in English and a "ski" at the end that I knew how to pronounce. I believe it's the name of a famous dead football coach, somethin' of that nature, not that it mattered where I scavenged my slander. Snappin' and joke crackin' and a thousand plays on that boy's name ensued during the course of that year. I even tried to rally the troops, talkin' loud and lookin' around as I clowned the pale problem, tryna encourage Miguel or Keisha or Free to join in. But they never paid me no mind when I got in that mode, almost like they knew I wadn't fit to be followed. I think I twisted it around in my mind that that was just another challenge, along with gettin' rid of the white boy, so I kept on with it, not lookin' to nobody to do my dirty work with me—I'ma spare you the sad details.

Krzyzewski, home-trained to a fault, called me Copeland, my full name. I called him whatever the fuck I felt like and waited for him to roast me back or throw a punch or respond somehow in kind, all the while knowing he wouldn't, knowing he couldn't, because he was too small to retaliate and because for a boy without friends all attention is good attention no matter how he gets it.

Eventually none other than Black Hercules hisself stepped in, which caught me off guard because by then DeMichael hardly even came to campus. He had his hand on my shoulder 'fore I even knew he was on the premises. A man's hand was clutching me in a school where wadn't a single male educator on staff. I froze dead. That hand of his could debone me back to front. It came to me quiet as it was kept right then, right there between the three of us that I wadn't only all by my lonely on my mission, I was just wrong.

DeMichael took his hand from my shoulder and someone else, probably Keisha or Free or maybe my conscience, said, "Leave it be, y'all, leave it be," and the next thing I remember the teachers packed up the lessons and the semester came to a close. School let out as the May rains dropped a curtain between me and my identity as a teenage torturer. It was only when July arrived and the sun decided to stay for a while that I emerged out of doors and came to the realization that my mission was unsuccessful as well as awful: Krzyzewski's fam had got ghost, U-Hauling it up outta there, which felt like an indictment against me, not a victory. Meanwhile, new invaders was arriving from all angles and in every ethnicity. The economics of America was gettin' critical, and with the shutdowns that just wouldn't quit and the job losses that that caused came the homelessness. Homeless camps on every corner, a new kind of ghetto flu. Old cars stacked bumper to bumper fifty, sixty, seventy vehicles deep, a windshield full of parking tickets to hide the whole family: Momma, Daddy, and the children living up in there. It was beyond anything anyone had ever seen. And don't get it twisted, you won't find Copeland Cane shedding a single tear for them hooptie hoppers. I hated that they was our new neighbors, crowding up every single side street in Oakland, even posting up inside the Rock amongst us hardworking people, like our lives wadn't turnt tight enough without they no-rent-payin' asses squatting in our space, what little space we could claim.

The rise in homelessness and the closeness of it shook me to the core. I knew my family was far from ballin'. I knew the homeless could be us and we could be them and wadn't but some luck standing in between. I imagined living on the streets my own self, huddled up amongst my homeless kinfolk in a car if I was lucky.

As things was gettin' worse, the town was steady gettin' richer at the same time: walled, privately po-liced compounds that housed people way wealthier and way whiter'n Krzyzewski. They appeared like so many aliens on the surface of East Oakland. And like the aliens in all the stories ever told, we never did see these folks. We just knew they existed and that they kept a distance, but not socially. We knew they watched us from behind high walls and maybe they watched us on the news, too, the Soclear Alert Desk news, if I had to guess.

One day I looked up and the Rock was surrounded by hella rich folk and dirt fuckin' poor people. That's when I started to see just how wild the world was—not just Caucasians versus the complected, but somethin' more complicated and crazier and deeper was happening to the hood. I came to regret my treatment of Krzyzewski and I wished that he would return. Forget coming back to our janky school, I wanted little homie to roll right up into Rockwood itself. Me and him would post up on the stoop outside our apartment and watch the ladies come and go. We'd hear them banter back and forth, the laughter, the snaps, the hair, the women who loved women and the women who loved men, not no division there to judge what was right or wrong—one community; the dreamer in his dream; the little things we ain't deserve to lose. Then Krzyzewski could take me to his place and show me somethin' that he knew. But that never happened. Krzyzewski was gone for good. Ain't no do-overs in life, I learnt that the hard way. I never did see young Slav sahab again and now I know I never will.

*

Snaps folks round the way used to say:

How the city makes a mural for every people priced outta town. Hella black folks playin' ball and blowin' horns and spinnin' records painted on walls in San Francisco.

Mexican food ain't had but two ideas, beans and rice, and soul food ain't had but one, diabetes.

And some things you just gotta live with, like your landlord, three-day notices, skunk weed, flu and mold fit to kill you, and mariachi music after midnight cuz it's always somebody's quinceañera.

Snaps that wadn't so funny when you thought about them a little too long:

Like how a black baby woke up with wings and told his people, "I'm an angel!" and folks heard that and hollered back, "Nah, nigga, you's a bat."

And that black don't crack, Jacq, it don't even grow old—we just drop dead one day.

*

If you have the first clue about this thing we call the "ghetto flu," you know what I mean by that last line, how folks just drop and whatnot. Hella hazards we had to deal with. Daddy told me that the man who owned our building, motherfucker owned half of East Oakland, and all you had to do was travel around that piece to see how the peckerwood played favorites. Ain't renovated shit but to put up a li'l old gate that don't keep nothin' out. "Whatever happened to that Polish friend of yours from school? Left out that quick? Learnt they was white?" He was talkin' about Krzyzewski and them. "Went somewhere got more than a dang gate goin' for it," Daddy could guarantee me that much.

Meanwhile, the run-down properties that our landlord was finna sell to the highest bidder got the rest of his attention and big checks, which left our hood, good old Rockwood, too black to love and too decent to improve. Wadn't never no inspections, no clean-ups, no nothin', not for us. And little by little, the Rock went from good to mediocre to downright moldy. Nah, I ain't stutter—my terrible teens was shamefully fungus-filled. That mess climbed up our walls, it fed on our restrooms, and plain ran trains on anything that collected a teaspoon of moisture, which, when you live in Oakland, ain't but about 95 percent of everything living and deceased. Matter fact, after low clouds and a hard rain it would be days where mold was our numero uno nemesis.

Mold could get all up in you, Daddy said, weaken your whole system. And then in the winter the flu would return and the city would shut us in and call our hood a health hazard, which maybe it was, cuz the sick would get ambulanced away every day, a lotta them folk never to return. If things kept up like this, the old man promised, wouldn't be no neighborhood left 'fore we knew it.

Fortunately for us, Daddy had a solution—*the* solution, he promised. It was just a matter of perfecting the thing, which smelled like gasoline, but once he got the mixture just right it would be a wonderful, strawberry-smelling cleaning agent, an antidote that would whisk away the stench and the grime that stacked up at the same pace as poverty in the nooks and crannies of our housing unit. After he got done cleaning our place, he could clean up the rest of the Rock and then make a business of it, take his solution all over the Bay Area, ending environmental injustice one health hazard at a time, meanwhile making hisself enough bread to kiss East Oakland goodbye.

But it's a lotta East Oakland, and a lotta environment, and even more injustice, so this whole plan was bound to be a while 'fore fruition. If you have ethics, which Daddy did, naturally you ain't trying to add to the world's problems, so even if the FDA ain't involved in your enterprise that don't mean you don't test and refine your homemade product 'fore putting it to market. After all, the thing still gotta fulfill its advertised promise and not kill folks in the process. So Daddy hadn't actually tested his solution. He was still working on the measurements and metrics, he told me. "Cain't rush a good thing," he claimed. "Alpha generation kids like you want aye'thing instant oatmeal, but that's not how life work outside the microwave, boy."

I couldn't understand the hesitation. Daddy was the first to raise a complaint about how we all probably had mold spores and black lung from sittin' up in these infestated-ass apartments. He pointed to the way things was changing around Oakland and how, hear this, the richer and the whiter the town got, the more news that came out about crime and poverty and illness. "They fittin' to move us out," he'd say. "They got big plans for this place that don't include us. Last thing they wanna do is improve these old buildings," he predicted.

Pre-diction: Cor-rect.

Yet his solution was to wait and de-liberate.

Every day I'd come home from school and see the men posted up outside our building, the boys playing basketball on the courts, and the girls princess-leanin' against the moldy walls waiting on they shattered Prince Charmings. And I never stopped to kick it. Never made time to relate and conversate. It wadn't that I thought I was better'n anybody or too good for the game, the girls, the mold. It was the simple fact that my old man would black my hide if I wadn't home for his brand of homework, which included not a single grain of instant oatmeal.

Meanwhile, the mold only got blacker. Still, I never raised my voice to question the man's judgment. Daddy was like the sun to me—you don't go questioning the sun, you farm your crops, have your ass in before dark, and say your prayers. I loved him like you love the sun, totally, unquestioningly. The sun wakes you and puts you to work. And back in the days, I didn't mind the work so much. I wanted to do what I could so that him and Momma could hit a gangster lean at the kitchen table, leaning against they walls without worrying what them walls had hid, not to mention not having to wash every dish twice just to keep the flu away.

About them dishes—Momma's favorite was a beautiful cooking pot that she had schemed from a swap meet in Inglewood. When I was still in my preteens, we would make these annual L.A. trips where Daddy dropped off money with his old lady from his past life. He would spend some quality time with his other children. These sons of his were fifteen, sixteen, seventeen years old, too big and too mannish for me to hang with. The swap meet and Momma's company was way more interesting, the place was packed full of reggae music and Caribbean food and loud bartering vendors and customers crowded shoulder to shoulder. There was a Jamaican with glammed-up gold dreadlocks and regal dark skin who stood behind his booth and held court, going ham about a particular set of silverware, kitchen cutlery, and dishes like they was the Queen of England's own—and maybe that was the case, cuz at least some of that stuff was very beautiful and very whatever the word is for old and fashionable and beautiful. I'm talkin' gold gilt edges and elaborately carved scenes of angels flying, fluting, dancing with demons, naked women posed in lush garden settings, the children of the gods at play. It reminded me of the pictures in my school textbook that the art teacher made such a big deal about because they represented Renaissance this and that. I could tell Momma was interested by the firecrackers sparking off in her eyes. She took me by the hand and rushed us up to the Jamaican's booth and peeled off her mask in a crowded public space for the first time since yours truly was rockin' diapers. Words I never heard her use, in an accent unlike anything ever heard in our home, came flying out her mouth: she was channeling the ancestors and giving his Jamaican back to him like second nature. They talked to each other, some words lilting the way the Nigerians speak, so sharp inflected, yet so truly proper, while other words and phrases had that lo-fi Caribbean bass, each beat biding its time deep in the back of the throat. The Jamaican, whose black-and-gold mask rode low under his nose, was nodding and smiling from the corners of his eyes. He let her handle his fine dishware, snaking his long arms around people in the flowing, waterlike crowds to hand one item then the next to her. But Momma was the one with all the talkin' now.

"G'wan do me one t'ing—sell it me if'n you cheap off ten percent. Deal?"

"Barter deal now, aye?" The Jamaican eyed her and chuckled, for there was no item up in that swap meet too good to be bartered.

Momma held firm to her request and met his narrowed eyes with her whole face. I felt her fingernails digging into me as she dug into the negotiation.

"OK now," the Jamaican conceded after a minute. He was looking at the crowd that had formed behind us, either to buy more of his best things or to witness the negotiation—the practices of a different country, I guess, though to my knowledge Momma had never came close to leaving our country; barely had she even been off the West Coast. "Ten percent i'tis. But that don't go for nobody else," he shouted. He pulled his mask all the way off so that he could stare a little bit better back at all the staring eyes that had gathered behind us, people as interested as I was in the back-and-forth between the two Jamaicans, one of them immaculately conceived by herself just a few minutes prior.

*

One night Daddy held court a little too good for our good. Told me how it had been hella schemes since 'fore I was born to get us up out the paint, outta Oakland en-tirely. Told me how the fallout from '20 was still fallin': most folks was broke, but them boys and girls in tech, they was gettin' richer'n Mansa Musa in Mecca, whatever that's supposed to mean. (Do you know what that means, Jacqueline? Cuz I don't.)* Anyway, instead of googling that mess, I thought about how if the old man wasn't crazy, wasn't a preacher without a church and parishioners, if he actually knew a thing or two, then we was straight up sitting ducks up in Rockwood.

I felt called, but prayer wouldn't get us nowhere. Momma's dishes would only be saved if someone on earth on the Rock did the saving. I stayed up till my folks fell asleep, then I snuck out to the hallway cupboard where Daddy kept the solution behind Momma's momma's momma's quilts. There was this spot of what I believed was mold on one of Momma's more beautiful dinner plates. It stood out black as the back of your neck on an otherwise perfect serving surface. Lookin' back, maybe it wasn't even mold, maybe it was just wear and rust, or

---

*Soclear Broadcasting, the only media empire great enough to span the globe and to answer the questions you and your S.O. discuss at the dinner table. *Soclear Business Daily: History Facts: Who's the richest guy ever?:*
The Elon, $600 billion
Jeff Bezos, $577 billion
Jack Ma-Mugabe, $495 billion
Mansa Musa, $400 billion
Vladimir Putin, $380 billion

maybe the imperfection had always been there. She had, after all, got it like she got everything, on first sight in a crowded market, bargained off a man from another land. But I didn't think about that. There it was, a plate that I tried never to eat off of due to its decay, the perfect test case for a cleansing. I didn't consider for a second that Daddy's solution could make the mold on the plate any worse'n it already was—either it killed it, or the mold lived on bigger and badder and blacker'n before.

Anyway, this spot had been haunting me. I shook every time it got brought out and food was placed on it, then shoveled into someone's moth. I shivered every time it was loaded with leftovers and placed in our fridge, which was bad enough already with its janky old freezer that froze these big ol' icicles that broke off and could damn near amputate your toe if you wadn't mindful. The fridge would start to smell as stank as Alameda Beach, and even though I've heard claim that Europeans consider molded cheese some sorta high cultural grace, I'm not about to eat nothin' that's green, gray, black, and blue, the advanced melanations of severe mold growth according to my studies in Shit Trying to Kill Me. So I took the solution and put it to action. Jacq, real talk, just like Daddy promised, that mess worked. Worked real good with a couple pours and a little sizzle and fizzle. Our solution whisked the contagion clean away.

I wadn't about to stop at an old English plate. The mold and the flu was all over our buildings, had been droppin' folks like flies for years. Some things gotta die so that we can live, and this filth needed to go. A gang of shit needed to go. Rockwood needed a revolution, am I right? Am I crazy to think like this? Or was I just taking matters into my paws when wouldn't nobody else do the damn thing?

The following afternoon, I hustled up some cowry shells from Miguel, who didn't guard each dollar like it was the queen's diamonds, the way Daddy did. I knew not to ask Keish, Free, or none of them others. They peoples was as stingy as the old man. Miguel was different, though. He would lend me some ends, no questions asked, no side-eyes turnt toward me, like either he liked me or it was more where his money came from, I couldn't call it. All's I knew was blood didn't need to ask his momma for shit, he kept his skrilla in his sock.

Now that I had my money and a purpose with mines, I moved quick, if not smart. I had my stuff together by the time Daddy expected me home to help him procrastinate his purpose some more. He put me on detail like usual, eating up all my hours till well after dark. Still, I slept light that night, and as soon as the sun shone, I got down to business. I knew I couldn't use up all Daddy's solution on some charitable, unprofitable shit like neighborhood sanitation. Him and Momma was trying to get up outta Rockwood, not beautify it.

I went and bought four one-liter water bottles as well as a couple other accelerants to the process. I emptied the water bottles out and filled them suckers up with the solution, which was beginning to smell like a car engine, not that that bothered me much. According to Daddy, Mr. Motherfuckin' MacDonald would use pesticides to spray and burn away the mold from his properties that he was fittin' to put up for a sell. Meanwhile, the peckerwood ain't do shit for us. So, with two and two coming together in my thirteen-year-old head, 'fore you knew it ('fore I knew it), I was walking the perimeter of the courtyard at the hour that kids is supposed to be heading off to school, grown folks is gettin' ready for work, day laborers is biding they time on boulevards, and hustlers and hoes is hitting that snooze button, and in my arms hugged up against my chest like several footballs I carried the bottles of the solution, which I now had it in my head was my brilliant black disinfectant.

A lady skinny enough to squeeze thru a shut door, totin' a cloth sack slung over her shoulder, approached me. The sack clattered with its contents, a bunch of aluminum cans. Every couple minutes she'd cough so hard I thought a lung was 'bout to jump out her throat. This woman looked and sounded straight out the homeless camp; that, or the ER. I was not lookin' to catch no new flu bug, but somethin' about her made me pause and hang around.

"You're staring like you know me from somewhere, youngster," she said, clearing a hurricane out her throat. "What you got there?"

I didn't say anything. I wadn't tryna have my mission stopped 'fore it started.

"Is you 'bout to plant a garden? What's that smell? Are we related?" Her questions came at me quick as a tweaker. "I'm related to half of Oakland. Are you a Montgomery?"

"I'm a Cane," I said. "Who are you?"

"Ah, shit." She sat her sack down and then stood to her full height. I could see the tat that ran down her throat: P E A C E. The letters fell almost unreadable within her sagging skin from right below her jaw down to her collarbone. I recognized her now: the lady who choked the shit out my teacher's neck five years back. "In AA, I'm supposed to apologize to you, make amends and whatnot. I slapped the bright out your eyes."

I remembered the back of her hand flying at me. The hand was thinner now and didn't seem attached to the same woman. If she hit me now, the only thing I would catch would be a backhand full of bones, which might hurt even worse. I drifted over to where the dumpsters stood, reeking, off in a corner of the complex. She picked up her sack and followed me.

"I'm so sorry, blood! I'm not like that anymore. I don't make a habit of snuffin' people. What's your name, baby boy?"

"Cope," I said, tossing some of the solution on the moldy ce-ment that surrounded the dumpsters.

"Cope's your government name?"

"Copeland," I said, moving on from the dumpsters.

"Sounds like an old plantation name." She laughed up a lung. "I'm Vista—you know what that means?"

"What's a vista?" I asked. I stopped tryna flee her.

"It's, like, a vista is where you stand and look out and you see everything. A lotta people never had that experience cuz they mind is on lockdown. It's so much in the world to see, but we never get to see most of it." She paused and snorted like a cokehead. "Blood, I don't want you to take this the wrong way cuz you seem like a good child and I did slap fire out you, but either you or what you're carryin' don't smell too good."

Every time the wind would break across the space between us, it would carry the scent of the solution up into my nostrils. My nose hairs would begin to burn and my peach fuzz mustache would tingle. As for its smell, I had got used to it. I ain't really smell it no more. I stared at her, slow to whatever it was she sayin'.

"I don't know what you're up to, baby boy, but you might wanna rethink it." She eyed my possessions. "Am I gonna see you again, blood?" she asked.

"I don't know," I said. It was a strange question. How was I supposed to know what was to be or not to be?

"You can always decide to be here tomorrow, baby boy," Vista said. "I learnt that."

I nodded and I was about to say somethin' about the solution, about how certain problems cain't wait for tomorrow, when she snorted louder'n I could speak, silencing me. Then she scooted off toward the Rockwood gates. I watched her go. She was scooting with a quickness, the sack of cans rattling on her shoulder while she shooed somethin' out the air with a wave of her free hand. I imagined her backhanding a bug like she backhanded me.

That was when I knew for sure that the solution was onto somethin'. Wadn't no bug she was shooing away. She felt some type of way about this solution. This solution could run off the woman who had whipped my ass. It was powerful enough to singe me each time a droplet jumped with the wind to my skin. It was everything the old man claimed it to be and even stronger still. This thing was fit to clean Rockwood all the way up. I watched old girl go her way and I went mines. I made my way thru the courtyard, dousing anything and everything even a little bit moldy, from walls to walkways and even trees. I imagined the pollution dying as soon as the solution hit it, but in reality I was moving too fast to study its effects. I just kept going, cleaning everything that looked questionable. I forgot about my friends, who wadn't fittin' to follow me; I forgot about the grown folks ready to head to work in the clear blue morning; I forgot about the day laborers and the sleeping prostitutes and shoestring pimps. Call it psychosis or some wild shit down from my daddy, but I started tellin' the onlookers, who had flocked up around me all of a sudden— all eyes were on me all of a sudden—to get away from the mold, the mold was about to be clean gone. I ain't pay the slightest mind to the way the solution sizzled on contact and the pop and crackle sounds that sprang up soon after. Maybe I'd just seen so many homeless cats light fires in garbage cans to warm theyselves on cold city nights that I figured that I, too, could perform a controlled burn—either that or I just ain't know exactly what it was Daddy's solution was made of or the consequences and repercussions that would come from high concentrations of that mug applied to wood. It was one thing, I now realize, to test it out on small metal objects, another thing to start bombing it everywhere like the pesticide I by now simply assumed that it was.

It's all a blur after that—the way the low sizzle turnt to a high buzz and then to a snap, crackle, and smoke that started trailing me and then catching up to me and floating alongside me like fog rolling in from the bay. Keisha and Free and Miguel and the other kids was all running up to me hootin' and hollerin' like we used to do when a fight would break out at school, except now I was the only fighter. The adults I barely remember, but I know from the po-lice report that frantic calls for 911 were made. People started yellin' about "Where are this nigga's parents? Yo, blood is a pyro!" And just plain "Jesus Christ! Hey-seuss Christo!" and a gang of saints I never heard of before but might get to know soon enough.

I remember wondering why they had to go and start acting like I was burning down the Oakland redwoods—I wadn't no arsonist, I was an environmentalist. This was the solution to our mold problem. I was no fan of fire, hated it when Momma left the stove burners on to warm the apartment because she couldn't tolerate the heating bill, hated it more when the dead smoke stench of Oakland's summer fires floated down from the hills and fitted a noose wove of oil and ash around our necks down in the flats. But I hated the mold even more, or maybe the idea behind the mold—I hated how we deeply complected complainers simply sat around and posted up and talked shit while Mother Mr. Fuckin' MacDonald poisoned us on the daily. And we never fought back. Nobody never took no action. Sure, if I could splash enough of this solution, which was seeming more and more unlikely with all the distracting shouting about 911 and "Why come yo' parents never gave you the ass-whoopin' the po-lice 'bout to?" A crosswind fled thru the courtyard and the morning marine layer descended upon the Rock, saturating the solution. Daddy's pesticide stood no chance, not because it didn't work but because folks and the weather wouldn't give it a chance. Even Daddy hisself never gave his product a chance to right the wrongs of Rockwood. A po-lice siren sounded, distant, then screamed closer and much louder. Most folks run when the cops come, but I had nowhere to run to and nothin' I should have to run from. I tossed a gang of the solution, one whole water bottle's worth of it, on a nearby tree that might not have even been moldy. The frustration was building in me. The weather and the people and the po-lice assembled against me. I would be branded crazy, out my rabbit-ass mind, sent to juvie, forced to do homework and Daddy's bidding for a thousand years. But what was the use of our freedom if we never did nothin' with it—

$*^{*+}$

The only story they have on me comes from some juvenile record, which is supposed to remain sealed, first of all, don't know how they can call theyself protecting law and order while they disrespect my rights, but anyway, ain't no record that can tell you who I am. Hella factual errors in what they allege, no receipts, they cain't even get right what went wrong. Wadn't no citizens arrested me. That simply ain't true. They think the whole world is in them documents when all that's there is them talking to theyselves, confirming they own conclusions, so they can close shop early and say I was bad from the beginning.

After the fire (which ain't even get lit), everything got tangled for me. Since I had no priors, I was classified a nondetained minor and released on informal supervision, terms pending, which sounds good if you don't know shit, which my dumb ass didn't.

---

*Insurgency Alert Desk, Third Bureau: Juvenile criminal records obtained by Soclear Broadcasting detail a long history of violent behavior that dates back to Cane's early teens, when he attempted to set an East Oakland apartment complex on fire and was subsequently detained in a citizen's arrest by appalled tenants of the housing development.

†Insurgency Alert Desk, Third Bureau: Authorities believe that convicted arsonist Cane is traveling alone and that he is armed. Anyone who sees Cane should assume that he is armed and should contact authorities rather than attempting to take the law into their own hands, no matter how justifiable such action would seem to be. It is believed that Cane is in regular communication with an associate, likely a coconspirator in activist circles, though law enforcement has not ruled out the possibility that this associate is from Cane's criminal network. Authorities do not believe that this individual is harboring Cane, but rather that they might be giving media information to Cane and that he might pass information about his motives and whereabouts to them.

First of all, them terms ain't pend too long. We received a slim little notice in the mail. I remember standing in the kitchen in nothin' but my boxers and reading it out loud to my folks. The exact words don't matter. It said that on account of the arrest, they was transferring me out the regular school and into the day school on Treasure Island. I would serve out the balance of the semester. This Treasure Island school seemed like a little prison: you got put out the regular school and they put you in this mug, where they had you locked down from the moment you came to campus in the morning till the time you left the island in the afternoon. It was only one step away from being locked up 24/7 for real. But that wadn't the half.

"Treasure Island?" Momma said, the name cracklin' evil on her tongue.

Daddy shot up from his chair at the kitchen table and took the letter from me. I remember him scanning it, reading it more'n once. I remember how he slowed down and held it in his thin hands, how the veins was standing out over the bones of his fingers and I thought I seen his grasp tremble a little. He was very quiet. He sat down.

"Promise me you won't drink the water," Momma said.

"Why cain't I drink the water?" I asked.

*

If you never been a juvenile offender, a Section 8 applicant, or a Job Corps participant, you won't know about the Bay's most infamous island, so let me tell you how the authorities do us: Treasure Island sounds like paradise or somethin' from a fantasy, heroes and pirates and beautiful maidens and all that—but that mug is anything but a fairy tale. Yes, it's sitting pretty in the waters between San Francisco and Oakland, but ain't hardly anything there but everyone that no one wants. Don't that strike you as suspicious? You don't gotta be a genius to know somethin' about that motherfucker just is not right.

"If it don't come out a bottle, don't let it even touch yo' lips," Daddy said, breaking his silence, slap-pounding the table. "Stuff out there is not natural. If you disregard what I'm tellin' you, boy, you'a be in a world of hurt, I can promise you that."

Here's the history, according to the old man: Treasure Island is an artificial island, man-made, straight-up landfill stacked and packed together from the bottom of the bay all the way up to sea level. As if it being trash literally wadn't enough, it gets dirtier, way back with World War II, when the government created the island. The government is God, my old man explained. Invent an island, flood the earth, or feed all its people for a hundred years, it can do whatever it wants. After World War II, them was the days, Daddy said, when the government was really being God. Them jokers was going to outer space and trying to take the world into nuclear winter at the same damn time. The purpose of the island, as far as he could figure, was to store hella nuclear materials and then liberally test them shits without repercussion.

I guess they musta did hella tests, judging by all the problems that's come to pass, but back in the day it all was swept under the island when the scientists out in Manhattan beat them to the invention of the atom bomb. Not only did they invent the thing, they went and used it twice. While the mushroom clouds was rising over Japan, back on Treasure Island the soldiers got busy puttin' the leftover nuclear waste in big steel drums and tossing all that mess into the bay.

Sometime later—Daddy didn't know exactly how long later, but he said it coulda been months, coulda been years, who knew, not like the authorities put none of this in no book—anyway, researchers eventually concluded that the drums had leaked into the land. How you like that for a treasure hunt? It's every cancer known to man on that motherfucker and a few new ones you might just discover for your own self.

If you need proof for these claims, Jacqueline, look at the yellow tape that surrounds so much of the island, like a whole hood just been shot up. The tape says in big black letters:

CAUTION. PRECAUCIÓN.
RADIOLOGICALLY CONTROLLED AREA.
AUTHORIZED PERSONNEL ONLY.
FOR ENTRY CONTACT...

And the real truth of it, according to the old man, is the whole island is polluted. "Ain't none of it fit for humans," he told me. "Watch ya'self now."

**

I couldn't run to Treasure Island like I could run to regular school. The BART don't run there. It's only one bus that goes there, and it picks up at 5:45, 6:45, 7:45, and so on every weekday morning. Folks who work on the island take the early buses, day school students like yours truly get on the 7:45, and all the trips after that is a mystery to me cuz who would come to such a place if they ain't have to be there to begin with? In the afternoon the buses fill up again with everybody headed back home. I know it's people who actually live on that mug permanently, and as hard as it is to find housing in the Bay, I ain't hating. Look, it's even a long list of wannabe Donald Trumps who've went and built penthouses on the highest hill on the island. I seen the skeletons of them shits every day of my semester served there, old empty bones just holding up the air.

Couldn't catch me sayin' nothin' but "yes, sir," "yes, ma'am," "hello," and "goodbye" while I was on that island. Spent half my time just trying not to get thirsty. If it wadn't a perfectly wrapped Snickers, I did not put it in my mouth. If it wadn't on a test, I didn't pay it no mind. Not that it was exactly easy to get in trouble even if I had had a mind to: armed guards manned the hallways and building exits. Even our teachers was retired law enforcement, hired to keep us compliant, not to teach us nothin'. And the curriculum they administered and the tests they wrote up was so remedial, designed for illiterate kids and compulsive criminals, that I was usually left with all day to twiddle my thumbs and dream about all the elsewheres open for escape. No

---

*Cope side note: You notice how much Soclear Broadcasting loves them some Insurgency Alert Desk reports. It's they audience, right? The American people love us some insurgencies and some alerts and some terrorists. But what we don't wanna hear about is things like the problems on the island, problems that won't plant a bomb or shoot a cop or pray to Allah. But courtesy of Copeland Cane, here's the dispatch of the day: "Insurgency Aftermath Desk: The weeds that rose up and choked the chief gardener wasn't weeds at all, but flowers spoilt by the soil . . ."

wonder Keisha and Free and them had started to play me distant on the Rock soon as I got put out the regular school and sent to the day school. Back then I figured they was judging me cuz of the situation with the solution, but now I know it was all about that island. Even if they couldn't say it, they knew and I knew somethin' about that muthafucka just was not right.

One day I finished my test so fast the teacher took pity on my literacy and let me leave class early. I followed the rules, was courteous, was late a lot but never disruptive, so she told the guards to let me roam the grounds. I was bored with nothin' to occupy my mind, and you know what they say 'bout idle hands, feet, and other body parts. I wandered into the two-foot-high jungle of weeds and standing water, muddier'n a mug. I was just beyond school grounds. In amongst the low weeds that ran all the way to the water, I peeped everything from broken bongs to shattered pipes, an old shoe someone left behind, its logo ate off by acids, an ancient flip phone bleached winter white by whatever's in that landfill foundation. I kept going, following the low jungle, watching my step, looking for anything but a weed that was alive. I wondered what but a human and a weed could survive. Wadn't even no birds flying above. It's the deadest place I've ever been, the other side of the moon is that island. I thought that maybe some rats got scooped up out the trash when they created the island and the rats mighta got buried underground inside the island and maybe they survived and maybe they descendants was right there, making they home right beneath my feet. Maybe gettin' kidnapped and took across the water and dumped with the trash to make the island had made them super strong. Maybe they was the smartest, toughest, meanest, roughest rats of all and wouldn't nobody ever know it. Back at home in Rockwood it was a rare thing for me to be idle long enough to daydream. I decided that this was one thing, probably the only thing, that was any good about the island.

It took a while for me to hear the groundskeeper yellin' for me to turn around and come back. Once I did hear him, I turnt and seen the hazard tape behind me. I had gone out too far. I started to walk back, but dude was yelling at me like I had stole somethin'. I didn't want the teachers to hear him and go and tell the security or whoever handed out the punishment. I started to run back toward the groundskeeper and the school, and then my foot hit a weak spot in the turf and I stumbled and came to an even weaker spot of soil and then I straight ate it, fell feet- and face-first, which idn't even possible, but fuck physics cuz I went head over heels and heels over head and then, just when I was finna touch turf and get my spine realigned, the ground fell in right in front of me. The soil gave way where I plunged with it. I scrambled against the sinkage and kept sinking, and that's when I panicked and it got worse. I screamed for help.

My eyes was closed with fear, cuz I was unaware that the groundskeeper had dove in after me. It's one thing to talk all this yang 'bout folks leaving off they differences to help each other, it's another to get saved by your friendly O.G. big homie groundskeeper inside a bottomless trash dump. A strong hand clutched my ankle, seizing me in place. My fall suddenly stopped. The hand pulled me upward, against the suction syndrome of all that shit. Then O.G.'s hand let go my ankle, but I could feel the force of the man's whole body like a great human plunger parting sewage and slime to get to me. He grabbed me again and yanked me clean out the muck.

I ended up lying on my back in the dirt looking up at dude. I brushed some landfill out my eyes and stared at him. He was twice my size.

"You hit one of them cocksuckin' sinkholes," he grumbled. He took off his mask, bent down, put his hands on his knees, and gasped for good air. "This ground is liable to give way any time. You're lucky you only fell a little ways. It's levels to this shit. These weak spots go way, way down where no one can save you."

I got up and dusted myself off, which only took a moment. I was surprisingly clean somehow.

"Y'all kids don't listen, don't read, don't see," my savior went on. "Are you out to lunch or what, boy? The boundary line's where it is for a *good* reason."

*

What was that reason exactly? That night in bed I couldn't stop my muscles from quaking or my mind from shaking out all the reasons, all the possibilities. It was levels to the island, danger zones if you stepped on the wrong spot. I knew what Daddy had told me about the island, that it wadn't no treasure. I knew yellow tape meant the same thing there that it did in Oakland, a place not to trespass. Back in science class in regular school in Rockwood, where they taught us things that took a brain to understand, I had learnt that the half-lives of radioactive materials lasted for about forever. Wadn't none of that shit from the 1940s dead. It wouldn't die for thousands of years. But I might.

The hood fireworks that rumbled all night all spring and summer and sometimes winter, too, trembled my room and shook my nerves. I knew especially after I went and wandered too far on the island that I was probably about a half step away from real jail. The island was a warning. It was more'n a warning, it was some toxic shit that could kill me. But if this is how they scared jokers straight in the free world, what kinda wild shit did they expose you to incarcerated?

I was already twitchy and kinda traumatized from my fall. I tried to put my fear of what I fell into outta my mind and think about other things, like girls, but not even jackin' off worked to calm me. Wadn't no girl fine enough to rid me of the fear of death. In the bathroom, I ran my hands over my head, my face, my chest, my ribs, my legs. Everything seemed OK at first, then I noticed one thing wadn't quite right: my hairline had shifted on my scalp. When I ran my hands along my head, the symmetry that had had barbers praising me from birth, complimenting Momma on her boy's bad hair, was gone. On the left side of my scalp the hair clumped thick like forest, deep gardens and tall trees of locked up, dreaded hair, while on the right my crown was desert thin and dry, liable to tear away. I knew in juvie they cut you practically bald, just like in the military. Anywhere where they took your rights, they took your hair.

I'm not sayin' that I could see the radiation at work, I'm just sayin' somethin' wadn't all the way 100 percent healthy. I seen my demise. First, my hair would go one side bald, then the other would dry up and die off. I would waste away to skin and bones. My lungs would fill with the ghetto flu and my throat would dead bolt closed to where I wouldn't be able to breathe.

I stared into my face in the bathroom mirror with the lights off. I showered in the dark and went to sleep in it, too, glad to still be black. I checked myself each night that I came home from the island just to make sure. I still do this some nights, I stand in a bathroom in the dark and tremble with my eyes closed, thinkin' that tonight's the night I'ma open them and be lit like the movie marquee, glowing like uranium.

*

I had a dream. I was older. My chest and shoulders had rounded and filled out, and for once I actually fit my clothes. I filled the body of an old black suit, a black vest, a white dress shirt. The pants was stiff from never being worn, but I forced my way into both long legs. I wondered how long it'd been since Daddy wore this old thing outta doors. I noticed the white pallbearer gloves that I wore and then I seen I was standing behind a pulpit and before an empty church. I looked down at my wing-tipped feet and instead laid eyes on an empty, open coffin. I knelt and closed it. Then I bore it away by myself, leaving the church and walking a great distance along lonely streets, deep into the thick woods and out upon unshaded, sun-bright paths. In the center of a mountain clearing circled up by a tight ring of trees, I lowered the coffin into a pit that God's fireworks had tore open in the earth. I unbuttoned Daddy's best suit jacket, his vest, and his dress shirt. I took off his pants and shoes and tossed it all into the coffin and knelt down and slammed its lid shut.

I woke stained with sweat and sperm. I showered for too long and left out the house twenty minutes late of when I was supposed to. It was 7:48 now. I could still catch the bus, but I would have to do it two stops down, about a half mile away, at High Street. If I could get there by 7:50, I wouldn't be late for school. What with traffic lights and bus fights and crazy people dancing in the middle of traffic and shit, I figured I had a chance. I broke out the apartment, past the gates, and booked down the boulevard on the dead run. A morning gale rose up against me, jailhouse g-force level of resistance. But I was fast and strong now. I dug deep and turnt my stride over and arrived where I needed to be at 7:49 plus a few pennies. Bus was late anyway, by minutes, not seconds, like always in rickety, raggedy old Oakland, so I had time to catch my breath, let it settle and relax. I felt slightly winded, but not tired like you would expect a half mile might make you. I wadn't even sweatin' like would be normal after someone's ran half a mile in under two minutes, which is exactly what I had accomplished. I guess I had known I was fast ever since the day Vista broke into our classroom, but no matter how fast I ran, I still arrived on Colored People Time all the time, late for everything. But after that day, on God, I ain't been late not a single date, drop-offs, bus stops, school clocks, and anything else where time's of the essence.

The sweat only started pouring once I was inside that tin can and we was headed over the bridge. Then my pores sprang the fuck open and the sweat came down like a hard, bitter rain on my forehead, pouring all in my eyes, soaking my mask till it seeped thru the fabric and kissed me.

*

I don't speak on it much cuz I'm polite with mines, but like any kid going thru puberty, my mind was on sex. Back in the day when Momma and Daddy had enough money to put me on a phone plan, I learnt about girls from Instagram. On Instagram, all the girls are gorgeous and happy that they're hanging out on the beach 365 days straight. Ain't no beach in Oakland. We got the lake downtown and the ghetto marina in the east. I admired the girls on the Gram, but I couldn't see not a one of them showing up in Rockwood. So for a long time girls was a foreign species to me, pedestaled in my mind. It was only when I started to notice girls at school that I could take them off the pedestal I had built in my head and see them for who they were.

At the day school, wadn't no one fit for a pedestal, not the three hundred boys, not the forty or fifty girls. But because it was so few females enrolled there, it was hard not to notice them. I didn't know they names cuz I didn't have a single convo with anyone, teachers included, while I went to school there. I stayed to myself, but my eyes roamed. The girls was pretty enough, but most of them rocked neck tats and other ratchet signs and symbols that scared me. Keisha didn't look like that. Free didn't look like that. They was my markers and these girls, in comparison, was way too scary. But after I got up out that sinkhole, I wadn't as scared anymore.

My body was the problem. Couldn't get no worse than radiation. Suddenly some tats and criminal charges ain't seem so risky. I decided to step to this bad Mexican bitch who all the guys talked about but stayed afraid to speak to. It wadn't that she was all that, but that she was the lightest-skinned girl in that piece that had them interested in her. I peeped that and seen how the black girls and dark brown indigenous girls got hella play from dudes, sneakin' off to the maintenance yard to smoke and have sex. Meanwhile, everybody kept they distance from homegirl, who they probably assumed was just too close to white, too close to a gringa, to give them none. She didn't make it easy either, cut eyes like straight razors at the other girls and would drop dead 'fore she met eyes with most boys. I think she was lonely, though, cuz when I did luck up and get her attention on accident one morning, absentmindedly staring at her, she looked back at me and the light in her eyes was like a welcoming. I could tell she had been wanting to talk to someone. I had not a word to say to her, but I did smile.

Between class periods, she came up to me. "You wanna get into somethin'?"

It was the most substantial thing anyone had said to me in my months on that polluted mug. "Cool," I said.

She mapped for me how to dip out the class and slide to the storage lockers in the back of the maintenance yard. "I just go there and smoke," she said, which I don't know if that was true or if she had been messin' around in the maintenance yard with hella dudes before me. At the time, I figured I was good as gone, wouldn't matter if I caught a disease, which is why I cain't tell you homegirl's name. It was a whole gang of things sexual I knew nothin' about. I learnt what I didn't know up in that storage closet in the maintenance yard that afternoon. I fumbled with her belt buckle, her bra hooks, and my own hands, not knowing how to handle any of the above. She took my clothes off swiftly and slipped her pants down. She was Mexican with long black hair and bright white skin that glowed in the dark locker like the full moon at midnight. "You got protection?" she asked, taking off her mask. Her breath hit hot against my face. It took a second for me to realize she was asking 'bout condoms and not about my mask or if my neked ass had a weapon on me. I stuffed my mask in my back pocket and grabbed around inside the locker till my hand hit some kinda grocery store plastic baggie. I took it and wrapped it around my dick. She looked at me like I was too dumb to breathe. "Nigga," she breathed even hotter and closer, melting into me. "Let's fuck," she said. She grabbed the baggie and tossed it away and pulled me into her. It was my first time inside a girl, and I had no idea what I was doing, but I kept going. Not wanting to get caught, we went slow, banging into each other like two quiet hands clapping. If she made a sound, I don't remember it. I looked away from her steady eyes. Then I felt her long nails sinking into both my shoulders like sharpened whispers tellin' me to stop. I stopped still inside her, fearful she had heard somethin' I had missed and we was 'bout to be found drawers down. For a few seconds I just held myself there inside her. "Don't cum in me," she mouthed, circling her hips in a subtle grind. She patted my back till I understood to start again. We got to clapping a little louder, but nothin' that would alert the authorities. She whispered in my ear, told me I was too nice for her.

Afterward, me and the girl went our different ways, she back to where boys and girls was men and women from birth, and me back into myself, whatever it was that I was. I peeped her here and there throughout the school year, but if we as much as spoke, Jacq, let alone let the other child know that they meant more'n a body in the dark, I cain't remember it now.

*

Daddy woulda jailed me his damn self if he knew I had got intimate with anything on that island, but nobody but me and the girl ever knew what went down in that storage closet. Instead I got reprimanded for trespassing into a chemically hazardous janitors-only area cuz that was what got caught on tape—like they say, it ain't what you did wrong, it's what they got receipts on you about. To my surprise, instead of maximum-security apartment imprisonment, Daddy took pity on me and removed me from his work crew, which meant I in turn got to spend my afternoons chillin' on my dumpsters bearing witness to Rockwood. Perched there, I seen beaucoup of nothin' new, brothers playing basketball, still talkin' about Oakland street ball legends from the eighties, while girls swapped gossip and spilt tea loud enough to split speakers. Vista wadn't new neither, but she was different. She looked at the world in a unique way that most people did not, so when she rolled up on me on my dumpsters one day to collect her cans, I started spillin'. I told her about my arrest, about being transferred out the real school into the island school. I told her about the trouble I fell into there.

She heard me out. "I mean, baby boy, I told you to live for tomorrow. You didn't wanna listen. Probably don't listen to your momma neither, do you?"

She eyed me stern than a schoolteacher.

"You got a bitch with a throat tattoo reprimanding you. That should be a solid hint to slow your roll, youngster. Look, I doubt that that sinkhole Nagasaki'd your ass or you wouldn't be sitting here speaking to me. But it might could be some new ghetto flu. You don't have to fall in no sinkhole. If that island's got it like that, probably it's all kinda mess out there that could make you sick someday. Maybe you should file one of them damn Freedom of Interrogation Acts, figure out what these devils got goin' on, cuz you know if it ain't one thing, it's somethin' else evil. It's so many atrocities that's been perpetrated it's hard to keep up. Thirty years of sterilization of black men in North Carolina. You heard 'bout that? Nah. Well, it's true as I'm talkin' to you right now. Tuskegee syphilis injections? How our cell phones and computers is investigating us 24/7?"

I shook my head at my own ignorance. I didn't know none of what she was talkin' about.

"Don't believe what I say," Vista said. "Read your ass up on the undercover shit that's being perpetrated. Side note: I apologize, real talk. You know what they say 'bout cocaine."

Apology accepted. I followed Vista's advice and read up on hella atrocities against us. It's a gang of them that you won't find in no school textbook. And besides mixing up some sterilized women with sterilized men and sellin' North Carolina short on how many decades they done did that shit, she did speak the truth. A lotta these conspiracies ain't theories—real talk.

*

"You're Copeland Cane?" the mailman asked. He was a young Vietnamese man who had only recently took over for the old black lady who dropped the mail for most of the years of my life. He was young and thin and had a scar deep as a buck fifty from his right ear down to his jawline. It was only, like, his second or third week on the job in our hood and he was still trying to match faces to names. I didn't know why he was trying at all, when all the job required was to drop the envelopes in boxes. Hella jobs been roboticized, but instead of armoring up a robot and having that nigga deliver the mail, here we have real live mailmen gettin' slashed across the face for they goods and shit.

But at that moment I was glad for the in-person contact. Never would a robot mistake me for my father and never would it hand over mail to a person when it could drop it in a mailbox. I nodded at his question and the mailman handed me a single envelope. I knew it was bad as soon as I seen the Treasure Island engraving and the little picture of a paradise island that they probably photoshopped off a Caribbean brochure or some shit—a white sand beach in the shadow of San Francisco, the bridge lights gleaming down on a tropical destination in the middle of the bay, baobab trees, coconuts, mangoes, and other mess that you will never, ever find between San Francisco and Oakland.

I walked into the courtyard where the mailman couldn't see me and opened the envelope. I read a statement of my infractions, nothin' that Daddy didn't already know. The school had emailed and called both times I line-stepped. But they had attached no penalties to it. I felt my body turning tense as I read on. I was feeling a pattern progressing: whenever somethin' real bad was set to happen against me, mugs put it in a letter and mailed it. Institutions wadn't messin' with no email and whatnot; when it came to the big verdicts, straight analog. The words "insufficiently compliant" jumped off the page at me like the logo embossed on an old head's FUBU jacket.

Hella befores and afters in my life—before I was grown, now that I am; before that letter found its way into my hands, which I didn't tell my parents about cuz I wadn't tryna get in any more trouble, and after the next letter arrived along with an email and a phone call. Daddy got the letter, Momma got the call, and we all got the email. I was in trouble, plain and simple.

It's these terrible moments that get stuck in time like old family pictures, if your family pictures only showed you at your worst. Momma has three pictures of me that she sets out with the other family photos. In the one, I'm a baby. She and the old man look dapper'n a mug, Daddy in that same suit out the Goodwill I keep seeing in my dream, Momma still losing her pregnancy weight, wrapped in some kinda shawl. They're holding me together. In the second, I'm older, able to stand on two feet; my hair's hella big and they actually have me dressed in some old-ass FUBU kids gear that I think they ganked from the '90s and forced me to wear. In the third, I'm like eight or nine years old and thin as spider legs. My hair's been cut low by the Muslims and I'm standing in front of the barbershop underneath they sign:

THE NATION OF ISLAM WAS FOUNDED ON THE BASIS OF PEACE AND AS AN ANSWER TO A PRAYER OF ABRAHAM TO DELIVER HIS PEOPLE WHO WOULD BE FOUND IN SERVITUDE SLAVERY IN THE WESTERN HEMISPHERE IN THIS DAY AND TIME.

But the email put different words over my head. Because I had been deemed insufficiently compliant with the day school rules, it read, it was the system's decision to allow charges to be filed against me—despite me being a minor and shit. And, yes, our passive-aggressive landlord charged that shit: brought arson charges against me and let me know by word on the street, phone call, email, regular mail, planes, trains, automobiles. We was headed to court.

*

My last supper I spent perched and posted at my usual spot. Vista was making her rounds and came and leaned against the dumpsters. "Boy, you should at least get you some pussy 'fore you go to jail."

"I'm going to trial, not jail, Vista. And it's the Youth Control, not jail."

"Same difference. You need to stop arguing words and go get laid 'fore this rite of passage."

"Nobody wants to have sex with me, Vista."

"Nonsense! It's so many fast little bitches lookin' to get fucked, you should get a gold medal for being a virgin, baby. How old are you?"

"Fourteen in a few days."

"They put fourteen-year-olds in jail?"

"I think so."

"Damn. It's a cold world where they'a throw a child in a cage. Now look at this, honey dip. Tell me she couldn't warm you up."

That's when I first seen you, Jacq. Across the courtyard. You was hella tall for a girl. That was the first thing that struck me. How long and thin you were. Vista kept talkin': "Baby girl need to save that natural shit for the white folks. Must be living with her daddy. Ain't no way one of these store-bought bitches would send her daughter out of doors lookin' like young Angela . . ." I stopped listening to Vista and made up my own story about you: you lived with your daddy weekends, but you was your momma's child. I pictured the return trip across town, your momma in the hills, a woman with status in her eyes, poised above you with a hot comb in her hand, unkinkin' it, flattenin' it, cussin' up a storm about naps and naturals and men's nonchalance.

Lookin' at you, honey-dipped, beanpole tall, and wire thin, with your highwater jeans, your Beverly Hills Polo Club T-shirt and face mask, and all that trappy, nappy hair atop your head, I couldn't imagine you living amongst us. The way you walked, so cautious, barely out the door and already had your arms crossed over your chest, bracing yourself for whatever might come next; eyes alive to anything that might be watching you. *What,* I wondered, *must she think of this new, old place?* Where living spaces, apartment doors, and porch steps melt into bedrooms and barbershops and beauty salons and homeless sleepers and Mexican tamale stands? Idn't it strange? Idn't it sad? Idn't it so much humbler here than the words that spill from the mouths of the rappers your daddy, your momma, one of them, maybe, probably both, never let you listen to?

You peeped me, looked my way with a stare more certain'n I imagined could come from someone who moved so cautious. We met eyes and yours kinda narrowed and got dark in the sunlight, and I seen that about you and I flinched and dropped my eyes to the plastic lid where I sat leanin' like a layer of human waste glazed across the dumpster. When I looked up again, you was already walking the other way.

"Baby girl kinda cold with it," Vista critiqued as, close by, a few fireworks crackled loudly, flaring 'fore falling silent, unexploded. "You seen that heel turn?" Vista kept talkin', not noticing. "Someone should tell the little girl it ain't no catwalk out here. Shoot, she probably wanted to holler at you, then seen this old lady choppin' it up with her crush, ain't want the competition."

I didn't say anything for a second, just watched you go. Then the fireworks went off, shuddering the ground like a earthquake 'bout to begin, or the warning 'fore a war.

*

Not a lotta news came outta Rockwood, good, bad, or in between, so when my misunderstanding transformed into an indictment and word got out around the Rock, boss, it caught a fire—so to speak. Negroes crammed theyselves by the dozens into the courthouse— not to support me, mind you, just to see the sentencing of the child who had tried to light Rockwood on fire. If I was acquitted, wadn't no one gonna scream "Thank Lord Jesus" the way they did when O.J.'s sellout ass got off for killing them folks. Folks stay shook about fire danger in California, a whole en-tire state suffering from PTSD, so even though arson wadn't anywhere in my intentions, these folks wanted me locked up. Most of the onlookers was probably rooting for a ten-year adult prison term. I did my best in trial, despite the odds, which was: all the evidence, plus the testimony of Mr. MacDonald and several tenants who did not appreciate they building nearly going up in flames.

Finally, Judge Kahn asked, "Why, young man, did you choose to endanger the place that you call home?"

I hesitated to answer. Now I had seen a couple court shows, hundred-year-old Judge Judy and whatnot, but a juvenile hearing works different. I ain't know the rules. I don't believe my public defender knew them either. I looked to the man whose rule was all I knew. Daddy stared forward, at me, at the judge, at the whole courtroom. His face said not a thing, a book with no words. I hesitated to try to explain his solution. I looked to Momma, who was masked up, but still I could see stress lines breaking like fault lines across her forehead, creasing her eyelids, making black crack like melanin wadn't magic at all.

For all her enchantments, she was still a sometimey saint who knew her way around a negotiation in the ghetto with her people way better'n she knew how to talk across a courtroom to a man in a robe with my life in his hands. I thought about her dinner plate, which the solution had saved. I thought about her Jamaican moment that had bought us the most beautiful of dinnerware, and I prayed for one kinda island insurrection or another to start up right there in that courtroom, Haitians, Jamaicans, whatever could set your boy free. But she remained silent. All there was, I realized, was my voice: "My mother's dinner plates were getting infestated with mold, sir. Smelled like a car engine, I remember, but it worked on a plate. It cleaned it. I wanted to clean everything. You know we got a high rate of illness in Rockwood."

The judge put his index fingers to his temples like two pistols point-blank to his brain. "Infested. The word is 'infested,' not 'infestated.' At any rate, proper English be damned, I believe the health hazard to which you are referring is, in common parlance, according to urbandictionary.com, the 'ghetto flu.' I've read the literature on this. Anthropological research. Apparently, culturally, it's related to the viral outbreaks of the past, '20–'21 especially. This is a kind of cultural residue from that dark time. A vaccine created by Stanford scientists was proven effective for the so-called ghetto flu years ago, pushing the most virulent influenza mutations to the margins of American medical concern. Nobody even wears those ridiculous, ineffective masks anymore. If illness is more prevalent in your neighborhood than, say, my neighborhood, why, that has to do with the poor health choices and genetic predispositions of the people who surround you, young man. It has nothing to do with any virus. Do you understand that point of scientific fact?"

Facts: There's vaccines for the flu, which is all good and whatnot, but it ain't like the ghetto flu is a one virus hitter quitter that you can bang a syringe into and call it cured. It's hard to keep still, let alone kill. It stays on the move, switches faces and names like a fugitive. You'd need as many vaccines as stars in the sky to truly get rid of it. I didn't know how to tell this to Mr. Your Honor, though, without pissin' the man off even more'n he already was, so I just kept my mouth closed.

"Did you ever think to ask your father what the ingredients were and why it smelled, quote, 'like a car engine,' unquote? What were its ingredients, young man?"

I knew enough not to look to my old man for the answer on that one. The white man had stole everything from the black man for five hundred years. He had a thousand ways to backdoor your brainchild, put a patent on it and call it his own. *And the A-rab's not no better,* he would say if pressed. *Tell anyone wanting to know your formula that the game is to be sold, not to behold.*

So I said what I knew the old man would say: the ingredients was bleach, vinegar, and Candomblé. They was Santeria, they was *Cuuuba* and *Afreeeca.* How could a bald man cut hair so good? Loas. How had a GED genius come near patenting a code-switching app? Orishas. And a lead detector and a mold remover to boot? *Ain't nobody's business but mines,* the old man would say if challenged. Heck, his own son knew not one single ingredient in any of his solutions, having never wasted the time it would take to ask him how he had invented his inventions.

But the judge wanted answers.

"Candomblé? Santeria? Young man, you disgrace those cultures, which you are totally ignorant of, which, as an African American, you ignorantly appropriate. Having vacationed in Dakar and Havana, I find your ignorance insufferable and your obstinance disturbing. I want to illustrate for you," Judge Khan said at sentencing, "that this was a very serious crime. Given different circumstances, your act of premeditated arson could have had a much more severe, even deadly outcome."

I couldn't see myself as no arsonist. I understood my actions as misunderstood, maybe ahead of my time. But that was not the moment to voice that idea. It sounded like I was about to get off light, so I kept my mouth on mute.

"Even many teenagers fifteen years and older are charged as adults in matters of arson. There's two categories of arson: 451 and 452. 452 is for reckless burning, which is what your defense claims that you've perpetrated: you were just trying to perform a neighborhood deep clean, you didn't understand you could hurt people or destroy Mr. Michael McDonald's property. I don't know that I buy this defense, given the smell that the solution emitted and the fact that your father went to such pains to make it inaccessible to anyone else in the home. But, then again, the public schools in Oakland have a fifty percent dropout rate, so perhaps my expectations are too high. Even in 452s, the reckless arsonist can be convicted of a felony and sent to federal prison. That is serious enough. 451s are even worse. Again, just imagine if you were a couple years older, son, and if we were to take seriously some of your statements to police and to the court that you view Mr. Michael McDonald as a, quote-unquote, 'slumlord' and a, quote-unquote, 'racist' and, rather paradoxically, a N-word 'who ain't been here in years.' Your subsequent actions could very well be construed as an attempt to willfully and maliciously destroy the property and displace the tenants of someone whom you have cultivated a racial animus toward. Wouldn't you agree that this might have been the way a judge, maybe even me, Judge Khan, might have seen your case?"

I was not about to cosign none of that, so I just stood there stone-faced, lookin' like every sociopath on the news feed. I looked at my parents. They sat still as lizards bakin' in the sun.

"If you were fifteen, we could move to have your 451 PC charged as an adult, and even though the damage was minimal to nonexistent, you would still be vulnerable to the following: One, 'if an inhabited building is burned due to malicious arson, the defendant can be sentenced to up to eight years in prison,'" the judge read off his phone. "Two, 'if the defendant's or someone else's property is burned as a result of the malicious arson, the defendant can be sentenced to up to three years in prison.'" Mr. Your Honor turnt off his phone. "You'll realize, given all that could have transpired, and not even touching on the potentially disastrous loss of property and life that your stunt could have caused, that you are a very lucky boy, son, even though I am not granting you the minimum juvenile sentence of a finger-wagging warning and a mandate that your parents not allow you on the internet for a few days"—his phone buzzed and he pocketed it—"nor even twenty-one days detention. No, your criminal behavior is rooted in an antiwhite, antiauthority attitude, the kind of mentality that brought about the damaging antipolice protests (riots, insurrections, really) of recent years. The root of all our country's troubles, the reason right-wing Americans had to rise up in retaliation." He was drifting off topic and I realized that I was drifting into jail. "Indeed, there is potential danger to the community from you if your mentality is left unchecked. Your anarchist, insurgent tendencies must be put a stop to, now. Detention is the best deterrence . . ."

*Urban Dictionary: The Ghetto Flu: 1) A popular culture phrase used to describe the multiple novel influenza viruses that came from Southeast Asia in the early '20s and caused the deaths of several million Americans during the decade, the vast majority of them black and Latinx; 2) The respiratory illness that emerged in '18 or '19, resulting in a pandemic and major economic losses worldwide; it was largely eradicated by vaccines in the '20s and only persists in sub-Saharan Africa and other pockets of Third World underdevelopment; 3) Hood slang that POC use to encapsulate all the challenges to their health and well-being that they face due to living in the hood; 4) A bullshit nonexistent disease that blacks blame for their self-created problems with poor diet, vitamin D deficiency, crime, history, and lack of exercise, now that blaming whitey for their problems is no longer believable because most white people fell for the *8:46 movement lies and are more pro-black than they are pro-America; 5) Whatevs.

+Soclear Health & Wellness Hour: On today's show, we will visit with andrewjacksonslaststand010621, an online account–cum–internet sensation who has made

As the Youth Control bus pulled off with first light, its shaky-ass acceleration was all I got for a goodbye to Oakland. It only took a few minutes rattling around like a quarter in a washing machine to leave city limits. Oakland is small. I had never appreciated that before. I was hella unappreciative before. Most mornings in my life had started with the sun, and I hated it because it meant I had to do Daddy's bidding. But now I appreciated how first light came in against the night, escorting the morning. It's the early-morning colors that I remembered when I was incarcerated and Homer, who gotta be a hundred poets given one name, spoke to me about the dawn, its fingers and roses. And even though when I was first in this motherfucker we call "the town" I had held most everything at a distance, now I knew I would miss all the common, normal shit: parties that ended in rowdy-ass second lines in the courtyard, brothers pirating basketball courts with East Bay funk dunks, the flashy Iranians in they plush velours, jewelry dripping off they necks and wrists as they stood outside they storefronts selling us they dreams.

Dogtown, Jingletown, Funktown, Chinatown, the Fruitvale, and Deep East, all our neighborhoods fell into my sudden past and we fled off to whole cities I had never heard of, places that to this day I couldn't point to on a map if you paid me; towns that was just orchards and vineyards and city limit signs that sprang up and was gone 'fore we could read them to know where we were; and the Youth Control bus just kept going.

Out there deep in the California countryside, we seen the sky turn orange. An official, judge-type voice came over the intercom, tellin' us there was a fire ten miles up the way, no need for concern. Someone asked, "Y'all got masks for us?"

The intercom clicked off.

The bus turnt into a straight-up oven and we cooked inside that mug. I looked out the window and watched as the sky filled with black

---

waves from Urban Dictionary to The Root by challenging Marxist groupthink, offering security expertise, and championing conservative politics. Over the next hour, they will be posting, texting, and emailing in response to our questions about a range of issues, from the legacy of insurrection and leftist terrorism to China and the link between public assembly and flu contagion.

flecks of ash that fell like so many black snowflakes on fire. The whole sky went black with smoke. A guard marched down the aisleway and snapped shut all the bus's windows, but not 'fore I tasted what I was pretty sure was a cinder. It crumbled into hot dust on my tongue. I put my head back and swallowed it and imagined that I was one of them cinders released by fire from the earth to wander the atmosphere, headed where the wind went.

*[*]

The California Youth Authority was abolished, I don't know exactly when, only that it was a punishment-based institution which ended its own life from hella corruption and brutality, COs setting up gladiator fights and whatnot. Around the time of the protests and all that, back when I was knee-high to a Nike shoe, folks got woke to the injustice of it all and realized that knockin' hard heads in they hard heads wadn't accomplishing anything but creating more and more super predators, or whatever it is Hillary Clinton called me 'fore I was born. COs lost they jobs, program directors got fired, and some good people came in and renamed the system Juvenile Justice somethin'-somethin'. They shut down all but a couple of the real-deal youth prisons and sent all the baby gangsters back to local detention centers. The good folks who marched for *8:46 got control of the justice system in California. They took it apart just like they tried to do to the po-lice, defunded that shit, one-eighty'd everything, and made policies to try and save us instead of killing us.

From what the inmates who needed a whole hand to count how long they'd been in told me, Juvenile Justice was the best of times, from handin' out new masks every day and lettin' damn near everybody go home every time an outbreak of the flu ripped thru the

*Insurgency Alert Desk, Third Bureau: Having been removed from the California Gang Member Database due to an algorithm error, records show that Copeland Cane was reentered into the database at around the time that he was sentenced to the California Youth Control. He remains in the database. Though he is not associated with a street gang, Cane is alleged to have ties to *8:46, the Black Panther Party, and other domestic insurgent organizations.

facilities—back when it wadn't a question that that shit existed—to sendin' kids to Buddhism camp for good behavior. Even for those who was fresh in and wadn't eligible for privileges or who didn't behave so properly, the local detention centers still hooked it up kinda nice. Didn't matter that a stocked library and meditation sessions and yoga and internet and gift cards courtesy of the State of California was like the last things you'd think to give a prison full of supposedly predatory children, it's what them white folks decided to implement. Mugs read and meditated up a storm and things was more peaceful. It was good times for some time.

Then somehow, some way, someone turnt out the lights on all that. While black people was paying bills and dying from the virus, the white people who didn't like the white people in charge, not to mention all the protesting and marching and murals for murdered black men going up and statues for dead white men coming down and cops being brought up on charges, took charge and took out they frustrations on us. The name of the facility changed again: the Juvenile Justice system, formerly called the Youth Authority, got turnt into Youth Control. Certain systems within the system got privatized. (This was years before there was private security all over Oakland, so back then I couldn't tell you what that meant, but I knew it wadn't good.) The rehabilitators and yoga teachers and librarians was out. Flu interventions was out. Masks was out. "Increased accountability" was in, whatever that means. I think increasing accountability just means counting shit till it disappears, but I don't know shit.

All's I know is I got locked up right when all them reforms to reform the reforms got formed. Like, inmates eighteen to twenty-five, who had been put in big-boy jail by our white allies, was crowded back into the Youth Control with us kids, just like in the old days 'fore all the reforms. The only perk that ain't get reversed was that the youth prisons that got shuttered ain't been and won't never be reopened. That would cost money, and one thing California ain't tryna do is spend more money on us. (It's also why they ripped the gift cards right 'fore I got there.)

Unfortunately, I found myself sent to one of the last of the last prisons still in existence way out in the middle of who knows where the fuck I was. I don't even think that town got a name since the only thing there is the detention facility. I found myself missing the Rock, but not like I missed it when the bus drove off. Then the feeling was a promise, a prophecy. Now the missing just sank into me like somethin' heavy I would have to carry. I felt the whole Rock hollowed out, evacuated by dynamite, fire, and foreclosure, a great big empty stone sitting inside of me, weighing me down despite it holding not a thing.

The state had seen the light, and then it heard I was coming and stopped paying the electric. New policy measures in the Youth Control got rid of all the females in the facility. I'm not talkin' about female prisoners. They have they own facilities. I'm talkin' about the yoga teacher girls with flowers in they hair in my dreams. They was replaced by a gang of no-neck dudes armored up and ready to throw down if we messed around. The one female still on staff was the Youth Control CEO or warden or whatever they wanna call her, head boss bitch Alannah Masterkov, a woman rumored to be an enforcer cold than the Financial District: "She will fuck you up somethin' serious," my cellmate, Larry, told me—more on that boy later. "Avoid her at all costs," he cautioned. I didn't want to find out how a female could get a rep like that. I made a mental note not to test Ms. Masterkov.

They say one of the problems with prison is that all the offender's friends end up locked up. Being incarcerated is no different than life at home, so there's no fear there. But I was not a typical inmate. I knew nobody except DeMichael, who was there when I got there. But blood acted like he didn't know me. He rolled solo dolo, and the few times I glanced in his di-rection and got on his radar, he turnt away. I didn't know what was up with him, but I figured maybe being one of the biggest boys in there instead of being the undisputed heavyweight champion had him feelin' vulnerable for once.

*

Policy-wise, meditation and fresh food was out, while anything that would keep us from mugging a tourist was in. For example, the library was not all the way abolished. We could still hit up the little room with the books during the daytime, but the selections was cut to the basics: textbooks on vocational subjects, a few canon classics, and nothin' radical, like no Malcolm, only Martin. No Garvey, just Atlanta Compromising. No La Raza, just los Estados Unidos. That's how I started to read Homer, not Socrates, and it's how I got to know about all the good Negroes without guns. These was the books Daddy had told me was nothin' but "boojie Negro bullshit." I always figured it was because my old man had no college and a big ego and a big brain with no books inside it hadn't been penned by Iceberg Slim that was the reason he felt the way he did. I mean, you gotta have a damn big pair on you to tell your charcoal-colored child that W. E. B. Du Bois ain't no more special'n the nigga doin' the weather on the evening news. Part of becoming an adult, I believe, is learning that Mommy and Daddy ain't God, they's just folks same as every other mistaken person.

Not that I condemn my folks for it. They was just doin' what they knew, which was gettin' by. If there was a college degree in Stretching Water and Rice Five Ways, Working for the Post Office and BART, and Never Taking Your Kids Nowhere, Black Americans would have a 100 percent graduation rate. They couldn't keep us outta PhDs in Not Learning Spanish and No Other Language, Having Your Ass Inside by Nightfall, and Not Fucking with the Same Shit White People Do. My parents didn't read books cuz books will not save your black ass. Books don't pay the rent. Books don't keep you safe at night. Cash money and a loaded pistol under your nightstand will, though. So I stayed fed and sheltered as a child, and always knew my way around a firearm, but I must confess I was dumb as a rock 'fore I got locked the fuck up.

With all them cutbacks, it seemed like all it was to do in the Youth Control was hang out in my cell, read stories, tell stories, and, according to my cellie, get ready for someone to test me. At first I thought him tellin' me that was his way of challenging me, but after a couple episodes of seeing other boys get ran up on without warning shots, the fights, the COs tear-gassing the whole world, including the two of us holding up the wall till we crawled back into our cell, I knew that boy was not about that life anymore'n yours truly was.

After the COs would subdue the squabble, CEO Masterkov would announce a lockdown so that it wouldn't be a round two. More cell time. The COs brought us each a book while we was locked down. Most fools just threw the book under they bed and never touched it. I did my share of diamond push-ups, too, don't get it twisted, but when my chest hit the floor and I could see the spine of the book staring at me, it was like it was talkin' to me, tellin' me that it had a story to tell that mattered as much as mines.

The COs who paid close attention knew I returned my books worn, the pages stretched and smudged. They would sometimes hook me up with multiple books so I wouldn't have to reread the same stories over and over. That's how I became a reader. That's how I learnt about Frederick Douglass pledging to fight every man at the docks just for the right to work, about Richard Wright by way of a down-ass Irishman sneakin' literature out the Memphis library and into his young mind, about Harriet Jacobs tellin' mofos how after the Nat Turner drama the slave masters got real particular about the love and forgiveness and Jesus part of the Bible. I would read about this or that harrowing affair that the author errantly found theyself in and I would think about what I would do, how I would move given the same circumstances, and if in the end I could survive like they did.

When I was reading, I was all good. I was under ancestral protections. But it was a whole 'nother story once the book was closed and I went outside my cell where others might read me, study me. I knew it wouldn't be too long 'fore they stopped studying me and assigned me my exam.

*

He was twenty-three years old, gang-affiliated, had hubcaps for shoulders from being locked up since Obama got in office. I'm pretty sure you coulda fit two of me inside old boy. He was a DeMichael Bradley–sized dude, maybe bigger. Later, I would learn his name: Mandela or somethin', some righteous black shit. Whoever named him ain't raise him, though, I'm sure of that, cuz as I was walking back to my bunk with my first care package cradled in my arms, I heard his whisper at my back. "You know a li'l nigga like you gon' get asked for that."

I turnt around. The care package was nothin' special. Edit that—I wadn't even sure what was in it cuz I had yet to open it and my parents never had been the type to just lavish me with gifts, especially after I went and fucked up and got locked up. I assumed they'd sent me some shirts and underwear, nonperishable snack food, maybe some music if I was lucky.

I was the opposite of lucky. Just holding the package in my hands and feeling home again was the best part, not the gifts. I just wanted to feel home in my hands, and here this dude was wanting me to hand over what little I still possessed. I looked around for DeMichael. He had the size to help me with this fool, but blood was nowhere to be found, as usual. It was just me and the monster. I wanted to tell him no, I did not consent to the monstrosity, and so, lacking impulse control and whatnot, that's what the fuck I did: "NO," I blurted, which surprised me. I could tell dude was surprised by me. Here was this little kid, not even a gangbanger, just a regular kid seeing fit to challenge him. For a long second, me and the monster just stood there staring straight confusion at each other. His hand, which was already outstretched to snatch the package from me, hung there in the air like a dead tree limb fittin' to fall on top of me. I was thinkin' the same thing he probably was, which was *What the fuck is this kid thinkin'?* When the stickup man asks you for your things, you give them to him and go the other way. Live to fight another day, as they say.

I don't remember what happened next, who unfroze first, me or the monster, or whether it was he who snatched my package from me, or if I bitched up and handed it to him. All's I remember is the weight I felt press against my empty palms as I walked back to my cell and Larry's expression once I arrived. The pity in his eyes. Don't nobody wanna be pitied, but there I was done had my cookies took, so how else was he supposed to see me? Nigga ain't say a single word, just let me climb in my bed and put the covers over myself, and still I felt weight where there wadn't any in my hands. My hands would not leave me be. I ran them through what was left of the separation at my scalp; I could still feel the difference between the two sides, even with my hair cut low. Still anxious, I started doing things with my fingers, contortions of triangles, circles, and cubes. I don't like building things in real life, never been much with my hands. But I started stackin' like the gang kids stack, one sign, one crew, then another and another. I discovered I could stack whole houses, massive architecture, cities and nations of gang sets. It's strange how you pick up certain things just from hanging around and half noticing the world around you and don't even know that you know all this stuff even though it's right there for you, hovering in the darker corners of your mind. The stackin' finally did the trick. Building a world by hand is hard. I got tired and teary-eyed. My hands were shaking as my mind drifted away.

*

I was visited. The old man peppered me with questions. How was I doin'? I was OK—not dead. Was anyone messin' with me? Nah. Did I like the comics they sent? They could send different ones if those wadn't my favorites. I would prefer some boojie intellectual books next time, but I was grateful for whatever literature they gave. What about the candy? You ain't let it get stale, did you? Nah, I ate it all. Were the guards civil? Yeah, no problems so far. Was I exercising? Was I reading? Was I depressed? Was I X? Y? Or Z?

"I'm good," I lied.

"Ain't no problems," I told them, even though, truth be told, half they gifts transferred ownership 'fore I could enjoy them.

"I just have to keep my head down and serve out my bid. No lasting harm will come to me," I assured.

I could tell Momma was verging on tears, but she kept them inside her mask. She is not the one to tell the world that she's hurting. None of us is.

"Stand up," Daddy commanded. I flinched. "You heard me, boy. Stand up. And lift up yo' shirt."

"What?"

"You heard me, Cope."

I heard him so I did as I was told. I raised up my shirt so he could see for hisself that no one had cut or in no other visible way abused his boy. But it's so many ways to be hurt and most of them you cain't see. I heard the way his voice relaxed, and it was then I realized all the fear hiding in him. I remembered his trembling hand upon the Treasure Island letter. His fear for me. His love, too. Love without protection.

*

There was the white boy, Larry. Larry, my cellmate, who I got along good with despite all the rules written and unwritten. The segregation of inmates was another area where reforms had reformed the reforms with poor results. Apparently, in the days of the Youth Authority, race relations was Jim Crow–ed badder'n a Birmingham bus before the boycott. Going to the pen was like getting drafted into the military, except instead of fighting for America, you had to fight for your race, be it black or Mexican or white or the others. There was no personal choice in the matter, just get to scrappin' based on skin color. Then the reform came thru like MLK and Obama combined, had people of different races and rival gangs, boys with drugs and guns on they records and blood anger in they hearts, bunked up in the same cell, like alliances and disputes and history wadn't shit. And that didn't go too good—nuff said.

Now, with the Youth Control taking over, the new hype was "limited integration based on past data." What had been shown to work to keep kids and officers safe while also "decreasing racial and gang tensions" would be "implemented as policy effective immediately." For example, the "newly processed inmates without gang-affiliated data," prime poodles like yours truly, might bunk with those of a different race, while them that had such affiliated data was placed back under Jim Crow.

Larry had a lighter sentence'n even I did, which was probably a complexion-related concession cuz cousin had actually put his paws on people. I was fit to be sainted by comparison, cuz, unless you count the back of Vista's hand, I had never been in a fight in my life. Meanwhile, Larry had got hisself kicked outta every public school in his town for fights that he apparently started and finished. That sorta thing was enough to get you locked up if you did it enough.

But the nigga was cool even still. What I liked about Larry, besides him being one of the few pale niggas in the Youth Control, making America a little more equal every day he was incarcerated, was he was entertaining.

When Masterkov had us on lockdown, which was most of the time, even my reading had its limits: I couldn't read 24/7. My eyes got tired, or my head would start to hurt, or I would just remember that I am not Malcolm X. And I could only do but so many body-weight exercises 'fore my biceps wouldn't move no more. Fortunate for me, Larry had him all kinda stories to tell, stories for days, that boy; he told me of secret orange grove opium farms and meth lab explosions, red-eyed rednecks and they rifles (which Larry said he used only for hunting, explaining to me how to endanger an eagle at any distance), and fishing trips on the water by hisself out in the middle of nowhere where the world is just trees and blue sky and a warm sun.

"Ain't nothin' better, Cope. I swear to you. One day when all this is over and we're grown, you and your wife are gonna come visit me on my land and we'll have us a big cookout. You'll get to appreciate country life. You might even decide you prefer it to the big city." Other times, though, his mood was sadder. "Where I'm from is a dying place, Cope. It's all addicts back home. People are either taking it to get high or they're making it and selling it. There's only two ways to make it out, by prison or that pinewood."

Really, Larry's decrepit old farm country sounded a whole lot like the so-called inner city. And sure enough, by the time I was finishing up my bid, a few more handfuls of white boys had been dropped into the Youth Control.

It took less than a week for one of them peckerwoods to show his ass and his ignorance, which only required that he get his hands on a writing utensil: NIGERS GO BAK TO AFRIKKA, he wrote on a wall in the kitchen. Wadn't even educated enough to put three Ks in "Afrikka." Damn shame. But most of them were all right, or at least no worse'n the rest of us.

The white boys came from Turlock and Hemet, Bakersfield and Blythe, but the hometowns and the color of the skin didn't mean much behind bars. The white kids just had on different birthday clothes, but everything after birth seemed similar: raw luck, bad decisions, bad breaks, diagnosed disruptive or retarded, now expelled, medicated, and incarcerated and segregated inside a facility where everyone was scared of everyone else even though we was really just one hurting child with however many different faces, different names.

**⁺

We ain't gotta hurry. They got a four-hundred-year head start on the story, ain't no few hours here or there gonna make a difference. These jokers can unseal whatever they wanna unseal and say whatever they wanna say. I don't give a yickety yack about that. I'm unsealing my memories so that it won't be a single thing they reveal about me that ain't already been told. After all, it's the life in between the incidents that's the real story, and only I can verify that. (And I don't think they know you quite as good as they think they do neither—but that's another story.)

Peep game: DeMichael Quantavius Chesnutt Bradley was the sole inmate besides myself who made the library room a regular part of his routine. But where I kept my head in a book for as many hours as I could, Black Hercules refused to spend his library time constructively. Black Hercules didn't read a single thing, he just sat in a chair in the corner drawing pictures on blank sheets of paper. When I think back on it now, I realize it wadn't time wasted, DeMichael was practicing conflict avoidance simply by staying clear of the other inmates.

---

*Insurgency Alert Desk, Third Bureau: Soclear Broadcasting has investigated Cane's juvenile record. We can verify not only his incarceration in the California Youth Control, but multiple incidences of violent and illegal behavior. It is also apparent that Cane is in communication with an individual who hails from Piedmontagne, California, a highly affluent suburb. This individual attends a university and is part of an underground insurgent network that uses dark encryption apps to conspire against government and the police. Law enforcement is attempting to gain access to university records that pertain to this individual.
⁺andrewjacksonslaststand010621: *8:46 lied about a lot, maybe almost all these cases! of police misconduct, brutality, and murder. When you do the research through the appropriate channels, you see that these "unarmed innocent black people" were thugs, killers, accomplices to killers, rapists, thieves, and the like. Let's unseal all the records! down to the birth certificates.

I knew he remembered me from school and the neighborhood. But DeMichael made a point of keeping his distance even from me. It was like he was taking the Fifth forever, in all situations. Like he had been programmed by his encounters with the po-lice to not say shit and not even to cast an eye at anyone. I found it sad that the biggest, baddest muhfucka breathing had had his lights dimmed like that.

And then one day out the silent blue yonder, he sat down beside me like we was back in elementary and shit. Just kids again, not inmates. Our shoulders bumped and I sank back a little. He gestured at the book I was reading, Booker T. Washington's autobiography. It was the kinda conservative, safe book the Youth Control allowed me to read. I flipped to the title page and showed him: *Up from Slavery*.

"You could write the sequel, call it *Back Down in that Motherfucker*. I never thought I'd see you in here, family," DeMichael's voice whispered, then boomed thru the room. "You was always so well behaved."

"They put me in day school on the island, then the judge went and got his back up and sentenced me here."

"That's how they do. They don't care about us. Blood, I remember the first time I got in trouble: I banked that crazy lady who was trying to choke the shit out our teacher, you remember that? They sent me to the island. That place, man, aye'body jokes about don't drink the water and the ghetto flu and shit, but *for real* for real, somethin' about that muhfucka just ain't right. I don't know anybody who got sent there who came out the same as when they went in. By the time I got back to Oakland, I was swole than a motherfucker. Twice as angry as before and could fight twice as good, too. I just kept gettin' in trouble after that, ended up here."

His linebacker-wide shoulder leaned into me and I looked at him without pulling away. I didn't know what to say. I don't even know what we talked about next. All's I know is, for the first time in a long time, I didn't feel alone. Eating dinner later that day, I chewed my food slow, trying to taste my tongue for Treasure Island poisoning. Does the flu taste a certain way? Can you marinate and grill toxins like you can chicken? Maybe it tastes like chicken, maybe we were tainted from the beginning and everything tastes like KFC—I cain't call it.

The next time we met, I told DeMichael some of Booker T. Washington's history of founding Tuskegee University and keeping the cracker happy, and he told me more about his history. Once upon a time when he was an even younger youth, he got locked up and then he went and fucked up and stomped out a kid for gankin' care packages from fellow inmates. DeMichael was sticking up for the kids who couldn't stick up for theyselves, went all violent Robin Hood, apparently. What he was unaware of was that the thief was thieving for a gang, not for hisself. When the gang sought retribution, none of the kids DeMichael stuck up for stuck up for DeMichael. Ever since then, my man had had no friends in the pen. "Don't try and do no good deeds for people. Roll solo, family."

"I did my last good deed the day I got arrested."

"On God. Real spiel, blood: Lay low. Do your time drama-free. But if someone do test you, you gotta let 'em know, na'mean?"

"Test me like fight me?"

"Hell yeah, blood. Don't act new to this here. If all you got when it do go down is these books, you won't survive."

"A gang member already stole my care package," I confessed.

"And I'm not gettin' it back for you." DeMichael laughed. His shoulders rose and fell like the green blips on a radio that mark the rise and fall of treble and bass. Between the laughter and the straining sounds made by everything he leaned on, DeMichael was a sound system his damn self. "You know," he said, lookin' at the Booker T. book, "what I don't understand is if niggas like this who wrote these books got so much wisdom to teach us, why is it niggas today stay gettin' locked up? Why we stay gettin' hated on? Why we stay gettin' killed by po-lice?"

"Maybe we don't read enough."

"Or maybe it's nothin' in these books we don't already know."

That line reminded me of Daddy. It reminded me that I missed the old man. I cracked a smile and sat back in my chair. "What should we do instead?"

"Look, when the white folks didn't like the way the government was treatin' them, they ran up in the White House with guns and spears and handcuffs and shit. Took that shit over. Ain't read no book on controlling shit, ain't listen to no nigga talk about it." He leaned back in his chair, matching my relaxation. "You cain't even get what you want in here just by readin' and thinkin'. Cope, it'd be a smart thing for a smart nigga like you to learn how to fight."

The next time we met in the library, DeMichael was ready to teach me to fight. Problem was, I was an unprepared student.

"Now, now," he said, "for starters, see how yo' feet is, you never gon' keep balanced standin' like a ramrod, blood. Loosen the fuck up and bend them knees, fool."

I studied his every word as he explained the repositioning of my terrified body, then the basics of how not to get hurt, starting with my breath. A couple years later in a private school on the other side of Oakland, I'd take an acting class where the teacher went on and on about our diaphragms and cycles of breath and all that good stuff. It made more sense coming from DeMichael, how if a fight was about to jump off, I would have to breathe deep into the scared places, the heart, the jaw, the shoulders. He had me breathing and settling into myself and standing balanced, and sure and then in the middle of all that good teaching, my teacher swung on me, I guess to put his lesson to the test. I seen his fist coming and ducked away from what was an intentionally wide, weak right cross.

The library supervisor was an ash-complexioned cat who looked like death eating a burrito. He was actually eating a burrito, and he looked up at us with tired, drooping eyes. Neither me nor DeMichael was bleeding. I figured that he figured that that meant that he was doing his job, cuz he chomped his burrito and went back to ignoring us.

I was posed up in my fighting stance, staring at DeMichael. "What was *that*?"

"Just me wonderin' if you was payin' attention, blood."

"All's you been teachin' me is how to breathe and stand still, not duck punches."

"That's where it starts, family." He began to circle me, left to right, right to left, and then taught me how to walk like the newborn I was: "Like this, like this, not like that, *like this*, side to side, slide, slide. Now if he's coming sidestep, don't be fallin' back like a bitch. Break his rhythm, come forward, flick out that left, just flick it, you got long arms. Ain't about hittin' nothin', it's about that distance." He showed me how to confuse a boy's feet, how to fuck up punching angles, how never to give up somethin' unless I was gettin' somethin' back for it, and only later to let my hands fly. Like I said, DeMichael Quantavius Chesnutt Bradley was a born teacher.

"And if all else fails, family . . ." DeMichael came close to me and whispered in my ear. ". . . just get you a weapon. Don't buy it off of none of these jokers, though." He gestured in all four di-rections, which I took to include everyone in the Youth Control, and he leaned back and laughed loud as car stereo speakers. "Anybody dumb enough to hand over they weapon's prolly too dumb to wash it. Don't wanna get AIDS off a blade while you in here."

My stomach turnt at the thought, but I was hella thankful to DeMichael: he taught me how to hold my own in there.

*

Despite the fact that the library supervisor never reprimanded us, me and DeMichael got summoned to Masterkov's office the next day. A summons in the Youth Control don't mean a letter in the mail and a court date, it meant gettin' handcuffed and strolled thru the facility at seven in the A.M. That was tiring and embarrassing enough, but it was the anticipation of what would come next that really worked my nerves. Where were they taking me? I wanted answers.

"Where am I going?" I asked one of the escorting COs.

He just looked at me, stitched up his lips, and shook his head. That seemed like a bad sign.

"Yo, DeMichael, you know where we goin'?"

"Jus' be cool, Cope."

We entered a great big back room office. The COs sat me and DeMichael down in hard-backed wooden chairs, uncomfortable than a mug. The COs stood back and watched us like we was liable to do a jailbreak. We sat and waited. I looked around at the oak-paneled walls and the Renaissance art portraits surrounding us and the sparkling chandelier above us and the plaques and trophies sitting on the floor. Then a door slammed and Masterkov appeared. This might sound like a cliché or whatever, but old girl was a statue of a woman, tall and thick and righteous and rigid. The tiles rang out against her heels like cymbals hit too hard and offbeat.

"Fighting in the library room," she began, putting the charge on the table not to be argued but acknowledged. We nodded like two animals already trained. Masterkov had an open folder in her hands which she was browsing as she rattled off our dates and hospitals of birth, our height and weight, hair and eye color, gender and race. She stopped browsing momentarily and looked up at the ramrod-ready COs. "You can go. These boys pose no danger."

The men left and then we was alone with the boss. I remembered what I had been told about her: avoid her. Instead I had gone fucked up and found this woman.

I looked at DeMichael to see if we should clarify the situation. His face was post-emotional. Masterkov was not a lawyer and this was not court, but whatever we said would likely be used and held and manipulated against us. Better to agree to whatever the punishment was 'bout to be and leave it at that. Anything else risked an escalation of penalties.

"Fighting's a definite no-no, boys. The purpose of the Youth Control is not punishment but accountability-based rehabilitation. We want the best for you. That's why we follow the science when it comes to adolescent mental and physical health. We cut spending related to virology and masking because the science changed and we followed it. We increased the budget for psychiatric care because the science changed and we followed it." She sighed and softened her tone so it wouldn't sound like metal scraping a voice box. "You two are both nice-looking, talented young men. You shouldn't be here. You're here because of poor choices you made and because of things outside of your control, like the intervention of the state to incarcerate you. That is your past. I don't want you to go backward behaviorally. When our security cameras picked up your sparring session, I figured now was the best time to nip this reversion in the bud. First of all, DeMichael, you're lucky you didn't maim this child. You're twice his size. I'd have to bring you up on child abuse charges at the least, involuntary homicide at the worst."

I realized that she was telling herself a joke. I looked at DeMichael, whose eyes was fixed on Masterkov.

"You boys want to leave here, graduate high school, go to college, get a degree, meet a pretty girl, live a good, clean life. Am I right?"

DeMichael nodded, so I nodded.

"We need to respect authority and situation and setting. Am I right? I want you to behave, whether you're in the library or in my office or wherever it is you find yourself in the future. Is that understood, DeMichael? You're nodding in agreement, but I'm not convinced that you're convinced." She snapped her neck at me. "You can go, Copeland."

In the Youth Control, you get used to gettin' orders given to you and you get used to doin' what you're told. Still, I didn't jump out my seat and run for the door. I looked at DeMichael next to me. His escape was yet to be approved. Masterkov didn't sound like she was 'bout to give him twenty-five to life, but I wadn't sure what would happen once he was alone with her.

"I can go?" I asked.

"Not if you insist that I repeat myself again, Copeland," she answered.

*

It's moments like that, when I look back on them, that cain't sit right with me. DeMichael got wrote up on the regular for his beefs with gang members, his shouting matches with COs; there was even a few punches thrown in anger on his record. I worried that Masterkov might over-punish big bruh. But only a few minutes after I returned to my cell, I seen DeMichael returning to his, uncuffed and unaccompanied, just like I had. And just like I wouldn't suffer no penalties for my actions, neither would he.

That made me feel better about leaving him behind by hisself, but it also surprised me. I was a first-time offender, but brother man's records had records. I knew punishments tended to be cumulative, with the bad shit you perpetrated previously playing against you when they decided how hard to whack you over the head for your latest infraction. But not with DeMichael. I started to see that keeping to hisself, not socializing with nobody, musta put him on the good side of the authorities, cuz he never got time added to his sentence or mandated to his cell 24/7. It was the type of thing that, once I seen it, once I looked at it long enough to realize it was a pattern playing out, I couldn't help but have questions. If we woulda been older and the crimes worse, I probably woulda wondered what po-lice paperwork my man had his name on. Once in a while, someone would ask me what I thought of DeMichael, since it was clear to everyone that I was the only person he could clique up with, and my answer was always the same: we was cool, but I ain't seen, nor heard, nor knew shit about whatever they was asking me about the brother. I kept my questions to myself. If any unwritten rules existed in that piece, the number one was not to get involved in nothin' that I didn't need to, not to ask no questions that wadn't mines to ask, and keep to myself as much as possible. And steadily, over time, I turnt out the light on that questioning part of Copeland Cane. I stopped wondering why this and why that and commenced to do unto DeMichael and every boy in that mug exactly the way that I did the authorities: I kept my head down, followed they rules, regulations, and the rest of it, and bounced as soon as they let me go.

*

My best inmate trait was that willingness to follow rules. I made my bed, kept things clean, didn't carry no contraband, and never spoke unruly to the COs. All this was notated day to day for 365 days straight in the logbook which they kept on me. They kept a log like that for every inmate. But where other kids had they records full of infractions, the only issue they had on me was my clinical depression, to which I say: Of course a nigga's depressed. A hundred percent of the boys up in there was clinical depressed. Hell, I bet if you put the CEO boss lady and her COs on the psychiatrist couch, they'd come up depressed, too. Every single person inside that institution was a depressive either by nature or by nurture. I was not unique. But where I had the other depressives beat was in the details: I followed the rules to the best of my ability, which was considerable, best of all being I was on time for everything—every bed check, every cell search, and every meal, which meant I was always first in line for lunch, which meant I grubbed pretty good in lockup and put on weight till I was muscles on muscles, rocked up like that river in Los Angeles. But it also meant I wadn't woke to what was going on behind my back till it was too late.

"DeMichael's boy." His voice rasped into my ear like a thousand years of weed smoke.

"My name's Cope."

"Nah, it's DeMichael's boy. You that faggot's boy. You a faggot."

I knew Shawn Barnes was right behind me. I weighed my options. Now, it's a lotta talk about how in jail you cain't let nobody punk you, this, that, and the third. I cain't speak for big-boy jail, but in the Youth Control it was beaucoup bad shit done went down that I won't speak of as it did not pertain to me. Lemme put it to you like this, I knew who not to squabble with and who I had to stand up to. I didn't really care that this future felon was pulling my card. The reason I turnt on him and put my chest straight into his chest was cuz of what he was sayin', or at least damn near sayin', 'bout DeMichael.

The boy didn't budge a step. We stood there chest to chest.

"Don't speak on DeMichael. He's a good dude."

"Where's the good dude now?"

I wadn't 'bout to look around for DeMichael. He never ate with the inmates at lunchtime. Everyone knew that. The boy was just wanting to distract me so I would leave myself open to an assault.

"He's my friend," I said, with my eyes right where they needed to be. "Fuck outta here."

I moved quicker'n a hiccup, shoulder rolling away from the force of the boy's first blow, just like DeMichael had instructed the smaller man should do. I felt the left coming and ducked it, too. I had seen this boy Barnes, high off prison-smuggled K2K, beat the dog shit outta enough inmates to know he wanted to get his hands around my neck and then start in with the knees to the stomach and related brutalities. I stayed low and drove into him at his waist and rose up with old boy on my back, and for the first time, y'all, I felt like a superhero. I had caught cousin mid-move, in the midst of lunging at me, so when I lifted him it was really his own momentum that did the throwing, even though to the untrained eye it probably looked like I tossed him over my shoulder and into the table and chairs behind us on some Superman steelo. I heard the crash of his fall and the "oooohs" and "oh shits" of the other boys. I turnt and looked at him lying there, sober as a dead body, and I considered jumping on him, hitting him hard enough to trademark his face. But I couldn't do it. Ain't have it in me to be that way.

Then the COs, who could be downright neutral and cool when things was tranquilo, immediately turnt into riot cops. Arms locked together and moving in formation, they tear-gassed us. The smart kids had cigarettes stashed in they socks and put them shits in they nostrils to filter out the fumes. The rest of us dummies cried for our mothers and hit the floor, gaggin' and chokin'. I just stood there watching kids crawl toward the bathroom. Then someone rabbit punched me in the back of the head and I went down hard, chest-first. I could hear the officers behind me herding people by race and gang affiliation into separate corners. I crawled for the bathroom and had almost made it when someone grabbed me by the ankle and pulled me back and climbed right over me. I took a knee to the head as he scrambled into the bathroom. Then another, heavier dude took the same route right across my spine. I checked to make sure I wadn't paralyzed and kept crawling. My head contacted someone's shoe and I scaled over him like was done to me, and then I finally wedged the bathroom door open one finger at a time. At least three of my fingers, I later found, got bruised black and blue from people slamming the door on them shits as I tried to claw my way in. It was like an evil rock climbing game where the climbers decide to push each other down the fuckin' mountainside instead of helping they brother make it to the peak.

Jacq, what I'm fittin' to tell you is a kiddie prison thing that don't nobody talk about. As inmates we never even spoke on it amongst each other. It was too stupid, too gross, too degrading. Inside the bathroom, kids was throwing hands like straight razors, aiming for vital organs, trying to clear a path to the toilet so they could take a dunk in the same place where we took our shits. I was afraid I would end up in a stand-up fistfight with a kid with sharp eyes who seen me throw Shawn and knew what I would try. I didn't really have no backup fight plan. I decided not to go hands. I kept low, put my head down, and scrambled toward the toilet. Right as I came within reach of the lid, I headbutted the backside of a boy with hubcaps for haunches. I went down again, face-planting into a hundred years of bathroom bacteria. The tear gas snaked underneath the door and made me weep just for breathing. I got up, half gagged, and put a shoulder into that ass and was knocked back again by the wall that was old boy's butt. This was not the ass of a teenage inmate, I realized. This was the ass of a twenty-somethin' asshole who ganked little kids for they care packages. As I fell back from him, an object fell from the waistband of his jumpsuit. I watched as it clinked and skittered around on the ground. It glittered up at me thru the waves of gas: a spearheaded plastic tool.

I picked up the shank and knifed old boy, driving the tool into his ass flesh. Motherfucker jumped out the way, his face dripping with toilet water. He was blinking, trying to see what happened behind him. He kept blinking and blinking and blinking blindly. I tossed the tool aside and leapt for the toilet. The relief was instant.

Jacq, you remember the scene in *Malcolm X* where the cops come for Malcolm on larceny charges? He's at the barbershop, gettin' his conk. I think Shorty Spike Lee is the one cuttin' heads, matter fact. Anyway, Denzel's got lye all in his hair and the shit's burnin' like a mug, so he runs into the bathroom and puts his head in the shitter to ease the pain and escape a scalping and whatnot, and then you hear "Nigger, get your head out of the toilet." It's the po-lice. Shorty's cuffed, and in a minute they both 'bout to be in blues. Well, in my situation my head's in a toilet, too, and it's COs in gas masks that make they voices sound like Lucifer on lithium screamin' on me. They barkin' at me to get my head out the toilet. It's total chaos. Only difference is that unlike in Malcolm's day, now behind they masks most of the COs is black and brown dudes from the same hoods that the inmates is from, so nobody calls anybody a nigger.

*

The boy who I knifed in the ass never did figure out who did it to him. The COs never figured it out neither. I made a clean getaway, or as clean and free as you can escape inside a jail. Unfortunately, there was other cats who knew exactly who punched and kicked and stabbed them. Usually, the fights for the toilet bowl was integrated ass kickin's, but for whatever reason this one broke down along gang lines. The consequences and repercussions wadn't confined to prison walls but instead made it back to the streets, where the aftermath went on for a long minute afterward. I was locked up at the time so I only heard tale about the street violence, but it didn't take long for the results to show up in Youth Control—beaucoup new prisoners, casualties of the gang wars. Combined with the influx of white boys from Larry's world, the facility got real crowded real quick.

*

"Copeland Cane, you are depressed, and as a result you are becoming violent and lawless," Masterkov spake and spoke and stated and shit from behind her desk inside her great office. This time there was no DeMichael around to help her forget I existed. "Your fight resulted in a full-fledged prison riot. Someone could have been killed. Several boys were injured. This is not good. It is a definite infraction. It's a sign that the antiauthority tendencies that landed you in this situation in the first place are beginning to reemerge. It would be a shame if you went down the police-hating *8:46 rabbit hole. Speaking of challenging authority, we've learned that your name has been included as a complainant in an inquiry into declassified information about a Bay Area environmental issue under the Freedom of Information Act. Do you know anything about this?"

"Declassified information?"

"It's information that's no longer classified. Anyway, that solves that. It's probably some kind of class action crap that's got nothing to do with you. Why would you be interested in the environment? Black people don't care about their environment. Too abstract. You care about getting out of here, right?"

I mean, that shit was racist as fuck, but she had me scoped out. I nodded.

"Copeland, we won't file charges against you for the fight. That wouldn't help anyone. While this place has certainly built you up physically, which is a handsome thing, nevertheless current research and political trends recognize the fallacy in locking young offenders up for long bids. It's just not productive. We need to find a better way to rehabilitate our youth offenders instead of simply punishing them for the sake of punishment. If society is ever to return to the safety enjoyed before the radical movements, we need to readopt the rehabilitative methods of the past, enhanced by modern science, of course, which is why medicinal intervention is so important. For decades, the State of California neglected its mentally ill. And what's resulted? Beggars, panhandlers, madmen, roam our streets and crowd our jail cells. The state is an utter disgrace. No longer. The Youth Control will end this outrage."

One second I was thinkin' how I just needed to stay silent and ride this lecture on out, the next second I had zero control of my tongue. The humble church mouse child who always abided his daddy's golden rule not to speak unless told to was replaced by a mouth that told Masterkov, "I'm sorry, I—I—I didn't wanna fight. I was just depressed. My daddy had me on task my whole life, and then one day he let me off leash and I seen this mold, which became my fixation, the new ghetto flu. I seen that this was just the latest way to poison us to get rid of us, so I knew I had to get rid of the poison instead. Ain't know that the poison wadn't in the mold, it was in man. Y'all put me on the island, y'all the real ghetto flu." I was an open book. You couldn'ta shut me up with my Miranda rights. If they add shooting Trump and killing the Kennedys to the accusations against me, you'll know why.

"Dynamic risk assessment and confession are complete. You are not a threat. We are done here," Masterkov said, drumming her fingers on her desk.

I cállated, kinda. Kept my mouth shut long enough to let her let me go. But whatever K2K and crack chemistry them fools dosed me with hit me hella hard, and the shit must stay in your system for a lifetime, cuz once I did come out of it, and on to this day, I cain't keep quiet to save my life. Anyway, the COs hustled me back to my cell, where I tossed myself onto my bunk like a sack of rocks and, Jacq, I fell deep asleep. Then I was falling and falling, crashing down levels of darkness. The dream came to rest in a burst of breath and a splash of light: I could see Daddy's black suit and the empty coffin. I looked at them floating there, so close I could touch them, tear them, break them. Then I knew I would one day bury my old man, and hell if I ain't start falling again. I fell face-first, my arms straitjacket style at my sides. A layer of landfill, dumpster trash, smoked-out fireworks, dog shit, human shit, old hanging cables, nylons, condoms, stained towels, napkins, bottles broken jagged enough to slice your neck, fire-scarred facades, and hazard tape, all in one big skim, appeared before me and I crashed thru it. I came out the other end with some woman's stocking stuck to my face, a thick cable noosed around my neck, and wearing an old man's dirty drawers. This was the dangerest, nastiest shit ever. How was it a superhero could go down like this? I kept falling. I knew I had to save myself. I wanted to save somethin'. The landfill flew toward me—or, correction, I flew toward it—and it seemed like if I hit it then it would be all bad for me, but I kept falling and falling, and then right when I was 'bout to meet that trash heap, have this spine of mines redesigned, I spieled out my superpowers one last, last time and hit a super swerve: I one-eighty'd and spun my ass back the other way, g-forces like a mug. Going up and up the other way, I avoided all that mess below.

As I flew, I peeled the nylon off my face, I tore the noose from around my neck, and I shook myself like a wet dog shakes itself clean, which got rid of them drawers. Everything fell away from me super clean, and I came back to the surface of the earth. I lay in my bunk in the dark with my eyes closed.

"Cope," a voice cooed, its tone healing as honey. "Lawrence Summerfield, the children at Treasure Island, your nemeses in the Youth Control, your friend DeMichael Bradley, whom we've been working with for years, with admittedly limited success, and the *8:46 movement, which I suspect you have sympathies with. All these negative influences. You can do better than them, Copeland. You can do better than them because you are better than them. You just need to give in."

I opened my eyes the way you do after you done slept dead off for what feels like forever. One eyelash at a time. The drugs hung hella heavy on my eyelids, but eventually I managed to see Masterkov's face above me. She was sittin' on my chest like a heavy-ass angel.

"Give in," she said. "Give in."

The bed grew warmer and softer with every word she spoke. I melted into its opiate embrace. My tired body found peace, my mind found peace underneath her voice, and my breath came slower and slower as her weight on my chest took my breath.

"Give in. Give in. Give in. You are better than those other boys."

I felt my chest sink under her weight. It did not rise again, but stayed sunken. I could breathe, but only real, real shallow. I felt the drugs taking me deeper under. I tried to pray them off my chest. I tried to pray her ass off my chest. But her spirit worked under my skin and sank hard into my heart, and I had to pray that much harder just to breathe.

They put it on me somethin' ferocious. Had me drugged to where I barely wanted to live. But you know the hero of the story cain't just die like that, not when you know he's still got shit to do 'fore he disappears. Maybe I reminded myself that I was my own superhero, even if I wadn't no one else's. Maybe that little notion allowed me to survive the Youth Control. But I wadn't thinkin' straight back then, couldn't even breathe with old girl on my chest like that, so I cain't call it . . .

*

Whatever that mess was they put in my water, it took me down bad and stayed keeping me down for days. I retreated, went back to my cell, my bedroll and book, and I tried to read, tried like hell, but the book and me wadn't on speaking terms no more, and that reality alone put fear into me. Afraid of what was happening to my mind, I kept my mouth closed and spoke only to myself for seven days and seven nights.

I recall like a bell rung clear in the dark the letter Momma sent me during that time. From Oakland, she wrote that Daddy's old lady in L.A. had sent a newspaper clipping and a photograph tucked in a manila envelope to our home. The news piece announced that the body of Daddy's estranged eldest son had been located deceased in one of the homeless camps that littered the city. The toxicology would take weeks to report, but the camp where he was found was known as an open-air drug market filled with the mentally ill, the formerly incarcerated. Overdoses was common as colds. *He was your half brother*, Momma wrote. When Daddy got the news, she reported, he just waved it away, said he wadn't gonna talk about it, that he would find the money and travel down for the funeral by hisself, that his son's addiction and estrangement was a long story without no real answers, just lotsa issues. I think Momma knew not to press him on it no further. It wadn't really her business, nor mines, she wrote. Daddy wadn't no deadbeat. He had fulfilled his financial obligations to this son, who was over eighteen years of age. An adult by law, at least.

The photograph his mother sent was cut from some other source, maybe a school yearbook, maybe a family picture. I thought about the woman cutting herself out the picture and sending the remains to our home. The dead young man was just a normal-lookin' young man with thin but broad shoulders, like mines, big starving eyes on a hard dark face, like mines. He was the color of shadows. He looked like me. Our uneven crew cuts was the same, our strong jaw was the same jaw, his face was my face just a few years' maturity and substance abuse apart, but the brother couldn't haunt me if his ghost tried. I did not know him from Adam. His image only made me want to know the man who connected us across time and blood and death. It was so much I wanted to ask Daddy, so many questions knockin' at my teeth that I couldn't speak. I wanted to know about his life before my life, all the years he had piled up on the earth without ever finding the trouble his sons couldn't stay away from. Obstinate and against the grain as that man was, how was it he had managed to keep hisself outta trouble? How was it he never taught his children that same common sense? But I never did ask. I knew I would have to sort that out on my own time, on my own terms. My questions wadn't innocent little things.

They threatened our whole family structure. I wanted to know why I had been raised as his little soldier, why I was brought into the world fighting, and what it was I was supposed to win. Mostly, I wanted to know him. I figured if I just knew him, the rest would make sense. But I didn't know him, not really, not at all. Who was he? How did he hold love and obligation for all of us, and why was his love so peculiar, parsed out like relief money if the relief only came when you ain't really need it? I imagined sweat cuttin' roads down his bald head, down the sides of his face, and the muscle between his thumb and forefinger bulging up and down on rhythm like a heartbeat exposed to the world.

*

Time passed. Larry, who loved nature, got hisself transferred to the firefighting unit, where inmates traveled around the state with real firefighting crews and battled the blazes that turnt California's mountains and woods into bacon year-round. I won't lie, I was jealous: Larry was gonna learn real fire science skills if he didn't get burnt up in the educational process. He would come outta jail with a chance to be a fully paid fireman.

"I can get a fresh start in the world," he told me 'fore he left.

Another complexion-related compensation, I thought.

Talkin' to the same boy every day for almost a year accustoms y'all to each other's thoughts and ways. Larry knew where my head was at literally and symbolically. "It's not your race, man, it's your record as an arsonist: arsonists can't be firefighters. That's why you need to fight your case and show that you were trying to do the right thing. Your heart was in the right place. Hell, Cope, you tried to save your apartment complex from mold damage. You're an environmentalist, damn near."

I wadn't no environmentalist. I hated my environment. And I didn't think fighting my conviction would do anything but scare the authorities into thinking I wanted to resurrect *8:46 from the ashes. Better to lay low and tranquilo. I turnt over in my bed and put my face in my pillow. Even though Larry was on the lower bunk and couldn't see me, I knew he knew by the sound of my movement that my mind was made up about folks having they mind made up about me.

The cell went quiet, which wadn't unusual. We lapsed in and outta conversation without any pattern or apology and would just start talkin' again whenever the spirit struck us.

"I'm the same as you," I said after a while, turning back over and unmuffling my mouth. "I'm a product of my environment just like you are of yours. My record is a product of my fuckin' environment. The only difference between us is my conviction."

"You ain't lying about that, brother," Larry conceded.

Then he was gone.

*

Due to not murdering nobody, I was soon transferred to a low-security detention center. Larry was in my rearview. DeMichael, too—too big to move. At the new facility, they stopped giving me crew cuts. My Afro came back, half Congo jungle, half Sahara desert. My depression diagnosis disappeared. Things got easier for me. It helped that everyone at the new facility was an actual child. Also, compared to the other jail, this place was not really a jail. On a piece of gated farmland, we lived in these long old shotgun shacks in rooms that everyone called "cells" but that were really just rooms like you'd find in a janky old house. We moved freer, too, tasked with chores to keep the facility running and hella "walking time," where we could socialize outside just so long as we didn't start nothin' nefarious.

In this re-laxed setup, I used my newfound talkativeness to keep myself on everybody's good side. Being incarcerated is not fun. People liked me cuz I was quick with my wit, always having funny observations about this and that, determined not to let our universal undiagnosed depression get us too down. That wit and determination, along with the way my body was bricking up, made me much less of a mark.

As my time ticked away and freedom came upon me like a brightening shadow, I felt a new kinda uneasiness. Brothers on probation will tell you that when they time is 'bout to be up and any little slip-up can have you violated and sent back to square one, you clinch yourself up in unaccountable ways. I started to notice little things, like the auras of white light that an early-morning sunshine will throw against uncurtained glass, calling you from your dreams with a suddenness that just opening your eyes never will.

I returned to my reading. Books and more books: *The Talented Tenth* and *Sister Carrie*, *Mrs. Dalloway* and *Black Boy*, *Another Country* and *The Sellout*. These stories spoke to me. I listened as I read, which don't even make sense, but hear me out: as I read, I heard how these writers built sentences, stirring and holding a cadence like a preacher; how they found the riffs and rhythms between the lines and ran with symbols and metaphors for days like the bridges in a song. I could see myself in the characters again, and again I thought about what I would do if I was faced with what they was faced with based on what I knew and what I had lived thru. I could see myself in Miguel, too, when one day he appeared straight out the blue.

*

At first, me and pretty boy just exchanged a few black nods, even though blood was mixed Mexican, Puerto Rican, Tongan, which makes him hella POC but only exactly 28.275 percent black.[*] The nod was just a way of sayin', *What up, Rockwood*, without the words. It was also a way of us lettin' each other know we knew the deal: a run-in with the law, Treasure Island day school, a run-in with the judge, and now baby-boy prison. Everybody's story was the same story.

I had always liked and admired Miguel. From genesis, we had spent time hanging out at the barbershop listening to men talk, and from them we constructed speech, learnt language, and got game. He had always had much more game than me, was flyer, flashier, and smoother with girls. He hustled, too. Had to. His fam was the type where both Momma and Daddy was liable to get laid off whenever

---

[*]Unless you believe Pacific Islanders was some African boatmen who got lost on the ocean and washed up on the other side of the world, which is what my daddy, my momma, and everybody else thinks went down. Given that fact, blood would be 73.8 percent black, to be exact.

the ghetto flu swept thru and the mayor closed the restaurants and choked off low-level labor. In the Bay don't nobody give a fuck about you if you're poor. Miguel's folks got laid off a lot. I guess the man of the house got tired of that shit and took one deportation chance too many, got locked up, sent back, and after that it was just my boy and his momma making ends stretch (and ain't met yet). Miguel had been hustlin' since Oakland was black, been sold fabrics, oils, weed, pills, whatever he could get his hands on and turn a profit. My situation was never as hard as his, so I never had to hustle like he had to. Was never about that life. But my life had gone thru changes; I had gone thru changes. We needed to speak, me and him.

"You just get here?" I asked one day, instead of nodding. I was down to a month left on my sentence. I wanted to learn from him how to make money so I could make my own way back in the world. I was tired of being ordered around by old men flashing badges; I wadn't tryna find myself back at home and back under the rule of my father, not when I knew it was a big world out there for me.

Miguel black nodded back, but smiled this time. "What up, blood. You know how it is. They say I messed with this one dude, happens to be one of my old customers. Muhfucka always comes up short and I cain't do shit but take a loss. He crossed me on the regular and I never responded, never sought no get-back. And they got the nerve to accuse me of puttin' these paws on him. They should know I'm too smart to do that. At least get my charges right, know what I'm sayin'? Sent a nigga to gotdamn Treasure Island behind the wrong thing. And speakin' of wrong shit, that island, blood, somethin' 'bout that mug ain't right."

"You're tellin' me, blood. That whole place is laced with poison. They don't put us there to survive."

"Word. It gotta be the devil. Have you wondering what's the meaning of life."

"Beans and rice, bruh. Everything else is just part of the poison."

"Cope, you're different. Somethin' about the way you talk and carry yourself. Like, you used to be quiet than a Chinese exchange student on BART after midnight. Now you done got talkative. Done got some height and weight on you, too, I see."

I nodded at Miguel's clipped braids. "Everything's different in here, blood." He was right, though. Once in a blue I looked at myself in the stainless steel mirror of my cell. My frame had me doin' double takes, like some bigger, older dude had snuck into my image of myself and was hogging the whole mirror. I knew what puberty did to the body, of course, but why was it that I was changing so fast and so much? It was like my life clock had sped up, like the island or incarceration had made me stronger. "I just wanna finish my bid," I said. "This place, it messes with you."

"For real, for real."

"I heard you was making ends downtown, though?"

"You know me, always got a hustle."

"What's the hustle?"

"What's on your feet?"

*

It just *had* to be the shoes.

That's right. Miguel had been hustling shoes. And not just any old shoes. You know who and what I'm talkin' about. Everybody and they momma seems to love this Negro. Hell, you probably love him your damn self. Michael Jeffrey Jordan's old unpolitical ass. If it was a championship in cigar smoking and not giving a shit, that dude woulda won all the chips. I'm generations too young to know his game, only seen a couple clips on social media and whatever, but what I know is that he keeps his distance from us. And, nah, don't gimme that *8:46 stuff. I was knee-high to his Nikes back then, but I remember they forced his ass into them statements and donations and shit, acted like he was Zuckerberg or some shit, like he just woke up one day and realized everybody ain't white and rich and beloved. Now, on the other hand, as someone who got political and got everybody and they momma mad at me, I gotta give Black Jesus his propers. He knows what he's perpetrating: just run, jump, dunk the ball, win the ring, don't vote, make that shoe money, snag a Cubana bitch, and smoke them big fat cigs like a boss. That's M.J., and America loves him for it. Even the hood, which he couldn't give two torn dollars about, loves that man. Blacks, Mexicans, Chinese, Vietnamese, white guys, black girls, everybody loves him and his shoes. You can put your hard-earned down and buy you a pair, hold them shits for ten seconds, then turn around and resell them at a major markup. Maybe black Mars Blackmon joked too true when he said, "Must be the shoes, money." Cuz it was all about the shoes and it was all about the money, and it's still all about the shoes and the money.

"You have any idea what you can get for some vintage Jordans on the resell market, loved one?" Miguel asked me one day.

Nah, not the slightest.

He answered his own question, kinda: "A grip of money." Point is, I got the point.

I knew I was going home long as I did not fuck up and commit no major infractions. On top of that, a brother wadn't trying to go home, recidivize, and return to that sunlight spilt across my windowpane. I remember Miguel assuring me that the shoe resell enterprise was 100 percent legal. "No doubt, blood. Nobody in they right mind wanna come back here. Keep your shit legal. I done made hella scratch with them shoes, all legit," he said. "The reason I'm in here is that my stupid ass went and got unprofessional, had my boy jack up a customer who had got over on me. Muhfucka went and snitched on me after he did the shit, said I told him to jack dude up, which is true so maybe I deserved to get sent here, but not behind some snitch shit. Learnt my lesson, though; that's the last fight I'ma get into *and I wadn't even in it*."

It's so much irony in life. "It's funny, blood, as much of a square as you used to be, I bet you you'll be a better salesman than me, more popular. You read and shit. That's necessary, blood. You gotta match these white boys book for book and you can do that. They be having the Kelley Blue Book on Jordan shoes and will quote your ass official list prices and shit. They come with real statistics like they the Better Business Bureau."

I might be smart, but I didn't have half his looks, which I bet probably sold half his shoes. "Don't matter, blood. Every nigga got they own audience."

Being in school would be the perfect front. "The student-athletes get gear for free. I ain't know that at first, was running all over the damn place tryna find customers. If I had known about the athletes I woulda went straight to them instead of fussing around with all them white people. All you gotta do is buy shoes off the athletes and then flip them shits at three times the rate at the shows and pocket the profits."

The system was stealing from the athletes to begin with, so it was only right that they sell the shoes the schools gave them. "You know how much paper these high schools and colleges be making off of football and basketball, blood? And do they pay the players a dime?"

I watch people's hands. Women know this; they stay watching a man's hands. Hands tell what the mind is planning, they tell what the heart is feeling. Miguel's hands hung open like doors he didn't care to close. He was generous like that, and honest, too.

"I don't front, Cope. I done things that was wrong, na'mean? Criminal shit. But ain't no shame in a legal hustle. Nobody gives niggas a chance. Niggas don't give niggas a chance. But I know a nigga who does."

The funny thing with all these investigations they wanna throw at my shadow is these fools cain't think to do anything but look up my records and talk to "school officials" and all kinda nonsense, like it's gonna reveal somethin' some way somehow. But I'm the opposite of official. My records don't tell you a thing about me. They don't tell you what I care about, who I love, the people that's made me who I am. Like, they don't know nothin' 'bout Miguel. You're not from where I'm from, so maybe y'all talk to the authorities, but I don't trust them jokers no further'n I can run from them. You cain't take a few notes from a file and know the truth about anyone, let alone someone like me who's lived half his life in a spotlight and the other half in a shadow. Anyway, since you're not the cops, I'ma tell you somethin' that's not in my records: me and Miguel shared more'n a street hustle. What we shared wadn't anything to do with what the investigators is after. What we shared don't really even matter to anyone but me. It was its own thing; it mattered to me and hopefully to him, which makes it part of my story.

When he spoke, Miguel liked to occupy his hands slappin' out a rhythm on whatever he had close by. In the silent breaks, I would hear him mumbling the song that came with the beat: We was working on the grave shift, or just was up too late, and definitely wadn't making shit. And at night, that song took us places. There was no out loud singing allowed at night, of course. If the authorities recognized you gettin' your Stevie Wonder on after lights out, you'd be in hella trouble. So at night we knocked out rhythms on the metal siding of our mattresses instead. The guards who patrolled the hallways never could tell one boy's beats from the next. But I knew Miguel's beat. In the dead of night, when I would hear it, I would stir from my restless half-sleep and try and mimic it, try and bring the beat back, but I could never get it quite right, or the rhythm wadn't what I thought it was, or whatever, cuz even when I hummed out the lyrics—the spaceship—that first back beat never broke, it just drifted off, past the sky and deep into the groove where I couldn't go. But I did my best nevertheless, just so my man would know he wadn't alone.

Jacqueline

There are so many pictures of you. I've seen them all because you've given them to me. They tell a story that words can't. The first are those of you as an infant in your diapers. Your mother can hold you easily in the crook of her arm. You are as small as the day you were born, as small and consequently as beautiful as you ever will be. These are the pictures that she will preserve and curate most carefully, for they symbolize a passage in time when she was everything to you and you were perfect. I am only a year older than you, but I can see these photographs and imagine holding you in my arms. Every woman and many men can imagine themselves holding you and they can imagine themselves as you. It is this universal bond that will assure that those who love you will share these photographs first with the world now that something bad has befallen you. They connect you to what we all once were and what we all one day may hold: the helpless human form only just come from the womb. We were all perfect children once, whatever we've become.

In a few months, upon your first birthday, you will become a gang member, according to a database, according to an algorithm, according to the news.

Then there are the pictures from your preadolescence. Your body, in stages, begins to take its unique shape. You are not round as the world, no longer the soft ball of your babyhood. You will never again be universal. You are you, or what your mother, your father, your world, forms you as. You wear the hand-me-down children's FUBU from your father's older progeny, his first family. Your bushy Afro has been harshly coiled and laid like overlapping vines into cornrows that fall into braids down the back of your neck. You look like a very small, very young, very innocent Allen Iverson. Looking at you like this reminds people not just of how young and beautiful you were not so long ago, it reminds them of other black men who used to be young, hard, and slender, with bright eyes and powerful energy. You are five, six, seven years old, but you are black so you have already entered the liminal space where you hover between the humanity that we all share and an existence that only your people and others displaced into diasporized and dehumanized space will know. People who are not black already count your calendar quicker than they do their own children's days, and because of that they may imagine that you are six when you are five, eight when you are six, ten when you are seven, or they may simply not notice if you die before you should. These images are unambiguous amongst black people, but they are up for interpretation in the haunted subconsciousness of the people who rule black people, none of whom are black. But this haunting is too deep, too bloodstained, too guilty to speak of, so these photos will never be published either unless we publish them and call you what you are: a child of God.

Ten is the age of darkness. By the time you reach it in reality, not in the imaginations of others, your body has thinned, your features have darkened, you look like your father except that he is bald and your hair is a simple tapered fade. You pose for your pictures now. You know how to hold your body in coolness, in seriousness, how to smile to approximate joy, how to be a schoolboy, a proper child, a momma's boy, your father's son, a feral thing amongst other wild boys and girls. Your photographers are your friends as often as they are your family members now. They curate you more coolly than your elders ever could, placing you inside the culture of the current moment rather than the memories of the past. You are, outside the space of their care, no longer anyone's child. These are the first photographs that the media will share with the public because they are the first photographs that feature a version of you that is self-possessed and personally defined to be both target and threat. Grown men are targeting these pictures right now, having plastered blown-up photographs of you upon the silhouetted, concentrically encircled bodies at gun ranges across America, so that they can fill you with bullet holes as personally as possible. You are only ever a child to those who love you.

The photographs of you at fourteen years of age are well known even to those who would never shoot a soul. This is the point: your image frightens otherwise God-fearing, reasonable people. They might want someone else to do something with you even if that something is only to arrest you. These images are evidence that you have been arrested before. At fourteen, your parents are out of the picture, photographically speaking. They might visit you in the Youth Control, but they do not live there. They cannot live there. You are out from under their protection. You are no longer anyone's child, least of all those who see you now as you were then. These pictures are like class photos if every classmate of yours is an inmate and the mandated uniform that you all must wear is a jumpsuit. All your classmates are inmates, your mandated uniform is a jumpsuit. It is an ugly dark green jumpsuit. You could be in the military if you weren't incarcerated, and by the looks of you—your sudden harsh crew cut, your broadening shoulders, your vascular biceps, the long, uncentered stare that looks through the viewer of the photograph and out to nowhere—you might one day. But in the timeless now of the photograph you are imprisoned, you are sullen, you are guarded. You are also worried about something no one understands: Did those days on that island suspended somewhere between freedom and incarceration contaminate and re-create your chemistry, your immunology? Nobody even knows that this is a thing except you and the others who were in limbo there, and me, because you told me. And none of us know whether this state of suspension, which is real, has really changed you in irrevocable, alchemical ways. What's the window period for annihilation? What's the half-life of genocide? Your whole life, every breath you've breathed, everything you've ingested, your environment itself in all its toxicity, has exposed you in ways that a photograph will never reveal. Lead exposure over a certain level is said to result in decreased impulse control, lowered IQ, and increased violence, and black communities in America experience lead levels seven times those of white neighborhoods. Our homicide rate is seven times higher than for white Americans. You can't see lead in a glass of water, let alone in the bloodstream in a photograph. You can't see what mold does to the lungs or the mind in a picture. You can't see epigenetics, trans-generational trauma, DNA and its ghosts; you can't see Greenwood burning. Some things simply go unseen. But at fourteen you call all these things you can't see radiation and your community calls it the flu and maybe you are both right.

I can't tell if you're omni-visible or totally invisible or both. There are no pictures in the news of you in high school; I have these pictures on my phone, tucked away amongst my private, locked albums. I'm sure other people who went to school with you do, too. I don't know if anyone has sent these images to journalists, but they should. I would if not for my fear of detection and investigation. Already, Soclear is dropping hints that they know that you are corresponding with someone. I don't need to tie their noose tighter around me. But these images could make anyone fall in love with you: your smile is sunshine against midnight-black skin. Like every boy, your eyelashes are the envy of every girl. Your bone structure is leaving behind its awkwardness, and your eyes are not vacant depths but warm, kind, and close. You are looking at me as I stare back at you from this side of forever. Time is such a strange thing, Cope.

You are eighteen in your last image. It is a picture that is widely circulated on the newswire, with your name, height, estimated weight, eye and hair color, all denoted below the head shot. Your eyes in this picture are somehow different, neither intimate nor vacant. Your cheekbones are rounder, wider, vaguer, as is your nose, which should actually be startlingly aquiline for a black boy but is, instead, broad and flat, your nostrils flared as opened caves. Your complexion, like the rest of the image, is a computer-generated composite of Negro manhood based on ancient ideas about skulls and racial traits and an artist's impression of the face of a black rioter in Atlanta, Georgia, in 2020. The artist remembers the emblem on the boy's torn shirt, *8:46; he remembers the car burning in the background of the photograph and the way it lit the boy's dark features in wild relief. He does not remember the child.

This image is not you, or it is the constructed, conglomerated you, the e pluribus unum you. Maybe it is the you that exists outside of time, that arrived here crowded out of all individuality, all names, all families, all tribes, all tongues, chained, massed at the shores of America four hundred years before your birth. Maybe this you has been here since the beginning. Whenever this image appears before me on one of my screens, in this fathomless news feed, I think how easy it is for black people to disappear.

Cope

Free finally, I was out and tight as a wasp with a memory. I touched turf, caught a ride back to Rockwood, and just as I was making my way to the gates, a Lexus coupe pulled up right in front of me. The female driver blew a kiss goodbye to the girl who opened the passenger-side door. You climbed out and appeared in the street. Had on that beautiful Pied-montay bomber, rose gold and gleaming, flashy as fuck and fuckin' flawless. Where I had went away with this still photograph of you in my mind, skinny and scared, your hair a mess, your face masked, your multistriped socks and highwater jeans a joke, twelve months later here I was returning to the birth of your cool. You was still skinny enough to slip thru a shut door, but now you had a confidence to your walk that was its own honey-dipped dance. Without the mask, I could see your high cheekbones and the rest of your pretty face. A professional had did your hair into tight cornrows with a long braid falling down each shoulder: one cold crown. And of course I loved the clothes.

You glided past the gates, across the courtyard, and into the apartment I had seen you appear from a year before. The Lexus pulled away only when you was safely inside. I took mental note, cuz everything had changed and ain't nothin' change. Funny how the world works.

I watched the Lexus peel past me, throwing up a gust of wind in its wake fit to give me chills. I walked up and seen somethin' else at the gate. The flyer read:

RENT INCREASE NOTICE
TENANCY AT: <u>ROCKWOOD HOMES</u>

THIS NOTICE SERVES AS A NOTICE OF PLANNED RENT INCREASE WITHIN THE NEXT **365** DAYS.

MONTHLY RENTAL FEES WILL ESCALATE BY <u>100%–200%</u> BASED ON THE SIZE OF APARTMENT AND LENGTH OF TENANCY. THE LAW REQUIRES NOT LESS THAN **60** DAYS' NOTICE OF A RENT INCREASE. IF THERE ARE ANY QUESTIONS, FEEL FREE TO CONTACT . . .

Just so we're clear, that's an eviction note, not no rent increase. I thought how you walked past it like it wadn't but a thing. Maybe that had somethin' to do with y'all's Lexus budget, but even still you mighta noticed it and taken a second to study it if it was news. Obviously it was not. The flyer had been there for a minute. My ass was just late to the eviction.

When I got home, the first thing out my mouth, 'fore anyone could even hug on me, was "What up with the rent note on the gate?" On cue, a cherry bomb shook the windows and rumbled the ground beneath our feet. Welcome back to the bomb shelter. Daddy waited for it to pass. He dropped his head and swayed a little, like an old church woman singing praises. "Gentrification," he muttered beneath his breath.

Gentrification. It was a word I had heard shouted like a curse from protest rally platforms downtown and seen headlining Oakland's many radical newspapers but never knew what it meant. Now I had a definition in Daddy's refusal to explain. Many moments like this would pass between us in the coming months, when word of Rockwood's demise would arise and Daddy would mutter somethin' to do with gentrification, and then he'd get quiet as a church rat and drift away into his inventions, not to be seen again for several hours. Momma had more to say: "Who knows, Cope. Maybe we'll have to do like everyone else is doin', move to Antioch, somewhere far away like that."

I only knew about Antioch—the Ock, folks called it—because it was one of them towns that the bus drove by as it took me to the Youth Control. I knew it for a dusty-ass little place where East Oaklanders went when they couldn't afford East Oakland no more.

"I am not moving to no Antioch," I told her that first day home. I made sure to enunciate each word of my denial fully, with conviction and confidence I ain't even know I had.

She was dicing limes in the kitchen for purposes unknown to me. Dinner was nobody's specialty in our home. I sure as hell couldn't cook. Momma liked to proclaim that she wadn't nobody's maid or slave, while Daddy, a tall, thin, knife-shaped Negro like myself, only ate as much as he needed to keep upright. Once in a blue, Momma would break down and cook an actual meal for everybody, four food groups and everything, but that was seldom.

"Juvie got yo' back up, I see," she said, a smile creasing the corners of her mouth. She patted me on my shoulder. I flinched. She startled. "What's wrong, Cope?"

I just looked at her. I didn't know how to answer. So much was wrong. You gotta understand, nobody touches you when you're locked up, or not often, at least, and not outta love. I couldn't explain that, though, without tellin' the woman who gave birth to me to keep her distance. "I'm sorry," I said, and hugged her quick and awkward. Then I confused not taking well to touch with voicing my feelings about leaving Oakland. I was outta practice carrying on regular conversations with regular people about regular things, like emotions. "I'd be a fish outta water," I said about the Ock.

She let go of my hold. "You're a fish outta water everywhere right now, baby."

"I'm just not feelin' the Ock too tough," I said, hanging on to that particular piece of outsider identity, which at least made me an insider in Oakland. "It's just, idn't much goin' on out there."

"It's lower rent is what's goin' on. You can get twice as much square footage for half the price is what's goin' on. Cain't survive out here unless you make at least $60K these days. See, this is where me and your daddy is different and where you and your daddy is so similar: I work for the hospitals. They's hospitals aye'where you go in this world. I could pick up and make a living in Timbuktu tomorrow. Shit, over there they probably hire more blacks'n they do here. If you ain't some kinda immigrated Asian—let me not go there. It's harder for him. The old man is in business for hisself. He don't have no institution payin' him twice a month. He gets what he gets from his community. Aye'thing he made, he did it in Rockwood and for Rockwood. That Negro can talk all the shit he want to about how he gonna make so much damn money and move on up, but this is his home. Born and raised on the Rock. He lived in L.A. for a few years, had them kids. It wadn't his life to live, though, and it nearly killed him. It'd be hard for that man to have to leave the Rock now. Y'all the same that way." She hustled the diced limes off the cutting board into a clear plastic container, which she then set on the dining table.

"Am I eating limes for lunch?"

"You got jokes now. Anyway, enough with this. We here for now, in Oakland, on the Rock. And we breathin', thank the Lord. And that's enough, thank the Lord. Now sit yo' free ass down and celebrate what we do have: you home, safe and sound and halfway sane."

Daddy came strolling in, a big store-bought pe-can pie cradled in his bony hands. My favorite. He was smiling like he was 'bout to get his picture took. It was one of the last times I'd see him smile bright and full like that. A moment later, I learnt that the limes was part of a Mexican, Yucatán-style dish Momma had learnt to make in a marketplace where not a single word was ever spoke in English. She could go into any market empty-handed and come out that bitch with the Queen of England's china and a recipe from every continent, that woman. She served me on her finest plates that afternoon. "Figured you'd like it," she said, as she blessed the plantains, ceviche, fish, and collards with lime juice.

She was right: I did like it—loved it actually—complected, conglomerated Californian that I am.

*

With Daddy's skills on deck most of my life and then being locked up for a year, I hadn't had to pay for a haircut in Lord knows how long. Back home now my hair was a natural mess. I couldn't let the old man go to work on my head, though, like wadn't nothin' changed. Everything was changed. I felt like I might break open if the dreamer set me down on the porch and memories of how things used to be came back to me. I might break if he touched me. I couldn't be in the apartment that close to him, his hands on my head, his love for me as close as his touch. He loved me too much. I couldn't deal with nobody's oh-so-careful attention all on top of me, holding me too close. I just wanted my space, my freedom.

I lit out for the new barbershop down the way. It was a cool outfit: clean, spacious. Good music. A food truck right outside. Portraits of the Obamas and LeBron and Jay and Beyoncé on the walls. Barbers who dressed professional. That was when I first realized that the masks was never given to us in the Youth Control cuz things had changed, not just cuz they didn't care about us, even though they didn't. Nobody in the barbershop, no matter how clean-cut and professional the brother happened to be, was rockin' a mask. Yet it was the most professional barbershop I had seen since the Muslims.

I stopped worrying about the masks and got free up in there, the barber cutting away the Mason-Dixon that divided my scalp, emancipating them slaves one nap at a time. I was cleaner-cut than an *Ebony* magazine model as I rode the BART train to a meeting in Berkeley, at the Shattuck station train platform.

Now, because I'm Bay Area turf by birth, I hate the BART train with a passion: dirty, virus-cooking, overcrowded, and just plain stank, not to mention too damn expensive. Bay Area Rapid Transit can go fuck itself for real. Now that the virus is dead, or whatever, and ain't nobody but my momma got a mask on, rich folks is back to riding the trains again, which of course means BART can increase the price of the tickets. I done spent so much money just to be miserable riding them tin cans, Jacq, breathing in bad air and whatnot. They're straight-up death traps, if you ask me.

On this day, I stepped off the train and onto the platform at the appointed stop, and I scanned the crowd. My man's people wadn't exactly difficult to spot. They had they hair all done up in multicolor dreads, red, white, and blue, full-on Americana for real. They had on flashy, shiny, studded, sequined clothes straight outta *Breakin'* or *Paris Is Burning*. I thought, *What the hell did I go and get myself involved in? Some kinda patriotic Folsom Street parade?*

One member of the crew, a big guy who could see above the whole crowd, met eyes with me, nodded and smiled. He sifted the swarm of BART bodies, sliding and spinning thru traffic like everybody except him was standing still. Hella lovely footwork. In a second, he was in front of me. Mr. America extended me a muscled, callused hand. "What's good, Cope! I'm the leader of the crew."

"Y'all sell shoes?"

"Hell nah. Did Miguel tell you that? Don't tell me that that nigga's gettin' his black people mixed up now?"

"I don't think he specifically said that. I think I misunderstood. What do y'all do?"

"We can show you better'n I can tell you, bruh. Come get on this next train with us."

I wadn't lookin' to hop on the train and breathe up the latest germs, but being broke is the flu, too, so I agreed to jump in and see about it. Wadn't much talkin' anyway; them brothers were performers.

*

It goes down like this: Mr. America walks into your BART train car and comes up the aisle like he's the president entering Congress to give the State of the Union, except don't nobody stand up and salute him. He makes his speech despite the disregard—it's some cold beautiful straight outta Obama game, about how all of us—black and white and brown, Left and Right, upside down and right side up—bleed red and blue and love the breath we breathe, the land where we live, etcet-era, etcet-era. The other two members of the crew low-key make they way onto the train, heads down, quiet, one with a phone that drips wires around his neck to connect to the speakers he has hid under his jacket while the other boy loosens his limbs to dance. The boy with the speakers wedges them things between the chair leg nearest the train door and the tin wall of the train with the phone resting on top of the speakers. After I started my work with the crew, it became my job to watch the speakers and the phone as the music cued.

The three boys always go in, dancing with Misty Copeland, Crazy Legs, and the Holy Ghost taking turns taking over they bodies. Breakin', flippin', flarin', they could be ballerinas, these boys with all the pirouettes on pointe and other mess they pull off; they could be gymnasts with the wild iron cross flips and pommel horse tricks they do from the rope ties and grab bars that run the length of the train ceiling; they could be anything that touches turf with all the pixelated poppin' and lockin', slow motion and vogue shit; they can hold forever on a train that never stops rockin'. Footwork from God. Balance like don't exist anywhere shit's easy. Cakewalk, moonwalk, pimp limp, church talk, whip that into some salsa and front flip to a perfect split. *BOOM-BAP.* They hang upside down from the beams, holding firm with just they feet and ankles, *BOOM-BAP*, and then against the laws of physics a boy will spill into a perfect somersault bleeding into somethin' triple-jointed like a comic book creation come to life, a human body turning itself into whatever it wants to be, *BOOM-BAP-BOOM-BAP*, a boy who can *Christ Jesus!* that ass from water to wine across motion and time.

They become the music, these brothers, the way they flow, transcend, and create on-beat and off-script. But the performance has rules. When I worked with them the act was as exact as clockwork. It always ran right to three minutes, never a minute longer, never a moment shorter, which was perfect timing because in the city the gap between BART stops ain't much longer'n that. It left just enough time for Mr. America to do the Obama act again and make an additional pre-scripted speech about donations. My job at that point in the proceedings was to shut off the music, gather up the equipment, and walk up and down the aisle, asking people to toss a few dollars into an upside-down Abe Lincoln top hat the crew had found in an alleyway and took to the cleaners. After I collected all the money, I flipped the hat on my head, making sure none of the bills slipped out. That was my performance.

Back and forth between Berkeley and San Francisco we went, same show all day long. An en-tire Saturday could fade away to the soundtrack of the same KRS-One and Slick Rick songs looped over and over and bookended by Mr. America's preachments on our human oneness. After a while, the smell-track of stressed, pressed human flesh packed tight and the screech of wheels and rails as we rolled along underneath the first hot layer of earth seemed almost like a second home.

The crew won't do a lick of dancing outside that chain of stops that runs between the two cities. Everybody knows where the money be at. Folks in Oakland and Richmond won't put down the jack to justify all the acrobatics they do. A lazy show is a waste of energy and won't net no money. Better to cool down and save the flavor for later, where the payoff is bound to be greater. Which is what I did, once I joined the crew and began riding the trains every Saturday, all day. North of Berkeley or beyond downtown, deeper into the city, we rested, lounging across empty seats like the homeless travelers who rode the train cars to nowhere day and night and day again.

'Fore the rhythm got radiated outta me, I had the same sense of time as everyone else. I could keep a beat and move my feet. Maybe I was no Miguel, knocking out Kanye's abstract stuff on bedposts in the dark, but I was on Colored People Time. So one day when Mr. America had the bright idea to make me part of the performance, at first I could just Soul Train up the aisle a few steps and be good. Our audience wouldn't care no way. The train car was full of European elders who was headed to the opera in downtown San Francisco. The kinda crowd that you couldn'ta put on a BART train at gunpoint back in the day with the virus and whatnot. There was even a couple of them who sported them little walkers with the tennis balls on the legs. Them things is unstable than a mug, liable to go sliding every time the train hits a corner. Meanwhile, the opera people was sippin' tea and eatin' muffins. It wadn't exactly a den of thieves up in there. Mr. America wanted to amp up the action. He pulled me away from the phone and speakers that I was guarding and caught a beat and motioned for me to battle him, and one, two, motherfucker, I tried to put one foot in front of the other on that rockin' and rollin' train and instead I stumbled into Mr. America because I was going right when he was going left. Then someone's walker slid into me and tried to dance with me. I walked it back to its owner, and then the train juked like Kyrie Irving on the fast break and I almost fell flat. Mr. America brought me back to the battle. How he could keep his feet, let alone stay on beat as he danced, was a mystery to me. I couldn't find the beat to save my life. The train tossed itself around a turn so sharp I lost my footing and fell ass-first into the lap of an old man in a tuxedo. He took it with a grunt, and some cussin', and slapped me in the back of my head, which I didn't take too personal. It wadn't his fault or my fault that I had fell; it was Mr. America's fault. Even if I still had had some rhythm, there was no way I could keep my balance on a stuttering, braking, twisting, turning train. No flares or back spins or any of that other mess was in my repertoire to begin with, let alone all them gymnastics them fools could do inside a moving vehicle. Gimme a piece of cardboard and a boom box, and all's you about to see is a cardboard retirement home for your busted-ass boom box to die in.

I couldn't help but be on time for everything but a beat. My dancing had turned into a disaster. I humbly found my way off of the old man's lap and back to the phone and the speakers, and I stood guard there, eyeing down the senior citizens as they made they trip to see Beethoven. And when our performance was over, I went around with the hat and collected the donations right on time.

After I collected the funds, Mr. America nudged my shoulder. "Blood," he whispered into my ear, "I don't know if anyone's broke the news to you, but you're a terrible dancer. Like, horrendous. Don't ever try that shit again."

"I didn't try anything. You made me dance," I hissed back.

"True. But still."

A younger audience came on board.

"Look," I said, "I used to dance OK, not special, but OK. But then somethin' happened. I lost all my rhythm."

"You just woke up one day ain't have no rhythm? All of a sudden? That don't make no sense, blood."

"It's a long story."

"We got thirty seconds."

"I fell into a sinkhole when I was going to day school on Treasure Island—"

"A sinkhole? Daaaamn."

The train seized and jerked itself backward on the tracks. Everyone in the Bay knows that jerk. It means the BART is ready to roll, which means the show must go on.

"They don't repair shit over there. Plus, it's all radiated and shit. I think I got exposed to some nuclear shit."

"*Daaaaamn, blood.* I thought the children was the future."

"Maybe Treasure Island is the future."

"*Blood,*" he muttered. "That's how they do us . . . Ladies and gentlemen, friends, Romans, Americans, Mexicans, please lend me all y'all's ears. I know you did not get on this train to listen to a brother speak, let alone to be enlightened and entertained by him. You were under the impression that you were traveling between entertainments, when in fact the real show is always the journey itself. You see, this train is a lot like the Bay Area and a lot like America: everyone's here, free and equal and oh so very beautiful. You all are looking fabulous this afternoon, might I add. You see, we're all one human family, even though the shades of our skin and the accents that we speak in might be a little, or a lot, different. We've come from all over the world to the greatest city in the greatest country on earth. And here we are sharing this moment! Me and my partners wouldn't want to be anywhere else but here with you. That's why we're gonna give you one beaucoup experience for the eyes and the ears right here. We are one people, one nation, shoulder to shoulder in a musty old metal cylinder going underground and into a groove . . ."

*

I don't dream much, and the dreams that I do have I hardly ever remember. But once in a blue, I'll have this dream where I'm riding the train, that bitch is bouncing along bad as ever. I got like two, three masks on my face, worse'n Momma, and then I hear that *BOOM-BAP. BOOM-BAP BOOM-BAP*. I look up and I see my old partners. They're dancing. They have the Holy Ghost all in them. The spirit is speakin' thru them. The hat gets passed by an invisible hand, and when it gets to me I pay them boys plenty, even when I'm down to my last dime.

IRL I moved on from the train hustle. Wadn't much I could contribute to the crew but to pass the hat on they behalf. But I was grateful Miguel had put me on with the crew. If not for him, I woulda been wandering East Oakland like Jesus in the desert lookin' for a job. Who was gonna hire a kid with my background anyway? The bank? The Chinese take-out joint? C'mon now.

Miguel was LinkedIn for the formerly fucked up. It had been many moons since me and him kicked it in the Youth Control. I figured he musta been sent home by now, but when I hit him up at his old cell number the mailbox was full and dude did not answer. I knew it was practically a rite of passage for a hustler like him to change out his phone. They stayed difficult to decipher. I had no idea what was up with my man. I would just have to wait and be watchful.

*

Them first weeks back home, all I wanted was to get my hustle up and make the world pay, literally, and in as many revenue streams as possible. I wanted to keep my folks in Oakland and, let me not be no liar, I also wanted some get-back for all the ways I'd got hustled, railroaded, radiated, and the rest. After all, hustling the system seemed like the best way to get ahead. Then news of another hustler hit Rockwood:

ROCKWOOD HIGH SCHOOL PRINCIPAL OUTED

Allegations of diploma fraud reached their zenith against local high school principal Sarina Jayachandra Campbell-Zayas when teachers union representatives voiced concerns on a conference call that the principal's alleged alma mater has refused to verify her graduation from its doctoral program in Educational Leadership. In short, Campbell-Zayas, it has long been suspected, may not have completed a PhD and may have erroneously and repeatedly over the course of several years' time listed the degree as having been completed on job application materials. Campbell-Zayas, it was also alleged on the same conference call, may have received her master's from an unaccredited institution. A source inside the school board has leaked to journalists that the Western Accrediting Association of Schools and Colleges, which oversees accreditation of Oakland-area public and charter schools, requested proof of the doctorate from National Student Clearinghouse. The appropriate transcripts were never produced, according to the source, but in closed-door meetings the matter was resolved despite the objections of faculty at other area high schools such that Campbell-Zayas has been allowed to continue as principal of the school. It is unclear whether Campbell-Zayas will continue to refer to herself as having earned a doctorate degree. The principal's Twitter feed advertises an internet-accessible graduation ceremony where she is to receive an honorary doctorate from the Todd $haw Music Institute of Oakland in Life Experience.

I read that story off my phone while perched up on my dumpster lid, and then I clicked over to her Twitter and they wadn't lying: there the lady was suited and booted, ten toes down in a big black graduation gown and hood, the whole lick. She walked the graduation stage to Jay-Z's "Hard Knock Life" and got robed and hooded, the whole deal. Then the lady styled and profiled onstage way past her time limit like she was lettin' them fools who tried to oust her *know* never to come for her head long as they lived. I remember lookin' out at Rockwood and just thinkin', *SMDH: Shakin' My Damn Head*. I had grown up in a tight little community. Not the best place in the world, I'll admit, but far from outta control. The planets of our universe rotated in steady circles. But now our issues was whirling outta orbit, out the atmosphere of anything that felt lawful and reliable. Maybe that was why I was so open to you, Jacq, when you approached me then.

"Hey, you."

I heard a voice which was softer'n and smoother'n anything I had heard on the Rock or in the Youth Control. I looked up from our unaccredited lead educator, half expecting to see Ms. MacDonald cheesin' at me, but instead it was you, Jacq, lookin' dead at me, serious but sweet, smiling.

"Hey."

"I'm Jacqueline."

"I'm Cope."

"I know who you are. I mean, I didn't know your name, but I see you every day on these dumpsters watching everything, watching everybody. I figure you must know about me and everything else that moves here."

"Only a little bit. Your momma be droppin' you here on Fridays after school hours. In a Lex, no less. She comes and picks you up on Sundays in that same Lex. I figure your daddy lives here. That light-skinned dude in 22A?"

You nodded. "He grew up here and moved back when they divorced."

"Why?"

You shrugged. "He doesn't have the budget of a corporate attorney like my mom happens to have. Piedmontagne is expensive. Rockwood's cheap—cheaper, I mean."

That made me think of all the things we could never afford. "You be rockin' that fly ol' bomber jacket: Pied-montay Prep. That's where you go to school?"

You confirmed. "I've got two of these jackets," you added, "this rose-gold one and another that's dusty rose. They're different."

"If you say so, Jacq."

"Jacqueline. And I do say so. You are right, though, I do go to Piedmontagne. Where do you go to school?"

"When it ain't summer?"

"I take college prep classes in the summer, but sure, when it's not summer, where do you go to school?"

"Rockwood. Right here. Ain't been enrolled for a minute, though."

I was expecting you to have somethin' to say about my unenrollment, but instead you said, "Piedmontagne's cool," like you hardly heard me.

"Yeah?" I said, since I was more interested in you anyway.

"I mean, it is and it isn't cool. I've lived there most of my life. And the school is highly ranked, so my mom really pushed to get me accepted there. She's ambitious like that."

"What's ambitious about Pied-montay?" I asked, and I didn't mean that in some kinda sarcastic way, boss. I just ain't know shit about y'all's city within a city or y'all's school or any of it. It might only be a few miles away, but like the Oakland Hills, I could count on zero fingers how many times I had been there.

"What isn't ambitious about Piedmontagne, or about my mom for that matter? I feel like they go together. She wants me to be multilingual. Piedmontagne has study abroad language immersion programs in Spanish, French, Farsi, Mandarin Chinese, and Arabic. She wants me to monetize my interests in social justice, literature, and new media. The school has a student-run newsletter with over five thousand subscribers, not including the students and staff at the school itself. It's kind of a big deal, and I used to write opinion pieces for the newsletter. I don't think I was great at being an opinion maker. Maybe I was a little scared to say things, maybe I didn't want to open myself up to people not liking me. Now I run the newsletter website as well as the data collection and analysis, not that there's a lot to collect and analyze, since the subscribers are the exact same people every year and the staff who read it are the exact same people every year because nobody's retired or been hired since my freshwoman year and it's against school rules to gather information about minors (that is, the student readers). But I play around with the software."

"What kinda things did you write about when you wrote?"

"You really want to know? Is that shrug a yes or a no?"

"Yes, girl—tell me." I laughed. "Why would I ask if I ain't wanna know?"

You laughed, too. "I think I just wanted to hear you say it. I wrote about private school admissions corruption, grade inflation, curriculum communalism—"

"Curriculum communa-what?"

"School curriculum, the stuff the teachers teach. A lot of it is based upon the Great Man theory. Like, this 'Great Man,' almost invariably a dead white man or a living very rich white man, did A, B, or C, X, Y, or Z. And that's it, that's history, that's literature, that's political science, that's science. When we communalize the curriculum, we'll make it more about everybody and everything, how what an entire community endured or overcame or protested about led to a historical outcome or landmark legislation or scientific discoveries, and it will be a lot less about what one guy wrote or did or whatever."

"And a bag of chips. Is y'all's school communified?"

"Communalized," you corrected me. "It has a long way to go." You looked back at the courtyard, which was definitely communified, communifried, communalized, and crowded than a mug with folks hanging out, playing ball, talking mess, watching they backs, coming home from they jobs, headed to they jobs, collecting cans, living homeless, shooting up, nodding off, and everything else under the sun.

"It ain't no Rockwood," I joked.

"I never said Rockwood was or wasn't anything," you said. "Piedmontagne has its own issues, especially when it comes to racial stuff. It's just got resources, like"—you paused over your sentence like a plane circling the Oakland airport in deep fog—"resources like a mug." You laughed at yourself for using some slang, which was kinda cute and kinda high sediddy at the same time, which confused me. "You know," you went on, "Piedmontagne's the only city in America that's surrounded on all sides by another city. They literally established Piedmontagne within Oakland as a separate jurisdiction from Oakland because they liked everything about Oakland except being a part of it."

"Damn."

"It's not exactly a diverse place. The copresidents of the Black Student Union are a black guy named Booker Taliaferro Adebayo and a white guy who wears boat shoes."

"What are boat shoes?"

"They're shoes—it doesn't matter. There's Chinese kids, of course, and maybe, like, five girls from Singapore. There's one guy from Dubai and a couple kids from another oil empire in the Middle East—they're census white, but not real white. All the other students are real white."

"Damn."

"My mom jokes around and calls me a 'social justice warrior,' which I think is some weird, played-out thing people used to call each other as an insult or something. She likes to say that all the best social justice warriors live with their parents and all the smart ones gave up and got law degrees. She wants me to go to law school, not work in media. I wish she would just let me do me. You know what I mean?"

Yeah, I had some experience with a parent who vetoed all my ideas and bossed me around like he was paying me. I just nodded, though, not wanting to start talkin' about me and the old man and all the ways he had me in check.

"Yeah, I'm on scholarship at Piedmontagne," you said, not really needing no prompting. "She made that happen. And she did pay for the study abroad immersion program, that she did do. I'm totally grateful for all of it, for real. I just wish she would ease up. And maybe have some sympathy and sensitivity for my position in that school as one of a handful of black people who aren't from Nigerian oil money. She has her whole AKA sorority of successful black women to lean on. What do I have? You know what I mean?"

*

Yay and nay on that one, homegirl. Your momma seemed like a superhero to me, she and all her AKA soros. I was in awe of all that black excellence. I would learn to live with whatever parental supervision and intervention I had to put up with if it meant I could study outta the country and learn to speak five languages and shit. Damn, I had to deal with the same shit and wadn't gettin' shit for it. I was too sprung and infatuated with you to tell you the truth about your problems. The truth was, wadn't no cavalry coming. What was your momma supposed to do, get you into Pied-montay for free on scholarship and then bring the rest of Rockwood with you, all of us delinquent, arrested, tried, and convicted mofos? What part of the game would that be, Jacq? Nah, Momma (your momma) was right: play that position, girl. Parlay that private school into a good college, get that law degree, and come back stuntin' on fools in your own brand-new Lexus, or whatever's above a Lexus. Buy that car and bring it back to whatever's left of Rockwood. Don't worry about us. We can hold our own out here. Or we cain't. We would survive on our little piece of Oakland. Or we wouldn't. Either way, it wadn't your issue. You wadn't even a Rockwood resident for real, turf by birth, loyal to the soil. You was just passing thru due to your daddy falling on hard times after his divorce—and wadn't nothin' wrong with that. If I were in your position, I would be hella optimistic, and maybe once I had it made in the shade to where I had the money to do somethin' for folks like Copeland Cane, then I would come back and do that.

Who knew if folks like me would be around by then. But again, that wadn't your fight. We was fighting our own battles. I was fighting, or at least hustling, or at least learning how to hustle.

*

Miguel might be a ghost, but that ghost stayed flying around in my thoughts. I remembered that he had mentioned a man named Guzzo. More than mentioned him, matter of fact: Miguel had made it a point to tell me that it was Guzzo who put him on the shoe game. I wondered what it would take to meet with Guzzo, get a supply of shoes, and start sellin' them bad boys at the sneaker shows that I knew happened online and in real life all the time. I had heard the sneaker heads in my hood boast about how much they kicks cost—jokers who couldn't do better than living in Rockwood was droppin' all kinda cowry shells on shoes. It didn't make the slightest sense to me, but so be it, I always figured. Like I said, fools love Jordan. That Negro is the American dream.

Now I did the math: If Jordan-loving Negroes in Rockwood would see fit to drop a hundred dollars on some shoes, what would people who actually had money be willing to pay for the same kicks? What if I could provide better shoes than what the hood rats of Rockwood would rock? What if I could get me a regular supply of Jordans from a trusted supplier and turn them mugs over at real profit?

My thoughts returned to Guzzo. Mr. Guzzo, that dude who Miguel had spoke so highly about back in the Youth Control. Mr. Guzzo, the Italian who would put you on if you had enough game to sell his shoes. He remained a mystery to me, this hustler or businessman or mixture of the two.

I had to go thru Mr. America to get to Miguel's cousin in L.A., who got Miguel on the phone from the Youth Control to call Guzzo and give him my number. When the grapevine finally got back to me, I had forgot I had even flown that kite. A 347 area code flashed on my phone. That was when I was still rockin' my old phone, which was newer'n this new phone. Telemarketer jokers and fools tryna talk me into signing petitions for stuff happening in Mississippi and North Dakota and shit used to call me all the time on that bitch. Sometimes I would pick up and listen to them just so I would learn what was poppin' on the other sides of America. "Hello."

"Yo," this strange accent that ain't quite sound like it wanted to speak English said across the phone line. Which was a surprise: ninety-nine times outta one hundred, if someone wasn't speaking English, the call was coming from California. But this call was from elsewhere.

"Who this?" I slipped out the apartment and into the courtyard.

"What kinda question is that?" That voice, confrontational as fuck. "Who says, 'Who this?' when they've just been cordially greeted by someone whose contact you've sought out?"

"Excuse me?"

"That's a little better, sweetheart. Let me introduce myself, since you clearly have no idea what you're doing: I'm Michael Guzzo. I run a pop-up shoe business. You're Copeland Cane, I assume?"

"Yeah. Yessir."

"You're looking to sell some shoes?"

"Yessir."

"You're flat as a board, kid. If you didn't sound black, I'd swear you were white."

That didn't make no sense. I didn't even know I was being insulted, let alone that I was down to my last seconds to impress this man. I didn't say nothin'.

"Look, kid, I don't have all day. I don't have all hour. I barely have this minute and the clock's ticking on that. Out of kindness and because I believe every motherfucker deserves a second chance, I'll kick your request back to Miguel and let him decide what to do with you."

"But Miguel's locked up—"

"You don't say? Criminals ain't the only people who can fly kites, kid. Look, while you're waiting on that shoe to drop, my advice is to lose the laid-back California dreamin' thing and go for yours every chance you get. Is that a deal?"

He ended the call 'fore I could answer. The silent phone went weightless in my hand. I sat there on my dumpsters processing backward. The call from Guzzo had finally came and here I was unprepared than a mug to shoot my shot with the man. I thought that I had learnt game in the Youth Control, maybe from the medication. But Guzzo only needed a few seconds straight out the 347, wherever that was, to prove me wrong.

I stood up on the dumpsters where I could see the whole Rock. It was no way in a neighborhood like mines, where every soul was some kinda character and every street was a stage, that I couldn't find not one Negro or Mexican or Tongan to hook me up some sorta way so I could entrepre-negro them shoes my own self. I spotted the chance right in eyesight, in the Rock's courtyard.

Trey was sporting the type of sneakers that I imagined Guzzo's vendors sold at the pop-up shoe shows. I got not just glimpses but two-hour movies of Trey's joints every day (and today was no exception): Trey hoopin' like his life depended on it. And maybe it did. Trey was one of them kids who would jump in front of a train for a basketball scholarship but wouldn't read a book if you paid him by the page. Being six and a half feet tall helped, gave him an easy-made identity to live with in the world. He was simple in that way that someone can be hella simple, even when the world that's spinning them around by the shoulders is totally complicated and confusing.

"What up, Trey?"

He dribbled around me and didn't say nothin'. Unmannered motherfucker. He was a whole drum line all by hisself, dribbling two balls at once on rhythm, between his legs, behind his back. I had zero in common and less to say to this dude.

"Where you get your Js, Trey?" I said.

Old boy kept on dribbling.

"They're nice," I added, going for the ego stroke even though I figured this must be how Mr. Guzzo felt right 'fore he finished his call to me.

"Fam." Trey finally stopped dribbling, the basketball spell broken. "Wha'chu think? Coach gave these to me."

That was the books of Genesis and Revelation of our relationship. Ain't spoke to Baby Jordan since, let alone done business with him. But I did take from what he told me that other athletes whose brains wadn't on strike for life might just maybe work with me.

(Full disclosure: I'm finna be hella vague right about now—the game is to be sold and behold, not to be told, especially when National Collegiate Athletic Association rules violations is in the mix and it's not just me I have to look out for but some never-to-be-named student-athletes whose scholarships and standing with they universities I refuse to jeopardize. Matter fact, Jacq, let's not even deal with no particulars pertaining to how I got connected. I'ma scratch and skip the record to where I'm jumpin' off BART at the downtown Berkeley station. I had an address, a phone number, and a name that I won't name. He was a college student-athlete.)

*

I approached his building, one of them tall, dingy, old, sad Berkeley buildings, which when you see it and realize hella students live in that mug, just beggin' for the virus to come and kiss them, it kinda makes you wonder why everybody and they momma wanna send they sons and daughters to go to school there. Inside, the structure was full of deep, empty hallways like sunken eyes, reminding me of Rockwood.

In his small room, I recognized the student-athlete. Ask me which shoes this brother, whose faceless silhouette decorated a downtown billboard that advertised the tickets to the next big game,* this brother whose dimly lit dorm room was the size of a shoebox, this brother sporting house shoes and high school hand-me-downs, eating Cheerios for lunch and shit—ask me what shoes brother man handed me to go and sell and I might could make some shit up, tell you they was a couple pair of the Air 12s with the white OVO leather that we marked up 300 percent and three of them red-and-black flu game joints, 200 percent markup, or whatever, but I don't remember and at the time couldn't tell one pair from another.

I took what shoes I could carry in the tomato-sauce-stained cardboard box that the athlete lent me, went down to the flea market, and did the best I could, which wadn't very good. After that first afternoon spent shoulder to shoulder with the vendors of essential oils and homemade tamales, herbs and incense and African scarves and African American memorabilia, I had sold just two of the five pairs of shoes I had came with.

I knew I would need to do better. I thought back on all what Miguel had told me. His voice echoed in my memory: *The train is the bloodline, blood.*

---

*
Silhouetted so the school or the vendors or whoever wouldn't have to pay him for his likeness.

According to what Miguel had told me back in the day in the Youth Control, BART riders made for the toughest audience on earth. These were folks had other shit to do, places to be, headphones to turn up so high they might go deaf in old age just to avoid you. *Blood,* Miguel's words returned now, *you need to peep the most straightlaced, professional-to-the-nines businessman muhfucka and approach that nigga. I'm not talkin' some nerdy techie: "Hey, Chad, want to video game it out on Friday night!?" Nah, not them niggas. We uppin' the degree of difficulty out this bitch. I'm talkin' find you a downtown lawyer, Financial District dude. Suit, tie, and briefcase; even better if he got on some expensive wingtip shoes since you wanna sell him on some basketball shoes and you know them business shoes is killin' his feet. He'd step out them joints and cry his eyes out, but he don't want people questioning his precious masculinity. You gotta understand, every man no matter his airs is insecure some sorta way. He wants somethin' that he don't have, or he's scared to lose somethin' that he ain't even sure is his to begin with. You find that dude who's frontin' the hardest and you rap to him. Your odds is, like, close to zero—I ain't gonna front—but ain't no other way to learn.*

Aboard the BART, it only took one stop for the perfect white man to appear before me. I'm talkin' a beautiful corporate muhfucka: expensive earth-hued suit, honey-toned tie, black leather briefcase, wingtips newly polished. He was standing in the middle of the train car, his legs straddled wide to balance hisself against its shakes and brakes. I thought about the downtown financiers, big men like this man, who would come from the Financial District down to earth where they would walk amongst the people. They would nod at the petty hustlers, complected men and boys like me who came up out the cracks in the concrete with cloth rags and tins of shoe polish. The big men would wave they ten-dollar white God at the little men. The big men would mount the grand old leather chairs that the city had sat out there waiting just for them like so many thrones right there on the street, and the little dark men would smile wide as East Oakland at the big men and thank the big men and praise the big men and kneel down at the feet of the big men and polish they shoes.

I got up from where I was chillin'. The car was half empty, so I knew the man would see me coming his way. I tried to approach with confidence, but then I said, "Sorry to bother you, sir," and like that I had handed him my manhood. I stopped a few feet from him and leaned against the peeling fabric of an empty seat. My stained cardboard box jutted into the aisle as I held it against my hip.

The businessman's briefcase sat in the floor space between his legs so that his hands stayed free to work the tablet that he held. He looked up from it only briefly. "I don't have any money to give, sorry."

"I don't want money," I said, lying without meaning to. I did want his money, just not in the panhandler way that he expected.

"That's what they all say." He made a point of jabbing his fingers into the tablet keyboard real decisive and shit.

I felt defeated again, at the get. This man could shut me the fuck down without effort. I considered just taking the loss and going back where I had came from, back to my seat on the train and back to the athlete in his little room with his unsold shoes. I looked at the man as I rocked in time with the train. He kept his eyes on his tablet. I needed to get my balls back.

"Who's the greatest basketball player of all time?" It was the last question I would ever want answered, but it leapt onto my lips because it had meaning in the world of men.

"Who cares?" The man jabbed the tablet like it had said somethin' foul to his momma.

"You do."

"Me and who else?"

"Everyone and they daddy cares who the greatest is."

"Oh, really? Enlighten me, genius. Who is the greatest of all time?"

"The Glove."

The man slowly logged out from whatever program he was working on, knelt, and dropped the tablet into a compartment of his briefcase. He zipped and locked it and stood to attention. "Not in a million years, man. Not in a million goddamn years. Did I hear you correctly? Kid, how do you even know who Gary 'the Glove' Payton is? I'm barely old enough to know who that is!"

"Everyone in East Oakland knows the Glove!" I shot back, stating the grand total of all I had heard said about this ancient athlete: "Is he not East Oakland's own, born and raised? Is he in the Basketball Hall of Fame?" I hoped the answers to my questions was yes.

"Yeah, bro," Mr. Financial District huffed, "but literally every great basketball player ever is in the Hall of Fame. So what? How does that make him the *greatest* of all time?"

"The Glove is East Oakland royalty." I stayed playin' my other card. "He must be the greatest."

"Are you serious? So now you're arguing on the grounds of a local popularity contest?"

I shook my head, and then it poured from me, every loud, cussing convo in the courtyard, every basketball court war of words which I'd witnessed from my dumpsters. All the sports pages scattered in the streets and on trains and in our hallways looked up at me in my sudden memory, names of players and teams and statistics of greatness that I had never noticed as anything but the noise of my neighborhood and the fantasies of men. "Oakland ain't local, my man. Oakland is a planet. The Bay is its own universe. We done raised up Bill Russell on these courts. The town birthed Dame D.O.L.L.A., J-Kidd, and many more. Don't lemme take it to baseball and football and track. Shit, what you know 'bout the first man to run ten flat was raised in the Oakland Flats? What you know 'bout Beast Mode?" I didn't even know what I was sayin', but it felt good to speak my speech. So often had I heard all these things said, and not just said but sermonized with the conviction of the Lord God Most High that it was almost like even though it was just me and this Brooks Brothers/Giorgio Armani dude arguing on the train, I felt I had a whole congregation in my corner, pulling me toward my pitch. "What you know 'bout the only man to look Black Jesus in the face like a straight Oaktown gangster in the NBA Finals and turn that joker into Black Job, just gettin' worked and made to suffer for the sins of humanity? The Glove made Jordan ask God why he forsaked him."

"That is the most blasphemous shit I've heard in my entire life! Is that what passes for logic in the world of East Oakland basketball? No wonder your Warriors moved across the bridge to San Francisco," the man said with real anger in his voice. "Michael Jordan won that championship series, by the way, not your guy the Glove. Jordan's poor performance in the one-on-one matchup against the Glove is basically irrelevant. He's far and away the greatest basketball player, athlete, and competitor in American sports history. There's no one who's paralleled Jordan's success on and off the court. He led the league in scoring for a decade, led his team to six NBA championships, made the NBA a global business. He . . ."

The preacher kept pushing his religion: Jordan this, Jordan that. It was like listening to a Sunday school teacher read out the begets in the Bible. But I'd started it and couldn't stop it now if I wanted to.

". . . And let's talk cultural impact and marketing influence, since you wanted to make this a popularity contest, which was a bullshit tactic, by the way, but it happens to be what I studied for my MBA at Columbia. The Jordan shoe is the most iconic piece of footwear on the planet. These wingtip shoes I bought from Brooks: six-hundred-dollar price tag, beautiful shoes, my wife loves them. I would throw these in a goddamn river if it meant I could get my hands on the red-and-black 86 Air Jordans."

I didn't say nothin'. I let him catch his breath and adjust his posture so that he didn't have to stand there stiff as a Roman pillar holdin' up the whole sky.

The businessman got quiet and looked me up and down like the cops do, and then dude broke out in the biggest chicken-eatin' grin I've ever seen: "Ingenious, really. You set me up beautifully. You captured my attention. You involved my emotions. You expertly shifted me from my entry point to your sales goal. Your abilities are rare. Are you in high school? It's always hard to tell how old you people—I mean, you African American people, you all just look amazing. The most beautiful woman I ever dated was the color of dusk and honey under dim lamplight, an absolutely gorgeous specimen of a girl. She looked years younger than what was on her driver's license, I promise you that. Here's a picture. Do you agree? *You are in high school.* Wow. OK, no more of those pictures for you. Don't report me. Anyway, you are an impressive, intuitive persuader. Here's the thing: I not only work in finance, I give back to my community. I create and maintain endowment opportunities for Piedmontagne Prep—"

"Pied-montay Prep?" I asked, thinking about you all of a sudden, Jacq, in the last place I would ever find Your Flyness.

"Yes, of course, Piedmontagne Prep, the most prestigious prep school in the Bay Area. You know of it, I assume?"

"Kinda," I confessed.

"There's no kinda when it comes to my school." The right reverend retook his pulpit. "You'd absolutely be a great scholarship candidate. I don't do kinda; I'll call my shot now. You have rare practical intellect. There's not enough of that in elite academia. Not enough African Americans in elite academia period—not sure why that is, maybe someone should study it, figure that out. Anyway, you should apply to our school, provided you aren't already at an elite institution, which does not seem likely given the circumstances under which we've met. Make sure to put my name on your application: Douglas Deadrich . . ."

I nodded and I promised I would, and as he kept on talkin', I thought about the shoeshine men in the Financial District. I thought about the street corner preachers in the Fruitvale who hawked they Bibles and ten-cent truths. I thought about my old man: more'n once, I'd heard him call nine-to-five suit-and-tie cats prostitute hoes, especially the black ones. And on the flip side, I had heard him praise them brothers who wadn't too scared to go into business for theyselves even if they suits was raggedy and the business didn't make a dime. I could just imagine Daddy praising me for the first time. *Go to that school and study, but keep sellin' them shoes, too. Be a hustler and a gentleman.*

A few minutes later I pocketed a clean $350 purchase off of playboy and snatched both my balls back. Later, I worked them bills between my fingers, just feeling all that crumpled cash. I thought about what I could do with that kinda skrilla, what kinda man it could make me, and then I thought about that faceless silhouette and them ticket prices and old boy wearing clothes that ain't even fit him, and I reminded myself how it couldn't be no parts sentimental, it had to be all about the money, but the fact that it was all about the money for me, all about surviving, all about doing what had to be done—all that meant it was about way more'n just money for me and for old boy. So I went back to his cramped little apartment and gave him all but fifty dollars from my profit.

*

By the time I got home, the sun was starting to go down, which in the Bay only means the light gets even brighter, like it wants us all to go blind by nightfall. I walked in. Nobody was in the front room. I could hear Momma from they bedroom. She was on the phone with one of her girlfriends. She liked to tuck herself in a corner of the apartment where you would barely know she was there till she opened up and started speakin', and then she and whosoever she had on that call with her got to talkin' like technology don't exist, like the cable lines and wavelengths and whatnot don't carry sound and they gotta holler from Oakland to Indiana and back to hear each other. You might call it annoying, but I liked hearing her inside doors without no mask just being herself. I imagined floating beneath the surface of her speech.

Below her loudness, everything else in the apartment hummed low. I figured the old man must be on the back porch. Wadn't no razor cords running beneath the door and wadn't no noise coming from back there, so I knew he couldn't be cuttin' heads. Which meant, by process of elimination, he was probably back there consulting hisself on how he was finna turn around the family fortunes. It ain't easy to make a fortune if you're not fortunate, though. I thought about my fortunate day, about meeting Deadrich, about seeing in his support a di-rect line to you and your school, and I thought how the old man had never had such fortunate luck that I could recall. I felt bad for him but good for myself. I wanted to tell him what I had in mind to do, from applying to the Pied-montay private school to hustling sneakers to all the rich kids up in that mug: I could get a proper education and enough money to at least attempt to pay our increasing rent.

I knocked on the door.

"What up, Cope?" he called in a low voice thru the door.

"How you know it's me?"

"Cuz you don't sound nothin' like yo' momma, now do you? Even your knock sound different. Y'all don't know how good I know y'all."

I opened the door. He sat in his barbershop chair. The sun had anointed his bald dome with one wide aura of white light.

"You knock fast because you young, don't quite know where you should be headed but you in a hurry to get there. That impatient shit will get you in trouble. Already has," he added.

I heard him, but I wadn't listening. I had somethin' to tell him. In a rush, I spilled everything all at once, almost in one breath— the train, the businessman, the prep school—I was finna get to the sneaker business and explain that plan in more detail when he sniffed loud as the BART train coming down the tracks. Ain't a mystery where I get my impatience from.

"Them jokers across the way be sellin' ramen out they apartment." He shook his head. "Cain't knock the hustle, but I can smell the sodium. Anyway, pump them brakes, Barack Obama. Look, now, you don't need to attend no high sediddy prep school. They ain't teachin' nothin' over there ain't in the books right here in Rockwood. Don't let them hustle you. You nothin' but a number to them. They need you for they di-versity records and that's about it. You don't wanna be in nobody's records no kinda way. Have you up in they brochure next to some Friscodite half man, half amazing, and a fake Indian with pigeon feathers in her hair, and all kinda other ol' bullshit you cain't even imagine."

Indisputably, Daddy did have him an imagination. But I knew that I was not a number to you. I knew that even if I was a number to Deadrich that he had some excellent numbers for me, three hundred some presidents in my palm to be precise. If it benefited me to add to the diversity of y'all's school, I didn't see the problem with it.

I heard the old man out, sitting there under what was fast becoming nightfall, smelling the sodium that our neighbors was selling, but I wadn't listening to a word that he said. Long story simple: he was too negative. I couldn't stand how he wanted me to see the world, everything an illusion. He was also becoming ankh-right-ish, which meant he was becoming a bigot, basically, against whatever it was he imagined y'all was. I didn't need his negativity. I didn't need his imagination. My imagination was made.

I left him on the back porch and went inside and fell into my bed. Ain't even undress, just dropped there on top of my bedcovers, underneath the noise of Momma's conversation and the old man's negativity. I didn't care how bad he slandered Pied-montay and all its privileges stacked like so many expensive suits in a shop he'd never see except from outside its window. I didn't want no Goodwill hand-me-down yesterday's fashion. I wanted to see the thing fresh and new, up close and within my price range, and of course I wanted to keep connecting with you, Jacq, and the only way to do all that was to transfer schools. It was time to get outta Rockwood.

*

I started scholarshipping: filled out the forms, figured out what my grade point average was and what my parents' reported income came to and the financial aid I would be eligible for (short story: all of it). I did it all and waited. And they responded. Y'all responded, like, out the blue in a letter to our apartment. I was asked to come in for an interview where I would meet with the principal and he would ask me a number of questions—and that's when I hit pause.

Don't front, boss. An interview? Why wouldn't I be thrown off? Ain't like you get interviewed to get in to public school.

*

"Ain't like someone interviews you to get you in to public school," I remarked next time I seen you.

We were both loners by then, you especially. I didn't kick it with my old friends hardly ever, and most of the folks on the Rock still took me for crazy. You, on the other hand, were a mystery and maybe a threat. Boys who knew they didn't have the education to keep your attention wadn't about to approach you asking for your number. They knew you came from somewhere other than the Rock, and wherever that somewhere was was not gonna include them. Plus, they wadn't tryna get rejected, they self-esteem smashed, so they social distanced from you and you from them.

"There also aren't tuition fees and scholarship and fellowship awards at public school," you rejoindered. "There aren't precollege Stanford classes or study abroad or virtual reality curriculum or private security personnel on call via every student's cell phone. It's just a different world altogether."

"It might be some crazy interviews if they start interviewing every kid round the way."

"Then maybe they should do that. After all, you can learn a lot about somebody just from talking to them, or just by letting them talk to you. That's all an interview is, right? Two people talking to each other?"

"Why you askin' me? You should be giving me game."

"It's not a game," you said. "Or maybe it is. The whole world's a stage—a game. You can play that game just as well as they can."

"You sure 'bout that?"

"Oh my God, am I? You're their dream, Cope. You're kind of my dream, honestly."

"You Martin Luther King now?"

"No. I just like you."

"I like you, too. But why would *they* like me?"

"Don't you see it? Maybe you have to go there to see it. You've never been to Piedmontagne, have you? I didn't think so, which is funny, not just that you haven't been there, really, but that I didn't expect that you had. It's right there." Your finger followed the line of the freeway stretching west toward downtown. "It's like ten miles from here, but it's a city inside a city, remember. It's a world inside a world, and in that world sits this elite, nationally recognized prep school that enrolls not a single student from East Oakland. It makes them feel racist."

"But what about my background?"

"You're gold."

One of them God-level fireworks thundered from below, shaking us sideways. Like Daddy would do, I looked at the ground and shook my head for no reason and let it pass. "Gold? You sure 'bout that?"

"Yes. Why wouldn't I be? Why wouldn't you be?"

"But what about my record?"

"What record?"

So, basically, you remembered a lot less about me'n I did about you, Jacq. You hold no memory of me from the long before which I think of as my innocence. Nor do you remember the day of my arrest. Where most of Rockwood still watched me like I was liable to go for my matches, you gave me the benefit of the doubt.

"If they ask you about your incarceration, just figure out something to tell them that will make them feel good about it. Say that you're a better person now, and then say that there needs to be more abundant options for the rehabilitation of troubled youth and that the state needs to invest in, you know, like, *innovative strategies*. They'll respect the way you manipulate the conversation. I'm pretty sure they view manipulation as a positive characteristic."

*

Momma spent all morning gettin' dressed for Pied-montay, and then she helped me put myself together. Only one problem: Daddy had the car keys and wadn't about to relinquish them to what he'd been calling my wild boojie goose chase.

"What you tryin' to get from goin' to that school anyway, Cope? Books is books. Teachers is teachers. Them folks don't have a magic potion that they sprinkle on yo' ass and make you new. And what's so special about them? Who died and made them the shit?"

I was not about to argue with him. The gap between us was growing beyond argument and beyond reason. It wadn't just that I had changed, turning hard and distant. He had changed, too. His voice fell away with a quiet fatigue, which was not somethin' that I remembered about him. It was new. He never talked openly about his notions and inventions anymore, where before he would go on for days. Now we rarely spoke.

"Hush up, old man," Momma said, sighing. "The boy idn't arguing with you." She opened her hand like he might actually concede her the keys, just drop them into her palm because she asked politely.

*

Me and Momma hoofed it, taking the train as close as it could carry us to Pied-montay. I swear, Jacq, Bay Area Rapid Transit must have a blood pact with the rich that it won't go nowhere close to they enclaves. You get off the train and gotta walk, like, a mile or more thru some twisty-windy cobblestoned streets just to get into that mug, and then you're there and you see the three-story homes and private po-lice on every street corner and you know that this ain't Oakland no more. This is different. Then them jokers smile at you and one of them up and gives you precise di-rections to exactly where you're going like they knew you was coming, and then if it wadn't clear to you before, now you really know that you don't know shit about where you're at.

We followed the heaven-sent officer's hand. As we took the route, we passed by the Artisanal Absurdity Shop, whatever that meant, and a storefront that's signage stated that it sold only luxury animal-skin wallets, and we passed by the Goodwill giveaway where Daddy got the fine suits that the people of Pied-montay got rid of all but brand new, like money wadn't shit, let alone real. Despite all the walking, we arrived at the campus on time, which surprised Momma but not me. I ain't never late, no matter the obstacles, that's just how it is. We came to the school and strolled along another cobblestoned walkway and underneath a stone arch that read FIAT LUX, which you let me know is Latin for "let there be light." The pillars that flanked the walk were draped in coils of flowered vines. Birds-of-paradise rose like leafy pelicans from the rock crystal–sprinkled soil that ran on either side of our path. And after the third marble water fountain and the fourth statue of a big-money benefactor to the school, I started to feel like this new world might just be some kinda paradise.

The interviewer was the principal hisself, Dr. Anthony Kennedy. His doctorate diploma hung in an expensive frame on the wall behind him along with several other degrees and certificates. I read the names: Harvard School of Education, UCLA School of Social Work, Stanford University. You couldn't fake these credentials.

The interview instructions stated that my guardian was to wait out in the lobby, where the principal's assistant had prepared for Momma a whole flight of mini-cakes and finger sandwiches and sleek literature about the school. Me and the man faced each other alone in his office now. Hella awkward, this next piece—he ain't even look at me. He stared down at the stack of paperwork in front of him. I waited for him to speak, but that wadn't happening. Instead, he ticked his finger along the page corners of each sheet of paper in the stack, like he had peeped it in the bookstore and was considering whether it was worth buying. I wondered if I was supposed to talk first, if it was initiative like that that an elite prep school was lookin' for. Part of me wanted to speak, to make statements, promises, predictions. Not just acceptance but tuition forgiveness was at stake, as well as the chance to hustle shoes to all the Douglas Deadriches of Pied-montay, California. I hadn't came all this way to sit quiet.

"Dr. Principal Kennedy, it's my pleasure—"

"Not yet. Just a second," he said. He raised a finger in the air and held it there.

I went silent but sat up a little in my chair, using its arms to lift me up like little kids do to get a better view—I wanted to see what it was the man was reading. When I glimpsed the form, I realized it was no paper that I recognized, definitely no transcript or personal statement or anything that was from my application materials. I was confused and stuck. It took me a moment to reseat myself properly and let go of the chair arms.

I waited, staring at the man's silver hair. His beautiful, expensive suit was silver, too. It was exactly the kinda thing Daddy would splurge for secondhand at the Goodwill if he had to go downtown for a permit or some shit. I imagined my old man wearing the principal's hand-me-downs, and all of a sudden I was glad he had stayed his contrary ass at home.

Kennedy finally spoke, his voice whispery. "I was just reviewing the projected budget. Let me start by affirming that we at Piedmontagne believe that diversity is the engine of our institution, white supremacy must be undone, and social justice must be our mission. Doubtless, you've applied to other area prep schools—Head-Royce, College Prep—and they are, I'm sure, enthusiastic to bring you into their fold. Those are fine schools, of course. But at Piedmontagne, we believe we offer more, beginning with our location not in Oakland proper but within the privacy of Piedmontagne."

He paused and looked down at his desk and his papers again. I wondered if you were right about me being Pied-montay's dream.

"We are prepared to offer you a full scholarship to our school. Your mother"—he gestured at the closed door behind me—"will not need to pay a dime. We also, and now I speak for my admissions staff as well as myself, are of the opinion that your presence will provide something that we lack."

"How can I help?" I asked, and remembered to smile.

*

Pied-montay Prep was hella—hella everything that the Rock was not. My first days of school, my eyes and attention stayed stuck on its structures: the big old pillars and beautifully architected buildings, the marble fountains and statues of previous principals, who had went on to govern colleges with famous names that even I knew, and of the billionaires that owned the online learning software that saved the American school system during the pandemic, according to the plaques that stood alongside the statues. Then there was the structures of the school curriculum: the classes offered included semi-basic instruction in literature and biology and calculus, shit like that. But then it was this other door you could walk thru if you had more'n just your tuition paid: the all-online Virtual Reality Education Elective Program. The study America and study abroad programs that took y'all all over the country and over to Europe and whatnot. The language immersions in Vietnamese, Cantonese, Farsi, French, and Spanish. The CEO and CFO Days. The field trips to Facebook, Salesforce, Twitter, and the companies that the men who had been made into statues had made.

One thing that didn't require no extra funds was the school newsletter. My contemporary American literature teacher wadn't fittin' to wait for me to get my eyes off the statues. Day one, during class, she told me to check my email. We was, like, doing a writing exercise or some shit, and here's the teacher tellin' me to get on the internet. A teacher up in Rockwood would scream on you, damn near threaten your life, for gettin' on your phone during schoolwork. Now

I didn't even need to reach for my phone. Y'all had computer laptops at every desk. Pied-montay would be very different.

> Dear Cope (the principal tells me you prefer this to your full name),
>
> I'd like you to join the Piedmontagne High Times-Picayune newsletter as a columnist. Though unfortunately branded by wayward hippies turned high school teachers in the 1970s, in the intervening five and a half decades the newsletter has come to belie its moniker, becoming a serious institution in the Piedmontagne community where young writers develop and readers of all ages are provoked to thought and reflection by the insights of our emerging scholars. Writing for the school newsletter will make you a better writer, a better steward of your own thoughts, and it will make our readers a better community.
>
> Sincerely,
> Mrs. Greenberg

I looked up at her. Why hadn't she just asked me in person? The way people do when they're being normal and shit. She reminded me of Ms. MacDonald, the pencil-skirt thinness, the yoga-type tats, Iceland white and whatnot, but she was older, so instead of coming off kinda nervous and nerdy and fun, Mrs. Greenberg just seemed focused. Her eyes locked on me and I didn't know how I would say no.

"Yeah, I—" I began, only to have her wave my answer away.

"Answer me via email," she said, rigid than a mug. "We can discuss the particulars at another point in time."

"Thank you for the offer," I wrote her while she stood there, like, three feet from me in the middle of a quiet classroom. The other students typed away on the assignment like this was normal, which maybe it was in prep school world. "I accept."

*

The point in time came for me to speak with Mrs. Greenberg after that Friday's class let out and the other students streamed away. None of them knew me, let alone spoke to me, but I seen a couple heads turn and notice I was still sitting there like the last kid left on the bus. I wondered what they thought I might be staying late for. I wondered what I was staying late for.

"Thank you for accepting the offer and for making some time for this brief orientation," Mrs. Greenberg began. "I'm looking forward to working with you on the newsletter. Positions on the school newsletter are highly coveted by our students. The journalism class that produces the newsletter is not a class that you can simply enroll in. I teach it on an invitation-only basis. I didn't want to cause unrest in our literature class by having you blurt out that you were accepting my invitation to be on the newsletter."

"Unrest?" I asked. It was a word I associated with protests, with insurrectionists and anarchists, with Trump and *8:46 and all that old back-in-the-day stuff. What did it have to do with the classroom where I sat? Pied-montay sure ain't look like the kinda place for people to plot rebellion, nor for black folks to protest the po-lice.

"Unrest," Mrs. Greenberg restated, real firm and convincing about it. "Our students take very seriously every academic opportunity that is open to them. Even opportunities that may not be open to them but that they predict might become so become turf wars. I wanted to keep you out of any conflict. Just keep quiet about it and show up for the class on Monday, OK? It will take the place of your physical education course."

It was like she was giving me game on how to stay safe in gang territory and how not to snitch on nobody, namely her. I did the same as I had done when I got advice like that in the Youth Control: nodded my head and kept my quiet.

"This is a very different scholastic environment than you're probably used to, Cope," she went on. "When people say that a school is, quote-unquote, 'competitive,' that's often interpreted as the school having very difficult curriculum, maybe that it's highly selective in terms of its application acceptance rate. All that is true of a prep school like ours, just like it's true of universities like Harvard and Stanford. But it also means that the students themselves are competitive with one another the way athletes are competitive. They simply want to win. There is a relentless drive to succeed, to take opportunities, and to outdo one another. It is not always as friendly an environment as it could be."

She stopped talkin' and let me sit with that a second.

"I suppose no one shared that bit of campus culture with you during the application process?"

"Nah, not really."

"Hmmm. Maybe they figured it was simply such a common feature of this school model, sort of a natural human response to this particular environment, that there was no need to talk about it. After all, you'll find the same thing at other similarly ranked schools. We're no worse than anywhere else. But even so, my advice to you would be to keep your friend circle very small on this campus. Don't get too close to people. Watch your back."

*

I was used to going places and not making but one or two or no friends at all. It was that way on the island. It was that way in the pen. But I was expecting better in private school. I was experienced enough to know that Mrs. Greenberg had been at the school way longer'n any student. She would know what she was talkin' about.

So I kept to myself and hung with you and with Booker Taliaferro Adebayo, until that joker said to me that me and you were the first upstanding African Americans whom he had ever met. He revealed hisself a whole fool for that one. I wadn't even sure how to respond or what to make of him after that.

You hung out with cousin, too, ate lunch with him and talked about y'all's goals, college things I had yet to contemplate. You had applied to all the Ivy League colleges, as well as some other dead-white-man-named schools on the other side of the continent, and Booker had already been accepted at Yale, Vanderbilt, and Oxford. It was good just sitting and listening to the jewels y'all dropped, even if I couldn't imagine jumping from East Oakland to some college on the East Coast that might be as prestigious as ten Pied-montays put together.

Yet and still, despite the jewels, or maybe because of them, I remember you warning me that it was more to Booker besides his impressive academic accolades. "Meticulously put together, upstanding brothers can be the absolute worst," you said. "Maybe that's why I like you instead."

Cuz you had jokes like that and cuz it was true—I didn't know the first thing about most anything at Pied-montay. It was also true, according to you, that Booker's fam on his father's side had been big in government in Nigeria. And then they had had to flee to the four corners of Europe and America on account of some shadiness. "Do you know what SARS is?" I remember you asking me.

"The virus? Like the ghetto flu but in Asia?"

"No, the Nigerian police force."

"Nah, never heard of it."

"It's not important that you know about it. It's just that his family was involved in some way wit' it back in the day," you said. "Booker isn't responsible for things that his relatives in Nigeria are alleged to have administered, or turned a blind eye to, or perpetrated. I just want you to know that he may have been raised with ideas about keeping certain people down."

After homeboy dropped that line about us being the only upstanding African Americans and I ran it back to you, all's you did was nod like you had heard it before. You told me, "I told you, Cope."

"But isn't his fam on his mother's side African American? What about them?"

You shrugged. "Cognitive dissonance is a thing."

Then why did you stay friends with him? I wanted to know. I was only just gettin' my feet planted and soiled in Pied-montay. I didn't understand how y'all maneuvered.

"He's not my friend. I keep my friend circle small at this school, very, very small. But I try to make my network as big as possible. Booker is in my network."

*

Not for nothin', I couldn't keep cousin in my network. I left y'all to y'all's lunches and did my own thing. You were a year older than me and were probably clockin' college dudes anyway. I cain't call it. I know I had enough of a crush on you not to want to embarrass myself by tellin' you about it. I didn't even know how to talk to you sometimes, or what to say when you mentioned certain things about Pied-montay that I wadn't even aware of, and when I thought about your momma's Lex and about Booker Taliaferro Adebayo's Yale and Vanderbilt and Oxford acceptances, that feeling of distance deepened. I knew me and you were friends, that we were doing more than just networking. But, yet, and still, when I thought of you, I saw your face, your frame; I saw your wardrobe and the things that surrounded you. But I didn't see you; I didn't know you—didn't know how to really know you. When I thought about who you were, it was like I was lookin' at everything around you, everything draped all over you, and also like I was lookin' up at you at the same time, like you were my idol or role model or somethin'. I had you on a pedestal for real, girl. Maybe I still do. Anyway, your boy don't have much sense, clearly, but I did have enough to know that I didn't know you as a person well enough and wadn't close to being on your level where I could have a relationship with you. I'm tellin' my story right now, but I wish you woulda told yours. I still hope you will once it's safe to speak. Ain't nothin' simple, let alone boring, about a fine-ass black girl from both sides of the city who knows so much, seen so much, achieved so much. Like I said, you're probably still on a pedestal in my mind.

Instead of hawkin' you, I lay back in the cut and applied the lessons that you taught me to my Pied-montay social life. Like networking: I decided that the journalism class would be the beginning of my network. Everybody in that piece was white. No Jacquelines, no Bookers. They didn't know much about me, but they also didn't say messed-up nonsense about African Americans, so we was good there. We could eat lunch together and not offend each other. We could talk about ideas and not get personal with it. We got along because, unlike black people, them white kids knew not to get too close.

It was with that distant friendliness that I was assigned my first story.

"After consultation with Mrs. Greenberg, I'm inviting you to write a piece for the upcoming issue," read the managing editor's email. He was a senior named Erick. He was tall, he was blond, he always wore Swarthmore shirts and hoodies for some reason, and he sat two seats to my right in the class. I looked at the back of his blond head. He was staring at the opposite wall. It was clear young Anderson Cooper had just wrote me this email five seconds ago from five feet away. I was schooled by then and knew what that play meant: your boy wadn't the only kid in the room who wanted that work. I looked back at my laptop. "Mrs. Greenberg and I think what would work would be for you to write a personal interest piece on the topic of your choice as long as it is relevant to social justice. Word limit: 1,000."

I emailed him. You already know my answer.

*

Because the journalism class took me outta PE, I was short on my physical education requirement. Every student, in order to graduate, was required to pass at least one physical education class per year or, as a substitute, play a sport. If I was gonna follow your lead into journalism, I would have to play a sport.

Back on the Rock I had never been known as an athlete. Sure, I had quicks, but nobody cared. Almost every kid on the Rock, no matter they gender, tall and short, fat and skinny, could hit the lights and be under the blankets 'fore the room got dark. Unlike me, the other kids could also play games where they threw, hit, caught, and kicked balls. Because they hadn't been doing a bid since birth, they had had time to play games and get good at them.

It was only when I came to prep school that people started hawkin' me to play this, that, and the Fifth. Real talk: the minute the coaches laid eyes on me, it was like the application interview process had started all over again. One coach wanted to know: How fast was my forty time? The only "forty" I knew was the malt liquor that them old, tanked-out dudes drank while they sat in they lawn chairs outside the liquor store. How fast could I drink one of them things? It might take me a month. I learnt later that the forty-yard dash is a race that helps determine an athlete's speed. Not being an athlete, I had been unaware of that shit. Nevertheless, the unanswerable sports questions kept on coming. Was I more of a lead guard or a wing? Was I ball dominant? Could I run the triple option, or was I a pocket passer? I know I could clean up my vocab some, but, Jacq, them coaches coulda started speaking to me in Gullah and it woulda made more sense.

The Pied-montay PTA was in the midst of a campaign to abolish football at the school on the basis of the research done on brain trauma and the fact that they kids wadn't a bunch of ghetto birds with no other means of gettin' a college scholarship. I wanted no parts of football and wouldn't mind if it disappeared like the Raiders outta Oakland. As for a brain-safe sport like basketball, it was somethin' to do with the games I seen on the Rock, Jacq, how brothers would practically be at each other's throats over a foul call. I couldn't deal with all that ruckus after being incarcerated. I hid it good, but on the inside I was still nervy than a muhfucka, what the psychologists call "hypervigilant." Anyway, my right elbow flared out like a bird's bad wing whenever I picked up a basketball and tried to shoot it. My baseball swing suffered similar deformities.

I would need to choose a sport if I wanted to write, if I wanted to stay enrolled for that matter. But I wadn't trying to be a part of any team that wanted me. The old football coach, Mr. Briggs, as part of his campaign not to get laid off for being a terrible math teacher, would approach me at lunch in the campus quad and say, "Hey, Cope. I hope you're considering the gridiron. We could use you in our option offense as a wingback." Or as a kick returner. Or a deep threat wide receiver. Or whatever other words he said to me that was supposed to mean somethin' but didn't. According to him, after he put an end to this abolition business once and for all, football would return like Christ Jesus.

Then there was the basketball coach. I didn't tell him 'bout the hitch in my shot, which I knew would only make me more of a candidate for his coaching, endless practice sessions, drills, camps, all that mess. Instead, I told the man that I feared being trash-talked by these kids I grew up with, cuz now I was seen as a sellout in they eyes, an Oreo, a coon, a crossover, for having went away to prep school. Black people, I told him, could be cruel that way. White people, real talk, love to hear us tell them that black people hold black people back, that we are our own worst enemy and that we would be so much better off if we could only get away from each other. The coach looked at me with somethin' between sympathy for me and frustration about his own damn self: "I understand. That must be hard. People of color are the real racists. But please consider trying out. Everyone knows we're a small prep school. We're not supposed to be competitive with the inner-city schools. It's like the reverse of standardized testing results. Those kids aren't really children anyway. I don't know what they put in the water over there, but something about it just isn't normal; they hit puberty sooner, they're bigger and faster and more aggressive. We don't expect you to work miracles, but you might help us lose by less. Here's a gratis pair of new Air Jordans. Aren't they beautiful? Think about my offer. Just think about it. There's more where those shoes came from."

Jacq, I flipped them shoes cold-blooded and avoided that man all year long.

And that only accounts for me and the sports people done actually heard of.

As for the boojiness, nobody in Rockwood could swim, so there went swimming, water polo, and rowing as possibilities for me. Matter fact, I wadn't even aware polo or water polo or lacrosse or field hockey or any of that prep school stuff existed 'fore I arrived at Piedmontay. Whoever wanna claim that black people is naturally athletic ain't seen black people naturally nearly drown in three feet of water or trip over ourselves doing whatever the fuck it is you do when you play badminton. The entire journalism class was on the junior varsity badminton team, by the way.

When she asked about my athletic plans, I told the rowing coach that her sport reminded me of the work of Roman slaves, and anyway, I'm from the hood, which means I cain't swim, which means our boat better never capsize. I told the water polo coach I couldn't even tread water, excused myself from badminton by claiming to hate Ping-Pong, and let the lacrosse coach hear all about my bid in the Youth Control and how I was liable to weaponize whatever you put in my hands.

I settled on track and field, because folks had seen me hustling from the bus to campus every day, so I knew that I couldn't claim that I couldn't run, and because with track and field the coaches wouldn't pay me any mind all fall since the track season don't begin till spring. That would give me the time I would need to get on top of my studies in the competitive environment of prep school and to try to write the thing that Mrs. Greenberg had told the managing editor to ask me to write.

*

When I was in grade school, my family plain didn't own a computer. The few PCs up at the elementary school was so old and outdated that the keys on the keyboard would stay stuck till you karate chopped them suckers back to life or they would pop out like big-ass bullets flying right at your face. Would you rather use the letter *A* when you write your book report or have both your eyes at the end of class? Fuck gettin' shot by the cops and going to jail and all the things people talk about when they talk about how hard it is in the hood, try typing two vowels down all the time. And you wonder why my vocab be lackin' and backtrackin'. My best bet back in the day was the public library down the way, but the hours would get funky when the virus broke out, which it often did. So I never could count on technology. I rarely dealt with technology at all, unless it had to do with some old cell phone I had came up on and figured out how to use. I'm that rare alpha generation kid with hella penmanship skills, print or cursive, you take your pick. Texting and typing just ain't the same to me as the handwritten word. If I've been writing and my joint comes up cramping after a little bit, that's just what it's gotta be: it's like I trust my words more the more they hurt.

I was supposed to write somethin' personal and about social justice. What was social justice? Justice for the society, I assumed. It sounded like a *8:46 slogan. I thought about it a lot. I could write about the shit that happened to me on the island or the things that went down in jail. I thought about all the stuff that I could write about, and after a while my thoughts clustered around the cops, the correctional school, the Youth

Control. I had no idea how to take all of that and melt it down to one clean thing.

One day slipped away, then a week, then another and another. I wanted to do what Mrs. Greenberg and Erick had asked of me, I just needed to figure out somethin' that was both personal and important to write about. I knew I needed to write about law enforcement somehow, 'bout how they jammed you up, exaggerated whatever you done wrong, locked you up, all the shit they put you thru once they had they hands on you. I would write about the system itself, the whole lick, everything that I now knew. I would write about it as a system, use the words that you would use, make it make sense in the way that I was learning in my other classes, to write from a thesis and supporting points down to a conclusion.

I stayed up late the night before the last drop-dead deadline date for the final feature pieces that would be published by the end of the school term. Then, in them final hours, I went down into the landfill inside of me and dredged up what was there. My joint did seize somewhere between thumb and forefinger, a hard, jealous fucker of a cramp that wouldn't let me go. But I kept writing and writing till the birds started chirping and my eyes started failing and my joint started shaking and I fell asleep. When I woke, like an hour later, I couldn't care less about beating two eggs together to make breakfast or dressing to impress. I had to proofread what I had put to page. But what I found on that page, Jacq, it in no kinda way resembled what I had meant to write. It wadn't in your voice. And it wadn't in mines neither. It was somewhere between us, like our child come into the world, except with only my experiences to speak of. I had told the truth, which was that the cops came at me guns already drawn. I was unsuccessfully trying to do away with that mold, had my bottle in one hand, shooing away people who was talkin' mess at me with the other. It seemed like the whole Rock was outside, and if they was my jury, I'm pretty sure they woulda voted a brother unanimously guilty without needing no recess to talk it over. But I had my mind on my mission and my mission on my mind. And then I heard the one warning I got:

"STOP. IMMEDIATELY. PARA AHORA."

I understood in two languages not to move one muscle, so I stopped. Stood froze like a dead man. I knew it was po-lice behind me, and my first fear wadn't guns but some outta pocket officer twice my size bum-rushing a brother and beating me into the ce-ment, several surgeries, months of rehab in the hospital drinking my dinner out a straw, learning how to speak and walk straight again. I was scared, but my mind was clear, which is where I think my luck was—most people either freeze and cain't follow orders for nothin' or lose it and do everything but what's being instructed, not because they're necessarily guilty but because that's the kinda shit that happens on the worst day of your life.

I was instructed to drop the bottle, which I did, its liquids flooding the pavement, sloshing and crackling away. Then I was to keep my hands where they could be seen, which I kept them. Palms forward right the fuck where they was and turn slowly around, motherfucker. I remember that the sun broke thru the marine layer, a few spears of light pooling its white blood on the ce-ment in front of me. I looked into the light and that's when I seen they Glocks, two men, two Glocks, four pavement-gray eyes all pointed right at me. To tell the truth, I wadn't as scared as I shoulda been. It ain't even process immediately; the cops was just doing they job, puttin' a stop to things in the only way they knew how. I was mad about the mold, vexed I couldn't kill it, especially seeing how every joker and they momma was surrounding me. I remember being thankful that five-oh acted civilized and didn't put hands on a brother. I remember being mesmerized by the pools of light on the ground so early in the morning. I remember seeing out the corner of my eye a figure the height and slenderness and rusted-penny color of the old man falling to the ground knees-first in prayer. I remember just standing there, girl. Standing on the edge between life and death. But that fact was too fatal to register in my living mind. Only months later, in the dead space of the Youth Control, did I sit down in my mind and let myself consider what coulda been, how I coulda died right then, and missed out on my own incarceration.

After I came home, I sat shunned upon my dumpsters and thought on it some more, what woulda became of my parents and whichever acquaintances would claim my memory. I wondered if Rockwood and East Oakland woulda burned. People held me at a distance alive, but dying young is the best way to get popular, the memory of you always worth more'n you was cared for alive. I wondered what woulda came of the cop, whichever one killed me, if he woulda been charged, even took to trial, and if his paid leave woulda came along with an involuntary manslaughter or murder charge, and in the end, when I was long since buried and the ashes of Oakland was wiped away by time and cold winter and the rain that washes everything underground, if the case woulda been dismissed, or settled, or if he mighta got a year, reduced to nine months for good behavior.

Many might protest the po-lice, but none but the two that bore me would mourn me. The hood might knock in a few windows, light on fire a couple cars, let off a few shots, and remember me with a mural and a little altar of candles and teddy bears and the Virgin of Guadalupe even though I'm about as Catholic as I am Mexican. The authorities would lay the law, might kill a couple more, and of course in the end they would pass verdict on theyselves and keep it moving. And life would go on the same as before. Another young brother would drop a week later, wouldn't matter from what, cuz once he was gone odds would be wouldn't nothin' come of it. And another would fall after him. And another after him. A different kid would meet you and interview for a scholarship to your school. And so on and on and on. So it was a lucky thing that your boy ain't—I mean, that I did not die that day, because, as I published in the paper, one false move and these words woulda spilt from me speechless in blood red and black on the Rock.

**+

---

*Soclear Security offers a variety of security and investigative services for both business and residential needs everywhere in the United States and its territories. Our services are customized to meet the needs of our diverse clientele. We are dedicated to providing the highest level of protection for homeowners, officers of the law, executives, ambassadors, dignitaries, celebrities, and companies.
+Insurgency Alert Desk, Third Bureau: The Harvard University economics major who was taken into custody and questioned by police in relation to the search for black identity radical Copeland Cane V has been released without charge. Authorities do not regard the individual as in any way connected to the case. This represents a major setback in the search for Cane and his accomplices. Authorities suspect that Cane's female associate may in fact attend a non–Ivy League university.

That piece, once it was published in the final newsletter of the semester, brought me beaucoup attention, thanks be to you. You hooked it up, Jacq: Insta ads in the student social network. SnapSlack audio of me reading my article. And that wild e-brochure of all the students of color with our backs turnt to the camera like we was either rejecting racism or 'bout to be stopped, frisked, and cuffed up—that concept, which was all yours, was dope. I loved it for the way it made people have to stop and stare and think which they really wanted, us standing up for ourselves or us getting cuffed up by law enforcement.

You was the real star of that show, but you knew better'n to get onstage and show out. (If only I could've figured out how to make the school happy and stay hid in the cut like you did.) You made me a sorta star and sent me into black excellence space, even if, as the same semester came to a close, the white kids from journalism class who had been lunchin' with me and whatnot kinda fell back and stopped talkin' to me for a minute, and when we would cross paths they would look at me hella sad, like I had been diagnosed with a terminal case of race and they was responsible for infecting me.

Whatever issues they dealt with was not my problem. I felt good about myself. I had successfully transferred to the best school in the area, first of all. My grades might not be all that, but I was learning I could hold myself down single-handed in the same classes as these kids who had well-schooled parents and tutoring for days. And now I had done somethin' that they couldn't do, that nobody but me could do: write my story. I had put to paper somethin' that forced folks to think about the complected people across town. I had put it down narratively enough to hold they attention and educatedly enough that nothin' that I wrote could be mistaken for somethin' I didn't mean. And eventually the white kids warmed back up as much as they ever would, lunchin', doin' dovetails off the things I said in class to support the points I made and never outright saying when I got some shit dead wrong. I was finding Pied-montay cooperative, not competitive, not like Mrs. Greenberg had warned me it might be.

*

Mrs. Greenberg had also warned me about sports even as she acknowledged that the system was forcing me to play. "You know and I know that you were brought here to serve a public role for the high school," she counseled via email. "They want you to be the new black face of the school, just as your friend Jacqueline was before you, and Simone before her, and Javon before her. Among them, Jacqueline is the only one who is not an athlete—I don't count junior varsity badminton as a sport in quite the way that I do, say, varsity basketball. Is that wrong? Anti-Asian? The entire junior varsity team, save for Jacqueline, is lily white, so there's that, I guess. Anyway, I haven't heard you utter a word about sports, so I caution you not to be drawn into any endeavor that is not of your choosing, nor any that present health risks to you. For example, if the football team is revived, please look into the research on head trauma before even attending a practice session."

*

The track was beautiful, all bouncy red rubber and gleaming white lane lines. I felt the extra bound in my spring-loaded steps just walking up the straightaway. I looked at the track coach, a thin old man whose body was doing the thing that thin old bodies do, which is wither away like a bar of soap. Old Irish Spring was leaning over at the waist, teaching two runners who I assumed to be sprinters how to set they blocks. It was one of them hella bright Indian summer days the Bay specializes in. I had to squint just to see clearly.

One of the kids was a skinny, red-haired white boy who looked like he could be the coach's grandson. Thru the white-hot sunshine I watched Old Irish Spring lose his patience with the boy and set the blocks hisself. I remembered my childhood races, alongside Keisha and Free and Miguel, using the handball wall to brace ourselves.

I watched the white boy leave his blocks and glide into the aura of light that the September sun cast. Next, a short, powerfully built white girl with the kind of ass I hadn't seen since East Oakland did the same rice cakes and flat water, despite her frame. The truth was, neither of them had any acceleration.

I knew I could hang with these kids once I got in good enough shape. I figured, come spring semester, after a week or two of practice, I would be ready to outrun my teammates. I looked down the way to where a handful of former football players were up to somethin' energetic and difficult. They ran and spun and jumped and yelled out complicated number sets inside another half-blinding circle of light so it was all one big hot white ball of invisible athletic fitness to me. Like, college-student-athlete-silhouetted-on-billboards-type athletic fitness. I didn't think I'd ever care enough about athletics to dedicate myself to it like they were dedicated or like old boy who lent me his shoes to sell was dedicated. All that year, I would prove me right about myself: I lacked commitment. I lacked work ethic. I lacked performance. I never even tried to train, let alone race in the meets in March and April and May.

Copeland Cane had other interests and concerns. Rewind me back to that first moment on the track in November of my junior year in high school: I blinked the light out my eyes and gazed back from the real-deal athletes to the track athletes who I chose to compete with. Old Irish Spring and his crew of subprime athletes gleamed back at me. I didn't let it blind me this time, though, and now I could see exactly what had blinded me. All of them wore gold track shoes. I looked back at the boys and they had on the same damn shoes, shoes that shone, that glittered, that price-tagged pretty good when I looked them up later. If I could get a complimentary pair off Old Irish Spring, them shits was gettin' flipped.

*

I accepted Irish Spring's offer and stuffed the shoebox in my backpack. Jacq, it was the end of fall, the beginning of winter, when that man recruited me with them shoes and I figured that I could chill on the sports thing for a few months. *I didn't know it was an indoor season in that sport and that it takes place in fall!* Did you know that, Jacq?* *Has*

---

*Jacqueline: I did not. All I know about sports is that Michael Jordan was great, Kobe Bryant is gone, and you are fast.

anybody alive ever heard tale of indoor track and field?! I rest my damn case. (And, needless to say, your boy was caught flat-footed upon learning that this indoor season thing existed and was already on and poppin'—I told the coach, "Hold up, I'ma see you in springtime.")

Anyway, being that I wouldn't be running races for a while, I didn't even think to open the shoebox that that first pair of gold shoes came in or try them on or break them in, none of that. You know I sold them suckers fast as I could, like five minutes after having them handed to me. (Side note: Pied-montay Ave. is a great place to sell shoes just so long as you can keep out of eyesight of the private security that's roaming everywhere. Hella people on that avenue will drop $100 on you easy as they comb they hair. This particular buyer was a white man about my height and build who wore a shirt that read BIG ISLAND ULTRAMARATHON: HELLA HAOLE! I remember appreciating that he didn't look me up and down or ask me a gang of questions that might attract the attention of the authorities, he just slipped me the skrilla and went on his way.

Back at home, I added the $150 to the $820 I had already banked from sellin' the silhouetted student-athlete's shoes and the shoes that the basketball coach had gave me. When winter break came and the schools let out, that number stopped still, no new revenue. Then the holidays and the flu showed back up and I had to pay for presents and flowers, and 'fore I knew it that number dropped like a dead body, decomposing one dollar and dime at a time.

*

When the spring outdoor season commenced, I was barefoot in track terms. No running shoes. That begged a basic question: What happened to the shoes? Old Irish Spring wanted to know. Without even really trying to be believable, I mumbled that I lost them. I was staring at my feet, my shoes, but I looked up at him after I said it cuz I had heard from somewhere that white men like it when you stare straight into they eyes. I could see Irish Spring's eyes didn't believe me and neither did the rest of his body. He usually held hisself kinda stiff, but now he was a damn dead man listening to me lie, ready for the pallbearers. He heard me out and ordered another pair of shoes, which took a couple weeks to arrive, which spared me from running in a couple more meets.

Me and him never did get along after that, not even after I came back as a senior in better shape, with somethin' more on my mind besides flippin' shoes and the system. I always sensed that stiffness in him, and he felt however he felt about me, I ain't finna climb into his mind. I knew not to sell my second pair and press my luck with him even though the student-athlete who shall remain nameless tore up his knee that spring and the billboard came down in Rockwood, re-placed by an ad for summer vacation in Venice. I was shoe poor and money poor then, which maybe Irish Spring understood, seen it as welfare or whatever, cuz he never did press me about exactly how I went and lost somethin' that was supposed to be worn on my feet. I cain't call it, but that unpressed silence between us was our agreement, and that's about all I can say about that.

*

Despite that shit, I was winning. By the time the spring semester got under way, I knew I could hold down the prep school academics. I had dipped out on every coach but the one who wanted nothin' to do with me, which meant I wouldn't need to take anything for the team. And best of all, I had told my social justice story, whatever that meant. It meant game over as far as I was concerned. Gimme the Grammy, or whatever it is they do for writers when someone notices them.

Mrs. Greenberg disagreed. In her expectation, my columnist career was just starting. She wrote me an email in which I was invited to enroll in the journalism class in spring on the condition that I meet deadlines this time. I thought to email her back and point out that I hadn't actually missed the drop deadline, only all the others. Mrs. Greenberg was not one to fuss with details like that, though. Her email was a whole soliloquy on how journalists have to always be on point, how they have to keep a calendar in mind all the time and that they must communicate with they editor in an informative and efficient manner no matter what.

On the first day of classes in spring, she kept me after the computer system closed the class period, the monitors went blank, the school anthem started to play from the intercom, and the other students filed out. She nodded silently at me to stay just in case I had any bright ideas 'bout leaving out with my peers.

Wadn't never no small talk with Mrs. Greenberg. "Good afternoon, Cope. How are you?" she said from her desk at the front of the room. I could tell she didn't care, was just asking cuz it's what you're supposed to do. "You seem like you're doing quite well. I will say, whatever you're doing, however you're feeling, you wrote a fine article, so you should feel proud about that. It's more of a literary accomplishment than most people will ever experience. You are so young, but already you have a voice as a writer that's all yours, totally unique. You truly are talented. You could be quite a writer. But to whom much is given, much is required. I think you can do more than tell the tried-and-true and well-worn story of a black man brutalized by the police."

I wanted to catch her and say that didn't nobody brutalize me, they just pulled guns on me, had Daddy prayin' on his knees, but wadn't no punches thrown or windpipes crushed, no brutality—but she kept talkin'.

"The way I see it, Cope, the police are but the butt of the spear. Or, rather, they're the tip of the spear. That makes more sense as an analogy. Here's a better, more historically grounded analogy: Mao Zedong said that power flows from the barrel of the gun, but he never said that power was the gun. There's a difference. The police typically deployed by city police departments are on the streets, armed, so they are the visible expression of state repression, but individual police officers hold very little power except for the right to arrest and the practical right to kill." Seemed like hella power to me, especially compared to me, cuz I didn't have a lick of power— but she kept talkin'. "*8:46 dealt powerfully with the problem that the police posed to black and brown bodies—or, rather, to black and brown people. Not to say that those issues are wholly eradicated, but I think it's important to look at the bigger picture. After all, it is more complicated than firing and prosecuting the 'bad apples' on the force, no matter how many rotten ones there prove to be. If the only thing we can argue for is the right of the oppressed not to be unjustly murdered in the street in view of the entire world, then this is a terribly primitive nation, don't you agree? And what about these police? Who are they now? Nearly twenty percent of police officers today in America are privately employed, oftentimes by companies that have ties to white supremacist organizations. Every policeman in Piedmontagne is privately employed. Many of these officers came to their private sector posts after the protest years. Now they aren't bound by the same regulations that regular police are, and sometimes when you look at an officer, you don't know if he or she is employed by the local PD or by a private company. Their uniforms are just a mess, with all those confusing insignia. The lines have blurred between public and private policing. Why is that?" she asked.

I shrugged.

She kept talkin': "The fault lies in the manipulation of our legislators. Our government, which creates the laws that the police enforce, has become increasingly repressive as a reaction to the protests of the recent past. They used the White House insurrection to pass new laws that mostly impact black and brown people even though there weren't any black and brown people in that rebellion. It's part and parcel of a cynical design. They used to deny that a deadly respiratory virus even existed; now the same people use it as a pretext to deny issuance of permits to protest in public space, which of course makes arresting protestors socially acceptable and politically palatable—and Soclear constantly propagandizes its viewers that all this somehow makes sense. It's a terrible era that we find ourselves in, Cope. We need our students and subscribers to think about how phenomena that may not be the most hot-button issue (like a man being killed in broad daylight by police) still severely affect life, and in particular the lives of the least fortunate, the same people who are most likely to be killed by that police officer in broad daylight. Obscure legislation is passed, the planet warms, sea levels rise, fires become more frequent, our water is polluted with new contaminants all the time. You are the student best suited to write about these things. You can become the conscience of our campus community. Let me send you some articles that will serve as inspiration."

*

Mrs. Greenberg was not asking my permission to inspire me. That evening I received an email from her entitled "Major National Newspapers and Journals: Back Issues." It was a gang of stuff, oceans of literature, and the first thing I thought was that the lady must be out her mind to think that I, a mediocre student, was finna read all this shit, do all my other homework, and wake up early as hell tomorrow, catch the buses, sprint my ass into Pied-montay city limits, into the school, and somehow stay awake in my classes. Luckily her email to me contained specific instructions about which articles I should pay attention to. I read them that she recommended, and in doing that I came to see for myself, from facts piled upon researched, verified facts and more facts, all the issues Mrs. Greenberg had spoke to me about after class. I could see that she had a point about how the government and the lawmakers moved slicker'n rainwater, gettin' things like the changes made to the adolescent incarceration system done on the low without the public noticing it or paying it any mind. I could see what she meant when it came to private po-lice. Shit, I didn't even know if the jump-outs who vamped on hustlers and prostitutes and homeless folks outside Rockwood and Ravenscourt was PD or private cops, come to think of it. I also read about the environmental issues she had raised. It wadn't anything in there about radiation, but the articles did inform me about all the lead in the water and its destructive effects, which disproportionately impact complected kids due to us being fucked over in general in society. I seen the big picture that she was talkin' about, a big ol' spinnin' globe full of nothin' but our troubles.

I also seen that *8:46 and all the other back-in-the-day protest actions had not solved all our issues with law enforcement. Like Mrs. Greenberg told me, when an officer did occasionally get brought up on battery or crookedness or even murder charges, it was often found that they had connections to some underground-militia-type stuff. If the fools didn't get locked up, they would leave the force, walk across the street, and go into private security work. The private cops worked with the regular cops and wadn't no way to tell who was who when they patrolled your hood, with the only difference being regular cops in California had to have that body camera on them and the private security don't. But filmed or unfilmed, black bodies and brown bodies kept stackin' in '22 and '23 and '24 and '25 and '26 and '27. And now the cases get lost in the sauce a lot easier without a po-lice chief and the mayor accountable and made to do press conferences about the shit. People who purchase private po-lice protection for they compound or company or whatever ain't tryna be hella public about every little killing and beating, after all.

Meanwhile, them bodies—a cop's bullet or choke hold seemed to hand some brother his walking papers every month, and as the dates of the articles came more current, closer to my present-tense presence in the world, the incidences came more like every week, every few days, some man or woman somewhere in America took ghost courtesy of the cops. But what really got to me was how the spokespeople for the security agencies and such would discuss the incidents on the Soclear broadcasts. The security agency spokesperson always started by announcing that the officer had been placed on administrative leave, whatever that means. Then they would talk about the need for improved community relations between they officers and the people, and they would call for charity events in the black community, basketball tournaments and shit. They would pledge a thousand dollars to a community center. They would cite one of these rich rappers whose mansion in the hills they protect like a head of state, like that's evidence of how they feel about our people in general. When pressed to speak on the case in question, though, them spokesperson jokers turnt into English teachers, wanting us to know all the context, the history of the site of the incident, the history of the company securitizing the site, then the backstory of each and every participant in the drama, the relationship that the officer had had with they parents, they relationship with they supervisor, who invariably vouched for they ass. They wanted us to know that the officer was married and had children and dogs and cats, they hobbies and interests and where this joker went to high school and what sports this joker played. They also wanted you to know the arrest history, psych evals, toxicology report, education level, and social media activity of the dead muhfucka. Then it was film school time:

The spokesperson would analyze the width and depth of the camera angle of the incident, even if it was up close and personal on a body cam. The spokesperson would go into detail about the color contrasts and how that mighta fucked up the footage or some shit, whatever's clever, the darkness and the light and the sound quality and the reverb and the feedback, the this and the that, the mise-en-scène and shit, and in the end they always concluded the same way, which was wadn't no conclusion to come to but to remain calm and to trust the ongoing internal investigation.

"I don't think I'm ready to be the conscience of the campus community," I emailed Mrs. Greenberg in the morning. It was all too much, too big, too crazy, too dangerous. And it also wadn't me: I was just a kid at a prep school doing his thing. Just because I'm black don't make me the spokesman for my community. It don't make me anything. I didn't know what I was, but I knew that I was more than the madness of the po-lice.

Mrs. Greenberg never did respond to my refusal. In class that day, she ain't speak to me not a once.

---

*Urban Dictionary: The Police: 1) The thin blue line between law-abiding citizens and the murder, rape, and thievery that certain "historically disadvantaged" groups inflict upon said law-abiding white majority; 2) A national terrorist organization harboring numerous violent white nationalists, a reality in keeping with its origins in post–Civil War racist revanchism; 3) Failed football players—the consequences of traumatic brain injury are real.

+Urban Dictionary: Stolz Jungs: 1) An offshoot of past militant Far Right movements, Stolz Jungs is an American far right–wing group heavily populated by law enforcement and ex–law enforcement, allegedly; 2) Let's take the Fifth and live to define other things.

*64:8: 1) A common figure of speech and internet greeting that is meant to signal antipathy toward the *8:46 police reform movement and support of law enforcement and right-wing politics; 2) Some dumb shit that a depressed Caucasian came up with in 2020 that won't go away, kind of like black dudes sagging their pants past their underwear—thanks, America.

Instead of becoming everybody and they momma's conscience, I was assigned a smaller story: I would interview and profile sophomore sensation Sherrod St. James, the smartest kid in East Oakland. Sherrod was an academic star, much like yourself, Jacq, except hood heritaged. This boy clocked 4.0 grade point averages like the cops clock bodies. More impressive, he had finished second in a regional robotics championship, building some kinda vehicle I cain't even begin to explain so don't ask. Boy was Tristan Walker mixed with that man who discovered how to do everything with a peanut sprinkled with homegirl from *Hidden Figures* compared to my academically mediocre ass. He also was opposite me in another way. He lived right across the street in Ravenscourt.

Ravenscourt was one of the most infamous neighborhoods, or projects, in all East Oakland. It was mostly known for being the home of Felix Mitchell, who died 'fore I was born yet his name still rings out, still has old heads reminiscing on the '80s, still has criminal-minded youngsters studying how he ran Ravenscourt and most of East Oakland. It was from the fear of shadows like his that I had never actually touched turf on those grounds.

Word was that if you was from the Rock, you needed to watch your back, front, and both sides if (not when) you went to Ravenscourt. Dudes who met girls from across the street had to check they nuts and consider carrying a weapon when they went over there. I don't carry guns—don't like them things at all. I can handle myself decent in a scrap, but that wouldn't help me if I got lost up in there looking for St. James and got jumped for my shoes by three, four dudes. It's things like this that people in Pied-montay don't think about when they ask you to talk to a kid across the street, and it's things like this that you ain't really tryna confess to them if you live in a place that's the exact opposite of Pied-montay, because either it's gonna make the place where you live seem scarier'n hell, or it's gonna make you look like a swaggerless punk for not checkin' your nuts and gettin' a gun to go see your girl, take your pick, neither one is good for the image of Black Americans that you're projecting to the people of Pied-montay.

I figured I would need protection, but I didn't have no weapons and didn't want none, so on the morning that I was to do my interview,

I found the next best thing to a gun: DeMichael. It might seem hella strange and slightly suspect of me to show up out the clear blue, given that we hadn't exchanged a single word since freedom, but I needed his help.

"Bruh, you askin' me for what now?" he asked from his apartment doorway.

"I need you to go over to Ravenscourt with me. Like, as protection."

"I know why you want me to go with you, family. That's not what I'm askin'. I wanna know why yo' ass tryna squad over to where all them wild niggas be at. Do you miss the Youth Control? You got a girl you tryna get with or somethin'? Pussy ain't worth gettin' jumped, fam. What about that tall, light-skinneded girl you be talkin' to in the courtyard? Her body hittin'. And she cute."

"She's too old for me. She's about to leave at the end of the school year and go off to college. I'm solo dolo, always have been."

"Then what's the deal? Why the field trip?"

"I need to talk to someone in Ravenscourt. This kid Sherrod St. James."

"I never heard of him. I doubt he's dangerous."

"He's not."

"So why do you need me? You his guest. That nigga should give you the hood pass."

I held my tongue. DeMichael was hard to argue with. I heard a fan whirring behind him real loud and a show on what sounded like an old-ass television with the volume turnt high enough to be heard over the fan. DeMichael filled the small doorway so totally I couldn't see nothin' behind him, almost like his body was a curtain between me and his home.

"What's up?" he pressed.

So I told him about Pied-montay and the article I was to write about Sherrod.

"Why they care what grades this crosstown nigga make?"

I shrugged. I didn't know. "It's a journalism assignment. That's all I know."

"Seems like they jus' want him for they school and they sendin' you there to help recruit him. Damn, I didn't know Pied-montay loved niggas like that!" he hooted.

"D-Michael Quantavius Chesnutt Bradley!" A thin, damaged, but powerful voice sprang like a rose rising from concrete. "Don't be cursin' inside this home!"

"Sorry, Granny." He lowered his voice, and I remembered DeMichael's granny picking him up from school all the way back to elementary. She was old back then. "Damn," he said under his breath, "it's like sometimes you can be standin' right next to her and she don't hear you. Other times she hear aye'thing."

"Don't 'pologize to me, boy," she called back. "'Pologize to your Lord and Savior. Who that is at the door?"

"It's my friend. His name's Cope."

"Well, bring the boy in here, child. Let me see him. Don't have him standin' outside like he ain't welcome."

DeMichael turnt down his gaze real sheepish, like he was actually obeying another person not cuz he could get somethin' out of them but from real obedience. "C'mon in, blood. Granny just wanna say hi."

I followed him into a little rabbit hole of an apartment. Maybe I had been inside his place before, but if I was, I was probably so young that nothin' looked small to me. Now I could feel how tight they apartment really was, a space way smaller'n the one me, Momma, and Daddy burst to the seams. The Bradley home's tight rooms was crowded even tighter by all the objects: furniture, a walker, that loud fan, a bicycle without tires, a camouflage hunting jacket, a big old grandfather clock, and hella other shit stacked on the floor, tacked to the walls, and hung from the ceiling. I followed DeMichael, inching along into the everything. I wondered if this was what people meant when they talked about hoarding, or if it was just the smallness of the space that made it seem like the two of them owned too many things.

"Well, hello, sweetie." Granny Bradley's voice fell out sweet as syrup over me. She closed the little laptop where her show was playing and laid it on top of unopened mail that cluttered the kitchen table. It wadn't Sunday, but you wouldn't know it by her outfit. She was an elderly lady whose long floral print dress had outgrown her. It was stretched thin in places and pooled upon the floor so that you couldn't see her feet. She wore an old-school church hat adorned with a spray of peacock plumes, which looked newer, like maybe DeMichael had bought it for her. "Your name is Cope?" she asked. "Is that short for Copeland? Yes, I thought so. Well, this be a first, now. Got one of D-Michael's friends up in this apartment. Had me half thinkin' this nigro ain't got no friends." I noticed the fray-edged Bible sitting in her lap.

I looked back at DeMichael, who stood beside me slump-shouldered. He lowered his head and scratched at it.

"So, what y'all two plannin' to get up to today?"

I was about to answer when DeMichael's head shot up. "Just kickin' it."

"Speak up, boy. I cain't hardly hear you."

"I'ma show Cope my room, what I do, then we fittin' to kick it in the courtyard and whatnot, nothin' much."

"Oh, that's nice. Copeland, did you know that my grandson is incredibly talented?"

"Granny!"

"Hush now. I am speaking to your friend. Now, I'm not talkin' 'bout no book smarts. I could give a damn what they wanna lie about in a book. My grandbaby gots real skills. He's a hunter, a marksman. Show him that shotgun, boy."

"Do I have to? I mean, I apologize—I was fittin' to show him exactly that!" He threw some fake excitement into his voice. "C'mon, Cope."

He led me into a small side room where a bed and a washer/dryer stood side by side. A rifle leaned barrel up against the washer. I didn't know a thing about rifles except for the facts Larry had dropped on me. I remembered his stories about hunting in the countryside somewhere far away and white, and I thought about that hunting jacket hanging in DeMichael's front room. "You hunt?"

"Yessir. I can spot and dot a bird at a couple hundred feet, prolly more."

"Where do you hunt that you can go shootin' at shit hundreds of feet away?"

"Up in the hills."

"You can hunt in the Oakland Hills?"

DeMichael shrugged. "Oakland Hills, Hayward Hills, Berkeley Hills. If you go up high enough, it's clearings where on a good day without clouds you can see aye'thing flyin'. It's not legal to shoot out there, but you know. It's shooting ranges out here, too, where you can go and buck shots all legal. It's whatever you want. If niggas can shoot each other in the hood and get away with it, you think you cain't go off to the middle of nowhere and shoot at some birds and shit? That's what yo' ass should be doin', go explore the hills, nigga, don't be duckin' these gang members in Ravenscourt. Ain't they about to tear that motherfucker down? They should get on with it."

"How often do you shoot?"

"Prolly once a month. It ain't easy to travel all the way up there. Not like Oakland buses have it on they route."

"How do you get there then?"

"You want me to have yo' back in Ravenscourt, right? Why you wanna know all these li'l details—unless you lookin' to come with me next time I shoot?"

"As long as we ain't gotta hitchhike to get there, sure."

"You think anybody would open they car door and let a NFL— nigga fuckin' large—lookin' nigga like me hitchhike with them? My probation mentor be takin' me up there."

"For real?"

"For real, family."

I didn't think too much of all that probation mentor nonsense. I stayed the fuck away from my mentor and he didn't fuss with me. But DeMichael sure seemed like he learnt a lot from his mentor: I watched as he took apart that weapon with a quickness, slapping sharp screws into my hand which snagged my skin. "Hold those. How 'bout this deal? If you gimme a fresh pair of Js, I'll show you how to put this shit back together."

He looked at me with bright eyes, and I realized that he had finally found somethin' that he was good at, somethin' that he cared about. More for him than for me, I nodded OK as I pressed my thumbs together to try and stop the bleeding from the little cuts that the screws tore open. "Go head, big bruh, go head."

Like a teacher, he showed me how to slowly reassemble the weapon piece by dangerous piece. My hand was still bleeding a little when I finished putting the gun back together. DeMichael took me to the one window in the room, pulled back its thin blue curtain, and opened the sill and the screen, and we looked out at the dark marine layer above us and the gray birds sitting on the telephone wires, which ran into and out of thick trees. On God, Oakland cain't even try and be safe about anything, I swear. DeMichael showed me how to load and hold the rifle, how to sight the birds, and how to ready my whole body for the shot. A little songbird was in my sights. I heard it go up and down the scales, singing different notes. My finger massaged the trigger. A breeze tunneled into the apartment and touched my face. *"Shoot!"* DeMichael ordered, and without thought I pulled the trigger. The song stopped and the bird scudded downward outta my line of sight. I raised up, expecting to see its body falling to the ce-ment, but instead I watched as it loop-de-looped and swerved and veered and disappeared unscathed into one of the thick-leaved trees. Then it hit me that I had just shot a gun for the first time. Had just shot a gun for the first time from an apartment window in the middle of Oakland. Stunned than I don't know what, I dropped the rifle and turned and stared wide-eyed at DeMichael. *"You made me shoot! Why'd you make me shoot!?"*

"First of all, family"—he held his hands up like I was 'bout to pick the rifle back up and turn it on him—"don't drop your weapon all careless like that. It might fire accidentally and hit one of us, or my granny. I just said to shoot. Ain't force you to do it."

"Why'd you tell me to shoot?" My breath came fast and hot. "Everybody on the Rock heard that! I'm not tryna go back to the Youth Control."

"Family." DeMichael lowered his hands, stepped forward, and pushed the rifle with his foot till its barrel was pointed toward the street. "Ain't nobody gon' say shit. They prolly gon' think it's fireworks. It is summertime."

"It's too early in the day for fireworks."

"It's too early in the day for yo' scary ass. Ain't nobody in the hood gon' call the po-lice 'bout no gunshot ain't hit nobody. I thought you grew up here. Private school must got you forgetful."

"People here know the difference between gunshots and fireworks."

"So what if they do, family? Ravenscourt niggas be lettin' off shots all hours. Ain't nobody here know how to locate a concealed shooter. They don't know what side of the street that came from." A smile curved his lips and he shook his head. "Here you are, wantin' me to go regulate on yo' behalf, yet you mad at me cuz I asked you to put in a li'l work, huh?" He chuckled, or whatever it's called when big dudes laugh and shake they head hella self-satisfied cuz they know you cain't steal on them and knock them out. "At least you ain't bitch out, Cope. At least you pulled that trigger. You are no coward." He squatted down and disassembled the rifle with a quickness. "C'mon," he said, hopping back up, leaving his toy in pieces on the ground, "I'm cookin' lunch for Granny."

Back in the cluttered kitchen, DeMichael fried eggs and cooked bacon, his head hitting every hanging plant and light fixture as he moved in tight little patterns in the tight little space. Meanwhile, Granny Bradley patted at her Bible with one hand and held the other still on her knee with one of them old oximeters latched to her pinkie finger. "I need to monitor my lungs in case they make another one of these viruses. All the viruses is made to kill black people. It's all we can do to check our health and pray. Do you have a church home, child?" she asked me.

I was still stuck on shooting the rifle. Had Granny Bradley somehow not heard it fire? Did DeMichael shoot at enough shit from his bedroom that she was used to it and just ignored it? I couldn't call it, but this was the kind of craziness I shoulda known to expect from a fool who had been in and outta juvie since he was nine years old. "Nah."

"Well, me and D-Michael go to the li'l old tried-and-true Baptist church right there on the corner. It's served me well all my life since I moved here from Lou'siana as a young woman. And as you can tell, that was a long time ago." She laughed, so I laughed with her, cuz I didn't know what else to do.

DeMichael set three plates of bacon and eggs on the small table and took his seat next to us.

"Copeland, I would appreciate it if you would do the honors," Granny Bradley said.

"The honors?"

"Pray, nigga," DeMichael translated, kicking me under the table.

Jacq, I cain't tell you when's the last time I prayed over some food. "Dear God," I said, "thank you for this food and for my friend DeMichael and for his grandmother Bradley—"

"My name is Charlene, thank you."

"My bad."

"Say it to the Lord, child, not to me."

"Forgive me, Lord. Lord, thank you for DeMichael and Charlene and for this food and for my health and safety and freedom. Amen."

"What about our health and safety and freedom?" Granny Bradley asked. "You ain't used to prayer, am I right?"

"Yes, ma'am. You're right."

"Well, you should come to church with me and D-Michael on one of these Sunday mornings. Or on a Thursday night."

"All right," I said, knowing that just like with DeMichael's parole mentor, I wouldn't go nowhere near that church. As we finished the bacon and eggs, the itis started to come over Granny Bradley. We watched her drowse off little by little. When she was all the way out, DeMichael nodded at the door and we both got up. I was out the door first. I let him lock the apartment door behind hisself. We had made our way across the courtyard and out to the street when Miguel called to us. "Hey, where y'all headed?"

I hadn't seen my old ace boon in almost a year. It was just the memory of his lessons rattling around in my head that had had me checking off boxes, hopping on trains and whatnot. But to see him was different: the Youth Control had done somethin' to him, hardened him. His face had thinned out like the rest of us so that he looked as raw and rugged as everything else on the surface of the Rock. He wadn't quite as much of a pretty boy now, even though his braids had came back in. He looked like a lighter-skinned Iceberg Slim in the powder-blue tracksuit he sported.

"Nowhere," we answered.

"Crossing the street," DeMichael said.

"When'd you come home?" I asked.

"It's been a minute I been back. I wadn't in there on nothin' too serious. A nigga just been traveling around a little bit, seeing if it's better business other places, na'mean? It is better other places, but I missed my soil. This is home."

I woulda stayed gone if a better opportunity elsewhere presented itself. I wondered about Miguel's schooling, if he still went at all. But I didn't ask.

"I hear you got in on that shoe hustle somethin' real, blood," Miguel said, slapping me on the shoulder where I stood, tilting on my toes on the curbside edge. I almost fell into the street.

"Just a little bit. Not too real."

"Real enough. How you think he got me to agree to go to Ravenscourt with his ass?" DeMichael laughed. "Gotta be the shoes, money."

"Ravenscourt?" The playfulness fell outta my man's demeanor. The housing project stood facing us from across the boulevard. It towered there within rock-flinging distance, but none of us ever went there, not inside they gates, and vice versa for them coming onto the Rock: it plain was not happening, not unless you was bringing your own security.

"Ravenscourt's across the street," my security said.

"Fact," I said, lookin' across the busy road at the baddest buildings in deep East Oakland.

"Y'all two be careful," Miguel said. "Them boys let off some shots this morning."

"We'll be careful, dog," DeMichael assured.

"C'mon, blood," I said, seeing a break in the traffic. I didn't want Miguel, who was smart as hell, school or no school, gettin' all investigative on me and asking a bunch of questions about my role as a reporter. He was the type to dead anything that even suggested dry snitching, and, truth be told, all reporting, no matter how minimal the story seems to be, is pretty much dry snitching.

I bolted into the street and raced to the other side. I stood there and watched DeMichael converse with Miguel another minute. Then his slow ass finally ran for it, diving di-rectly into the traffic. A busted old Lincoln Continental braked in front of him, inches from clipping him and coming up totaled. Black Hercules breathed heavy as he found safety on the Ravenscourt side of the street. He huffed past me and immediately began scaling the fence that separated the Ravenscourt apartments from the street. He huffed up the fence and huffed on over it like a six-foot-plus, two-hundred-fifty-pound-plus Catwoman or some shit. Who knew dude could climb like that? I watched him drop into enemy territory and followed him over.

Then we was in. I took a second to scope it out and soak it up, Ravenscourt, the infamous stomping grounds of Oakland's old drug dealer kingpin, Felix Mitchell. After selling more drugs'n the pharmacy back in the day, Felix Mitchell was arrested and sent to prison in Kansas, where he was stabbed to death over some Oakland shit. The famous funeral procession began here, this tenement: limos and a black Cadillac hearse led the way, followed by a horse-drawn carriage where the great man's body lay in state like the president. President of East Oakland. People crowded the boulevard. Meanwhile, the national news reported on how messed up black people was for stepping out they doors and doing the same damn thing—lookin'— that they had sent newspeople from all over to do. Try and have that happen today. It'd get shut down so fast on account of a report of looting or a virus or some other shit.

DeMichael tapped me on my back shoulder. "Family, you see them jokers cross the street? Stay woke now."

I checked the scene: a big open courtyard in the same design as Rockwood's except that this one had no basketball courts, no benches, no nothin'. Clearly created for poorer people. DeMichael nodded at three female Jehovah's Witnesses. They was going door-to-door. I watched as curtains was peeled and then shut closed with a quickness when the people behind the curtains seen who was knocking.

"It's practically an I-raq war up in here," DeMichael whispered.

As we was wandering lost thru the empty, mostly vacant, stripped-clean concourses of Ravenscourt, we came upon the Witnesses again. Each woman was dressed in a big black gown and a black head wrap. They reminded me of the Musliminas, but instead of lookin' away or droppin' her eyes, one met my gaze. She nodded at me and DeMichael. DeMichael nudged me with his big shoulder, knocking me off stride—his way of messaging me to drop my eyes: *No eye contact with Witnesses.* The nudge worked cuz I almost fell into the third-floor railing. "You don't know your own strength, big bruh," I hissed at him.

"Brothers, good afternoon," one of the women, a pleasantly parchment-complexioned sister said. I could tell by the way she floated in her gown how small she was, and somehow that made her big, ellipse-shaped eyes all the prettier.

I cut my eyes at DeMichael and then smiled at the woman as she and her sisters approached, the other two with covered heads bowed.

"Be careful of your surroundings, brothers," the pretty Witness said. "Some of the residents told us that it was a gunshot fired this morning from across the way. Everybody is trepidatious of a gang war."

"We'll be careful," DeMichael said, which surprised me cuz I thought he was anti–free speech. Then I realized he had the situation studied a couple steps ahead of where my mind was: he spoke to the woman over his shoulder and kept moving so that she would have to double back from her sisters and pursue us if she wanted to proselytize. "Not to trouble y'all," he said, "but y'all know where apartment 13-2B is? This place is organized real wild." He stopped walking then, but now we was at the opposite side of the concourse from them.

"Oh, that's easy," the pretty Witness said, and proceeded to explain how to get to the apartment we had got very lost trying to find.

"Jehovah Witnesses always know how to find they way around," DeMichael whispered under his breath as we passed thru double doors and onto a separate section of the walk. It was true.

I rapped on the apartment 13-2B door. No one answered. I knocked harder. I knocked a third time. My hand started to hurt so I used the big brass door knocker to wake the dead, or whoever happened to be lying up in there. I figured I'd come this far, I should at least see Sherrod.

Finally, the door eased open and a small woman emerged from behind it. Her hair was hived in a du-rag and her yellow Warrior T-shirt hung loose from her shoulders. She had a raw yellow tint to her eyes that I had only seen in the homeless and people half dead from the virus. She studied me and the big man behind me: "Who you is?"

I introduced myself and DeMichael. "We're here on behalf of the *Pied-montay High Times-Picayune*," I said.

"The what?"

"Our—my school newsletter," I explained.

"Boy, y'all don't look na'n official." She put her hand over her chest and coughed and laughed at the same time. "What you here for, my nephew Sherrod? They oughta be 'shamed of theyselves, got y'all black kids recruitin' each other like it's a business."

"No, ma'am. I'm actually here to interview Sherrod—"

"Sherrod don't need to answer any questions. As far as we're concerned, he's happy to go to school right where he goes to school."

"I'm here to interview him for the school newsletter, not for recruitment purposes."

"Child, get woke. It's the same thing. I imagine they ain't pay y'all to do this?"

I shook my head. The only person gettin' paid—in shoes—was DeMichael, and that didn't feel like it was worth explaining.

"Well, they damn sure gon' have to pay me. You know, they fittin' to tear down Ravenscourt. Already done cleaned out half of it. Then where we gonna go? What good is an education in Oakland or Pied-montay if we don't have nowhere to live in Oakland or Pied-montay? Here I am with three kids ain't even my own who I gotta shelter, gotta feed, clothe, and send to school. Ain't just Sherrod. Just cuz his brothers don't get straight As don't mean they eat less or they don't need a roof over they head. We need money, living money, not just some old tuition forgiveness."

"I'm sorry," I said. "We can leave."

"Look here," Auntie said. "It's got nothin' to do with y'all. I don't want y'all to think we don't got no love for y'all cuz it ain't the case. How about this? Sherrod don't need to talk to you right now, but I do need to talk to whoever run y'all's school. Whoever has his hands in that budget is who I need to speak with. So I'ma give you my number and my email, and you're gonna go back to that school and tell the man with the money to contact me. Can you do that?"

I nodded, not because I agreed with the plan but because I had no idea what else to do. Kinda stunned and impressed that she wadn't too scared to make demands, suddenly I was wondering if this was how I shoulda handled my interview with the principal.

"In the meanwhile, write yo' little article. Tell them people how good a student Sherrod is. And tell them how he has to live. Tell them what you seen today in Ravenscourt. Half the apartments vacant. A fire in the western quadrant, might as well be the Ghost Ship over there. Tell them how it's nowhere for children to play here. Tell them these things. Tell them straight. Where y'all came from?"

"Rockwood."

Her eyes widened with surprise and she cocked her head to the side. "Well, hell! I woulda figured y'all for some downtown nigroes. Well, at least you." She looked at me. "Yo' friend behind you's clearly yo' bodyguard. Y'all be careful in Rockwood, ya hear. It's a gang war on the Rock right now, nigroes firing shots in the morning time. Ain't safe."

We thanked her for her time and walked back along the concourse and down the floors. It was nothin' there to be scared of, contrary to everything I had ever heard. We seen the three Witnesses again and the prettiest one smiled at me. We seen three girls dressed in they school uniforms playing double Dutch on the second-floor concourse. We seen four boys on the bottom floor playing trampoline on a dirty old mattress someone had put outta doors. We seen two more lighting firecrackers at a far edge of the courtyard. We seen an old man the color of winter midnight with a big white beard and a white Afro as round as the world crouched like a grasshopper upon an empty oil drum. He was singing in Spanish. We seen homeless crowded in front of a food aid station in the shadow of the burnt western quadrant. We seen a woman sellin' empanadas and a man sellin' roses and a boy and a girl who was blowing bubbles back and forth to each other, laughing and smiling, and a mural that read:

THE CITY IS COVERED IN OUR DEAD FRIENDS NAMES

Maybe I was just a pawn for Pied-montay. I couldn't call it. Still, I decided that I would write about Ravenscourt, all of it, everything that I had seen. I couldn't guarantee Sherrod the money he and his fam actually needed, but I could tell they story.

As we crossed the street and walked back onto the Rock, DeMichael said, "It's like birds. One has its song, another has a different song. Hella different songs. But they all jus' birds, and if you shoot them out the air, they all gon' fall the same."

*

Later, at night, when it was just me and the explosions sounding away lonely as I was, I wrote my piece and I wondered about things. If we were all just the same kinda bird with so many songs, like DeMichael said, then what made my song special enough to write up in the *Picayune*? What was so special about me that I might become the "conscience of the campus community" one day if I could commit to communicating with my editors in an informative and efficient manner while also staying on deadline? It wadn't too much to ask, which was why, when I thought about why I hadn't done that shit to the best of my ability, I realized that somethin' was holding me back. I knew I could do what the newsletter required of me, and I knew a gang of other folks who could do it, too, who would never even have the chance cuz wadn't no one checkin' for them in the first place. Why was I important enough for Pied-montay and for the newsletter and all that yang while DeMichael and Miguel and the others had to stay theyselves on the Rock? I asked myself this, and the only answer that came to me is ain't shit special about me, not special enough at least.

Maybe, I figured, it was just a matter of quitting the newsletter. Writing was complicated and compromising and uncontrollable in ways I couldn't even explain to myself, let alone to anyone else. Maybe I should just drop the Sherrod story and drop the journalism class, and then I could take regular PE and I could quit the track team. I pictured my responsibilities falling like dominoes and a dude in the Rockwood courtyard scoopin' up them bones by the handful and demanding his money right then and there.

I wadn't in no position to go demanding things of the prep school. It was them that had brought me in on they dime, not the other way around. I couldn't just go making my own rules. Nor could I just go being a normal-ass student. It would not work. I was there to fulfill a public role. I knew that and they knew I knew it. I might not mess with the "conscience of the campus community" thing too tough, but it was no point in pretending that I could drop everything all at once.

Plus, quitting wouldn't change shit. It wouldn't change the fact that people in Pied-montay lived longer, lived better, had more money, more education, more everything, compared to people in places like Rockwood. It wouldn't change the fact that either you was one of the lucky ones to be born or be brought there, or you was one of the unlucky ones not to have that happen for you. I was one of the lucky jokers. It wadn't a thing I could do or write or quit that would change that.

I wondered about you, Ms. Jacqueline, because you traveled between the two realities, the two communities. Maybe you thought of yourself as uninteresting because your suburban story was too similar to the white people who do most of the reading, but it's somethin' unique in you cain't nobody else claim. It's that you're black and it's that you're you and it's that you see how to tell a story without having to grab a mic and go in. It's so many other stories in you.

And who would want my story anyway if to tell it they would have to live it? You're a much better storyteller, because you can sit between these two worlds and not have to be dipped so deep in either you might never get out long enough to tell about it. That's a kind of luck, boss. You're lucky as rollin' seven and eleven. Like the luck that you wadn't stuck with your pops in Rockwood 24/7/365. If that was your life, you would see what living in a dying neighborhood was really all about: your landlord hawkin' you, threatening you with eviction even though he already got the rent on time. Junkies rollin' up on you with holes in they face, asking questions no one can answer. Shoestring pimps all up in your business as you try to walk to school in the morning, wanting your number, your name. Cops callin' you out your name for walking down the street after dark. Cops who would tell me to get my ass inside like we was under curfew after dark. Negroes who didn't give a damn about no po-lice but hated each other all day and all night. Mexicans who hated each other all day and all night. The noise all night long. The fireworks, the fires, the gunshots at three in the morning. Seeing all that would get in your soul and might silence you even when you spoke, just like it did me for the longest.

It was only luck—that superstar momma of yours—that kept you safely off the Rock five days outta seven. And it was only luck that I had met a man on the train that was the reason why I was able to transfer away from all the drama of the Rock to a better place, a better school. So I was lucky, too, even if not as lucky as you. But you was making real moves, earning the type of grades and meeting the caliber of people that would pave your way in the world. I was a mediocre student, a bad networker with no connections of any promise besides yourself. I felt absolutely ordinary, just another bird. Which was why I was only gettin' tuition forgiveness, not no extras. I thought how Sherrod's auntie would probably get that money she wanted. After all, Sherrod was actually exceptional. He was not lucky one bit living hell up in Ravenscourt, but he was thriving yet and still. The article that I would write about him would show why the little homie deserved a duffel bag full of funds. But what it would say about me and what I deserved, I did not know.

*

In philosophy class, our teacher Mr. Marquard dropped jewels on a daily basis. "Do we have free will?" he asked us one day as the computer monitors clicked on and class started. "Or are we simply selected by circumstance to be who we are?"

Some girl with school-spirit-dyed brick-gold hair got on her phone and reported that "free will is the ability to choose between different possible courses of action unimpeded." She smiled a perfect pearly smile. It's more dentist offices in one square block out there than in all of deep East Oakland.

"Thank you, Wikipedia," Mr. Marquard said. "Do you think that you have free will—that is the question. You won't find the answer on your phone." He stared down the girl with the perfect pearlies and bricks of gold for hair.

"Yes, of course," the boy J. Northcutt, who would one day be our valedictorian, said.

"Why are you of that opinion?" Mr. Marquard asked him.

J. Northcutt tapped his boat shoes, making a beat that actually slapped pretty hard—I ain't gonna front, dude had rhythm. "People do not have free will in material terms. A person might go to school, work really hard, get straight As, perfect scores on all of his standardized tests, SATs, all the etceteras, but his academic success is still overdetermined by certain factors: parental guidance in his academics, like the fact that both my parents are college professors; family wealth, which might allow him the time to study rather than work to help support the family—not to mention that they'll be able to afford tutoring for him—"

"Even the neighborhood you're from is based on how much money your family has at their disposal," the girl who would compete with him all that year and the next for that valedictory status interrupted. "There's a million reasons why we don't have free will. You don't need to list each and every one of them to make your point. There's no free will."

"But he maintains that there is," Mr. Marquard insisted. "Why?"

Northcutt stared some daggers at homegirl and got back into his groove. "It's the mind. Ralph Ellison writes at the end of *Invisible Man* that by going underground he whipped everything but the mind. No matter how deleterious the circumstances people have found themselves in, they have always made art, song, music, poetry, dance. Think about London during the blitz, when people held waltzes in the bomb shelters. Even if you're chained to a stake in the ground on a desert island, you still have recourse to your mind. You can think, fantasize, philosophize, dream."

"And you would define that as freedom?" Mr. Marquard asked. "Chained to a stake in the desert?"

"Desert island," the valedictorian noted. "Let me ask you, sir, was Jesus free?"

"The government jailed and crucified him," Mr. Marquard responded. "But I concede that spiritually he was free."

Checkmate like a mug.

I sat back in awe of this young nigga Northcutt's unwhipped mind. Here I had came from the Rock and from the island and from the reformatory, where my mind was steady being whipped, flipped, and fucked with, and somehow thinkin' I might have anything to say about anything when I was only an empty cipher. I was even celebrated for my story about almost being shot, like that's somehow original in the hood. Only to find that it was kids like the valedictorian who were so far advanced of me that we might as well be from different centuries or somethin'. I was so impressed by these kids who could reference world literature and history in the same sentence just to make a point about philosophy. These kids who didn't even flinch at holding it down in intellectual conversation and debate with teachers who was damn near Stanford professors in they own right. I determined to get on that level, the valedictory level, in my mind even if my grades, which was weighted down by Rockwood, would never show it. But about that free will thing . . .

"The issue that Althusser—remember, he's the crazy French guy who killed his wife, we read his essay on ideology—that guy would take issue with your argument," Mr. Marquard rejoindered, "because it romanticizes the intellect. It presumes an inviolate status for the intellect when, in fact, the intellect is imbricated by the ideologies that surround and overlay it and that, in a sense, have brought it into being. If you've learned to speak by mimicking your parents and babysitters, the fundamental means by which you articulate the world around you is already predetermined by their ideologies. You don't know what a boy or a girl is, you know what they are called. That's why when someone transitions from one gender to another, they enter a second space that people don't quite understand because there are so few names for it (not for *them*, you see, but for their social role; we *are* our social roles). For that matter, you do not know yourself, you don't know who you are except in the context of how you are known by the social world around you. You know your role, or, put another way, you know only how you are hailed."

*

In the end, I think we're all hella hailed, am I right? Ain't no way to know what we do cuzza pure free will. Whatever white folks call freedom, we know we ain't free from them, let alone from ourselves. Very few black folks is ballin' financially and spiritually free to where they can just move however they want. And if you cain't move however you want, you ain't free by definition. How could it be any other way when they brung us here as property? A hundred-somethin' years since slavery and what can we claim? We don't own no private schools. We don't own no banks. We don't own the po-lice that po-lice us. No codes. No laws. No religion. No government that's our own.

In the dark when I'd think about you, Jacq, and the school, it wadn't the philosopher who killed his wife that I thought about, it was the principal, it was the po-lice, it was prison, it was the island. I don't wanna say we was slaves, cuz what slaves you know ever had the things we was given? But we damn sure wadn't free.

*

I remember the day: we was at school, of course. I got no idea what you was up to, homegirl, besides being brilliant, but I know I was well into writing my B+ essay exam for the existentialism section of Mr. Marquard's philosophy class when two BART cops arrested the crew of train dancers right there on the downtown BART platform. His sahabs took the cuffs quietly, but Mr. America wadn't having it, wouldn't take the harassment, and bucked back by refusing to silence his speakers. I wouldn't be surprised if the big homie kept on dancing right in those cops' faces. Four officers beat the crap out of him, knocked the Nikes he had bought off of me half price clean from Mr. America's feet and wrenched my man's shoulder from its socket as they busted him up right there for everyone to see. But somehow wadn't no video footage, no body cams, and word was the cell phones of bystanders was confiscated, the recordings scrubbed by some presidential technology that law enforcement has now.

That very same day Milwaukee PD, who apparently wadn't as woke to the new methods, messed around and released the body cam footage of officers using excessive force against a college basketball player. Three separate body cams show the athlete being confronted by cops in a Walgreens parking lot where he'd illegally parked his car. The first officer calls for backup and then, like they had heard the bat call, beaucoup squad cars is on the scene. The athlete remains calm, explains hisself while the officers hover around him like drones. Then he puts his hand in his pocket and on cue the cops collapse on him, wrestling his slender ass to the ground, beating and tasering the brother till he's left limp.

Meanwhile, in Miami, the Olympic weightlifter Richie Prosciutto went 51/50: while in the midst of a workout at his local gym, Prosciutto, it was reported, started raving 'bout the FBI having a vendetta against him. He blocked the gym exits with weightlifting equipment. He chucked dumbbells at his fellow patrons, breaking out a window in the process. Po-lice arrived on scene and took the Olympian into custody on an involuntary psych hold without arrest, let alone tasers and batons.*

*

The day after my Sherrod story went online, Mrs. Greenberg emailed me. Even though the piece was garnering attention, revealing to people on the other side of town what it was like to live a few miles east, Mrs. Greenberg didn't pay much mind to it. Ravenscourt was dated for demolition. The place was old news. And it was a simple story of poverty and loss. It was small picture, with a lowercase *s* and a lowercase *p*.

If I couldn't write about the big picture, the least I could do for my next story would be to write about a big event. She emailed me a flyer: there would be a town hall the next night in downtown Oakland to address what had happened at the BART station. Persons involved, as well as local celebrities and academics, would discuss it. "The community came together in the case of the bigoted barista of 2025. Now is the time to address injustice in our community once again. Si se puede!"

---

*andrewjacksonslaststand010621: As a former member of the American military and a public and private sector security personnel/police officer based in a major metropolitan area, I laugh!! at shit like this. These news stories are about bad cops. They confuse their gun with their taser. They get scared if a black flinches at them. They bust guns at any opportunity. Real police don't do that shit. When law enforcement decides to wage war and take this country back, trust me it will not be a matter of one black beaten up here, another shot over there on the other side of the country! We have the ability to coordinate and act tactically and massively!! We exercise restraint relative to our capacity for violence!!! But the Time is coming.

I had a sinking feeling as soon as I finished reading the flyer. Not sinking like the sunken place, more like sinking into all that stuff that I seen in the Youth Control when they had me all drugged up, except now instead of falling thru landfill, I was falling into somethin' hella suspect and basically boojie. Mrs. Greenberg needed someone to cover the event and write a story on it. I knew it would be pointless to ask her if any of the other students would step up and do the job.

"Can you send me bus fare?" I wrote back.

She Western Union–ed me some cowries and like that I was dispatched downtown.

The integrated lakeside church sat in the shadows off Grand Ave. at the edge of a park underneath a crew of trees that seemed to stand guard like so many COs. The line to get in was hella long and diverse, young and middle-aged and elderly, black and white and Latin and Asian and Pacific Islanders who reminded me of Miguel lookin' hella long-haired and light-skinned Creole, if Creole people was huge enough to hoist up houses and shit. Ever since '20, you don't see people of different races stand in line shoulder to shoulder breathing in each other's stank, dank breath. Least you don't see hella white people thick in a crowd with the rest of us.

But that night was different. I spotted a poster peaking between swaying, waiting bodies. It reminded me of the speakers for the evening, a three-person panel that would discuss the BART brutality incident: a Berkeley ethnicity, education, activism, and American studies professor, a comedian, and the white dude who called the cops on Mr. America. I got the feeling that the event might be about everything and everybody but Mr. America.

Inside the church, I peeped the scene. People was milling around, socializing and speechifying. It was brothers in dashikis and Jordans and brothers in BART worker gear and brothers in business attire, Asian cats in basketball shorts and Jordans and Asian cats in Financial District fits, and white cats who looked like Men's Wearhouse models and white cats with long blond dreads who looked like they had took every spray can in the store to they clothes, all the colors of the rainbow and none of them matching. Complected women both black and brown dipped in deep Afrocentricity, rockin' headdresses to the heavens, Angela Davis shirts, and camouflage fatigues, shared space with black, brown, and white women who all somehow sported the same steelo, that downtown San Francisco, on they *j-o-b* and too busy to be bothered business suit.

I overheard a man whose voice sounded smooth as a Soclear newscaster say that he used to work in the VC space, but now he was funemployed, taking time off to see how the other 99 percent controlled their blood pressure. The chuckleheads around him laughed like they was inside his joke. From the outside, I had no idea what any of it meant. Another cat with the same unsoiled speech which coulda sprouted anywhere in America spoke to a circle of women who looked up at him like he was 'bout to drop some jewels. "Everything," he said, "is cyclical, it's a cycle of sorts, a feedback loop where you get out what you've put in on all ends. Businesses' investment in our communities," he told them, "must be matched by the community's investment in business. That's why Trump was such a tragedy. If you looked past the racism and psychosis, the man did have a plan for Black America, but who looks past racism and psychosis these days?"

I guess it was good to see so many people of so many different races and ethnicities and fashion choices in the same space, sharing the same air. I knew networks was important. But what did any of this have to do with Mr. America?

I dipped thru the networks and made my way toward the stage. The techs worked away at the back of the stage. They performed the sound checks and light checks, making things buzz and thunder and *boom-bap* and go dark all of a sudden, and then bright spotlight the one man who sat still behind a foldout table in the middle of the stage. It was not the comedian and it was not the professor. It was Deadrich. He sat there calm and cleaner'n a muhfucka in his bone-white Brooks Brothers and his red-and-black authentic 86 Air Jordans. He sipped water from a paper cup while the techs zipped around him. He sat behind a long table with an empty chair on either side of him and a microphone in front of each chair. I tried to process the scene: Was he the person who called the po-lice on Mr. America? Was I gettin' my white people confused? I had took Deadrich for a comrade, or at least as someone who wadn't in conspiracy against black folks. Or maybe he didn't have nothin' to do with the incident. Maybe he was just sitting there receiving free water cuz he could. Maybe he knew nobody would question him if he just went and sat up onstage like a boss.

The techs seemed to think he belonged there. They kept refilling his cup from a giant pitcher of water. I wondered when the event would begin and what role, if any, he was there to play. I watched his wondering blue eyes wander the church, taking everything in. They wandered from back to front and from one set of pews to the next. I could see that he was about to see me when a commotion broke out at the back of the church. A group of masked protestors burst in. Wadn't no time to think about what was about to happen, they entered so fast, but a memory of the Capitol fully on fire and the White House on lockdown flashed up.

"*8:46!" they yelled.

NO JUSTICE, NO PEACE,
NO LOVE FOR PO-LICE.
NO JUSTICE, NO PEACE,
NO LOVE FOR PO-LICE.

They masks all read *8:46, and I could see behind they masks that most of them was POC, black and tan and olive-complected, but a few were white as well. In the audience, folks of all colors leapt out they seats and threw up they fists. "FUCK TWELVE!" someone yelled. "Fuck twelve, fuck twelve / Fuck twelve, fuck twelve, fuck twelve!" others began to sing. Folk cheered and chanted over the obscenities: "No justice, no peace / No love for po-lice."

"DEVONTE!" a masked protestor stepped forward screaming.

"*SAY THEY NAME!!*" the others cried back.

"GEORGE FLOYD!" a woman screamed.

"*SAY THEY NAME!!*"

"ALAN BLUEFORD!"

"*SAY THEY NAME!!*"

"TYISHA MILLER!"

"*SAY THEY NAME!!*"

"TRAYVON!"

"*SAY THEY NAME!!*"

"BOBBY HUTTON!"

"*SAY THEY NAME!!*"

I lost consciousness of the man on the stage and leapt up and yelled with them: "*SAY THEY NAME!!*"

"*OSCAR GRANT!*"

"*SAY THEY NAME!!*" I yelled again.

*

The sound system roared awake like a giant, crying higher and higher till it drowned out the chants. The people in the masks ripped them joints off. "No more fake investigations. No justice, no peace! Let's settle it in the streets!" a high yellow lady with a big Afro and reddish-brown freckles declared. Then she turnt on her heel like you did that one day when I first seen you and walked right out the church. The other protestors followed after her, and some folk in the audience ran behind them. I started for the exit, too, making my way back into the networks of people. I weaved between the stunned funemployed folks and made for the door. Then I heard Deadrich's mic'd voice burst across the church.

"YEAH, YEAH, COOL, I GOT YOUR SOLILOQUY OF A TEXT MESSAGE. I'LL MAKE SURE TO READ IT. NO, WE HAVEN'T STARTED. WE'RE RUNNING LATE FOR SOME—IS THIS GODDAMN MIC ON?"

The whole church went silent as all eyes turnt from the protestors to the stage. Deadrich stared back at us, all of us, and turnt actual, not racial, white. For a second, nobody in that piece knew what to do. Then Deadrich said, "Well, I guess we're getting started. I apologize for my language. Can we cue some music?"

The techs scattered behind the stage curtain and Stevie Wonder started singing.

---

*Insurgency Alert Desk, Third Bureau: Copeland Cane remains a fugitive from justice. He has twenty-four hours to turn himself in.

Deadrich looked back to his phone and stood up from his seat, picked the mic off the table, and stood. He made a throat-cutting gesture and the music stopped mid-Stevie. Who was this dude? I wondered as I made my way to a seat amongst the networkers. And what was this event I was fated to witness? And what did any of this have to do with the po-lice and my battered friend?

"I'm Douglas Deadrich. I'll be the moderator for tonight's event."

"Nah," someone yelled from the audience. "You the cracker who called the cops on that boy, got him beat up!"

"No, no, no, no, no," Deadrich said, shaking his head. "Not me."

"Then who is you?" a voice that probably wadn't draped in business attire questioned.

"The white man who called the police, precipitating the terrible incident that we are here to discuss, is not here tonight. I apologize for his absence."

"No need for you to do that," the same woman said. "He should apologize for his own self."

"Punk-ass white boy!" someone shouted.

"Again, not me," Deadrich pointed out. He went to his phone and started reading from it louder'n people was yelling. "'Due to concerns over his safety, John Henderson, a local business owner who mistakenly'—hear that: mistakenly—'called police on a BART train dance performer, has asked me to appear in his stead for tonight's event.'"

"What about that boy's safety!?" someone clapped back, and I found myself clapping along with half the audience at the comment.

"Coward ass!" another voice yelled out.

"I wouldn't say that," Deadrich said. "John Henderson has been a friend of mine since childhood. We went to school together and we do business together. I believe that I can express his perspective, his thoughts and feelings about the matter, in a fair and honest manner. I'll vouch as a community member, business leader, and activist myself that John and his wife, Armineh, have always supported opportunities for minorities and the underserved. He acknowledges that he made an error in judgment . . ." The apology, which was a lot about what his friend did for the community and not much about what he had did to

Mr. America, rattled on and Deadrich read every word of it. ". . . and that's why I'm confident that we can make amends tonight and move forward as one community," he concluded.

Stevie Wonder started singing again, and the comedian, who towered over Deadrich despite Deadrich being over six feet tall easy, came out from behind the curtain and took the seat to Deadrich's right. He leaned into his mic and laughed loud enough to break a window. That got Deadrich to stop talkin'. "I apologize, too," the comedian said. "Sometimes I just laugh for no reason. Nothing's funny. It just happens. Douglas, can I ask you a question?"

"Sure," Deadrich said.

"Can you sit down?" the comedian asked. Everyone laughed.

Deadrich sat. The music stopped.

"Can I ask you another question?"

"Shoot."

"I'd rather beat your ass than shoot you, and I'd rather interrogate you than fight you—c'mon now. My second question: Do you think people need to call the police on black people less, or do you think the police need to de-escalate and interrogate more and shoot and beat less?"

"Both."

"But if you had to choose?"

"The police are the ones responsible. My friend isn't trained to react to a crisis."

"Is he trained to see a crisis where there isn't one, though? That's the question."

Deadrich didn't respond.

I remembered that I should be taking notes. I started scribbling, "What is this man doing here??" That was not journalism. I reprimanded my own self. I needed to get on-task and take notes on what was being said, not ask questions that nobody was gonna answer. But I did wonder what Deadrich's intentions actually was. Was he really just there to speak for his friend? Was he tryna bridge a gap between black and white people? Or was he an agent on the low for law enforcement?

"Can I tell you a story?" the comedian asked.

Deadrich nodded, and the comedian told us a story that began with how great his life is: hella money, beautiful wife, millions of social media followers and whatnot. This brother was living so good that he figured shit was sweet to where he could act like he was free, smoke his weed, throw on a face mask for the cold air and whatever new germs was flying around, and take a walk by the lake as the morning sun glorified the earth. He told us that if he got his walk out the way by dawn, he could return home and fall back asleep right about the time his wife would wake up. Then she couldn't nag on him for not taking care of his health, not to mention she would have to deal with the munchkins while he went back to snoring. Two birds, one stoned rock star, he quipped. But one dark morning a new cop fresh outta elementary school pulled up next to him, braking hard. Kindergarten cop leapt from his car, barking orders and drawing his taser and shit. The comedian stopped stock-still, wondering what he had done wrong. The cop yelled somethin' about a masked burglar and motioned at his real firearm and threatened to shoot the comedian where he froze. Old boy explained to us that if not for his years of onstage ad-libbing, he mighta reacted slower and met his Lord and Savior right then and there. Instead, the cop ordered him to the ground and the comedian dropped like he was stolen goods. He told us how he hit the pavement flat nose and fat lips first. That was painful enough, but the worst part, he said, was that even though he escaped the taser, his fall scuffed his vintage Jordan rookie sneakers beyond mint condition. "The problem is perception," the comedian said. "Someone, whether it was the cop or whoever called the cop, perceived me to be a thief, not because I was masked (wearing a mask in public is a civic good when you're as ugly as I am), but because they wanted to see me that way. That was their preexisting perception of me, and that perception precipitated action, ergo: Fuck your friend, whoever smelt it done dealt it."

Deadrich didn't respond, just nodded kinda noncommittal. I couldn't call it if the comedian was just a good talker, or if it was some truth to what he was sayin' and some intelligence to how he said it. I eye-hustled the room: the black people was split on whether the comedian was funny or not, the white people looked like they was about to shed tears for some reason, and the Latins and Asians was somewhere in the middle not knowing how to feel about the shit.

As the comedian concluded, a woman dressed to the tens came from behind the curtain. This was the Education, Activism, and American Studies professor from the posters. Late as fuck, I thought, but fine as hell. Her freckles spotted a face the color of dust. She was wearing a skintight black blouse and black yoga pants over her slim-thick frame. I know I'm wrong for thinkin' looks first—my own sin of profiling. Did I mention her red-and-black Air Jordan high heels was hittin', too?

The lady took her mic from the table and walked out in front of the table like we was her college class and she was finna lecture us for the midterm. "Hello, everyone," she said. "My name is Sarina Jayachandra Campbell-Zayas, principal of Rockwood High School in East Oakland, visiting lecturer at the University of California."

It was one of them "come again?" moments, Jacq. Cuz I had seen the Rockwood principal's candy-red Corvette, but I had never actually laid my eyes upon the woman herself. Here she was, not just our principal but a professor, too. And what about that degree again? And what about Mr. America?

"We have a tendency to localize state-sanctioned white supremacist terror against marginalized persons," the principal said. "I said, we have a tendency to localize state-sanctioned white supremacist terror against marginalized persons, and we have a tendency to universalize crimes committed by marginalized persons against the powerful. I said, we have a tendency to universalize crimes committed by marginalized persons against the powerful, brothers, sisters, and trans folks. We must think more systematically, we must think more *systematically*, we must think much more *systematically* about the violence meted out by the state against marginalized persons, particularly against women, trans women, trans women of color, and people of color generally, particularly African-descended people, particularly African-descended persons. The systemic threats encountered by the constantly surveilled black body in our white-dominated postbellum apartheid nation-state . . ."

Dear Jacq, I was, cross my heart and hope to die peacefully, truly attempting to understand all that gum-flappin', I swear I tried. But as she just kept going in and going on, I just got more and more confused. I felt the audience around me get just as sideways.

"I've learned a lot tonight," Deadrich said after the professor finally sat down.

I waited for someone to say different, but all the outta pocket audience members had been removed or hushed up or talked at into silence. And wadn't a single mention of Mr. America. The comedian had hovered around it, but he only spoke about "perception" and about hisself and about Henderson. I wadn't tryna learn how not to call the po-lice and I wadn't really tryna teach white people nothin'. I wanted to know what reparations would come to my brother whether a lesson got learnt or not. Mr. Henderson seemed like he was breaded up pretty good; why couldn't he just chunk Mr. America off some money? Why couldn't Deadrich, or any of them jokers, do that, instead of teaching and learning and acting like we was in a classroom? Who were we here for, really?

"Not only have I learned a lot from this discussion," Deadrich said, "I feel inspired. I'm realizing how I personally can take action and I hope everyone here feels the same way." I remembered Deadrich was the moderator and realized that he was 'bout to segue some shit, but what he said about taking action caught hold of me. "Let's open the floor to questions for the panelists," Deadrich said in the same light-bright-and-all-the-way-white way he said a lotta things.

It was automatic, Jacq: my hand shot up and so did the rest of me, rising from my seat. Deadrich pointed toward me. "Yes, right there."

We met eyes, me and him. I could tell he really was inspired to take action by his glittering, hopeful gaze. But he was also confused—not about the actions to take, but about me. I could tell he recognized me, but he tripped over my name: "Yes, yes, young man. What is your question?"

This nigga, I thought. *To him, I'm nothin' but the nigga done sold him his shoes. If he cain't remember my name, does he even remember my scholarship?* I wanted action and I wanted to be recognized for who I was, which, put simpler, simply means that I was hella tight when I started to speak. "Let's talk about taking action," I said. "What y'all, any of y'all"—I looked from Deadrich to the comedian to the professor—"plan to do for—for"—Mr. America? Captain America? Captain Black America? I caught myself in the void and realized that I didn't know my man's government name. I didn't know his name. His crew never called him nothin' but street names. Nobody at the event that night had spoke his name cuz they did not know it to raise it. I lowered my voice. "What are you doin' here?" I said. I cut him off 'fore he could answer. "Why is we listening to you when you don't know why you're here? We know why we're here, but they got you directing shit like we don't know our own problems?"

"Now there's no need to use profanity," Deadrich rejoindered, still all smiley and hella contradictory. He turnt so he wadn't lookin' straight at me anymore but at everyone and no one at the same time. "This has been such a rich evening of discussion. There's so much to process. I'll come back to you, OK? Other questions! Yes, you in the beautiful red head scarf thingamajigger."

I wanted to stand up again and take some kinda action, but instead I looked to the woman in the head wrap, who knew what she wanted to say, but it wadn't OK, the evening wadn't too rich, it wadn't too much for me to process. It troubled me somethin' bad that I didn't know my brother's name.

Deadrich started parlaying again, answering the question posed by the lady in the headwrap, but I stopped listening. The only action I could take that would mean anything was to get up outta there. I needed to bounce. It didn't matter if I disrespected Deadrich. He wouldn't remember me no kinda way. I knew it was only one person I had to listen to in order to write my story and he wadn't in that church.

*

As I rode the BART home, I decided I would ask Mrs. Greenberg for time off from the next day's class to visit Mr. America at Highland Hospital. And for the money to take myself there.

I remembered how empty the trains was back in the day when the ghetto flu was really hunting. How folks was afraid to get in these tin cans and catch they death of recirculated air. Now the trains is packed all day, plus plenty more come rush hour. Round midnight it gets thick with fiends nodding laid out across the seats or in the aisles and crazy people talking to theyselves, threatening the air, certifiable insane with no psych ward to go to. I made sure to keep my back to the wall and to socially distance from everyone.

At Coliseum station, I de-boarded and ran home. Fireworks sparked above me and pulsed like heartbeats beneath my feet as I went. When I seen the homeless encampments like a little village up ahead, I knew I could slow down. I walked past the homeless and into Rockwood with my eyes on alert. You never know with these cats; one day this man who lives on the street is A-OK, polite as you please, just minding his own business in his little tent and not bothering nobody, the next day he's liable to be off his drugs and decide you're the devil. Might scream on you; might try to kill you. It's why I'm no fan of these homeless camps, Jacq. I wish they would disappear. But idn't that what people wanna do with us? Would it be better if the po-lice came and cleared the homeless out? If they decided to do that, wouldn't we be next on they list for forced removal? What if they brutalized folk in the process? What if a good dude like Mr. America got caught up and beat down in the mix?

I worked the old lock on our front door till it gave way. I was pretty sure my parents passed on the WD-40 just so they would know whenever people, meaning me, was coming and going. Sure nuff, Daddy sat in the shadows lookin' straight at me. He was set up in one of our folding chairs behind a tray table. A deck of cards was spread like turkey plumes across its surface. I never knew my old man to play cards. He was always too busy with his ideas. But somethin' about the man had turnt.

"Hey," I said.

"They keep y'all out late with this reporting mess, don't they?"

"It ain't mess."

"You know what I mean. You got a article to write?"

"Yes, sir."

"You got a deadline?"

"Yes, sir."

"Well, you just make sure you don't miss no deadlines. Always make sure you deliver on an obligation."

"Ain't think you cared."

"Boy, I don't want you at that school, you know that. But now that you are there, I want you to do yo' very best, represent, show them folks the knowledge you got up in that big brain."

"It was a panel discussion on po-lice, excessive force, things like that."

"Like I done told you, Cope, you got more to teach them folks than they can teach you."

I nodded again even though I couldn't cosign that. It was whole colleges of knowledge I knew nothin' about. Now that I was attending a high-ranked prep school, it seemed like the only thing I knew was how little I knew. I just had my experiences, my opinions. I didn't even know what I would write about that night. But I couldn't tell him what troubled me, not in the way that I wanted to. I couldn't imagine just up and speakin' my mind to the man, not in this lifetime. I started to speak on the journalism class, on my story, on the school, and I think maybe I got caught up in it and said too much, or I was tryna justify in ways I didn't know how the value of the prep school, but I went on about it too long cuz after a minute, or a while, I heard a gentle rumble coming from the shadows where he sat. I put myself on pause and listened to the rumble as it rolled like a radio signal from a far-off frequency. I walked over to him. Up close I could see that he lay back in relaxation that his wakeful form never knew. His head was tilted up like a man in the last moments of prayer, and I remembered him falling to his knees in prayerful fear as the cops pointed they guns at me, and for a second, Jacq, I wanted to weep. Then his jaw fell open, drawing the low rumble of his breath in and out deeper and lower and rougher. I had never known him to fall asleep just like that, the way old folks do. That was the night I realized my old man was really an old man.

*

At six in the A.M. I woke and emailed Mrs. Greenberg: "I need to know more to write this story. I need an excused absence to visit the victim. And I need some funds for the trip."

A reply email hit my inbox almost immediately. Like, when did this lady sleep? "Don't worry about class today," it read. "Go to Western Union at nine A.M."

After scoopin' the centimos, I paid for a taxi to the hospital. During the ride, I scanned article after article about the incident in search of Mr. America's government name. I finally came upon it as we came upon the hospital: DeVonte Baltimore. I remembered the protestor that screamed that name: DeVonte. Baltimore. The blackest name in history. I should really be calling cousin Mr. Black America, but you know how first impressions work: I'ma always have his all-Americanness in my mind no matter how black his name is, no matter how many times the cops wail on him, even if it turns out his middle name is somethin' blacker'n DeVonte Baltimore. And peep this: What if being hella black is the same as being all-American? What if being second class, treated like trash, is the American way, it's just don't nobody wanna call it what it is?

*

DeVonte Baltimore was hooked up to hella tubes, oxygen, machines, EKG, this and that. His big frame was covered loosely by one of those hospital smocks with the little floral patterns. Like he was someone's grandma. Like they was sho nuff tryna finish off my man's humiliation up in that hospital ward.

"You're the first person who's found me," he said when he seen me.

His breath wheezed outta his throat like someone near death, and I remembered what it was like seeing elderly hauled out into the courtyard on stretchers as they coughed out they lungs. I remembered how they jerked around tryna find air they couldn't get. I remembered they eyes staring darkly into Oakland's perfect sun, clean air, blue sky, as they breathed they last.

"How'd you find me, blood?"

"I read the news, boss. It's all there, your name and everything."

"Really?"

"You're big news, homie. Or, I mean, what them mofos did to you is news."

"Nah," he drawled out, his voice rattling outta his chest. "Niggas get they asses kicked by cops every day. Ain't nothin' special 'bout me. Maybe if they had killt me."

"How you doin', big bruh? You recovering?"

"Yeah. I feel better every day. Might not look like it, but the doctors say I'm young and my shit fittin' to heal with a quickness. Just gotta be patient. A patient must be patient." He cracked a smile, and his oxygen tube fell out his nose. I leapt toward him to re-situate it, but when I got to his bedside he held his left forearm out like a guard rail. "Chill, my nigga. Chill. It's just precautionary all this shit they got me hooked to. I promise you, a nigga ain't one nostril tube from death. It looks way worse'n it is."

I fell back and observed, remembering I was there to tell Mr. America's story, not save his life. For real, though, dude looked terrible. The left half of his face had a blue undertone to it like underwater jaundice. His whole face was puffy from the painkillers they had him on. He had hella stitches along the middle of his lower lip and he breathed deep and heavy, like an old house making noises. The morphine drip on the opposite side of the bed made a *tick-tick* sound every time his pain surged and he had to hit it to subside the shit. His left arm sat in a sling, the sign of a separated shoulder.

"You sure about that?"

"It looks terrible so yeah, Cope, I'm sure. If they want me to stop dancing on the trains, they best come with a shotgun next time. These is just a few bruises and things."

Mr. America might be banged up, but if he was emotional about it, he wadn't about to show it to me. The first thing he had said was that no one had found him. I wondered who was lookin'. If he had family, why hadn't they looked? Why wadn't any of them at his bedside? I saw how alone a boy is when he turns eighteen and he idn't a child no more. That would be me soon. Super alone with no one to call on but myself.

"Why'd you find me?" he asked.

"You have a story to tell," I answered. Then I realized that I did, too. "Look, I transferred schools," I said, and proceeded to catch him up on a life he knew only so much about just like I knew damn near nothin' about his life. "So that's what's brought me here," I finished.

"After all that, why not just tell your own story? Why search me out?"

"You're more interesting."

"A nigga who dresses up like Uncle Sam and moonwalks for white people's money, then gets beat up by cops over some nonsense. How you figure that's interesting?"

"Sounds interesting as fuck to me."

"I'm a living, breathing stereotype, blood. You're unique."

"How do you figure? I got locked up. A million black people is locked up. Ain't nothin' new there."

"Ain't nothin' new 'bout gettin' beat up by some cops neither!"

"But people don't hold town halls and rallies and shit for kids who do a crime and get sent to juvie. Incarceration is just a statistic; they literally make you a number. You sittin' here all broken up, tubes in you and shit, that's not a number. It's, like, the apotheosis of all the injustices."

"Apotha-what?"

"Never mind."

"Boy, I wish I could go back to school and learn some of this shit you know. Maybe I should become a journalist."

"Maybe you should. Can I take a picture of you?"

"Oh, *helllll* nah, blood! I look too good to look like this for eternity."

"Fair nuff. Bump that. How 'bout I write a description of the way you look? For the story."

"Freedom of speech, blood. This is America. You write whatever you feel you should write."

"Cool then. You wanna tell me what happened, or should I just go with what the po-lice reported?"

*

That's how I got the homie to speak. And I did describe as best I could how he looked without making it too ugly or disrespectful of his dignity. Them cops tried to take my brother's dignity, I wadn't fittin' to do him dirty in print. Never that.

At least that's what I like to tell myself. At least that's what I told Mrs. Greenberg when I submitted the story, and it's what I told you when we discussed it back then, and it's what I woulda said if Mr. America had ever questioned me on it. I don't know how he truly felt, though, cuz he never said A or B 'bout it, least not to yours truly. I have no idea what it feels like to have someone write about you in your weakest state. Even now, with Soclear wanting to define me as some kinda monster, one thing they ain't said is a brother's weak, na'mean? But Mr. America had no choice in the matter. They beat him like a runaway slave and laid him up in the hospital for the fun of it. I tried to tell myself I had repped him right in my article and, real talk, anyone can look it up: I think I did a good job with it. You thought I did a good job with it. Mrs. Greenberg thought I was gotdamn James Baldwin out that bitch. It was hella people who read it and found that they sided and sympathized with big bruh in the hospital, not with the local celebrities who did all the talkin', let alone the cops who put him there. I was proud and thankful that the story did its little part to shift the local dialogue away from the nonsense at the church to somethin' that truly mattered.

But maybe where I went with the story mattered too much. I couldn't get the thought, the image, the memory of Mr. America, DeVonte black than Nigeria Baltimore, laid up like he was, with his underwater jaundice and his morphine drip and the whole helpless scene in that hospital, on the page without feelin' some type of way about it. Puttin' my brother in print like that felt like a violation even though I had had his consent, even though I had my First Amendment rights, even though I had y'all's approval. It felt like he was too much on display. And I knew that I, too, was too much on display. I was just as out front every time that I penned somethin' for publication. Aye'body white and they white mommas was staring at us in our devastation in the hospital, in the street, in the scholarship application process. I felt like I was lettin' these people who wadn't even my people, seeing as my people didn't need the lessons my stories was teaching and half of them only wanted an escape that would name-check Kamala and Barack back in the day and Black Excellence all the time—I don't even know where this sentence started, Jacq, let alone where it's gonna go. But you hear me now? You understand me? It wadn't somethin' I could sit easy with, this completely neked birth of words into a watching world.

It was then that Daddy's dislike of literature made sense to me. The old man was not insane after all. I realized what was wrong with writing, especially writing like Mrs. Greenberg wanted me to write. From writing for the newsletter I came to see what it was to be a writer and it fucked with me bad. A writer goes inside theyself and shovels out what's in there, they fears, they sins and confusion. They take all that they find and put it on the page. It's a struggle, like a lotta things is. But what's it for? For who, for what? Books change your mind but they cain't change shit in the world. Like the train dancers spilling out all they soul for a few dollars, or some scattered clapping, or a cold-ass shoulder. These writers wrote they lives away, took theyselves apart and put it on the page for people they would never know who would read it when they felt bored, or shallow in theyself, or so they would have somethin' smart to say to they friends at some function someday, but never for the only thing that really mattered, which was to know someone and love them anyway. The only love I knew was the unconditional love of my mother and the conditional love of the old man, the exact terms of which I wouldn't be surprised is probably bullet-pointed in a pamphlet somewhere.

So many people had spoke and wrote about black people gettin' fucked with by po-lice. They spoke after Tulsa in 1921. They spoke after Harlem in '43. They spoke after Watts in '65. They spoke after Rodney King. They spoke after Sean Bell and Oscar Grant and all them folks who was killed 'fore I was born. And then *8:46 happened. I'm old enough to remember it happening and things changing and how it had aye'body and they momma thinkin' this at last would be when the po-lice would get defunded and killer cops would be sent to jail and this, that, and the third, fourth, and fifth was 'bout to change for once, for all, and forever. And I bet it was all kinda Yale- and Vanderbilt-accepted black people writing speeches and essays and whatnot. But what actually happened? How many— apologies to my daddy—n**** hunters been locked up? How many of these out and out Ku Klux Klan members been stripped of they badges, fired from they jobs, and had the cuffs clapped on them? What's actually changed when it comes to the po-lice that ain't get flipped back around and made even worse? Mrs. Greenberg said it herself: the cops went and switched clothes, done traded in one set of laundry and one kinda badge for another, meanwhile leaving they body cams behind. And now in the private sector they ain't have to worry about background checks or gettin' caught out with some tat that revealed what they was really all about. It was almost like you couldn't have a damn inch of progress in America without a half-circle reversal.

What was the point of any of it if nothin' changed, or if it changed and then changed back, or went some way that was way worse? What was my words gonna do to fix any of our history, or our present, never mind our future? What could I do? Teach whoever ain't hear or somehow forgot a lesson they shoulda learnt along with they ABCs? If someone wanted to know black people's elementary problems, they didn't need me to spell that shit out for them. They needed to take theyself to the Fruitvale BART—not for no history in no movie, but for what's right there right now: bear witness to the brother posted there. He's there every day; you cain't miss him. Old boy is hella yoked. Looks like Michael B. Jordan in *Creed*. He holds court, this cat. Walks the length of that train platform shirtless, impressive, with an orange Super Soaker water gun cradled to his jet-black chest. "You must smite them," he proclaims, like he's performing Shakespeare or some shit. "Y'all must smote them. Every small mammal, every little bird, every offending insect, down to the grasshoppers. If it flinches, if it makes any furtive movements, if it fails to maintain eye contact or to comply with all orders given, take it out! Blast it into oblivion! Wreck shop. Shoot or risk repeating yourself. Kill or be considered a member of your community. It is y'all's duty, it is y'all's obligation, it is y'all's birthright and religion to defend this nation against all enemies foreign, domestic, terrestrial, arboreal, subterranean, mitochondrial, fantastical, chimeric, the whole lick. Oakland shall not be safe until all these forces hath been smited."

$*^{*+}$

Writing wouldn't change the world. At least not for black folks. But I lay low and played my role: I kept writing, hitting all my deadlines. The year spun itself out, one unconquered crisis to the next. I learnt how to live thru the news. The bad headlines and the human problems behind them was endless. I threw myself into every inch of ink.

Copeland Cane lived from one newsletter to the next, Jacq. Yeah, I did all right in my other classes, passed them and kept my scholarship, but journalism was my priority. My only clique was you and the rest of our class of newshounds. I seen stories in my sleep and ate and drank them awake. I missed the Rock even though I lived there, maybe because I only came home to sleep and wake and went weeks at a time without seeing Keisha and Free and them. My eyelid started twitchin'. My whole body was on alert, just like when I was in juvie. I only saw the Rock in the dark when I got home from school and barely spoke to either of the people who had put that roof over my head.

By the time summer arrived, announced by God-level fireworks that rocked the earth beneath Oakland like so many small earthquakes, I was barely surviving. The same could be said of the Rock. Mr. MacDonald announced via email that our apartment buildings (which were really his apartment buildings) would come down one at a time so that construction on the new luxury lofts, the Redwood Homes, could begin a-sap. This was bad news for the Rock, but good news for us. My fam's building was scheduled to get the dynamite last, which meant we would get extended four, five, maybe even six more months past the new year 'fore our rent jumped. That would give me enough time to finish high school, maybe, hopefully, but not a minute more.

---

*Insurgency Alert Desk, Third Bureau: Recent complaints made against Soclear Security police officers allege a conspiracy among a wide network of police officers to covertly menace people of color. The Insurgency Alert Desk's investigation has found that these complaints are totally without merit.

+andrewjacksonslaststand010621: I'd be honored to put a bullet in Copeland Cane's head. He can take the .45th. *64:8. Stolz Jungs. Fourth Reich. God bless America.

The email displayed a sketch of the renovated Redwood Homes as they would appear after Rockwood was demolished. It would be four gigantic luxury lofts, two that would look like spaceships angled in all kinda unique ways, high rectangles and low squat squares of clear glass, the other two done up like huge log cabins made of redwood, fake redwood. The whole shit felt fake. The center of the courtyard would be converted from a basketball court to tennis courts and a Neiman Marcus, entry to which would be fingerprint-recognition software ensured. The same software would regulate entry into the new buildings, the technology implemented in order of construction. The email listed the construction schedule.

I read the schedule and thought about when Rockwood's residents, the ones I was close with in particular, would be forced out. Trey's building would be the first to go. Jacq, you had your bags packed for a college far, far away, where all this broke-ass Oakland lollygaggin' and scallywaggin' wouldn't mean a thing, so I wadn't worried about you. But your daddy's building would be the second to fall, which couldn't be good for him. Vista, rehabbed and rehoused, was the only person I knew who lived in the third building, the one that would be zapped from the map on New Year's Day. Finally, the rest of the folks I knew happened to live in my same building, which was why I knew them in the first place. It's like they say about crime, you do it to them that's closest to you. It's the same with everything else: the people around you become your people. Y'all don't choose each other. It's destiny.

I stared at the email, which was its own kinda destiny. It felt like the whole world was right there, the new world, and it was cold and real and expensive as shit.

*

I tried to read that summer. Searched out the same books that had spoke to me back in the day, but the meanings escaped me into mystery: Baldwin was just words and words and more words, a sermon of impossible complications. But Homer seemed too simple: all his people and gods was this or that symbol with a meaning that manifested like magic in the world. Richard Wright told on hisself too much, opened his heart in the heavy, raw way that Mrs. Greenberg wanted me to open mines. Truth like that was its own death wish. No wonder brother Wright never did see his old age.

You can only speak to the page when the page speaks to you, so when my books stopped talkin' to me, I stopped talkin', too, by which I mean I stopped talkin' to the page. I couldn't write. I mean, edit that—I could write a text message, I could write an email, maybe I might could even knock out a term paper or two 'bout some shit I couldn't care less about, but I couldn't write nothin' that would move people to do somethin', to want somethin', to make somethin' better. I couldn't move myself. I couldn't write for the newsletter no more. Couldn't stay they spokespade.

As I came to terms with me and the pen and the page no longer being on speaking terms, I had to confront some other realities as well. I did the math on my mediocre grades, my below subprime performance on the track team, and the little issue with Irish Spring and the shoes. I couldn't just drop the journalism class and the newsletter columns without picking up some other profile. PE would not be enough of a replacement. Pied-montay had accepted my application and waived my tuition for a reason. I was there to make it known that I was there. I couldn't afford to lose my scholarship. I couldn't afford the tuition. My $611 and two quarters stashed in a shoebox beneath some clothes underneath my bed would melt away in a minute and my ass would be back studying at the public library in Rockwood. But I couldn't write no more.

*

Forever. Ain't put pen to pad or fingertips to keyboard for nothin' nonessential since. My email to Mrs. Greenberg was simple and plain: "I've decided that I'm done writing for the newsletter. I won't take journalism this coming school year. With my academics and training for indoor track, I won't have the time. This is the best decision for me."

Finito negrito—cain't see myself writing ever again unless it's fittin' to change at least this small earthly square where I stand.

*

I knelt at the starting line at my first track meet of the indoor season, straight up and down dreading my fate. Our opponent was another preppy private school. I had heard that private schools, especially the Catholic ones, took sports super serious. Many were athletic powerhouses. De Sales. Blessed Sacrament. Our Lady of Guadalupe. Pied-montay, for whatever reason, was not. Maybe if we had Jesus in our school, our sports teams would be better. Maybe if our campus was planted in hood soil like a lotta the Catholic schools happened to be, we would be better. Keish had run track at a small private school in the Fruitvale the year I was gone, starring and going to the state meet. Free followed her, enrolling and running there despite her religion. The school wadn't tryna convert them, which was good, or teach them much of anything, which was bad, which was why both girls transferred back to Rockwood at year's end, switching places with Trey, who cared more about playing basketball in a gymnasium paneled in stained glass than the schoolwork they shorted him on.

Pied-montay Prep's plushed-out facilities were as state of the art as it could get. Way better'n any school in the hood, public or private. Our track, football field, baseball diamond, and gymnasium were all kitted up cutting edge, high tech, deep-cleaned, updated, interactive, and whatnot. You couldn't blame no insufficient funding; no, Pied-montay was not shy on spending its shells. Nah, I believe our underperformance across sports was solely the result of poor coaching. Irish Spring would run practice by taking us off campus grounds, pointing down the road, and ordering us to run to the freeway overpass or up into the hills to the horse farm and back. Back on campus, on the track, we never had no system to how we trained. We never did the same workout twice, never built, never sharpened. We just ran random workouts day to day. Nobody cared; nobody went to Pied-montay Prep to play sports.

Even though I had spent my first year at the school telling myself that I was pushing so hard with the journalism jones cuz it was my passion and it was hella demanding and I didn't have no time to train for track, I realized as I looked at them looping white lines in front of me that part of my reluctance was in not wanting to lose—not just taking the L itself, not losing by a stride or two, but that I was liable to be made a whole fool due to my lack of preparation and Irish Spring's swaggerless, subprime coaching. It was one thing to feel like I was fast as I ran to the bus stop, clipping past old, obese Fillmore Slim wannabes and grannies and nodding junkies; it was another to set foot on an actual track in a real-deal competition.

In the days leading up to the meet, I had dreamt about being exposed and humiliated. In the dreams, the gun sounded and I lit out into the lead. The other runners stalked my golden-shoed steps. I hit the halfway mark, took the second turn, and began to feel my lungs collapse or contract, and all of a sudden I couldn't catch my breath. The track stretched on endlessly. Wadn't no halfway. The race went on forever, and with each step I slowed and the lactic acid sank its fangs into me. Eventually, everyone passed me and I chased after them, no finish line in sight. I chased them off the track and back to the Youth Control, across land and water to Treasure Island, and back across time to that boy I used to be back when the world was new.

I knelt and tried to set my blocks. I fumbled with the equipment. For all the times I had seen other kids set they blocks, I couldn't do it myself. The boy in the lane next to me tapped me on the shoulder and peered down at me and asked if I needed some help. I turnt to look at him standing over me. It was finna be a very bad race. I got up and let him help me. I remember watching him as he nailed my blocks into the rubber track one whack at a time. His skin was the same color as the beige rubber. He glistened with sweat. I was bone dry. My mouth was a desert. Tension spasms ran along my calf muscles, threatening to turn into full killer cramps at any moment.

After he set the blocks for me, I knelt again and fixed my feet into them like I knew what I was doing. I got so set in them joints that my body set poised dead rigid as I waited for the gun. When the shot rang out and the other runners leapt out they stances, I stood straight up. It was a second where I almost stood still just watching everyone else move. Then I started running, but I was already behind. The boys in the lanes ahead of me increased the stagger and them that was in the lanes behind me breathed down my back. I was neck and neck with the boy one lane below me and losing contact with the lanes ahead. I drew dead even as we came along the first straightaway, yards, not strides, behind. I tasted hot grease in my throat. My feet fell heavy underneath me, the whole sole touching turf each time I took a step. My body was just waking up. I fell farther back. I remembered the day in elementary school when I discovered that I could run—but that was in competition against a bunch of little kids, not nearly grown high school athletes. I remembered other runs for school buses that picked up far from Rockwood—but the only competition then was time, the time of the bus schedule, not Colored People Time, which I had lost somewhere. All my nightmares was coming true when it happened: my muscles woke up. The powers that visited me in the Youth Control came back. The boy who looked back at me in the stainless steel cell mirror came alive inside me. I eyed the boy one lane ahead and shortened my stride, putting power into each step. My legs turnt into levers that hit the ground as hard as they could, then snapped back just as fast, then down into the ground again. I cut into the stagger as we hit the turn and I drove hard along the inside of my lane till I passed one boy then the next and the next. I was in the lead as we headed down the backstretch. I became a superhero as I ran, flying on my feet, fuck physics. My arms caught the wind and I felt godlike. I crossed the tape steps ahead of the others with a forty-nine-second four hundred meters. Ain't even feel tired either, if you wanna know the truth.

Later that same day, the boy entered me again, and I ran like my life was under threat and I took the half mile by five meters, which idn't even the same number system, not that that shit matters when you only have to count to one.

*

Mrs. Greenberg sent me one last email:

> Dear Cope,
> It's been three weeks since you resigned from your
> column at our school newspaper. I emailed you

immediately asking for a meeting, but you haven't
emailed me back. This email is not an attempt to
change your mind. Please suspend judgment of me
and my intentions and keep reading.

   After taking some time to think about it and
reflecting on my overtures toward you, I think I
might understand the undue pressure you felt in
your role as a writer for the school newsletter. I think
that I was overly enthusiastic about the idea of you
being some sort of disruptive force, enlightening
the Piedmontagne populous about issues related
to social justice. I fear that now that I've been a
teacher here long enough to earn tenure three times
over, perhaps I've magnified the importance of this
school's politics well beyond what they really are. It is
just high school, after all . . .

It was cool and all that she took the time to write me and explain
herself, and I have to admit that she was good people and all, I guess,
given everything and whatnot. But I never did write her back.

*

From that day on, wadn't no static about leaving the newsletter.
Sure, Mrs. Greenberg's last email sat in my inbox gathering dust
and distraction. I even remember receiving a text from you, Jacq,
writing me all the way from the East Coast. You said somethin' 'bout
politics taking an interest in me if I took them to be interesting. But
by then your daddy's apartment building was being demolished. I
thought about you. I had feelings for you that I knew would never
go nowhere, because you're a year ahead of me and academically
you're generations, centuries, and maybe even Ivy Leagues beyond
where I stand. But still, maybe I shoulda took things a step further,
asked you out, tried to kiss you, connect with you, like I did with
other girls at that school who I didn't share shit with, which made
them approachable and forgettable and you the total opposite of all

of that—not approachable or attainable, let alone a girl I could get out my mind. Maybe I shoulda tried in some way that I didn't. I played it safe instead, and now here I was, all messed up in the game, with you texting me from thousands of miles away with some social media caption wisdom, like you was my guru tellin' me what I should do. I wished we could be on more equal terms, which would allow us to be closer. But it wadn't to be, not in the way I wanted it to be. We wadn't even on the same side of the continent anymore. I had to accept these facts. So, for the simple fact of that and since you wanted to text me to teach me things, I treated your text like I did Mrs. Greenberg's email: let it fall to the bottom of my inbox landfill. And like landfill, it got mushed down with everything else in there and I knew I would never see it again.

Now I don't even own the phone you texted me on, number gone, the whole lick. When the authorities trace my old phone number, they'a probably find theyselves talkin' to someone named Teneisha who's got classes at community college to study for and don't really have time for this, plus she got an open window or some thin apartment walls and some loud-ass neighbors talkin' over her, so this call might as well come to an end sooner'n later. It makes it easier not to get caught that way, but now I cain't read and cain't remember exactly what I wrote to myself (pretending I was writing to y'all) to explain why I had to leave journalism behind. I was having trouble writing my thoughts by then, so I don't know that even as I wrote to myself that I ever truly put in high-def clarity what it was that made me quit. But in the end, it was this simple: writing was too dangerous and too meaningless at the same time.

Anyway, I knew the newsletter wadn't changing the world, so why should it run my life? If I left the news alone, I bet that it would leave me be.

*

I bet right. Don't nobody check for the indoor track season. The newsletter and the news itself left me alone all fall and all winter. Meanwhile, I got busy on them tight-turning indoor tracks. The boy visited me and I won with him inside of me. He was everything that had made me, he was the island, he was every chemical chain that laced me there and the drugs they dosed me with later on, and every diamond-fingered push-up and doorframe pull-up and all my anger. When the boy didn't show, I was just another slow Pied-montay nerd. I was just another middle-of-the-pack nobody. But I knew he was somehow there inside me. I just needed to learn to call on him in the right way at the right time.

I decided to stop listening to Irish Spring, whose sometimey workout schedule tested my patience, and to do my own circuit runs and hill repeats and intervals on my own time. If I ran fast enough in the meets in spring, I doubted the old man would object. I suspected that the decision to lean on myself as my best and only coach would bring the boy into me more often. I wanted him with me every time I touched the track. He might be from my past, but he was pushin' me forward. I knew I had this man-child in me, Jacq, who just needed to be brought out, and come the outdoor season I was liable to take off and embarrass folks.

*

Come February, the third Rockwood building fell, and I ran away from that reality. At the Mt. SAC Relays, I clocked 47.7 in the 400 and 1:49 in the 800. At Arcadia, I won my 400 race with a 47.5 and finished third in the 800 with a 1:50. The boy didn't leave me now. He was I and I was him.

March, the second and third Redwood Homes started going up, and at the Stanford Invitational, I dropped them shits like stones off a cliff, running times that not only won both races but had my name ringing statewide, wherever kids ran races. Just know this: when I say your boy could fly on his feet, I'm not talkin' yang. I had been thru hella changes, had a whole new chemistry to me, and each time I touched the track, it showed. I showed out. My times were the truth. So if the cops wanna come for me on the dead run, Jacq, them jokers can save they breath, best look into extradition.

*

As the outdoor season transpired—now there's a Ivy League word for your ass, transpired—I received more and more attention for my athletic exploits. The students who had read my articles on race and the po-lice and fell back from me like they was still social distancing and I was the virus now rolled up into my personal space like we was kinfolk. My whole rep and persona changed, Jacq. I learnt how to be popular for the first time for real. It wadn't like the newsletter, where everybody knew you but only an unknown number less'n half would have your back or even care to speak to you. This was different. People liked me and wanted to get in my vicinity. The boys who wore boat shoes would cross the campus to congratulate me and to tell stupid jokes about how they could outrun me if something was chasing them and how they wanted to kiss me and compare dick size, all that weird white boy shit.

As I opened up and let myself laugh at how stupid these smart kids could be, new things opened up to me. I learnt from one kid who was headed to Harvard in the fall that the arches and pillars of Pied-montay were an example of classical Roman architecture. I learnt from a girl in the drama class who wrote my name on her tits and flashed me when the teacher wadn't lookin' why the peacocks in the campus's urban garden had such beautiful plumes, what the plumes were for, and how she, being a natural exhibitionist, was akin to a plumed peacock morphed into human female form. *So you're not tryna get with me?* I asked her, still thinkin' about her tits. *No, not right now,* she said as she held qigong tree pose. *Maybe when I enter estrus. Research that.*

And a boy whose father CEO'd for Pixar informed me that the birds-of-paradise that rowed the walkways and tilted toward us, open black pelican mouths sprouting blue and pink flowers, were the only genus of *Strelitzia reginae* to have been cultivated at a school campus anywhere in North America. Our en-tire overachieving senior class, who loved us some ancient Egypt facts almost as much as we loved geeking out on extracurricular activities and overachieving at shit, kept a running joke all year 'bout our "Hierakonplishments," which was the kinda silly, nerdy shit that wouldn't get you nothin' but sideways looks in Rockwood but that I found myself laughing at and repeating as much as anyone. I loved it cuz it was silly and stupid and smart all at once—just like Pied-montay Prep.

The teachers who had an interest in sports let me turn in my papers late and leave class early. Principal Kennedy shouted me out in his weekly announcement of achievements. And, best of all, now that I was somebody, I could connect with college student-athletes solo dolo, no intro. The shoes that they received for free and needed flipped, I could now flip to more and more customers: Mr. Guzzo gave the good word go-ahead to some understudy dude, who gave it to Miguel, who passed the approval to me. I didn't care that he wadn't tryna speak to me; he could put his blessing on the back of a dirty dollar bill if it meant I could vend at his shoe show pop-ups at SportsZone in Oakland and the Metreon and the Palace in San Francisco.

The shows revealed a whole 'nother side to the game: these were the people that made sports big business. Hella Douglas Deadriches descended on these shows to window shop, authenticate, barter, talk shit, and buy shoes. These Deadriches were white and black, Chinese and Filipino, Mexican and Puerto Rican; they dressed in everything from Financial District fits, suits, and shit to high-end, on-trend shoes and signatured jerseys and custom-engraved caps. A few was even female. What they all had in common, other'n money, was that they was set on that swoosh and that jump-man image: Jordan suspended in air, one arm extended, his hand cupping the basketball, while his other arm trails behind and his legs fly out at a perfect ninety-degree angle, like Da Vinci's man in the circle.

That man Guzzo knew what he was doin'. Freelancers like me had to post off in the back while his vendors set up in all the best spots, the corner booths and whatnot. I only made one sell at the Metreon, two at SportsZone, three or four more at the Palace. But just being up in that mix let me see how much money was moving. Guzzo actually was everything Miguel had promised him to be: a real player.

After working the shows, the wealthy people of Pied-montay slid off the pedestals I had put them on. As I started to see them walking on the same earth that I was, it made everything easier. I even sold shoes to a teacher or two—ain't sayin' no names, y'all don't need to worry. And back at home, I thought how maybe the changes that was coming wouldn't be all bad. The new residents would have hella disposable dollars to spend on shoes, as long as my folks and me could afford to live next to them.

Despite the demolitions and the Redwoods rising up all around the Rock, and the arrival of private po-lice in our neighborhood to hold the line between us and the new residents, my senior year was speeding along lovely: I was running fast, stacking my Hierakonplishments and holding my own on all levels, set to graduate with a diploma that would carry weight out in the world. I was also stacking my side skrilla.

Rockwood might be coming down all around me—scratch that, it most definitely was doing just that—but I couldn't stop that. And when winter came to that dying neighborhood where I still lived, a few folks peaced out from a flu that was supposed to be dead its damn self—but I couldn't do nothin' about that neither. I confess that I escaped to that dreamlike little city within our big sad city and made my own make-believe within it. But, no lie, I was loving what little was left to me.

*

Me and Miguel's paths tended to cross at our gates. I sold a pair of sneaks here and there to our new neighbors, but Miguel went way harder on the homeland. He made sure to post where he could face the boulevard. Passing cars could see all the shoeboxes full of consignment shoes that he had built like a fortress along the gate railing. He would make eye contact with each driver, his eyes always scanning even if I was out there with him and we was parlaying. If one outta every fifty people who looked his way pulled over and asked about some shoes, it was a good day.

Of course, he was smart enough not to actually sell the shoes right there on the street. That would be solicitation without a license, the kinda shit they be choke-holding brothers to death in broad daylight for. Instead, he got phone numbers of those who showed interest in the display. Later, he would call them up and transact the deal. The display was just for show. If twelve rolled up and questioned him, he was hard enough to keep his composure: *It's just for show,* he would tell them. *Ain't even an advertisement. It's just me flashin' on fools, showin' them what I have.*

Miguel had a quick, daring mind. He had the math on how much a pair of vintage kicks could be sold to a Redwoods resident for and how little a Rockwood tenant would pay for the same joints. It might as well have been the same scale that separated our rent from what the Redwoods was charging on twelve-month leases, numbers that made my little shoe money look like two flat bicycle tires in a city landfill.

Miguel had all type of stuff down to a science. He even knew the new Redwoods po-lice patrol schedules. Knew when they would come by and harass him down to the minute, no different'n if he was waiting for a bus. When a certain officer joker would roll up in a company patrol car and jump on the intercom, Miguel was already way ahead of the warning:

> **Miguel:** Nothin' good goes down after dark, fellas. Move along.
> **Intercom joker:** NOTHING GOOD GOES DOWN AFTER DARK, FELLAS! MOVE ALONG!!
> **Miguel, still side-mouthing to me:** Don't you boys have girlfriends? Time to stop the circle jerk and go the fuck home. Don't you have girlfriends? Stop the gay shit and go home.
> **Intercom joker:** DON'T YOU HAVE GIRLFRIENDS? TIME TO STOP WITH THE ASS GRABBING AND GO HOME.
> **Miguel:** Get ghost, just get ghost.
> **Intercom joker:** GET GHOST, NOW!!

After we would retreat behind the gates, Miguel would shake his head and tell me, "Them dudes is robots, Cope. Punch they code and you can predict how they gon' react."

I wadn't tryna deal with no po-lice codes, no interactions, reactions, or infractions. I sold in safe places, at least places I considered safe:

Pied-montay Ave., the skeleton of the Neiman Marcus store that was being built, the shoe shows. But like the contradiction that I am, I kicked it with Miguel when I would see him in his unsafe spot. When the officer who talked hella shit in his company car came thru in his Oakland PD uniform and Oakland PD Escalade, he just glared at us. Him and his partner. Whether they was suited and booted for the city or the Redwoods, I knew it was some danger there.

But somethin' drew me to that spot. Somethin' drew me to Miguel. Maybe it was the genius of his hustle, maybe it was somethin' deeper. I cain't call it. I would see him standing in the shadow of Rockwood and instantly I vibed with that steadfast swag.

Three-fourths of the Rock was already gone. It was a small four-building rebuild, but it was big to us. It was everything to us. So it was hard to stay safe or to think too much about po-lice who took it too far. It's po-lice lookin' to run you down wherever you go in this world, cain't worry too much about them in your backyard even if your backyard is a boulevard.

So we posted griot-gang against the gates, two sahabs talkin' shit about the stingy niggas who wanted to act like we shoe vendors was working Wall Street and the careless muhfuckas who spent money on Jordans like they was printing it theyselves. When it got late and law enforcement ratcheted up the intensity, Miguel would concede the space. I would help him pack up his shit. We would retreat into Rockwood, where now hella apartments sat empty. Folks was beating the bulldozers by leaving a few months 'fore they had to, and I wondered how long it would be 'fore Momma and the old man decided to do the same.

*

Me and Miguel found us a vacant with the front door ripped off the hinges, just an open doorway. Inside, we sat amongst the shoeboxes and smoked weed. Miguel always had weed on him. My lungs couldn't handle the shit; I knew it was terrible for my running. But I smoked with him anyway cuz smoking with your friend is about the only way two boys will let each other dream.

"I've been visioning this since back when we was in the Youth Control, Cope," he said, speaking on the future. Cuz that's what we did when we got high. "We'll have our own shoe show right here in Rockwood. Bring this shit to the hood. Booths out front on the boulevard, tables and display cases, the whole deal."

"That's what's up."

"And we'll need some music. Real classical Oakland shit: Tony Toni Toné, Too $hort, E-40."

"We gon' have that spot on lock so tight, the po-lice is even gon' pay respect. Shit, they'll set up a perimeter to protect us instead of acting like we're the criminals, chasing us off."

"You know it, blood."

"And what about advertising? We need our shit on 106.1 and all the other hip-hop and R&B stations."

"Rock stations, too. 'Bout to be hella white cats up in the Rock, blood, buying shoes and all kinda half-price new shit. Cope, we're 'bout to be so paid out this bitch, I'ma make it big and retire my ass into management and ownership. Fittin' to manage and own things."

"I feel you on that, bruh, cuz, for real, though, I don't give no fucks 'bout no Jordan shoes. I could be sellin' grits for all I care. It's not about the product, it's about the prosperity."

"Prosperous as shit. Cope, I want enough money to buy me an island like Marc Benioff and just plant weed all over the muhfucka, be smokin' 24/7."

"Weed is the last thing I'd spend my millions on."

"You're smoking now, nigga."

"I'm just keeping you company, lonely nigga."

"Well, fuck weed then. You ever had some good-ass whiskey, Cope?"

"Nah. I never had a glass of whiskey."

"Me neither. But it's the type of thing men of distinction drink, so I'ma buy it and drink it when I'm distinguished."

We laughed our damn asses off, laughed at our dreams and our bullshit and at each other. In the Youth Control, we never could let our guard down, least not till we was in for the night in the dark and everything was invisible. But here we could be ourselves, the closest we ever got to just being kids.

*

My speed was the perfect disguise for all the deeper things I felt and knew. In my prep school life, I became the black star that the city that Oakland surrounded seemed to want. When I ran, people cheered me and colleges recruited me. Meanwhile, the boy that I had discovered inside of me, radiated and medicated and incarcerated, ran with me, but quietly, invisibly. No one who watched me run could see that other me. It wadn't like when I first showed up at the school and messed around and wrote my stories. Then, he had been on Front Street. Everyone could see him in my words. He was not new. He had been with me for years, ever since I stared into that stainless steel mirror and seen a boy lookin' back who was nobody's child.

Quitting the newsletter, I took him from y'all, all y'all. On the track, that deep part of me that I call the boy showed up in a way where nobody but me could hear it, where only I could feel what he meant, where only I knew him. Which was all that I wanted. The tension and anticipation 'fore the race forced me inside myself in deep and beautiful ways. The pain that came after the first few seconds of the race, as my body, at my command, fully committed to the pace of the race and the denial of that po-lice siren that screamed at me to drop to my knees and put my palms to the sky—the pain drove me deeper into that hurting boy inside of me, and I looked that part of me in the face where I was completely afraid and still angry and full of confusion. The island was there and my fear of it, the Youth Control was there and my fear of it, you was there and I knew it was somethin' in me, girl, that when you was here was too afraid of you to know you or to let you know me. I ran into everything that held me prisoner. Below the crowd and the cheering and the nervousness and the arrogance and the peacocking, it was just me, myself, the prison, pure pain, and dark, deep silence. By the backstretch of every race I ran that season, I lost my hearing and my eyes fell closed as boarded windows. My teeth chattered and my whole mouth tasted like burning pennies. The world went dark and the boy screamed inside of me again and again.

And either I would win or I wouldn't, but that wadn't important. After the race, we would stumble off the track and into the infield or under the bleachers and lie down in exhaustion. Our throats stayed raw and tender for hours so it was no point in talkin' even though everything inside of me was screaming and crying. I'd sit there with all the lactic acid in the world burning inside of me. I'd lie down and close my eyes and wait for the boy to go quiet, which took a while, but it always happened. And then there I was at peace. I don't know what that means. I don't know if anything I'm sayin' means anything to anybody, or if it's socially just or politically important or whatever. It had nothin' to do with being black or being a victim or a perpetrator or an athlete or anything you might give a name to and put out on Front Street some type of way. It was just me and everything that hid and showed out inside of me. You cain't put this in a news article, cain't write it and have it mean this or that, but maybe it's what them who read and write the news should know.

*

I ran in the devil heat of Fresno. It was April already. On the backstretch, I looped behind, around, and into the lead, outracing the short Mexican kid who had led from the start. We was fifty meters from the finish line and I had him bodied. The boy screamed inside of me as the wind gusted between our bodies. I took the inside lane, surging ahead. I shut my eyes and tried to tighten and power to the finish line. I heard above the screaming inside of me a huge burst of sound from the people in the stands, like it was a fight up in there or someone had got shot, but as I opened my eyes I realized they was cheering the two of us, but especially the Mexican homie, who had found his own spirit inside of him and had returned from the dead. He surged to my shoulder. He strayed into my lane and we tangled hands and elbows as we ran for the line. He dug an elbow into me and I felt somethin' sharper than bone and hungry as my loneliest night as he pulled past me for the win.

It was a great comeback. I bent at the waist and gasped for air. Staring at the heatwaves that floated over the track, I tried to make sense of what had just happened. I hadn't seen him coming till it was too late. My arms was tying up and my feet was punching holes in the track by then. I had already made my one and only move and couldn't respond to his kick. The boy, not even lookin' winded, loped across the lanes and tapped me on my shoulder. I raised up a little and seen him nod at the bleachers. *This joker,* I thought. I couldn't hardly move and here dude was, clearly not too tired to talk. I wondered what he wanted that required a mission beneath the bleachers, but I was still too winded to ask. I dapped him up and bent back down and undid the laces on my spikes. Even walking off the track felt like a fantasy.

Eventually, I hobbled my ass under the bleachers. My competitor was there, and he wadn't alone. A girl was with him, and the two of them walked into and outta the light and shadow display that the bleacher planks above us created. In the years since I went to the Youth Control, Keisha Manigault, who had been fast since grade school, had taken it to a whole 'nother level, becoming the state's best girl long sprinter. She gave me a hug, flecks of sweat and her long braided extensions flying into my face.

"I be seeing you around, but you hardly even say hi, my nigga." She smiled. Sharing the same building meant that we had seen each other in the wind for years even if we rarely spoke. I had watched her change over the years, her height topping out around six feet, her body filling out from ass to shoulders, her hairstyle flip-changing every few weeks. But that didn't mean we socialized. We weren't in grade school anymore. We weren't even in the same school anymore. But this time under the bleachers, it felt different, like we shared somethin' again. Her face softened into a question. "I heard from Miguel that you had the hookup with the shoes? Brand Jordan and shit?"

"I just hustle a little bit here and there. Nothin' special."

She laughed. "You sound like you're pushin' weight, my nigga. You can chill. Don't nobody care that some broke-ass student-athletes give you they shoes to sell."

"It is against the rules," the Mexican kid pointed out, speaking for the first time.

Keish, not one to be contradicted, cut her eyes at him. "This is Innocente. Y'all raced just—"

"I know, Keish. I have a short-term memory. What's he want? How do y'all even know each other? Ain't you from Fresno?" I asked a flurry of questions of both of them.

"I'm from Visalia, next to Fresno," Innocente answered.

"We know each other from track," Keisha said. "Been watchin' this nigga in the state meet ever since freshman year. We both got the Nike scholarship to go to Oregon University full-ride in the fall."

I dipped my head a little at that. I was late to the scholarship game. All the fast kids had been offered scholarships early in the year. I would need to figure some other way to get into a school with a relevant track program for free. "What y'all want?"

"The shoes, nigga."

I went into my bag for the Brand Jordan track shoes I had brought with me to the meet. I mostly flipped shoes at the little shoe shows in Oakland, but I also took extras when the team left town. They were small, easy to pack away and pull out real quick to flash at potential buyers as I walked around the hotel lobby or strolled thru the stands at the meets. It's not somethin' I wanna speak on more'n I have to cuz I ain't tryna get no one caught up in a rules violation. Plus, like hand-to-hand drug deals, once you know what you're doing selling shoes, it is not exciting. I don't wanna give the people a false impression: I was a part-time merchant, nothin' more. Still, I had been steadily upping my hustling as the school year went on. It had been a long time now that I had been serving as a connect between those who wanted shoes and the broke college athletes who was lookin' to get paid without the risk of a rules violation. I knew I was subject to similar rules and that I should stay careful. Which was why it was kinda sketch to me that these two had just came out the ether already knowing my hustle like a website manual, like someone had clued them in on me.

I knew Keisha wouldn't snitch. She was the homegirl. But I didn't know this incredibly fast, resilient, unwinded nigga Innocente from Adam. I only knew it was no come up in a future Olympian like him going to the authorities about me.

I held the Brand Jordans up by they laces. Inside the dark shadows cast by the bleacher planks, the two shoes looked like South America and Africa fittin' to cross the water and reconnect.

"Aye, I love them," Innocente said. I could tell by the apologizing tone in his voice that he couldn't afford what they cost. He tried changing the subject. "Did you get offered by . . ." He hesitated, wanting to match my time and place to one of the schools that had offered him a scholarship.

Above us, the meet announcer's booming baritone rang out. He was prepping the crowd for the final races, the girls' and boys' mile relays. "I need to go," Keisha said. "I have a race to run. You sellin' them shoes or not, blood?" She gestured at the female version of the same shoe, which had fell out my bag and lay gleaming on the ground.

"Do you have $150 cash on you?" I asked. Cuz by that point, I was Iceberg Slimming them joints. "And $175 for the men's shoes." I nodded at Innocente.

"Oh, it's like that, Cope?" Keisha asked.

I shrugged. "Yeah, girl."

"Cool. I can respect that shit. Who spends that kinda money on spikes?"

"White people."

"I see your hustle, Cope. I respect that, I feel that. Innocente, you tryna get in on this big-money spending?"

"I'll save up," Innocente promised. "I'll see you at the state meet and buy them then—after I beat you."

"I love it!" Keisha said. "A man with a serious-ass plan. I'ma buy mines then, too, after I wax you, Cope." She laughed her way back out from under the bleachers and into the light of the stadium.

Then it was just me and dude standing there with ego and competition and money and poverty running between us. It felt like I was back in the Youth Control. Months later, in the heat of the protest, I seen Innocente take his shirt off and took note of the chest full of tats he sported: Día de los Muertos masks and skulls. The Santa Muerte draped with an ammunition belt. A burning marijuana leaf. The Virgin of Guadalupe weeping blood.

*

I was memorizing lines for my role as Mercutio in our drama class—*A pox on all y'all houses*—deep in Mercutio's characterology. (Here the nigga is, caught between two worlds that only wanna fight each other. Ain't no one even attempting to extend a hand or listen to the other side. Here Mercutio is tryna make some kinda peace, and the audience knows from jump that the peacemaker, the bridge builder, is bound to get got.) Then I seen that New York number in my inbox and a text: "Cope. It's Michael Guzzo."

Why would he wanna contact me without go-betweens? Ever since that first phone call, he had played me distant. Before my thumbs could respond another text came in: "Let me cut to the chase: I have reason to believe that your scholarship may be in jeopardy due to a business issue."

I froze. Mercutio disappeared from my mind after the third text: "Freelancers can make an impact, but they take a risk on behalf of their client. Vendors who work for branded resellers transfer that risk to the business entity—and they can make much more money."

A fourth text gave an address, a day and time, and told me to have myself there.

*

The next day in drama, I played a mean Mercutio: *They done made worms' meat out your boy!!*

I remained everything Pied-montay wanted me to be, for the time being.

*

I discovered that San Francisco's Financial District was freezing now that I had to get out the train and walk the streets to a high-rise, all-glass, see-thru building. Guzzo's office was on the fifteenth floor and had no furniture. The space was just one long hallway with a few posters taped to the clear glass walls: Jimi Hendrix burning his guitar in Monterey. Ice Cube holding up his platinum plaques. The Ramones rocking out. President Obama brushing the haters off his Armani shoulders. The day's light shone in from all angles, and I could look out on the city: the skyscrapers all around me, the blue bay in between and beyond the buildings, and the hills hovering above the fog, piled with homes like hella dominoes fittin' to fall. It's the highest I've ever been. Only less than two years before, I had been locked up, incarcerated for no good reason, and now here I was. I drank in the difference. Lookin' out at the city, I breathed in everything and damn near caught a contact high off Guzzo's cologne.

"I rent this motherfucker by the hour when I need to meet with an employee and speak," he explained. "These are not official company facilities. Figured out during the pandemic that company facilities are totally unnecessary. I like to think of what we do, our business, like a ghost. There's nothing tangible about us except our product, the shoes that we buy and resell. We just fly in and fly out, know what I'm sayin'?"

I nodded. But I felt his heavy movements vibrating the office walls, the opposite of a ghost on the premises. Guzzo was all torso—high, rounded shoulders and barrel chest—a big silverback gorilla of a dude who stalked his Financial District digs slow and dramatic, his head always up, his eyes and face always the black shadow beneath his Yankees hat. He took space, his and yours. I thought of my hustle like the ghost that he spoke of, light and fast, barely there and gone quicker'n a eye blink.

"I like how you move amongst those Pied-monty fucks," Guzzo said, kicking off the meeting. He paced back and forth in a tight line. "This Kennedy character, I guess he's a school principal, the rancid Irish fuck. Apparently, someone dimed you out to him for selling university-provided shoes for college student-athletes and for conspiring with my vendors in the process. The motherfucker's harassing me with phone calls, telling me not to allow you to vend at our pop-up shoe shows, rules violations, yadda-yadda. I told him one, I don't employ you, I just allow you and a dozen other freelance motherfuckers booth space at the shows; I can't control what you and Miguel get up to outside Miguel's work hours. Two, I'm A-rated with the Better Business Bureau. Three, if he doesn't leave me the fuck alone, I'll put enough cash in front of you to make you quit school. Fuck a rules violation. Fuckin' pussy."

Guzzo talked faster'n Innocente ran, and just like with that little dude from nowhere, I couldn't keep up with this man. I had never met anyone like him. "Kennedy's cool with me," I said, almost defensive about it as I remembered the finger food platter he gave Momma on the day of my interview, meanwhile forgetting that he had made her wait in the lobby. It had been almost two years since I entered the prep school. I was used to all its little put-downs and whatnot; it was the price of the ticket. "I think he's just lookin' out for the school's rep," I said.

"Exactly, motherfucker. Exactly. He's looking out for the school, not for you. You need to look out for yourself. You have a gift that has nothing to do with athletics. You might not sell a lot of shoes by my standards, but I've never seen a seller who has the kind of athlete access that you have."

"That's cuz I'm an athlete. I'm not a shoe seller, not really. I sell some shoes here and there."

"Whatever. Let's get philosophical: Is anyone what they do? No, not necessarily. But you claim to be an athlete because it's something that you do. You also would call yourself a student because you do that, too. But you've sold shoes longer than you've run track, and you've made more money vending than you have by going to that stupid prep school. Academics is ninety-five percent bullshit. I say, fuck school. Run your track races for a club team and work for, no, with me. Not only can I pay you a decent wage right now, I have a long-term goal that might interest you."

He whipped out his smartphone and played its keyboard till its screen glittered to life. The image of a beautiful basketball shoe dissolved into gold dust, and the gold dust remixed into an island that looked hella like Treasure Island. "That's Treasure fucking Island," Guzzo said. Pixeled properties sprang up on the island, and I noticed that they massed in areas I knew to be off-limits due to the pollution. This was not what I expected at all.

"The shoe game's been good to me, but it's time for me to diversify and make some real money. That means real estate. With the Bay Area housing crunch, local government has lowered regulations," Guzzo explained. "Certain shit is being back-burnered, OK. The island should be open for development within the year." The words RENT CONTROL rose up in puffs of white lettering like skywriting by an airplane, hovering above the golden apartments. "Do you know how much the government will pay you to provide rent-subsidized housing? It's bananas. I plan to get some of that development money. To do that, I need to build my brand. I propose that you, with your unique access, serve as a community ambassador for me: you bring me the best amateur athletes the Bay Area has to offer, perhaps help me organize and promote a series of outreach events, basketball tournaments and the like, on the island."

The mere mention of that place triggered me. I flinched.

Guzzo arched an eyebrow. "This gentrification thing is a mother-fucker. I'm not insensitive to your situation."

"How do you know about my situation?"

"You think pretty boy Miguel got anything less than a homicide-investigation-level interrogation from me when he recommended you? I didn't pass the bar to play patty-cake with motherfuckers. I know that you, your family, and everybody else in your building will be evicted within the year. I can, you know, hook your family up with affordable housing options on the island. That way you get to stay in the Bay, I grow my business, and ultimately, once we've worked together and these plans have come to fruition, we're able to rehouse your whole community in a location that boasts the best vistas in the Bay Area. You win, the gentrifiers get fucked, relatively and figuratively speaking. That's what back home we call a 'virtuous cycle.'"

He stopped pacing and tipped his cap up so that I could see his eyes. I seen my image twice over, treacherous as the third rail, black as midnight. Then he laughed in the same megaphone tone that was his voice.

"I'm bullshitting. No one in Bensonhurst, Brooklyn, has ever used the phrase 'virtuous cycle.' Fuck outta here with that Bay Area hoodoo voodoo. Yes or no?"

He waited.

"I sense your hesitation," he said after a second. "Look, I'll admit, the nuclear waste thing is rather problematic. It's a bad look. But the way I see it, there's no perfect solution. Either people of color will keep getting displaced by gentrification, or these wine-and-cheese San Francisco fags will cry about the nuclear waste this, the soil contamination that—clutch those fucking pearls, Becky. You should see the pigsty I came from: pollution for breakfast, larceny for lunch, and corruption for dinner. But look at me now." He flexed and his mountain range of a biceps rose up. "Who knows, maybe there are physical benefits to environmental degradation that haven't been researched yet."

He stopped flexing and produced from his track bag two of the smallest drinking glasses I'd ever seen along with a very big bottle of liquor. I read the label, ISLAND RUM, and below those words a sketch of palm trees overlooking a sunlit beach, a few stark-neked slaves serving Deadrich's great-great-great-grandaddy.

"You drink liquor, kid?"

"Nah."

"Not even jailhouse hooch? Well, goddamn it, I guess Hollywood's been lying to me about prison life. Imagine that. Fuck it, there's a first time for everything. You're about to *take a shot for me!*"

He poured the rum into the two small-ass glasses and handed me one. I took it and watched him watching me. I did what I had seen men in movies do and tilted my head back and lobbed the rum down my throat. It burned instantly. My throat and then my stomach and then my en-tire body lit up like Christmas lights downtown.

Guzzo took his shot and muttered, "Jesus Jordan."

"Jeez—"

"Jesus. Jordan. Consider my offer, please."

"But I hate Treasure Island."

"I think you're overthinking this shit. Remember that the auspices of my business provide a protection that you'll otherwise be without."

"But you yourself said Kennedy is threatening you about employing me?"

"Yes, he is. But the dumb fuck doesn't have a legal leg to stand on. Only one of us is a lawyer and it isn't him and it isn't you. The Constitution is crystal clear on this, despite whatever these scholastic athletic organizations that restrain the income-earning ability of student-athletes will have you believe: restraint of trade laws protect all adult-aged citizens."

"But I'm not—"

"A citizen? Where'd you immigrate from? Detroit?"

"—eighteen."

*

On the BART train back to East Oakland, the liquor closed my eyes, somethin' I advise you never to let happen on public transit, don't matter where you're at, but especially not if you happen to be riding round the hood. Still, when I woke, I looked at the other riders and not a one of them looked like DeMichael or Vista or Guzzo. One upside of gentrification: no one on the train that night had the balls to rob me. I looked out the window at dead old East Oakland. The town would be hella safer and untroublesome once all the DeMichaels and Vistas and Guzzos and Copeland Canes was gone. But what would become of us? What would become of me and mines? Clearly, I couldn't just run across town and be at home there. Someone at Pied-montay wanted me gone and outed my hustle to Kennedy for that purpose. It hurt to realize that my dream city might just be another nightmare. I felt flung open inside myself, exposed the way a flu rattles inside your chest.

The only question was who at the school had snitched on me. The handful of kids and even fewer grown folks I had sold shoes to, any of them could be the culprit. Or was it someone from the outside? Innocente? Keisha? Anyone and everyone else who knew anything about me? I couldn't call it. I would probably never know. But I realized my hustle had an expiration date on it. The cold reality of it was that it didn't matter who the snitch was. The truth was Mrs. Greenberg had warned me about the predators at Pied-montay. I was fool enough to ignore her. I was fool enough not to watch my back with them folks and for it I was caught slippin'—a mistake I never woulda made on the Rock, which might make me a racist on top of being stupid. What else but race would allow me to lower my guard around these white cats, yet watch my back, front, and both sides with black folks?

I deserved to get caught just for that.

Or maybe not. The rules I broke by selling shoes is only there to keep me and my people broke and begging. The rules themselves is the real problem and everybody knows it. That's why I violated them without apologies. That's why I ain't really try and cover my tracks: because I knew what I was doin' wadn't wrong.

I had to keep thinkin', had to keep pushin', I told myself. I couldn't give up and just wait to get expelled or evicted or both. The problem was every opportunity canceled another one out: I wadn't tryna earn my diploma and find myself homeless for it. If I went with Guzzo, I would have to give up on Pied-montay, which was maybe OK if I got paid out the deal, but what about that island now? I couldn't see myself shaking the memory and the fear of its earth opening wide and eating me alive, pulling me into its pollution. Wadn't nothin' changed about that place, meanwhile everyone who spent a season on it went thru hella changes. I couldn't handle no more change, no more upheaval in my life. My only options was no options at all.

*

I got home, opened the janky door, and walked in, and there was Daddy posted up at the kitchen table. He held a letter in his hands. "I been waiting up for you, Cope."

I didn't wanna lie to him. He knew I flipped shoes; wadn't like I was slingin' coke. "I had to go talk to this shoe supplier person."

"Out late only for that?"

"That's all," I said, hoping he couldn't smell the alcohol on my breath, hoping he would just leave me alone.

"You be careful in these streets, Cope. Oakland ain't nice. I don't wanna lose you, boy. You gotta understand, I failed as a father by not keepin' my son close enough to me. Given a second chance, maybe I've failed oppositely with you, done held you too close and now you rebelling, don't wanna listen to me for nothin'. That's probably my fault. I'll wear that. But be careful. Will you promise me that?"

"I promise," I said cuz I didn't want the old man worrying about me. The rent was enough to worry about without me.

He nodded and almost smiled. "I trust you, Cope. You know, I heard you just the other day practicing them lines—hella clean. Was that *Romeo and Juliet*?"

"We finished *Romeo and Juliet*. We're doing a new play now."

"Did they have you be Romeo?"

"Mercutio."

"Who that?"

A text message pulled me away from any explanation I could give him. "It don't matter," I said. "You don't care about no Shakespeare no kinda way."

He didn't say nothin' to that and my words hung there between us heavy and mean. He laid the letter on the table edge nearest me where I could see its Pied-montay logo and the school colors. It balanced just barely, momentarily, before falling on the kitchen floor as quiet as a breath. He bent over to pick it up, sinking outta sight. I knew what I said was wrong, but somethin' small and spiteful in me wouldn't let me turn back. I looked at my phone instead as I walked past the old man. It was Guzzo texting me, drawing my attention away: "You're a genius, kid," the message read. "Keep hustling. But exercise caution. Destroy this cell phone and buy a new one. Don't get caught up. The law does not protect you."

Daddy's words about whatever it was he had just said fled from memory as I took that legal opinion under advisement.

*

The first chance I got the next morning, I snuck off to the ghetto marina, which is down Sixty-Fifth, just a few minutes from the Rock. It's not a real marina with miles and miles of coastline like the Berkeley Marina. What we got is a small strip of land in between warehouses. But I believe the water runs out to the bay. I bet you can find apartments downtown that are bigger than Oakland's little marina. But whatever, I'm not tryna make a point, that's just where my phone went, drowning in the water as the sun rose above the city.

The old men who had parked they cars in the little parking lot that surrounds the mini marina watched me while they smoked. I could tell they wouldn't care if I dropped a body in that bitch, let alone a little phone. Probably it's a million phones and other things floating there, people like me treating it like just another landfill.

*

Piedmontagne High Times-Picayune
STUDENT-ATHLETE SCANDAL
When You Know You Done Fucked Up

Imagine that meme. But even though that headline only existed in my nightmares, the truth was I was not safe. An actual attorney had told me that the law as it's written would not protect me. I feared everything from expulsion to reincarceration. Selling shoes wadn't illegal, I knew that for a fact, or how else could a nigga like Guzzo run his shoe business out in the open, holding trade shows in Berkeley and Oakland and downtown San Francisco? From what I could tell, it was a business that was legal for everybody but me and my fellow student-athletes.

If you commit a crime, or whatever you'd call what I was perpetrating, it's best to do it by yourself and to get ghost as soon as it's done. But I couldn't sell them shoes to myself. I couldn't act alone, and Lord knows I couldn't lay low as a high-caliber athlete. It was really no way out for me but to hope the world just spun in my favor.

I was finishing out my classes, working toward my diploma, meanwhile wondering if each day would be the day that I got caught out, called in, and expelled. I had that rabbit-eared anticipation, no different'n when I was in the Youth Control. I won't front: I had GED daydreams, Jacq, like I was only one step away from losing aye'thing.

Good Enough Degree or prep school paperwork, I would need a college scholarship, and I knew the best way to get one in the twenty-fourth hour of college admissions was to win state in the 400 or 800. It might also be the only way not to get expelled: make them realize it was better to keep me than to kick me to the curb.

But winning state wouldn't be easy. Innocente had took my heart and outdid me, outdid me in the 800. No one who had seen him let me take the lead only to rip it back from me in a matter of moments would give me a chance against him. I didn't even give me much of a chance against him. Whatever he had in him was easily the equal, plus some, of my haunted self.

My best bet was to stay away from him. He didn't run the 400. I did. I had run fast at the Mt. SAC and Stanford relays. Then at a dual meet on our home turf, I slid thru in 46.6 seconds, which placed me third in the state. I was a legit contender, even if the two boys with times better'n mines looked like they was on Guzzo's workout plan, like they had swallowed all the radiation and flu in California and had only grown stronger from it.

I turnt my attention to speed and power as I trained and counted down the days to the state meet. But before I got there, an email from the principal hisself finally summoned me to a meeting.

"So what is it, Cope?" The old man stopped me in the kitchen that same evening the email came. Momma was there, too.

I felt my heart drop. I could see the tight, drained disappointment in his face. I didn't dare look at Momma. They had to have received the same summoning email since I was a minor, still just a student. When I started to speak, it was stammers coming out.

Daddy caught me off. "I know it's hard, leaving Oakland. Me and yo' momma, we're ready to go. We got a good nice place out in Antioch we can rent. Makes this little apartment look like a tent underneath the freeway."

I slowed down my breathing and looked from the old man to Momma and back from Momma to the old man. Her face was shiny with sweat and enthusiasm. I studied the old man's face and wadn't nothin' there waiting to take me to task. He appeared not to know a single detail about my issues at school, which I could only figure musta got lost in the sauce, what with them having to pack and move and not keep me informed about it, just like I had got lost in that same sauce spending all my time training for the state meet and selling shoes and smoking weed with Miguel and trying to keep from being expelled. Our minds occupied two completely different places, two different worlds, and it wadn't anger I felt, or anything else really, but just empty. I was vacated, like the last apartment in Rockwood when everybody was moved out and the wrecking balls and dynamite was set to do they thing.

"I know y'all been at this for a while and Momma been wanting to move to the Ock—"

"For years." The old man finished my sentence for me. "She was the one went and got the deal done out there."

"But I want to finish out the year at prep school," I insisted. "I want to graduate from a good school, not some wack old Antioch school. What schools is even out there? Have y'all looked into that? What does y'all moving now even gotta do with me?"

"It's gotta do with you livin' under our roof and this place finna be leveled and it's a deal on the table right now out there," Momma jumped in. I might could sway Daddy on the matter, but wadn't no swayin' her, and her sway was what was leading this decision.

"You can get that diploma piece of paper anywhere, Cope," the old man said. "It don't matter the name of the place. I know you're in a little trouble at that school. What they call trouble, at least. Don't trip, Cope. I ain't mad—but you could finish out school elsewhere and not have to deal with none of that mess."

Here I was worried about gettin' expelled for violating a rule that wadn't even a law when right in front of me, in plain sight, my family was planning to move for financial reasons (the very reason I was sellin' shoes to begin with). They wadn't even slightly tripping about the trouble I was in. They wanted me to move to Antioch, which would mean I would have to finish school online on a home computer Daddy had saved in the 1989 earthquake or some shit.

"I'm just tryna bank some money," I tried to explain, but he cut me off.

"That ain't my concern, Cope. I'm just sayin', it might be easier somewhere where they ain't watchin' you like some damn hawks. Look, I know Antioch ain't your dream city. You ever known anyone to say, 'Hey, let's take a vacation to the Ock? I wonder what the hell is poppin' out there in Antioch. I caught myself daydreamin' about the Ock.' Nah, you haven't and it's a reason for that."

"Oh, now you got jokes, old man," Momma said over her shoulder.

"At least I tried to make somethin' of myself—more than you did," I said, and I know it came out cold, colder'n I wanted it to come out, like I couldn't care less even though it's the only thing in the world I cared about.

Those words shivered the space between us, reached out and froze us both.

"I still have ideas," he said. "And whatnot. But if that's how you feel, Cope, the less said, the better. I'm not lookin' to argue with my son. It's your world, boy. You can come with us and do like I said, or if you can find one of your friends whose momma will let you sleep on they couch, then you can go and do that, try and see if they'a come up off they little rule book long enough to let you graduate." And he said other things, and so did I, and none of it was even memorable, no curse words or insults. But it was mean, the things I said to him, and frustrated, the things he said to me. Mean and frustrated in the ways that two sensitive people can be toward each other when they nerves is shot and they feel empty and nothin's what it should be.

*

After classes, I took the walk that I'd been dreading like a mug: the path that led past the birds-of-paradise and the fancy pillars and all the other things that first welcomed me to the prep school, all the things that it felt like might get snatched back now. All my trying was turning against me. I walked into Principal Kennedy's office, a place which was hella intimidating now that I was inside of it in some trouble instead of in his good graces.

He didn't waste no time gettin' to the point: "You could potentially find yourself in a great deal of trouble, Copeland. You do know that, I hope."

Don't admit to shit, I thought. *Don't say shit.* I looked at the table between us and kept my quiet. The green light of Kennedy's custom-made desk lamp pooled out like weird waves of water across the carpet, and I remembered physically, in my muscles and bones, the courtyard and the cops and the Youth Control and the cops. Principal Kennedy was just another officer of the law.

"When we granted you your scholarship nearly two years ago, we might not have done our due diligence. Douglas was so hot to trot that we more or less took you on as a fully known, fully vetted individual, even though what we knew about you was based on your description of your past. Of course, I did some background checking. I found that the facts of your past as you presented them were true and that your dynamic risk assessment and parole mentor evaluation scored you in the lowest risk category, all of which suggested to me a basic solidity of character, which was what I felt was necessary to know to make the decision to enroll you at that time. Obviously, I was in error. Since then, we have been notified that those evaluative algorithms are being reevaluated. My concern is that you may have missed out on this critical bridge in your rehabilitation."

I kept keeping my quiet.

"Do you feel that you are fully rehabilitated, Cope?"

That question put me in a corner where I had to respond. I nodded.

"Are you experiencing stressors at home or in your community that might have caused you to fall back on some of your negative modes of behavior?"

I shook my head. If I was stressed out, so was the whole community. Rockwood was being re-placed around everyone, rents was rising everywhere, hustlers and homeless was everywhere.

"All right then, Cope. You don't have to respond, though you can if you wish without repercussion. There's no need to treat this as an arrest. You also don't have to worry about what you say being used against you at a later date. Nothing here is being recorded, nor will I make a record of it after you leave. You have my word and state law on that. (In case you didn't know, it is against state law to record anybody without their permission, and I'm doubtful you'd permit me to record this—you seem quite cagey.) In light of how street smart you evidently are, I think you and I are both best served to come to an agreement."

Was this a good cop routine? If that was the case, where was his counterpart, the dirty, crooked-ass cop? Or could both roles be played by the same person in the same confrontation at the same moment in time?

I could only figure that the man meant exactly what he said: he was speaking the truth, he had no intention of treating our meeting as an arrest or a trial. He was no Judge Khan fittin' to throw the book at me. Principal Anthony Kennedy was a different authority figure completely, smarter'n Khan and, to use his word, quite cagey, cagey like a muthufucka, too cagey for me to out-clever.

"Name a college. Name a university," he said, in the same way most dudes talk about which rims to put on they car. "Name one that you would realistically seek to attend given your total profile—grade point average, athletic and other extracurricular accolades, personal narrative, ethnic background."

I stayed silent. That lamplight was starting to look downright radioactive. I looked at the degree plaques on Principal Anthony Kennedy's wall. He'd graduated from the elite of the elite universities. So had his children. They family graduation pictures displayed them in Ivy League regalia. Kids at Pied-montay talked exclusively about Ivy League schools and Stanford, with Williams and Amherst and Emory thrown in for diversity's sake. I knew that the elite schools was altogether out of the question for me. My GPA was still recovering from Rockwood. With all the schools that my rehabilitating grades excluded, no one at the private school had ever told me where I might be *included*.

Principal Kennedy stared square at me. I noticed how easy he filled his suit and how easy his hubcap shoulders and hubcap head filled the ergonomic leather chair where he sat. He had paperweights on his desk. Each paperweight featured the mascot of a different college floating inside its clear glass shell: a roaring bear, a beaver dressed in orange and black, some kinda big cat, too small to be a lion, too white to be a panther, and a Roman soldier, and a red bird, and a duck standing upright wearing a green-and-yellow hat. I felt suspended like I was the mascot suspended inside the glass shell of Pied-montay Prep. People with nothin' better to do was eyeing me in my enclosure, examining me, admiring me, and there I was, prized, sought after, but suspended, caught in mid-float, unable to move. The green lamplight shone over the paperweights, bathing them in its color.

"Perhaps the conversations around campus and in your counseling meetings are a bit skewed," he went on. "There are four-year institutions beyond the Ivies, beyond Stanford. I have a niece who is at Amherst. We're proud of her nonetheless."

"All right," I allowed. Speaking, I found, made me feel no less floaty. I wondered about the logos, if each animal was in eternal limbo when they wadn't parading around at homecoming celebrations and football games. Were they as trapped as they seemed to be?

"Think about schools on the West Coast with strong athletics programs and good academics: San Diego State, Long Beach, Fresno, the University of Oregon. These are all credible institutions. As an athlete of some note, you will be more prized than most. I can practically write and sign your scholarship myself—not for this year's fall term, those enrollments have already been capped. For the following school year, however, I can place you at the university of your choosing. I've done it for other student-athletes. Our connections here at Piedmontagne run very, very deep. The only problem in your case is that information has come to light which might jeopardize your candidacy. Frankly, I've known ever since Douglas Deadrich told me about how he encountered you on the train that there was the potential for this kind of problem. I braced myself. I planned ahead. I thought about contingencies. That's the essence of being a lead administrator, taking the long view and envisioning multiple options rather than locking oneself into a predetermined path."

He stopped and stared me down. Where was this headed? Kennedy had this all planned out, had had this in his back pocket the whole time, just waiting on me to give him a reason. This was it.

"I'm good at what I do. What I need you to do is to get better at doing what you do. If you want an academic and an athletic future, you will need to forego the California state track and field championship, as this rules violation prohibits you from further competition. The school might incur sanctions if you run; we need you to forego all competitive athletics for the time being. Also, you need to stop selling the shoes and discontinue any future meetings with Michael Guzzo, as well as his associates. Lastly, I ask that you agree to serve in an institutional liaison role. It's not an unusual thing for our graduates of color to engage in. It's good for the high school and it's good for you. Whatever you want will be yours, collegiately speaking."

Jacq, I realized the man wadn't about to expel me. A brother took his first easy breath in I don't know how long. Then I considered his offer just like I considered going with Guzzo. I hated the idea of not running the championship meet. It was my only chance at a full-ride college scholarship, but if Kennedy was telling the truth, then I would only need to wait on my come up for a year and then he would hook it up somethin' lovely. I wouldn't have to worry about expulsion, which would kill any chance at a college scholarship. I could graduate. I could go to college. And all I would need to do was help the school out some. I nodded as much to myself as at him. "All right," I said.

"Good, Cope. Great. Good," he replied quickly. "Piedmontagne is an exceptional institution. Its diploma, its stamp of approval, is unique. Its benefits follow our graduates their entire lives. Which is simply an elaborate way to say that you won't regret your choice. The robotics whiz Sherrod St. James has decided to join us in the fall term. He says your visit had a profound impact on him and he'd like to continue your legacy here."

I remembered my "visit" with young sahab St. James. I remembered Deadrich congratulating me on the article that I wrote, which was about Ravenscourt really, not the boy, and I remembered Deadrich asking about Sherrod and how I took that opportunity to drop the auntie's request on him. Ravenscourt would be razed in a matter of days. Sherrod and them needed the money. That was the story. And, of course, Pied-montay paid up. I would have no such luck. I was damn near graduated. They wouldn't be chippin' me off nada but a promise. But that promise was my best bet.

I shook Principal Kennedy's hand, which he locked on me dead stiff, like when you shake hands with one of them AI robots in a downtown display and you realize being human is hella vulnerable and soft. I felt a whole mess of humanity just under the surface of what me and him was sayin' to each other with our hands clasped, and like usual I didn't know what to do with life when it got complicated, so I slipped out of it, bounced, turned around and left out his office quicker'n a hiccup. I walked over to the bookstore and spent my shoe money on that rose-gold bomber that you used to sport, Jacq. Cut the tags right there in the store: no going back.

*

I bussed and walked home and went and sat up on my dumpsters till the sun started to set in sheets of itself, colors that fell off like melting crayons from yellow and bronze to liquid red. A church choir of clouds rose over top of the color show like transparent foam. If I stood up on my cans, I could see out to the bay. With my en-tire weight pressing on the dumpster lid, I felt it about to give way. There was a gang of shit in my life 'bout to give way, from Rockwood's last building (my building) about to be razed along with Ravenscourt, to Momma and the old man gettin' ghost.

I looked around the Rock and the Redwoods. Across the high gates of the tennis courts and the clear glass siding of the Neiman Marcus, a gang of junky old cars sat jam-packed out front of Rockwood. Hella folk gathered amongst the cars in the shadow of the fancy shit that was off-limits to us. I remember thinkin' that this was the most complected people congregated on the Rock since the rebuild began. If the cops had it in them to harass Miguel for hawkin' shoes, what would they do if someone from the Redwood Homes or Neiman Marcus or the tennis courts called 911 on the whole black population of Oakland, which was now crowding around Rockwood? It wadn't actually a whole city full of folks there, but based on my studies of Staying Outta Trouble When All It Takes Is One Wild Muhfucka, it was enough for it to become a problem.

"Aiiiyo, Cope!" Keisha called from the crowd. I couldn't see her in the swamp of cars and people, but I recognized her voice, big as East Oakland. "Come over," she shouted.

I leapt down from the dumpsters and made my way over. "What's there to celebrate?" I asked as I waded thru weed smoke and the cars stacked like rusted old dominoes.

Keisha leaned against a bucket-lookin' Datsun. She didn't even pretend to answer my question. "You know I love you, Cope," she said. "So, since I love you, bring your ass in here and eat and drink and enjoy your damn self."

Being as strong as most teenage boys, Keish took me by the hand, almost tore my arm out the socket, and hauled me behind her into an apartment that was so thick with people, we had to do the robot just to get past the front door.

To Pimp a Butterfly pumped from behind a wall of bodies and a veil of weed smoke. *King Kunta / Black man, taking no losses.* A raft of balloons floated across the ceiling—someone had shaped them into the words ROCKWOOD GRADUATION.

"It's a graduation party," Keisha yelled back over her shoulder at me. "We walk in a week."

"How come y'all's school year is so short?"

She raised her hands palms up and shrugged her shoulders like that old "who knows?" iPhone emoji. "Rockwood does its own thing," she called back. "A diploma's a diploma, right?"

Not really, I wanted to say, *it's a reason Rockwood gets out so soon and matriculates its graduates to McDonald's.* But until I see another group of people celebrate a demolition and a graduation at the same time, you won't catch me badmouthing anything outta Rockwood. Those was, is, and always will be my peoples.

We slid deeper into the party, where it was finally some space to breathe and talk like normal. A banner that read CONFERENCE CHAMPIONS! fell from the ceiling, or somewhere, and landed across my face.

"Slash a celebration of our team's conference championship in track," Keisha added. "I was the only girl on our team to qualify for state, but our team still did good. I'm proud of my girls." Keish pointed me toward a table full of fried chicken, potato salad, mac and cheese, and several sweet potato pies.

*

I told jokes I cain't remember and made people laugh whose names I cain't recall. I found myself wondering if I'd made a mistake in going to Pied-montay Prep when I coulda stayed my ass right on the Rock with my people. After all, I was now a bona fide prep school problem child, barely allowed to graduate with my class, replaced before my departure by a better black kid, while Keisha was a public school star, a bright shining black girl, somethin' I would never be. Come fall term, she would be on scholarship at a university, somethin' else I wouldn't be. "I'ma major in religious studies," she confided. "My family thinks that that means I'ma learn the Bible backward and forward and come back to Oakland to run a church or some shit like that, but what it really means is I get to study the way people all around the world see God."

Free would be there, too, just on academic instead of athletic scholarship.

"It's ironic: you got the high school scholarship while we was going to school in the ghetto, but now the tables done flipped and it's me and my bitch who get the free money. It's funny. You should come with us, Cope. I don't want you scrimpin' and scrappin' out here."

"The fam's movin' to Antioch."

"The Ock?" Free questioned. "Say less."

A big dude with a lilting accent off some island walked between us. "Sistren, bredren, if you need to speak and you're far away, then you need a cell phone."

"Hella presumptuous with your bad self," Keish cautioned him.

"Maybe so, maybe so, sistren. But lemme show you something, nah?"

"Only if you promise to be nice about it."

He smiled at her and produced a shoebox full of cell phones. I had to respect the hustle.

"Hold up," Keisha cried. "Is that a prepaid flip phone? Is you runnin' hoes in the nineties, bruh? You cain't get these joints nowhere."

"Not in America," the man informed. "It's the cell phone of the Caribbean."

"OK, Trinidad James," Keisha said. And if you were to see this hella random brother and then google an image of Trinidad James from back in the day when we was knee-high to a Nike shoe, then you would know how funny what Keisha said was.

I started laughing.

Dude snapped back like a skull cap, somethin' about a well-seasoned jerk chicken sandwich any day over the unhealthy shyte we eat in Black America, which I have to admit is true. Not that I know much about jerk chicken, but I'm guessing anything's healthier'n the straight-up radiation we eat in America.

A little crowd formed around us, which reminded me of the swap meets I used to visit with Momma back when we was a family, back when we loved and trusted each other.

Trinidad flipped open one of his old phones, which, I realized, was actually new, just vintage. He showed off its beautiful basicness for all to see. "The jerk chicken of cell phones, don'tcha know," he boasted. "Twenty dollars."

Vintage prices, too, I thought. And you might think that that price is indicative of its quality, and you might be right, Jacq, cuz this mug is the Bermuda Triangle of phones when it comes to losing numbers off your SIM card and dropping outta service whenever it feels like it, with no rhyme or reason whatsoever.

Still and all, a gang of folks, Copeland included, bought phones off of our visitor. Seeing how quick the crowd cleaned him out, throwing Jacksons at him like we wadn't about to be evicted due to insufficient funds, I started to understand why people had bought them old Jordan shoes off of me. Wadn't shit to do with my salesmanship. It was the past that they wanted. You don't love what you have till you lose it, and then you look back at what's lost and what's left of what's lost and it stirs somethin' deep inside you. You might spend the rest of your life lookin' in nooks and crannies for any remnant reminder of your past.

"I can put some of our best Caribbean apps on here," Trinidad offered.

"Nah, it's all good," Free said, looking closely at her purchase. "I'm not trying to pay your cousin $9.99 a month for his personal reggae channel. Pass."

"That's hella prejudiced," Keisha said, "but I'm with you, bitch. Pass."

But unlike the rest of them jokers wasting they money on a vintage phone they would never actually use, my phone was swimming with the rest of the radiation in the bay so I actually needed that thing, apps and all. And so it came to pass that your boy was the only one in the party who didn't pass on the Cayman Islands of applications, this untrackable, prehistoric Pre-sage shit, which is why I'm freely contacting you while the rest of them fools got tracked by the new technology (the up-to-date phones they already owned) and is in custody now. Funny how things work, or don't work, or whatever.

*

Motown mixed with Sugar Hill disco and hyphee tracks took us back in time, and trap music that swerved sideways into some next shit vibrated our souls even though none of us had a name for it. I felt Colored People Time revisiting me, sitting down in my soul. If you can talk, you can sing. If you can walk, you can dance.

The hustlers from off the corner, Miguel and DeMichael, came thru, partook of the liquor, danced and dozened and mourned the last days of the Rock. The party pushed into eternity. Darkness descended over the skyline and over our emotions.

One of Keisha's momma's people got too drunk and hella disorderly. The O.G. just up and started yellin', "COLONIZER! COLONIZER!" Then he walked over to Miguel and waved both his hands in his face. He got right up in my man's grille and hollered, "COLONIZER." Then he grabbed Miguel by his ponytail braids. "COLONIZER." Ain't every day you see someone, let alone your close fam, get yanked by his ponytails. I was about to jump in and fight dude, but then Miguel put his hands up the way the cops tell you to do, palms out, level with his head. He kept his quiet at first, then he said, "I'm respectin' homegirl's apartment. You need to pump them breaks, unc."

"*COLONIZER. COLONIZER. COLONIZER.*"

That was all the time it took for DeMichael to get behind the old man and put him in one of them jiujitsu-type choke holds that po-lice use. Old dude gasped for air and let go of Miguel's braids. DeMichael let his neck go and controlled his arms. He walked the old man outside into the shadow of the Neiman Marcus. Standing there on the strip of green space that held the new construction separate from Rockwood, the two of them looked like lovers talkin' out an issue after a real bad argument.

The party fell away, and me and Keish and Free and Miguel took the last six-pack of beer up to the rooftop.

We drank and laid down and looked up at the stars, our heads the four corners of the box that we was all stuck inside, our little universe. A cherry bomb rolled the earth beneath our building and we shook along with it.

"Y'all Negroes fittin' to say somethin', or are we just gonna sit up here pretending to be shy and shit?" Keisha called on us.

"When did I become a Negro?" Miguel asked.

"When the cops started hatin' your ass," Free said.

"For real, my nigga." Keish laughed.

"I cain't believe y'all ain't bring no smoke," Miguel said. "Why do people even like beer?"

"Why do you like marijuana?" Free rejoindered. "Maybe if you're trying to fall asleep, OK, but not if you want to dream."

"Or see God," Keisha added.

I imagined one last firework blast which would finally, after all these years, bring down the building, taking us all to God. I wouldn't be against it.

"Public service announcement for that ass," Free announced. "Don't do drugs, pretty boy."

"Teetotalin'-ass females," Miguel roasted back, which idn't the kinda thing I'd expect him to say, since he hadn't been in school in who knows how long, but people will surprise you if you let yourself care about them.

I watched as he leaned back and tossed his empty beer can with a flick of his wrist. I got up and walked to the rooftop's edge just as the can slid off the side. It fell into the emptiness below. I heard it go *clang* against somethin' that wadn't empty, and I listened to the echo of it vibrate from our building, past the tennis courts and the Neiman Marcus, to the luxury lofts that surrounded us, towering over us on three sides: the Redwoods. We were history, the kind that's never recorded. That reality sat down in our circle and spoke to us in the silences between what we was sayin': the Rock was all but broken apart beneath us.

*

I moved to the Ock, which was dusty like a brother who's still rockin' his FUBU fitted from the twentieth century. Dusty like a wardrobe full of clothes two sizes too small. Dusty like the dust that gathers as sure as mold in a rainy, wet place if you don't keep everything clean and dry.

The Ock ain't rainy and it ain't wet. It's located inland somewhere, which means it's hot as your attic in summer and dry as our shoreline in drought. It's also ghetto as hell. I'd bet all of Ravenscourt and the Rock and North Richmond done moved there. The home Momma and Daddy decided to move to was way bigger than our little apartment back in Rockwood, which was definitely a good thing, but I was gettin' all the familiar ghetto vibes every time I walked outside and peeped the abandoned warehouse just up the way, not to mention the two, three, four liquor stores hemming us in north, south, east, and west, not to mention the homeless encampment only one block over. Then there was the issue of how stripped out our own home happened to be—I'm talkin' no blinds, no running water, no heating, no air-conditioning. Them jokers straight-up sold us (check that: rented us) a skeleton!

By the time we had rattled our cage enough for the landlord to unstrip the place and put all that shit back where it needed to be, a week had passed and I had had time to see that our new neighborhood was crammed full of these skeleton houses. Apparently, trifling landlords exist everywhere, not just in Oakland. Squatters had set up in some of the stripped-out homes. In others, families would move in one day and then jump out the next as soon as they realized they had rented only the outline of a house. Only those who couldn't afford nothin' better accepted the situation and lived where we lived.

We wanted a better life, but from what I could see, the Ock was just a way station between where we was from and wherever it was we was meant to be. Back in the day in the Youth Control, if they had told the COs to let half of us walk out into the empty countryside to set up shop solo dolo for ourselves, the society that we woulda built woulda looked a lot like the Ock: free, yessir, but without the basics that makes freedom matter.

*

Meanwhile, I was hardheadedly splitting the difference between finishing things out at Pied-montay and doing Daddy's plan out in Antioch. The prep school had an online virtual campus run via its website. I decided to try and do my schoolwork on my new phone.

It was a prayer that, like the old folks said, ain't get above my head. Half the apps and portals and mandatory interactive elements that made up Pied-montay's virtual education was incompatible with my Caribbean technology. The phone had problems with the Bay Area in general. It and Antioch ain't get along either. The wind was always blowing way too hard out there. It's hot and dry, and not a tree in sight sometimes, depending on what dusty spot you find yourself. Which meant that my phone was always struggling, its connection a constant sometimeyness. I got the feeling that the phone just wadn't meant for America—and that I might flunk out my senior year due to it. I remembered doin' school from home back in the days when the virus shut down the whole state, how the kids who lacked the proper technology or who couldn't stare at a screen all day basically just fell so far behind it was like they missed a whole grade level and never got it back: I was turning into one of those kids. My Hierakonplishments were well in my rearview, almost like some other, smarter kid had Hierakonplished all that.

I called Keisha up 'fore I fell too far behind. I begged her and then I begged her momma to let me stay with them till graduation. Keisha did some convincing and a door opened for my return to Oakland. I told Momma and Daddy the deal, not asking for permission, just puttin' it to them straight up: I was fittin' to flunk if I didn't rehouse where I could attend school in person.

I left Antioch and returned to the Rock. I slept on Keisha's momma's couch some nights, her daughter's bedroom floor others. I remember feeling in the air of the apartment the warm closeness and craziness of community, of all the people who had left and all the people about to get ghost. I remember hearing in the silence at night the sounds of the celebration that took place right there between them quiet walls. I caught the buses across town and ran when I had to and returned to school in physical form. I got back to work in my classes and got to where I would graduate. If you look at my transcripts, you'll see that my grades was on point all the way till the end. My diploma was due me. Just ain't make it to the ceremony.

Meanwhile, my hood matriculated toward destruction. Ravenscourt came down, turning mostly into a memory for those who used to know it and staying a story in the imagination for those who had never trespassed into its reality. Ash and smoke from the demolition hung in the air for days and never really went away. I remember that it held like a veil over us, hiding us away from the rest of Oakland, let alone the city within a city on the other side of town.

*

One Sunday morning I went with Keisha and her momma and them to a religious service in this little falling-down church house the size of two apartments pushed together, where the preacher ranted 'bout Christ on the cross and the blood of the lamb. He ain't read from the Bible not a word, but went in with all haste and fervor about scriptures that don't even exist. The book of the City of Dope Cain't Be Saved by John the Pope. Psalms E-40. Todd Shaw 25 to Life. He held the Good Book in the air and slammed it on the pulpit platform, and danced in a circle in the middle of the stage, and sat on his butt right in front of us and swore he was fittin' to start speakin' in tongues if that was what it would take to bring the Lord into this house this very morning. I looked around the small church, the walls smudged off-white with a million people's paws, the broke ceiling fan rusted black, the thin lines of mold and old earthquakes running the length of the ceiling and the side walls, and I looked at the few parishioners, old ladies mostly, and a few girls like Keish, young and doin' they best, and only but one other boy besides myself. Of all our folks, Jacq, who did I see up in there but old boy DeMichael Bradley, sitting all proper, hands on his lap and shit, next to Granny Bradley. He sported a suit that didn't fit him right. Looked like he might burst out that mug any moment. The old woman wore an ivory-white skirt and blouse and a pink jacket and a flapper hat the same bright pink decorated in roses and daffodils. The two of them sat in real solemnity in the far corner of the little church, fanning theyselves with the pages of they open Bibles, nodding they heads at the strange sermon. After a while, DeMichael looked over at me where I sat next to Keisha and he nodded a welcome.

Because her folks wouldn't cotton to no second scripture, Keisha had to keep her real feelings about the church and the minister to herself while we was worshipping. But after church, she got alone with me and disclosed that she didn't like this latest church home. "Them fools pass the hat every half hour on the hour, singing, *Monay, monay, monay / Monay!* and shit, like they dancing for dollars at the club and shit. Homie with his Holy Roller act been tryin' to holler at me on Instagram ever since I turned seventeen and my ass started to fill out my jeans. Quiet as it's kept, the way he misspells things in his text messages, I suspect he cain't read most of the scripture he be claiming to cite in church."

I remembered how Daddy used to create scripture outta thin air when his customers played him short, the way he would grasp at anything to make a point about other people's profligate ways. Back when he was a wild emergency tucked inside some muscle and bone. But at least the old man wadn't tryna run no church, didn't try and pass hisself off as a man of God.

The two-faced-ness of church don't sit well with me. I prefer the heathens. The next night I showed Keish the vacant where me and Miguel would smoke and bullshit. I smoked and she talked about her future: Oregon, college, religion, track and field. And I listened cuz my future was on hold and outta my control. I wished I had good options like she did, not just the Rock and dusty old Ock.

Even in May, the cold-ass bay wind blew in, skirted underneath closed doors, slipped thru the rooms, and found us where we lay. The wind lay up with us, hugged up on us and chilled us, as it listened to Keisha and talked to me in its quiet way about how things end, how they come to die. The wind felt like the flu, felt like death even in summer. I didn't hold myself against it. I made friends with the wind, welcomed it into me with all its ills. I fell asleep somehow. I remember Keish one minute, then nothin' the next. And then I fell. I'm not talkin' that teenage falling dream we all know so familiar. This was different. Your sahab went suddenly subterranean, sinking thru sludge, thick layers of landfill, black and thick as syrup cut with oil, and then I seen some boosted bicycle locks and chop shop car parts and a rusted wrench and a dumpster's worth of tore up trash bags weighted with mulch and weeds and paper plates and used Magnum condoms and emptied vials and cans of gasoline and antifreeze and soup and sardines and other cheap shit, sewage, one perfectly unused Steph Curry basketball shoe, and baby formula behind bulletproof glass, and an en-tire West Oakland housing project in free fall, and pages from textbooks floating like fall leaves, and sheets and sheets of curled and permed and braided and dyed real Indian hair falling, shell casings and waterlogged guns falling, a green shipping container marked for an American city falling, the Marcus Garvey Building falling, the Java House, the kung fu movie theater, and Oakland's last strip club, and a crack pipe and a heroin spoon, an MC Ant poster, *Life Is . . . Too $hort*, 8-tracks, a box of vinyl records, a pair of bell-bottom pants and one worn-out platform shoe, two hair picks, Huey's spear and wicker chair, the orange fins off some old-ass muscle car, and a newspaper advertisement reading "The Detroit of the West," and the city charter and a single jar of lye and an ad for skin-bleaching ointment and hella newspaper clippings about everything that had ever happened in Oakland and one, two, three, four badly punctured metal drums that leaked highly radioactive nuclear waste, down and down I went till I came to my old man at the bottom of it all and I heard *Love thy father!* and I fell farther below the bottom and I heard *I love you* in the dark. It was just me and Miguel dreaming out loud—

"For real, Cope. Finna rock niggas this summer. Picture this: banners all over the Rock and the Redwoods. Me and you, the headliners. Our display cases is all glass lit gold, and they're like columns, like ancient Roman columns lit by classical Roman candles. Every shoe finna be lit bright as the sun. The best DJs, the best rappers. Aye'body and they momma rockin' and shoppin'. Finna be hella beautiful. I had crazy visions, Cope."

"I think I heard that line in a song."

"Dreams don't got owners, Cope."

"That's kinda deep. I feel you. I love—I got love for you, blood."

"I love you, too, Cope."

*

I woke alone in the vacant and felt my phone rattle against my forehead. I grabbed it and investigated: it was a text from Keisha.

"Don't trip, I had to go home or Mama was gonna kill me. You were too heavy to carry."

"Lol—all good."

"I was thinking about your situation & I have an idea."

"What it is," I wrote back, jamming my suddenly fat fingers into the phone's miniature keypad. I was gettin' used to it, typing as fast as I had on my old phone. I wandered into the Pre-sage app and some of the other curious-ass apps cousin had uploaded for a flat $100 annual fee. To my surprise, they looked kinda cool, like they own little mysteries, not old school or on trend, and definitely not American. I might need to break for Trinidad if everything there was as cheap and as unique as these apps. I played with the apps a little longer 'fore my mind started wandering across the continent and over the ocean. Why was I even living in this extremely expensive city, in this beaucoup expensive state, where the nights was cold and complected people got pushed around like pieces on a puzzle board, when there was other places on the map that was so much friendlier to us? Maybe my goal shouldn't be to stay in Oakland or Antioch or Oregon, but to get out altogether from America.

"Do you know what a rabbit is?"

"Run that back??"

"Do you know what a rabbit is?"

"You want an animal emoji?"

"Stop playing. In track the rabbit is the runner who goes out to the front and sets the pace and then steps off the track."

"That doesnt make sense. You run to win."

"Of course it makes sense. The rabbit can't win. The rabbit is there to push the pace. The rabbit is there to break up the field so that the fastest runners separate from the slower ones. No pack running. The rabbit helps records to be broken. The rabbit helps other runners make qualifying times. The rabbit sacrifices for the field."

"But what does he get out of it?"

"1st of all who said the rabbit is a he? It could be a girl. They had to outlaw men rabbiting for women's races."

"Why?"

"The men pushed the pace so fast that the women kept breaking records—women's records."

"Isnt that a good thing?"

"Idk. Off topic. Real talk I think you would be a good rabbit. It's a college meet the day after the high school state meet. I could get the Oregon coaches to let you pace their 800 runners on the college day. It would be a good way for you to walk on to the team and it would get you on their radar for next year when they make their scholarship offers. You up for that?"

"Its a plan."

"Will you do it?"

"I'm down—but what if the rabbit goes ahead and wins the race?"

"Don't play Cope."

I was so short of sleep it was all I could do to end the text exchange without typing her a text the way people do when they run they whole hand across all the piano keys. I didn't wanna run races where I was not a competitor. That was whack. But it was way less whack'n what I would be doing if I stayed in Oakland in the vacants, barely able to eat and dress decent.

I could almost see myself as U of O's rabbit. Sprint races don't need rabbits. I would need to work the half mile and the mile. Those would be my specialties. I could do the half mile no problem, but I would need to gain more stamina and maybe reduce my muscle mass for the mile. The mile. Four laps around the track. Three laps and some change for the rabbit. As soon as the gun would go off, I would light out like the only smart black dude ever cast in a horror flick. My adrenaline would carry me thru the first lap, a quarter mile of pure painless speed. The chase would be on and poppin' behind me, but I would lead them around with a couple strides' lead over second place, a pace I would pay for sooner'n later. A lesson in fire and brimstone was on its way: the pain would no-knock bust thru my doors like the po-lice. The lactic acid would shoot into me like the fires of hell, the devil in my legs, my chest, my throat. By the third lap, heatwaves would be hovering over the track surface. The pace was set now. Another day, another job well done.

But it would come a time when I wouldn't be satisfied with a job well done. I wouldn't want my rabbit role. I would be way out this rabbit-ass mind of mines and I'd fight back pain and the job description and lean into everything that hurt. The first command would come loud and clear—*Kill the rabbit!*—as I completed the third lap and tore into the turn, leaning and digging the rubber out the track. *Kill the rabbit!* the call would come again. My whole life, I'd been the rabbit, I just didn't know it and didn't know how to play it. I was the rabbit when Vista attacked our teacher and I went running 'fore anyone else to find help. I was the rabbit when I took action to sanitize our apartments. I was the rabbit when I wandered too far on the island. I was the rabbit in the jailhouse library, and I was the rabbit when I left the hood for prep school. *Kill the rabbit!* Pain would pepper my legs like rounds of buckshot burning into my skin. I would be way ahead, not just winning the race but on rabbit record pace, and them jokers in the infield would be having a fit. Just when they was about outta they own minds, about ready to tackle me and make me taste turf, I would do what I now knew how to do from all my rabbit runs: step off the track without breaking the rules, doing the job. It would take a couple seconds, which in a race is forever, 'fore the other runners would pass me. It would still be the race they wanted, with me out the picture just in time. The rabbit cain't win, after all, even when he's supposed to.

*

Run, rabbit, run. I fell asleep and slept easy, Jacq, for the first time in a long time. Just tucked up and dreamt some easy dreams. When I did come to, it was to a screaming phone full of messages.

"Where are you Cope?" Keisha asked.

"Where are you??" her second text read.

"Where are you???"

"Where are you Cope?" a text from Momma questioned.

"Cope???"

I texted the woman who gave birth to me back first, writing the first excuse that came to me: "I'm ok I kicked it w/ Miguel last night."

"What happened?" she wrote back immediately.

"I'm fine. I'm still in the vacant," I wrote to Keisha.

"Nothing happened," I wrote to Momma.

"What happened to Miguel?" she wrote back.

Keisha ain't write back.

I began to notice noise filtering in from outside. A low rumble. I went to a window and looked out. The Neiman Marcus threw the green space and everything else beneath it into deep shadow, but the rumble of talk or music or whatever it was still sounded, source unknown, too loud to ignore.

"What happened to Miguel?" I wrote, meaning to send my text to Keisha but sending it to Momma instead.

There was no response.

I hurried outside and realized that the noise came not from inside the complex but from the street outside the gates. I only had to run a few steps toward the sounds to see yellow-and-black tape ribboning a crime scene on the street outside. The tape kept a small crowd from coming closer. The ambulance and po-lice car lights discolored the darkness, flashing crisis colors, red, white, and blue.

It was a cold, smoky summer night. I could taste the ash in the air, probably from a far-off fire. The air held still, the smoke sitting there thick enough not just to taste but to see and to touch. You imagine that if someone gets shot, it'll be hella folks crowded around the yellow tape wanting to know what happened. But it was only a couple dozen people barriered off by the yellow tape, if that.

Up in the mix, the noise of the crowd didn't seem loud at all. It was barely enough people to call it a crowd, matter fact. I remembered Keisha's party, how the cars stacked like dominoes and the people crowded in even closer, double sixing every square foot of the Rock.

I could see an ambulance and some cops in the restricted zone. They wandered back and forth, unworried and kinda aimless, just like the people without badges and uniforms on the opposite side of the tape was wandering around and not doing and not saying anything.

I wanted to ear-hustle the facts of the situation, but everybody was whispering to each other or they was on they phones, deep in virtual space. Finally I peeped Free behind a wave of bodies. She was up at the yellow tape, leaning into it like a runner about to win a race. She was so short she was easy to miss, especially as short as it still was. But there she was, leaning over the tape and stretching it to where it might snap, and then slipping under it and walking right up to the scene of the crime. I watched her walk up to the ambulance, which had its back doors open. She was talkin' to someone inside the ambulance. The first thing I thought wadn't who was in the ambulance but how she was able to walk right into the restricted area. Back in the day, police woulda beat her ass, if not killt her, for trespassing like that. They feared us nuff to kill us, which ain't but a box in a paradox, am I right?

I've seen my share of folk die on the Rock. This was different. Free was practically inside the ambulance. Both her hands gripped the retractable metal ramp, not allowing the medics to raise it and run away. She stood there like that talkin' to them for forever, maybe three, four minutes. Maybe whoever was inside the ambulance was already outta danger one way or another, I thought.

Then she let go of the ramp and it raised, and a medic came and shut the doors behind him and the ambulance drove off. Free came back across the crime scene, weaving between wandering officers. She jumped over the tape and ran back toward our building. I had to sprint as fast as I could to catch up to her.

"Free, what's going on?" I called as I came level with her at the entranceway into Rockwood.

She stopped and stared at me, and I knew by the dead wild look in her eyes what she would tell me 'fore she had to say it.

Jacqueline
Cope?

Cope??

Where'd you go? What happened? What happened to Miguel?

Cope

I wanna believe the sidewalk outside our gates was all blinged out and glamoured up that night. That Miguel and them boasted lit-up display cases ten feet high with racks on racks of Jordan shoes and Lamelos and LeBrons and even them Dr. J Reeboks from when my old man was knee-high to his dreams. I like to imagine they had a DJ playin' all the slaps and it was crowds of customers, a huge show with whatever me and him used to dream, and that that was what brought the cops all overaggressive to the scene that night. That they just couldn't stand seeing my dude on flash like that and they just had to take him down a few. But it's not true. It was a quiet night by all accounts. Miguel and DeMichael was posted no different'n most nights. Wadn't no one out there but the two of them and the occasional customer dropping they number in Miguel's hand. Maybe they expected to see me. Maybe if I had came by and we had smoked, or whatever, figured out a di-version, any di-version, we woulda been off the street sooner, 'fore nightfall. Then the po-lice wouldn't be no problem—at least they wouldn't be our problem. But that's not how it went down. The only way to change your history is to lie about it, and it's more lies in the next news bulletin than I've told in all these hours.

What happened to Miguel? Ain't no story to tell 'bout how Miguel got got. It's body cam footage of the altercation that'll tell it for what it is. Footage that the po-lice won't publish if they don't have to. And they don't have to unless arrests is made and charges is filed.

*^{*†}

---

*Code 4-1117: As an extension of the right of law enforcement personnel to turn off their body cameras in situations that present as highly dangerous, law enforcement review boards may also hold sealed the footage of all incidents that bring about citizen complaints. This right does not protect against search warrants for said footage

"What happened to Miguel?" Momma had asked me and I asked it to her right back, cuz that empty circle that our question formed told the en-tire story. Now I wrote her back the only truths I knew besides that emptiness: "Miguel got killed. By police I think. I wasnt there."

We been seen it before, so many times, just wadn't no camera phones for this one. Wadn't no video of Alan Blueford, or Tyisha Miller, or the homeless dude over by the hospital who Free seen get shot dead for resisting arrest when she was five years old, or the boy po-lice shot in the back of the head while he ran past my auntie's house on the same day that Oscar Grant got murdered. Hella people been murdered off camera, don't mean they're any less dead. Ain't no video of Emmett Till gettin' got. If you need to see it happen (I don't), go peep everything that's online going all the way back in time and walk it forward one black body at a time: Philando Castile. Eric Garner. Walter Scott. Laquan McDonald. George Floyd. It's plenty more names I could name—I ain't forgot a single one.

---

in cases where felony charges have been filed against officers or in class action civil suits against police departments and/or their administrators.

[+] *San Francisco Chronicle*: While San Francisco, Berkeley and Oakland Police Department officers are required to wear body cameras throughout their time on duty, private security has no such requirements. Oftentimes, Bay Area police officers work both for the police department and in private security, oftentimes in the same locale, making enforcement of the rules and laws pertaining to their use of body cameras difficult.

[*] Code 4-1117: As an extension of the right of law enforcement personnel to turn off their body cameras in situations that present as highly dangerous, law enforcement review boards may also hold sealed the footage of all incidents that bring about citizen complaints. This right does not protect against search warrants for said footage in cases where felony charges have been filed against officers or in class action civil suits against police departments and/or their administrators.

[+] *San Francisco Chronicle*: While San Francisco, Berkeley and Oakland Police Department officers are required to wear body cameras throughout their time on duty, private security has no such requirements. Oftentimes, Bay Area police officers work both for the police department and in private security, oftentimes in the same locale, making enforcement of the rules and laws pertaining to their use of body cameras difficult.

I woke ahead of daybreak. My body had clammed up cold on the cold floor of Keisha's apartment. I had to shift around this way and that to warm up. I turnt onto my side and looked at the black outline of two bodies, Keisha and Free wrapped around each other like the swirls of an old-school barbershop pole if its colors was midnight black and honey brown. I looked at them for a long time. It's hard for me not to hate my own midnight-black body, let alone love anyone else's. Everything in America teaches you to love what you ain't, Jacq, especially if you're black. But Keisha was as beautiful as anyone on earth that morning.

The *Avatar* blue of first light spread over us, and after a while the girls awoke like one hurting body come alive to its pain. I let them rub the cold out they eyes and get theyselves cognizant 'fore I said what I felt, which was the only reason me and Free had come to Keisha's place to begin with.

"It's a crime," I said. "That cop killed Miguel. That boy was way too smart and calm to fight a fuckin' officer."

"I know," they said on the same beat.

(Jacq, law enforcement can claim that I instigated the protest. I cain't even say they're wrong for that. I spoke the first word and that counts for somethin' in the Bible and in life. Everything came from that beginning, but everything afterward was all of us in movement together.)

Keisha and Free, being girls with a thousand pictures of theyselves and Instagram followers for days, got it poppin' with the social media. Unlike me, they knew how to organize from following behind they older siblings and cousins back in the day when *8:46 was rollin' deep at every protest action. They could bring people together quick as you comb your hair. And 'fore I knew it, 'fore lunch time, matter fact, Miguel's murder became a movement. We had folks not just in Oakland but all around the Bay and beyond, that whole Oakland exodus network of folks, planning to meet that night at the biggest church in deep East Oakland.

*

That night, fireworks sounded out, not like God but like they own little protests, sounds the po-lice cain't stop. The sky was smoky with it.

We tasted it thick in the air and dry and sulfurous on our lips as we hopped the Allen Temple Baptist back fence and followed Keisha thru the church back door. We passed by church dressing rooms, restrooms, and storage closets. I could hear what sounded like the chatter of a thousand people up ahead. The noise grew louder and louder as we dipped thru the rooms. We turnt a corner and came thru some double doors and walked on to a wide, wood-floored room bathed in stage lighting. At the far end of the room was a black curtain.

A tall, broad-shouldered man in a gold-colored suit parted the curtains and we glimpsed beyond it: a pulpit and pews and balconies and folks, folks, folks, folks, folks.

"Pastor Jeremiah!" Keisha called out.

The pastor strode toward us. "Girl, I remember you when you were knee-high to a grasshopper. Look at you now—almost tall as me. I believe you're eighteen now, youngster. Where you and your peoples went to? I don't see hide nor hair of y'all."

"Some went to Antioch, others back to Arkansas. Momma just found her a different church home, though."

"Well, I'll be." The pastor sighed. I could tell he was more moved by the church home changing than the folks having to leave outta Oakland for the four corners of America, but he played it off solid. "It's sad that the young brother's death is what it takes to bring our community together in this House of the Lord, but the Lord works in mysterious ways. That's why when I saw your social media posts, I knew that our church had been called to a great convening."

"Thank you for calling the people, Pastor."

"I was called, Keisha."

He looked back at the curtain as it waved open and closed behind him. I caught glimpses of the crowd: it wadn't one audience sitting in pews politely waiting on us. Everybody was up and moving around. Little cliques had formed. I could tell that this was already way beyond our control.

"But it wasn't the Lord, Keisha. You called me," the pastor said, turning back to us. "You called all this together." He looked from Keish to me and Free. "The community is healing tonight because of you—all three of you."

That was a lot to take in. Part of me was playing the wallpaper, just watching it all happen in front of me, while on the inside the rest of me rattled and shook with thoughts of Miguel. What happened? How did he get shot? What was the particulars? I split in two and admitted the obvious: "We cain't organize all these people, Pastor." He bucked his eyes at me, surprised that I had spoke. "I'm just sayin'," I said.

"But you don't need to," Pastor Jeremiah assured. "There are more experienced organizers here, like myself. I was on the front lines of *8:46 along with my church brethren. You already did your biggest job. What I can do is come out onstage, make an announcement to introduce y'all to the whole church, and then y'all can introduce y'all selves to whomever you'd like to work with. Does that sound like a plan?"

It didn't. But I didn't know no better.

*

There was angry black folks in that church and curious white folks and bottom-line-eyed people of all colors, all of us sharing that same suddenly unspiritual space. My fellow student-athletes was there. There was Trey Marshall. There was the brother who used to be silhouetted on the billboards above Rockwood. There was your Creole father, lookin' more'n a little like everybody on earth. There was DeVonte Baltimore and his crew of dancers from the train, each of them decked in they red, white, and blue. There was Guzzo. There was Deadrich. Principal Morgan and Sherrod St. James. The memories of the virus and the distancing still stuck with me, so to see this group of young and old people, people of different races, riches, and cultures, huddled close up and unafraid of each other was a very strange and beautiful thing. There was the groundskeeper from Treasure Island who saved my life, and Vista, who backhanded me into existence unofficially, and a couple of the brothers whose barbershop burnt to the ground. There was my grade school teacher Ms. MacDonald and my high school teacher Mrs. Greenberg. And there was DeMichael Quantavius Chesnutt Bradley, too, all by hisself, holding up the back wall of the church next to the exit doors. I knew that if anyone had witnessed the killing and could tell me how it had all went down, it would be him.

"DeMichael," I called, and raised up a hand for him to see me, simultaneously dipping and slipping past people till I got to him.

"What you here for, Cope?"

"What do you mean, what am I doing here? Me, Keisha, Free, we started this, blood."

"Really?"

"Nah, Negro, it fell out the dang sky. You ain't seen the social media we put together?"

"Nah. I don't be on none of that shit."

"Don't be cussin' inside the church, blood. How did you know this was happening if you ain't on social media?"

"Blood, aye'body and they momma is in on this."

I looked around the church at all the known and unknown faces, folks from as close as down the street and from well past Pied-montay. It still felt like I was hovering over the whole scene, watching this wild shit happen. I didn't wanna organize none of it or be around for none of this setup. I needed to know what happened to Miguel. I reached past DeMichael and pushed open the door behind him.

"You kickin' me out, family?"

"Not unless I'm kickin' my own self out."

I slipped past him and shouldered thru the swinging exit door. An automated buzzer sounded somewhere over our heads as he followed me out the church. We stood there in the parking lot for a second just lookin' at each other, not ready to speak about anything so sad.

"Can you tell me what happened?" I finally asked.

DeMichael peeled his eyes in all di-rections and kept quiet. The exit door buzzer had already drawn attention to us where we stood. It didn't make sense to play statue on the street side of a thin door and talk to Black Hercules, who had concert speakers for vocal cords. We needed an empty, quiet place.

"Let's keep walkin'," I said. "Did you see what happened to Miguel?" I asked him as we walked.

"Did I?"

"Did you?"

We came to Ravenscourt, its remains. What once was a whole city block of housing was nothin' but stones and ce-ment lying loose on the ground, and screws and shingles and door hinges and the skeletons of showerheads and so much more. It was like if you turnt any house, or all the houses on any street, upside down or inside out and just let all the insides fall where they may and then let the scrappers come thru and snatch the metal outta anything that could be turnt around and resold. There were a few stacks of scrap and rubble that rose as high as we stood and some spaces of wall that wadn't completely brought to the ground. In the dark, I couldn't tell how high them things still rose, but it was clear that the demolition people wadn't done.

"Family." He shook his head.

"What happened, DeMichael?"

"Cope, you ever notice that these fools who shoot at cops never shoot nobody who actually killed someone? My parole mentor was breakin' that shit down to me and it made sense. He said how it's definitely killers on the force and shit, cops that need to get got. But it's never those ones who get shot. It's always some unsuspecting new guy, just got his badge, playin' on his phone and shit—these cowards will blast a cat like that for no reason."

"You ain't lied yet." I looked around the ruins. In the night, the vast space looked like a limitless graveyard, every fallen pillar and piece of rubble a tombstone. Thousands of tombstones. There was enough junk piled in Ravenscourt for a whole landfill, not to mention driven holes every few feet. It wouldn't be hard to stash ten weapons in there. Standing in the ruins, I looked old boy up and down. "DeMichael, what happened to Miguel?"

He looked around like we was being watched. "Li'l bruh." His big voice shrank to a plea. He shook his head again. "Can we keep walkin'?"

We walked across the street to the Rock, what was left of it, our one building and the Bradley apartment within it. DeMichael closed the door behind us. I could hear his granny snoring. DeMichael signaled for me to remain quiet. We slid into the narrow little kitchen and sat down at the table.

"Look, li'l bruh," he whispered, "it was like this: Redwoods security rolled up on me, like usual. Them same two cats that always be out there. They was giving me all kinda static. Miguel started talkin' yang to them, callin' them fools out for not wearin' they masks. He was, like, readin' the city regulations to them off his phone and shit. (Family, I ain't seen not a single officer wear a mask in years, but my dude was on one that night. Wadn't tryna see them fools mess with me.) One of the cops starts jaw jackin' right back at Miguel and totally loses interest in me. He goes and gets in Miguel's face. I remember Miguel turnt off his phone and the street kinda went dark, and that's when the second cop asked him what was that in his hand. He left me where I stood and rushed over and put paws on cousin. He got him on the ground and he's yellin' about 'don't resist arrest' and shit like that while he's got bruh-bruh on his stomach, hands behind his back. He has his knee in Miguel's back and he's steady punching him in the side of his face and shit. It's kinda hard to stay still when someone's got you like that, na'mean? So Miguel's squirming around, tryna cover up and whatever. I thought about jumpin' in, family, I swear I did. I thought about fightin' them fools on the spot. I thought about takin' one of they guns. I took a step toward them where they was squabbin', and the cop who was still standing seen me and turnt on me and yelled, 'Don't move!' I could tell that he wanted to put that tool on me. I wadn't tryna get shot, blood. I wadn't even tryna get arrested. I backed up and that's when the cop on the ground stopped yellin' at Miguel and the shot rang out. Have you ever stood that close to someone when they shoot a gun? When you ain't expecting them to shoot it and then it just goes off? I couldn't hear nothin' and I think I closed my eyes. I remember opening them and seeing again. He shot cousin in the face."

I didn't say anything and silence sat down between us.

"Cope?"

"Yeah?"

"I didn't even see the man reach for that tool. Next thing I know, it's blood everywhere."

The only thing I could think to do was ask about the facts. Everything else was too much, too, too messy, too terrible. "He shot him in the face?"

"That's what I said."

"How do you—"

"Miguel was, like, halfway on his stomach, halfway on his side. The cop had him penned and shot him in the side of his face. Family, I've never seen no shit like that before. The blood. The body. That boy just laid out like that. I looked away real quick."

"Where did you go after that? I came outside after the shooting. Didn't see you."

"I left out quick, blood. Went home. Po-lice wadn't tryna question no witnesses."

"Would you talk to them if they did?"

"I don't even know. I shoulda called my mentor—shit. I was wildin', li'l bruh. It is what it is. Look, if you really 'bout this whole protest march song and dance, that's cool, but it ain't gonna change shit. *8:46 ain't change shit. You gotta be willing to move like the po-lice move, na'mean?" He looked at me in the total dark of the apartment. With his granny still snoring over his words, he whispered to me, "Cope, I came back—last night, after the shooting, while the cops and the ambulance was still there, I came back. You just ain't seen me cuz I went out the back gate and walked the long way around. I had on my winter coat and had my rifle inside it. You remember that rifle, right?" He reached behind him, reached beside the 'frigerator behind him, and tapped the long gun. "It's easier'n you would think to hide this bitch. Last night, while the cops was still out there cleanin' up they mess, I walked right behind them, right over to Ravenscourt, and I posted up right there where it's hella scrap to hide behind. I thought about shootin' right then and there. I was right there, I had a clean shot and aye'thing. I couldn't do that shit, though, not last night. I started lookin' around and I seen that if my big ass could hide like that, I for damn sure could hide a rifle, right? I didn't do that neither, not last night. But I'm still thinkin' about it. Y'all gonna have hella cops out there tomorrow and won't none of them be thinkin' about a ditch on the other side of the street. Know what I mean?"

He picked the rifle up and showed me its empty mouth. He passed it to me and on reflex I reached for it. Then I pulled back.

"It's not loaded. Why you pull away?"

"DeMichael."

"One of us gots to hold it, Cope." He placed the gun carefully on the ground. It sat there like dried shit in the dark.

"We don't need to take it there, bruh-bruh," I said. "I need to get back to the church." I started up from my chair.

"You sure about that, Cope?" he pressed deeper.

I didn't leave. I wadn't about to pick that thing up and go and bury it like a dead body in the Ravenscourt ruins, but I understood that one of us was gonna have to hold that part of our pain, the deep, real part of it that don't wanna pray or love or do nothin' but what's been done to us. I looked at the gun on the ground and sat back down. "DeMichael, I don't know what to do."

"Neither do I, Cope. Neither do I. Shit, I need to talk to somebody."

"Am I not somebody?"

"That's not what I mean."

I don't know what he meant. I let it lie. "I need to get back to the church," I said. This time I started for the door, making sure to sidestep the rifle.

"You know where it'a be at, though," DeMichael called after me, loud enough to wake somebody. I looked back. He nodded at me.

I nodded back.

*

My phone was all full of texts asking the same question: "Cope, where are you???" Running the half mile back to the church, I didn't know what I wanted, but I didn't wanna plan shit. I had no intentions on digging around in the dirt and finding DeMichael's rifle, though, I can tell you that. It was a plant, not a plan, that gun. And like any plant, I could choose not to mess with it, just leave it in the soil. But that plant made me not wanna even think about planning. I opened the church doors anyway.

Inside that piece, I could see that everybody had either peaced out and promised to come back by morning or was fully focused, sitting like clenched fists as they debated tomorrow's plans. Along with Keisha and Free and several folks I had never seen before, the planning circle that I came back to included Ms. MacDonald. It still caught me some kinda way to see that many folks who ain't really know each other collabing that close.

Shit went late. The church emptied out except for those who fell asleep in the pews and the seven of us up in the pulpit. Like a C student, I stayed up just enough to catch the basics. The plan was actually simple when you peeled away all the personalities and focused on the fundamentals. Redwood Homes is designed in a simple four-dimensional box with the three buildings that stand there now, plus the one they'll build when they tear ours down, set off into four quadrants. An electronically controlled gate rings the buildings. The west quadrant faces downtown. The east quadrant faces a side street and, beyond it, the rest of deep East Oakland. The south quadrant faces the water and the airport and whatnot, while the north quadrant gates open onto the boulevard and the ruins of Ravenscourt. Miguel was murdered on the sidewalk outside those Ravenscourt-facing gates. Already a ghetto altar of rosary beads, a statue of the Virgin of Guadalupe, several skeleton Santa Muertes, a few empty liquor bottles, and a couple baby pictures of Miguel stood there. This memorial would be the center of the protest, it was decided, because it was highly visible but set off from the road, not impeding no traffic, legal as a law book. For those folks who didn't fear arrest, though, a second action was planned that would block traffic at the entry/exit points for the east, west, and south quadrants. This was where most drivers entered and exited the complex because it was off the boulevard.

"Drums," Keisha said.

"Drums?" the whole circle asked.

"Yeah, drums. We need to make some noise, let the Redwoods know."

"Let them know what?" a man in a Habitat for Humanity jacket asked.

"That y'all cain't hide in the buildings y'all done built on top of our bones and not hear about it."

I nudged Keisha but she ain't budge. It was clear she wadn't gettin' sleepy, not one bit. But my brain was worn out by everything that was happening. I tried Free, whispering, "Peace, loved one, I gotta get some sleep."

"You cain't sleep," she hissed back. She grabbed and held me down.

"The drum reaches everybody," Keisha said. "Slaves used the drum to communicate and plan escapes and revolts. The slaveholders never understood what the rhythms meant."

The name-branded organizers from Habitat for Humanity and Black Excellence and other organizations I ain't heard of didn't say anything to that history lesson.

I looked at Keish, who looked at Free, who looked at me.

"Oh, hell nah. Y'all not about to have me playin' no damn bongos at this rally," I said.

"Nah, you ain't got na'n rhythm, my nigga. But we can put you in charge of finding whoever's gonna play the drums," Free explained.

I was too tired to debate it. I pushed away from the circle and found my way to an empty closet. I curled up inside it and shut the door and set my cell phone alarm to ring in two hours, and I closed my eyes and tried to let myself fly away for a little while.

But I was only walking along the street where Miguel fell. Toward the ghetto altar. I bent down to give my offering, an unspent shotgun shell. That was when I felt the weight of DeMichael's rifle strapped over my shoulder. The sky was that hard metallic blue that if you could taste it it would be like cold steel on your tongue. The air was crisp with morning. The marine layer was hours from fading. My feet knew where I was headed even if my head didn't have the slightest understanding. This rabbit-ass mind of mines. I came to the gate that led to the front entrance to Redwood Homes. This was where I had always entered Rockwood, except that back in the day, way back in the day, there wadn't no gate separating the Rock from the world. Things was different now.

I tried to open the gate, but it was locked with a code that I didn't know. I tried squeezing between its bars, but they was spaced so close penniless Jesus hisself couldn't slip past. I thought to climb it, but it rose too high. Since the gate barred me out, I set my sights on the clock that rose from the center of the complex on a high pillar. REDWOOD HOMES, its etched insignia read. I took DeMichael's rifle from my shoulder and sighted that mug. It was time. I aimed and fired and the recoil threw me to the ground like Vista backhanding me back in the day. Meanwhile, the bullet flew for what felt like no time and forever. An explosion broke open the clockface and giant shards of glass flew every which way. In the clear of day I could see that the shards was the picture of the world: the sky, the sun, the oceans, love and betrayal and murder and the license to commit murder, and the power of the state and the power of the people, all imaged. I seen people, the people in the church that night, and other people, too, Momma, of course, and the women from Daddy's porch stoop salon, and you, Jacq, I seen you, too, brighter and beautiful as the morning sun. I seen Miguel, his braids catching the air perfect as anything and flying past the sky, just like in the song. I sat there in wonder, marveling at how one shot could scatter the whole world. And then one shard, big as a truck tire and sharp as a knife blade, came flying for me. I wanted to look at the image it held. My instinct was that it had to be the old man coming toward me, finally ready to reveal hisself. I went to stand up to see him better. I watched it fly toward me and waited for the spinning shard to turn sideways so I could see him, but I realized the shard was flying too fast, it was too close to me, and it would never turn. Wadn't no time to dodge out the way. I didn't see Daddy. I seen my death instead. I seen my own image, the rabbit, and then the hunt was over and I knew that death was coming for me, and I thought of a book about the power of myths that I had read in the Youth Control and later in a high school class. Every people has an origin story, the author proposed, and in each story it's a hero at the center who is born in the womb and dies as he's borne wailing from that womb into the world. Then later on he dies from his childhood to his manhood, and then he dies from his manhood to his sacrifice for his people. I thought of that literature and I knew that my death had arrived. The only thing left to do was embrace it.

I came back to life sweaty and nervous as a crackhead, and boom-bapped my head against the side wall of that damn church storage closet. That woke me the fuck up and brought me out my dream and back to basics. I checked the time on my janky phone: four in the A.M., hopefully accurate for Oakland, not the Caribbean.

I wanted to think about the dream, what it might mean, but I knew Keish would slap the sleep out my eyes if I didn't figure out this drum situation. I dipped between church pews till I came upon Mr. America and his crew. Good money: these were some real performers. They were all bangled up in the old red, white, and blue costumes like they just came off the train, which maybe they had. They lay in layers upon each other, all arms and legs and torsos crisscrossed like old railroad tracks drove deep into the street. Mr. America's face was jammed what looked hella uncomfortable into the back of the pew, which stuffed up his nose and made him snore. When he snored, his bangles jangled in rhythm—everything about these boys stayed on beat.

I shook them awake, and the whole crew tumbled like dominoes to the floor. Mr. America landed on his bad shoulder and grunted in pain. The whole crew came to pulling theyselves apart, cussin' up a storm and promising vengeance. Then they looked up at me.

"What up, family? Why you wake us up? What hour is it? I thought y'all said eight? Sun ain't even out."

"Y'all can drum, right?"

"Yeah, sho nuff."

"Where can we find some drums?"

"Basement," Mr. America said. "What church don't got a basement?"

We used our cell phones to navigate the church's underworld, eventually coming to a locked door marked MUSIC.

"Ca-gotdamn-ching."

"Called it like a mug."

*

Everyone in the church was awake by 6:30. We proceeded out to the Redwood Homes under a cold-ass orange-red sky. It didn't look like morning, that's for sure. It looked like afternoon and midnight shuffled together, like a dream that I was dreaming while awake.

I looked across the crowd as we moved toward the Redwoods and the Rock. Hella folks from the Rock and other parts of East Oakland headed up the procession. Keisha and Free walked together. Vista and Ms. MacDonald marched arm in arm, waving flags that read INVESTIGATE THE COPS and SHOW BODY CAM FOOTAGE, respectively. I peeped a few people from Pied-montay in expensive school gear and wondered if they was there for well or for ill. Guzzo and Deadrich and some other businesspeople was there for PR purposes, bringing up the back, they own little briefcase-and-bankroll squad.

Chants went up from the Rockwood folks in the front, filling the air. I heard Keisha and Free close to me. They was talking, not chanting, about the sky above, and a fire, and the way the whole world seemed to be falling in on us.

I didn't talk to nobody, didn't chant nothin'. Again, that feeling had came over me like I was watching the whole movement of people and our message, our mission, and the signs held high that said it all in so few words from outside and somewhere above my body. Even amidst all the marchers, I was alone, alone with my actual dream and the rifle and the clockface breaking away and my mind wandering back again and again to DeMichael and his rifle. Big man was right, somebody had to hold it. My hands was empty and I felt how heavy emptiness always is, the worst weight in the world.

I looked across the heads of the people. Amongst the African wraps, dreads, bald heads, and signs reading JUSTICE 4 MIGUEL, JUSTICE 4 MIGUEL, JUSTICE 4 MIGUEL, I didn't see his face. I knew better'n to expect him to be out here marching. Brother man had told me exactly what he thought of our protest—that it wouldn't do nothin'. I took note of my fellow marchers and felt the same: How could all these people, so different in so many ways, really all be on the same page? Of course they was here together to stand against a boy being shot down like a bird out the sky, but what else did they have in common? What else could they come together over but to mourn Miguel? What strategies would they agree upon to stop the same from happening in the future? How many of them in the back was paying for they own private po-lice, putting these trigger-happy fools in the streets all over Pied-montay and now even guarding compounds and gated apartment complexes in East Oakland? How many might call the cops on some boys dancing, like Deadrich's friend did, and jump out the window when the cops roughed him up and folks got angry about it? Was that man in our march? I didn't know his face from Adam, so I cain't tell you if he was there, but I wouldn't be surprised if he was. People's sympathies wadn't the same as they priorities. How many of these people was gettin' evicted in the same month they got they diploma? How many of them was forced into the priorities that me and Keisha and Free and DeMichael faced? And even if all the marchers did somehow agree on enough things to protest injustice with a solid purpose, what was our little, half-created crew gonna do head up against a Hercules organization like the po-lice, especially the private po-lice, who was fully suited and booted, trained and organized to a military level? How could we do anything to change or overcome them when they had all the power?

DeMichael wadn't wrong. That rifle of his wadn't wrong. But it wadn't right either.

*

We blocked the housing complex from all four di-rections. Partitions. Picket signs. And bodies, peoples upon peoples upon peoples. The Escalades and Teslas that was set to drive thru the open gates got blocked in. Redwoods residents lay on they horns and cussed us out. But we held our line.

I stood on the sidewalk before the boulevard, arm in arm with two Mexican women I cain't say I seen before that day and definitely ain't seen since. The sky painted both of they brown faces the colors of fire. It painted the whole human wall of us somethin' both magical and nightmarish. I heard a voice behind me say somethin' about social distancing like we was still living in '20 and it caught me how deep some fears run amongst us. Fearing the virus. Fearing the po-lice. Fearing ourselves and each other.

Redwoods security rolled up in little two-car teams that couldn't tear open wet bread. They parked right in front of our line, which was right in front of the gates that led to the Redwoods buildings. I felt my biceps pressed backward as our line fell back a little. Maybe the arrival of the cops had people shook. Me, personally, I didn't give a goddamn about being arrested that day. Miguel was gone and so was just about everyone and everything else. I had spent two years ten toes down, avoiding anything that might violate a law, and this was where it had got me, standing in front of a home that wouldn't be mines much longer, head up against a bunch of armed, armored, masked-up po-lice. Private company po-lice. The sky had repainted them as well, in the same radiation-red reflection as everyone else. Maybe it was just me, but in that same glow, they looked so different, so crazy, when I compared them to the people that I linked arms with. Here we were, holding back all these vehicles that cost more'n most folks make in a year, and we looked like folks, just hella people, with no armor, no guns, no corporation insignia from Soclear, no nothin' but the clothes we went to bed wearing. It was a certain menace to these men who stood across from us, hidden from us by all that armor. It was only but so many options with these private security forces—they would either rush us, shoot us, or stand there and take notes on us.

They didn't look like they was fittin' to rush us or pull triggers. For the moment, at least, they was just holding they side of the line, forming a perimeter to the protest. I didn't fear them, Jacq, but I confess that I felt closer to death, to my own murder, than ever before. I thought about that rifle once more 'gin—I didn't need to defend my life yet, but it was no tellin' what the next moments might hold.

Meanwhile, Mr. America couldn't care about no violence, no officers, no masks. I heard his drums calling from the boulevard. On impulse, I broke out from the line and went lookin' for the sound. His drums sounded from the core of the crowd at Miguel's altar. I pushed thru the people, which was easier cuz it wadn't a picket line up there but an audience instead. Trust, my brother had them joints going, singing, hollering, crying, testifying. His bad shoulder was all good all of a sudden, or he had just caught the spirit and was playing past the pain, cuz the polyrhythms he beat into those animal hides sang out like beaucoup gods, beaucoup saints. His crew started singing, which surprised me. In all our train travels, I hadn't heard them bust out with not a single bar. But now they went in singing for real, with voices wild and haunting. Several of the protestors who I had never seen, never met, people who had came from who knows where, some white, some black, and others brown and beige and butter pe-can, they all surrounded the boys and these people sang, too, voices flying to the cold fire and the dark sun above us. I was visited by somethin' I cain't call by name, and I walked up in that mix and the only words

I heard was *love* and *death*, and I started to sing in time, in rhythm and on beat for the first time in forever. And there we all were together in that moment, at that memorial, one wild voice, one haunted heart, one human being. And from deep inside that oneness I held it all suddenly and tragically, the whole protest, the people, the po-lice, the Redwoods, Rockwood, my momma and daddy and every mother and father and child, my city and my country. I remembered the rifle and I thought about DeMichael sitting in the dark, thinking how he could hide it and find it and take retribution, and then I thought about Miguel's face tore off in the street, and my heart broke across all of it and I cried out with the last of my voice.

I pushed my way back thru the people and out the crowd. I lit out across the boulevard, swerving in between traffic. I made my way into Ravenscourt's ruins and searched the rubble, kicking away ce-ment slabs and shards of stucco. I got down in the dirt and dug around, finding screws and bolts and plastic cups and paper plates and anything and everything you might think would be there but that gun. I couldn't find it. I looked some more. Every damn ditch in that mug was an empty grave, a grave without no body. Desperate than a motherfucker, I kept at it, kicking up dust in all di-rections. I'm sure my fingerprints is on aye'thing down there and that don't look good for me. But the reason I was rootin' around like that for that gun was outta my total, two-souled desire to find it and take it apart piece by piece and free all that love and courage up on that boulevard from the one threat of further violence that I could control, and at the same time to hold that tool in my hands, fully assembled, to place it on my shoulder, Jacq, and sight that thing like I meant it and hold one of them boy's, one of them officer's, life in my hands just like they hold our lives so careless and often in contempt every single day. I confess that I wanted that choice.

But I couldn't find the rifle.

A few walls still halfway stood in that massive lot. But only one apartment building wall still stood to its full height, undemolished. I had noticed it the night before, but it jutted out different in the daylight. It's probably twenty feet tall, like somethin' you might see in a schoolbook about World War II and what little still stayed standing after the war was over. On the backside of the wall, facing away from the boulevard, is the skeleton of a stairwell. The railing is gone, but the stair steps is still there linked by a ce-ment base below each step. I didn't know if the steps could support my weight. It looked like a fifty-fifty, maybe so, maybe no. I wondered if I should climb them and find out. I wondered if DeMichael had put the rifle up there—I had no idea.

I went up, my feet touching light on each unsteady stair step. The final step was set just below a window. The window was already blown out, had no pane, no screen, no nothin'. It looked out on that sky and that scene below. I looked into the heavens. It was the most frightening and beautiful thing I ever seen, Jacq. I cain't even explain that vision, the way the sun shone like the sky, taking in its colors, and how such darkness overwhelmed the daylight. And below it, the protestors and the po-lice still waiting each other out, facing each other down like opposing armies, with one side having all the weapons, of course—ain't no fair fights in America, after all. And I could see Mr. America and his crew. I could see the altar beside him and the banners our people had draped across the gates:

INVESTIGATE THE COPS
SHOW THE BODY CAM FOOTAGE
JUSTICIA!
LAND, BREAD & HOUSING
NO JUSTICE, NO PEACE, ABOLISH THE POLICE
THERE'S MANY A MILLION GONE
OUR LIVES MATTER

Insurgency Alert Desk, Third Bureau

In the wake of the killing of an officer of the law during a political rally that itself was ostensibly held in protest of a shooting of an Oakland civilian, numerous persons fled the scene. The protest organizers have been sought as suspects in the shooting of Officer Colt Bergen: DeMichael Bradley, 20, of Oakland, arrested in the ruins of a recently razed housing project adjacent to the Redwood Homes; Keisha Manigault, 18, also of Oakland, arrested the following day in the basement of a nearby Baptist church, where authorities were able to trace her by her cell phone GPS satellite positioning; Ayesha Ali, street name "Free," 18, also of Oakland, boarded a flight at the nearby Oakland International Airport, according to authorities. Ali landed in Detroit and from there made her way to the home of a family friend in Dearborn, Michigan. She was finally captured several days after the shooting because of a tip given to police by the spouse of a family member. The final protest organizer and suspect in the shooting of Officer Bergen, Copeland Cane V, also of Oakland, remains a fugitive. Law enforcement says that Cane is likely armed and very dangerous.

Others detained at the rally include prominent local businessman Douglas Deadrich and Piedmontagne Prep School principal Anthony Kennedy. Both Deadrich and Kennedy were released without charge. Piedmontagne released the following statement via its social media accounts:

> We at Piedmontagne Prep grieve the deaths of both Officer Colt Bergen and Miguel Ngata. It is our understanding that the protest action where Officer Bergen so tragically lost his life was organized with the intention of peaceful protest against police brutality. Our principal joined the protest in this spirit and we support his peaceful protest. It has been determined by law enforcement officials that he did nothing wrong. Piedmontagne Prep upholds the American right to freedom of speech and freedom of assembly. Piedmontagne Prep also values deeply and has extensive ties to California's law enforcement community. Copeland Cane V is currently enrolled as a student at our high school. We have no further comment upon this matter.

The time and place for the public memorial to the fallen Officer Bergen has been set: 8:00 A.M., tomorrow, First Congregational Church of Alameda.

The arrests mark the culmination of a series of events that suggest the depth of Oakland's problems with lawlessness and leftist violence. According to multiple police reports, on the night of May 17, Redwoods security officer and Oakland Police Department policeman Abel Enriquez was executing a routine investigation of a complaint of unlicensed solicitation and drug trafficking outside the Redwood Homes in East Oakland. Miguel Ngata, 19, of Oakland, was detained for questioning by Officer Enriquez. Under Freedom of Interrogation legislation, the right of officers to detain and question in public space is protected. However, Ngata became uncooperative and refused to reply to standard questioning. Officer Enriquez tried to take the teen into custody, at which point the teen, according to reports, cursed at the officer and charged toward him. Officer Enriquez, acting in self-defense, discharged his weapon. The teen died at the scene. The Oakland Police Department has ruled the incident a justifiable homicide. No charges have been brought against Enriquez, who is currently on paid leave.

Social unrest swiftly ensued, leading to the shooting death of Officer Bergen.

Insurgency Alert Desk, Third Bureau

It has been reported by CNN and MSNBC that prior to her arrest, Ayesha Ali placed a request for information related to ballistics and forensic data taken at the Ngata homicide scene under the recently repealed Freedom of Information Act.*

Insurgency Alert Desk, Third Bureau

Authorities have recovered a rifle that they believe was used in the murder of Officer Bergen.

---

*andrewjacksonslaststand010621: Attempts such as this show how deep the terrorist criminals take it b/c they will stop at nothing! It shows how committed we need to be to take them out By Any Means Necessary!!!

Jacqueline:

No, Cope.

Cope:

No, what?

Jacqueline:

No, you didn't. You didn't shoot that cop. You didn't play any role in the shooting. Not any active, creative role, anyway. Those forensics don't mean anything. They don't even start to tell your story. Every piece of *your* story points to DeMichael's involvement, not yours. I know it and you know it. By your own admission, you've only fired a gun once, at DeMichael's direction—other than that, all you got were a couple pointers from that white boy in the juvenile facility, whatever it's called.

Cope:

The Youth Control. If you think it was just a couple convos, you're underestimating how many times two intellectually limited, locked-up muhfuckas can discuss the same exact shit.

Jacqueline:

Only an intellectually limited person would think you're intellectually limited. We both know who did this. Admit it, Cope.

I'll tell you what I believe happened. Let me enter the following into evidence: DeMichael is highly susceptible to law enforcement influence. If the police were looking for someone to disrupt the protest and shift focus from Miguel's murder to the murder of one of their own, then there was no actor better equipped for sabotage than a compromised person like DeMichael Bradley, an individual whom they may have trained themselves. DeMichael's been in and out of various incarcerating institutions since he was all of nine or ten years old. That's more than enough time to have been turned, especially considering the concerns you yourself mentioned around his relationships with authorities that date all the way back to the Youth Control.

The evidence is there, Cope: DeMichael never formed bonds with anyone in the Youth Control except for his childhood friends, whom he already knew. Everyone else rejected him, or he rejected them. He was most closely aligned with the authorities and received certain perks, which is why he was not there in the cafeteria that day when you fought Shawn Barnes, a fight which resulted in the first attempt at your recruitment—well before your days in prep school. You came home from your incarceration and transferred to Piedmontagne. DeMichael bopped back and forth between Oakland and the Youth Control, always unable to keep himself out of trouble. That's a lot of arrests, a lot of charges, and maybe a few deals along the way. Don't you find it unusual that a twenty-year-old black male with such a long juvenile and adult criminal history could even legally possess a firearm and take it with him to hunt? And who do you think taught him how to shoot that weapon? His absent father? His dead grandfather? His half-gone grandmother?

In a sense, the whole purpose and motive force of law enforcement is reactionary, but I would argue that all it would have taken was one reactionary individual to make DeMichael not just another informant in the black community but something much worse. Law enforcement had all the incentive in the world to use him to divert attention from them. The better question might not be if he did it, but whether it was vengeance or under orders.

Cope:
DeMichael ain't do all that complicated shit—

Jacqueline:
I don't know why you're protecting him.

Cope:
Cuz he protected me.

Jacqueline:
That's just a story you tell yourself, Cope. Not every story you tell yourself is true.

Cope:

So what do you want me to do? Roll on a brother who had my back from knee-high, who taught me how to handle myself, who's been thru the same shit I done came thru? And all that when I cain't say what he did or didn't do? You're trippin'.

Jacqueline:

I'm tripping? You're a fugitive on principle. Who's tripping? I swear, you black boys, black men, whatever you are, you will protect each other no matter what—way more than you'd ever protect me or Keisha or any other black girl, or black woman. So, I get that, you're not going to go against your guy based on some sort of misplaced loyalty. Whatever. The only question I have for you is why you want to involve yourself in all this, when you can probably get out of it and get back into some kind of a normal life if you just take it to court? Shit, Cope, is this even about the policeman's murder for you? Why am I even asking you that question?

Cope:

OK, you win, boss. One year you've been in college and I couldn't debate you if I tried. I'm not tryna argue with you, though. I don't have nothin' to argue, nothin' to hide. I bounced, plain as that. Got my ass up outta Ravenscourt and out that whole piece. Ain't seen East Oakland since. As far as where the gun mighta gone to and who pulled the trigger and all that, I ain't said shit and ain't fittin' to say shit about it.

Jacqueline:

So you are hiding something?

Cope:

Nothin' that's mines to hold. You know what I mean? I ain't seen that shit and don't know shit but what I've seen. And I done said all that I've seen.

Jacqueline:

OK, I respect that. But if it wasn't you who did the crime, then what are you running from?

Cope:

A fucked-up, biased-ass jury for one. And friends who'll start flippin' on each other for another.

Jacqueline:

So take the Fifth and don't snitch. The evidence is on your side. I know it and so do you. There's really no reason for you to keep running—is there?

Cope:

It's so much more to it, though. It ain't even about that man gettin' got, may he rest in peace. I don't wanna rent no room in a burning house, Jacq. And this house we call America, either it's on fire, or it's just hotter'n a mug where we stay at. You know what I mean? I'm not tryna argue. I don't have to exonerate myself. I'ma be free. You feel me? Let me finish the story—then maybe it'll make some sense.

Jacqueline:

Go ahead. No one is stopping you from speaking—yet.

Cope:

OK, the end: in Antioch, under a blood-orange sun, I made my way from the train station to the home Momma and Daddy is renting.

When I hugged my momma and told her how much I loved her, she became the first person on record to smile and keep a straight face at the same time. Ain't seen her wake up to joy in a long while. Really, she looked the same as ever, not happy, not too sad, not a pound lost or gained to stress, still thin, with her short hair, her pretty light brown eyes. We hugged and she held me close for a minute, gripping me by the shoulders so I stood suspended in her grasp. I looked her in her eyes and seen how complicated it was up in her soul behind her mask. Then she let me go and I seen the old man. He looked not just old but aged all of a sudden. His face and hands had turnt into the desert floor, light brown skin full of fault lines and depressions and the occasional canyon where his eyebrows fell away and his eyes sat back in the dark cave of his face. He worked his hands in that tense way that I remember from every tense moment in time, the ball of muscle between thumb and forefinger rising like a sudden tumor in his hand.

"I cain't stay here," I said. "I just had to see y'all."

"Did you do it?" Momma asked. "Did you have that man shot? Tell me the truth."

"Nah," I said. "But that don't matter. I don't see how I'ma get a jury of my peers right now. They wanna make it so I won't have no peers."

The old man shook his head. "Gotdamn it!" he thundered, hustling up from his chair in a burst of energy that almost laid him flat, cuz in a moment he sank back into his seat lookin' worse for the energy spent. He didn't look good. He had always been a thin man, but where before he had had so much free energy, now he looked frail and tired and caged by time.

"You couldn't save me," I said. It was the opposite of what I had come there to say to him. I wanted to talk about my accomplishments, but my heart was hurting in deep ways.

"I'm sorry, Cope," the old man said, his voice falling. He looked me in my eyes.

I looked at him without anger. "I wanted to be like you—like you wanted to be. I wanted to save our neighborhood. I wanted to make some ends at the same time. I did do that—the ends—but you ain't even ask how much I made. I worked so hard at that school and y'all wadn't even there for it."

"You know how I feel about all that."

"And you're right to feel it! But the thing of it is, I passed my classes, I won the races, and was all but handed my diploma. But it didn't mean a thing to the hood, it didn't help nobody who needed it but myself, so I tried to make it mean somethin' to someone—to you. But you wadn't having it. And that's the problem: it's no way to work this system and have it mean anything for anybody but me." I held his gaze.

"Cope, the only system I know is gettin' it how a brother was living."

"What do you mean?" I asked.

He seemed to weigh with his rigid jaw the risk of what he would say next. Then he spoke and, Jacq, he said a whole life to me right there. He put it to me like this, that he was from that '80s generation, which musta been the most confused bunch of Negroes in history. His words. He said, like, that he came of age under the shadow of complicated men, men who survived a war that they own government lied them into, and that lie was why when them brothers came home half of them went and turnt to the Panthers, only to see that dream infiltrated and they close partners knocked off by this same government that calls itself our protector. Jacq, he told me how them old heads turnt to they very enemy and got hooked on government heroin and government cocaine. And how the young sahabs, him and his boys and a million others like them, seen those troubled souls and sold them the drugs, not knowin' but a dollar. They wadn't tryna build no community, they was hustling the community, they was harming the community. He told me all this, how he used to hustle up in the Tenderloin in the city and in Ravenscourt in the town.

"I moved to L.A. a hustler cold-blooded," he said. "Money-minded. Criminality-minded. Met the wrong woman (and I for damn sure was the wrong man), so I stumbled into my family responsibilities, and then I had no choice but to hustle. Got locked up eventually and had to defend myself once I was in that mother. Caught another charge, which is why won't no employer hire me now. My record's got records—a few rent strike protests is mixed in there, too, but mostly it's dirt I did. Cope, I had to give my life up to find a new one. I came back home, met me a better woman (and made myself a better man), and we had our own son. I wanted to lead you better'n I did my first children when I was young and stupid and wadn't fit to lead no one. I wanted to teach you to make yo' own and have yo' own so it won't even matter if these fools who run these businesses don't wanna hire no one darker complected than theyself. I wanted everything for you—I still do. I had dreams. I had plans. I wanted to save the Rock, or at least do somethin' for it. I wanted to use what I had learnt to teach you how to help somebody. I wanted you to be yo' own man and I wanted to show you what that looked like by my example. But we cain't teach what we don't know. That's black folks' problem: we don't know shit. I was the wrong messenger, just a old hustler not even knowin' how to turn over a dollar in this changing world. I failed you and I apologize from the bottom of my heart, Cope. You already outdid me by a mile, boy. Ain't nothin' left for me to teach you."

I took all that in, Jacq, or as much of it as I could. I knew him finally, my old man, and ain't even matter to me how ashamed he felt cuz of his past, cuz I know every man and woman got they past and the next perfect person will be the first. The only way the old man ever did me wrong was not to let me know him. And then when that wall he had built and maintained came falling down right there in that house in Antioch, it felt like more of my world might make sense. It felt like I could be true to myself, which is all that matters, not no judge, not no jury and po-lice and records and documents and shit.

"You a leader, boy," he said. "You did that protest. You stood up for your friend, may that child rest in peace."

"When Miguel got got—"

"Say less," Momma said. "We know you ain't kill nobody."

"These people want me dead, though. That's why I cain't turn myself in."

"Yeah," Daddy said, "definitely don't do that shit."

I caught myself about to laugh and let go his gaze, and all of a sudden, I felt the future arriving. I looked around the living room where we sat and it was so bare. None of his things was there. The loose papers and old notebooks and tapped-out laptops and cardboard and pasteboard and this and that and the other. I seen how much of it was missing and I realized how much I missed the sight of his half-created ideas, the buckets of thoughts spilling everywhere even if they ain't go nowhere, or at least seldom did. None of it had came with them from Oakland. That father who I never really knew but by his commands was gone, and in his place was this revealed and frail old man. He sat there open to me, and I wanted to praise him and mourn him and mourn the god that died so that I could see the man for who he truly was. I felt the air in the house lose all its tension, like all the smoke and fires that was hawkin' us was put out with one bucket of water. And I didn't know whether what I had found in Antioch was better or worse, but I knew for damn sure it wadn't the same. And it wadn't just my old man and it wadn't just the home that was different. I thought about how much I had changed. It had been a long time since I had stood in the old man's home with his presence my sun, his word my scripture, his rule my law. I realized then that my changes couldn't be put down to the island or its poison, but that it was a more complicated maturation that had changed me over many years and across many environments, not suddenly, but slowly, into myself.

"I have to leave," I said.

"To where, though?" Momma asked. She looked out the kitchen window at the unnatural sun, and I followed her eyes into what looked like a whole 'nother world.

"I don't know," I answered her. "Out there."

"The boy gotta lay low, Sherelle. He understands how to move. He needs to get where he can see them but they cain't see him, where he can speak freely and then say his side."

I nodded with each word he said.

Soclear Broadcasting
Insurgency Alert Desk, Third Bureau*

We come to you from inside First Congregational Church in Alameda, California. As we look in on this rather remarkable and of course altogether tragic sight, you, the viewer at home, can see the processional making its way up the aisle. Dignitaries and the deceased's family will take up the frontmost pews. Here is Officer Bergen's wife and their two wonderful young children. American hearts are broken. We've all fallen in love with this grieving family. We mourn with them.

Behind the family you see the processional continue: the mayors of Pleasanton, where the Bergen family resides; Oakland, where Officer Bergen, of the Oakland Police Department and of Redwood Homes

---

* andrewjacksonslaststand010621: This is America.

private security, a subsidiary of Soclear Security, was murdered; and Alameda, where the funeral has begun.

The head of the Fraternal Order of Police, former Allan Creek Township police chief and National Security Administration regional administrator Antonio Marciano, leads the representatives of law enforcement. Here comes the Oakland police chief. Also, all of Officer Bergen's fellow Oakland beat cops are here. These are the men who patrol our roughest streets and keep the good citizens of this tough town safe day after day and night after night. If you're hearing some rather passionate cheering in the background, that is because the embattled officer Abel Enriquez is part of that group dressed in full police uniform. Officer Enriquez was involved in a tragic confrontation with an Oakland street thug that precipitated the mob action in front of the Redwood Homes in East Oakland where Officer Bergen was murdered. You can hear the pastor calling the congregants to order, but some things aren't about law and order, like honoring our brave police officers whether currently serving, under investigation, retired from the force, or fallen in the line of duty.

And now we have the governor entering to a smattering of cheers and jeers. We might not agree with his liberal politics, but it is safe to say that the jeers are in poor taste given the gravity of the moment.

Coming to the stage is Antonio Marciano. You see the congregants rising to applaud Mr. Marciano as he makes his way up to the pulpit. Let's listen.

"Policing ain't easy. The thin blue line is the only barrier between the good people of America and the immorality and chaos of the criminal underworld. It is the job of our police force to hold that line with integrity, with justice, and, where necessary, with appropriate force. We keep the people safe from the bad guys, simple as that.

"Colt Bergen graduated from high school, and instead of going the easy route, enrolling in a university and getting blind drunk like the average twenty-year-old, he went in a different direction. Now, in fairness, if I had to listen to the enemies of the state who teach college, I'd probably need to throw back a few shots of tequila on the way to class myself, but that's beside the point. Colt chose to be police. It was either that or the military, he told me. Either he would serve country or serve community. Colt chose community. He graduated from the academy in good standing and went to work. He was an easy mentee, never slacked off or thought he was too smart to learn from those who went before him. Over the years, he made a name for himself, a true police.

"He never fired a shot in anger, a sign of a policeman that knows both courage and restraint. Was good with the mitts, which is something we see far too little of these days. You want to know how to reduce the number of unjustified police shootings and quell civil unrest? Make sure each newly hired officer is experienced in no-holds-barred hand-to-hand combat before they join the force. We need gym wars in our academies. We need fighters. Officers have to be ready to go up close and personal, not just reach for their gun. Colt was one who was not afraid to handle things with his hands.

"Colt was a hero, no doubt about it, just like every man and woman who wears the uniform, police department or private security. A coward took out a hero. A sick animal took out a hero. It's an ugly fact. But it's one that the brave men and women who protect America accept. No, policing ain't easy. But it's what we do. And I promise you that the blue line will prevail. May God bless you and may God bless the United States of America."

You're hearing thunderous cheering for Mr. Marciano.

Now, proceeding to the pulpit we have Mrs. Colt Bergen and Officer Dondra Blanton. Some moments simply deserve our silence. Mrs. Colt Bergen is exhibiting incredible emotional strength simply to be here today at her husband's public memorial, let alone to offer us her words. Officer Blanton, I assume, accompanies her for moral support. It seems like Officer Blanton will begin the remarks.

"Ya know, y'all, it's been a strange few days, a rough few days. Don't nobody on the force wanna experience this tragedy, but we all know it's a possibility every time we put on the uniform. That goes without sayin'. But some things that shouldn't go without sayin' is that Colt wadn't no racist and he wadn't no sexist. He helped train me, a black female, when I came on the force. He was the best mentor a minority could have in this job. Honest, fair, straight shooter. That was Colt.

"Ya know, part of dealing with diversity is being smart enough to understand the different ways different people from different backgrounds come at you. Some of us like sweet potato pie for Thanksgiving, others of y'all like apple pie. And ain't nothin' wrong with either, sugar. Colt was a straight-up corn-fed white boy from the burbs, but if you put in an honest day's work at his side, you was his brother, you was his sister, no ifs, ands, or buts—and he might could just hook you up with some private sector work. See, it don't matter the color of your skin, your sexual preference, or your gender. On the force, we all bleed blue. That needs to be put on the record: blue lives do matter."

"Thank you, Dondra."

Mrs. Colt Bergen is now taking the mic, beginning to speak.

"All praises to Jesus Christ, my personal Lord and Savior. Only the mistakes are mine. I know there were people in the community who pressured Dondra not to speak, just like there are some people on this side of things that don't like wives of officers who speak our minds. So I appreciate Dondra from the bottom of my heart.

"I met my husband during our junior year of high school. I remember helping Colt with a few math problems—math was never his strong suit. I was surprised when he asked me to the Christmas dance because I wasn't a cheerleader or the kind of girl who people praised for her looks. I always considered myself average looking, and guys like Colt aren't average. But Colt asked me out and I thought, Why not?

"If I was maybe not the closest thing to a supermodel, that didn't matter to Colt as much as the fact that I had a good heart and a smart head on my shoulders. I think he saw that I was the kind of girl that he could make a life with. Six years ago, I gave birth to our eldest son, Aryan. Then I gave birth to Abyad, our youngest. They are Colt's greatest contribution to my life and to this world.

"The person who killed my husband was, according to the news reports, barely older than a child. He probably does not know the true meaning or value of life. That ignorance allowed him to commit murder. I don't know what's on God's mind. I don't presume to understand His ways, why He brings certain people into the world and removes others, or why evil is allowed to flourish in this land. I don't believe that that young man who killed my husband was intent on murdering Colt Bergen. I think he meant to kill a symbol of something he hated, that he's learned to hate. Maybe a policeman treated him like he wasn't a human being, or maybe he just watches the news and sees the instances of unarmed black men who have been killed by officers. Police are not perfect; they are human beings with human imperfections. My husband was human, which means he was fallen. Scripture teaches us that we are all fallen beings, that we all must seek forgiveness and grace. Please, if you can hear my voice, hear this heartbroken plea that we see each other for who we are, one life, one person at a time.

"I want to thank the union. I want to thank Colt's police chief, his security team at the Redwoods, and all those fellow officers who were honorable in their service to their community, as well as the instructors who trained Colt in the academy, and his high school and grammar school teachers. I want to thank his parents, who accepted me, the child of refugees, who revealed to me the Word of Christ Almighty so that I might be reborn a follower of the one true God and His Son. I am grateful."

And there she goes, a woman who is the essence of honor, of stoic grace under terrible circumstances. Today, despite her personal tragedy, Mrs. Colt Bergen has risen to the challenge of this terrible moment to mother us all, to tell us as a nation that despite this horror, we as a people will be all right. We still have protectors in this world. We are not truly lost, only finding our way.

And now please rise for the president and CEO of Soclear Security, Inc. Here he is, flanked by heavily armed personnel, at the podium:

"In my executive capacity, it is my honor to address the men and women who wear the badge and protect and serve in both their public and private sector capacities. When Officer Bergen was murdered by a street animal who cloaked himself in political protest, this nation passed a threshold. Law and order came under siege. Police officers came under siege. God and country came under siege. From here forward, I pledge to end the carnage that has beset our urban areas. Here, today, this terrorism comes to an end. The gang violence, drug violence, human trafficking, and animalistic assaults perpetrated on our brave men and women in law enforcement come to an end. Do not believe the fake research from the Marxist university propaganda machines that claims that crime is not skyrocketing. Do not believe them when they tell you that gentrification has changed the demographics of our cities and made them safer. Do not believe them when they tell you that you are safe. You are not safe.

"Our cities are under siege. Gang cartels have made urban America's streets free-fire zones, where women and children are gunned down in cold blood every day. The murder rate has never been higher. Criminals reign like warlords over slum neighborhoods. Homeless, psychopaths, and sex offenders lurk in the shadows. Immigrants and insurgents use racist, antiwhite activist front groups for their destructive mission. How do we bring an end to this carnage? Gentrification alone cannot end the carnage. Mass incarceration cannot end the carnage. Stop-and-frisk cannot end the carnage. We need a War on Urban America to save America. Only this war can bring peace. Our brave men and women in uniform are trained and prepared to retake America, and they will do just that by any means necessary. We are the great insurgency; with God's blessing, we will prevail. May God bless you all and may God bless the United States of America."[*][+]

Cope:

And may God bless Miguel. Where's my man's high-esteemed funeral? That's what I wanna know. Where's this CEO and this Fraternal Order of Police joker when it comes to us? Where are they? Where's the po-lice and the government and these companies when it comes to us? Where are they?

---

[*]andrewjacksonslaststand010621: We need this Man and Marciano! on the same ticket. We need them in the White House! If there has to be another insurrection then so be it.
[+]Insurgency Alert Desk, Third Bureau: Ahead of Officer Colt Bergen's public memorial service, there is major news in the search for a culprit. The state is announcing a single charge of premeditated first-degree murder against DeMichael Bradley. The state is charging Keisha Manigault, Ayesha Ali, and Copeland Cane V as accomplices to murder. Cane is sought as a fugitive from justice.

Jacqueline:
Where are you, Cope?

Cope:
I'm where the priced-out, pushed-out, exiled folks is at, Jacq. Where if they don't kill you or break you, you might just escape to. It cain't be that everyone who been moved out is living in some homeless camp under a bridge. We cain't all been moved back to our people in Louisiana. It's somethin' else for us out here.

California is named after the myth of an island where black Amazon women and griffins rule, but in reality it's an island for all of us who nobody but they momma and maybe they daddy love—for all of us who can confess how scared and scarred and fucked up we actually are, and how much and how long we been wanting to get ghost. This island is everywhere that the powers that be done condemned, done put outta sight and sense, which is why they won't find your boy even if they come lookin' for me with a candle in daylight.

From your perspective back there in the world, it probably seems hella sad that things went down like they did, but from where I am, the truth is that I gave one life up to get another, just like the Copeland Cane that came before me, na'mean? Except I found the freedom in exile that he'll never know. All's I ever wanted was to know the man so I could love him and bury him and be free, and I did that, Jacq.

You know, girl, at first I thought this story was the defense of my character. I was dead set to prove to the people all the reasons that I'm not no monster. But then I realized it don't even matter what people who don't know me and won't never meet me take me to be, not unless they're sitting on my jury, and seeing as I ain't tryna turn myself in, a jury's not in my future no kinda way. I know you believe I can win my case. I don't, but even if I did, I'd still have to live in this bitch, and how you think I'ma do that? I'm just the rabbit—and the rabbit cain't win. I'm just the sacrifice, which makes me the executioner, too. And maybe it's no honor above being chose for the race, your life and death the example, but I for damn sure can think of cooler ways to live and better role models for the young ones out there. So it don't really matter 'bout me anymore, Jacq.

It's only in coming to the end that I realize that this story that was mines to tell ain't mines to keep. I said from jump I would give it up to you and now it's all yours, to do with what you see fit. I just hope someone out there will listen to it and open up they mind a little more. But America ain't fittin' to stand still in a mirror long enough to judge me fair.

Jacqueline:
America can change. I don't want you to disappear, Cope.

Cope:
Jacq, I ain't fittin' to fight these folks forever.

Jacqueline:
I hear you, I hear you. I just want to believe that there's more for you to do and to be if you work through all this in the courts. I want to believe that America is more than this hate and contradiction and all of these escalating tragedies. I want it to be more, which only means that I want us, all of us, and especially you, not to disappear.

Is there more? Are we more?

Cope?

Cope??

Jacqueline
(Later.)

Copeland, despite that sudden end, did not disappear entirely. I made sure of that because I loved his story and, in a certain sense which I hope is not misunderstood, I loved him. I loved his truth, however complicated it may have been.

He told a few lies, that boy, but he held a lot of truths big and small. Small truth: About the encryption level of the Bahamas-based Presage app, he was not lying. Presage is impenetrable; in other words, Cope did protect me. He also left me with whole sole control over the recording.

I transmitted the piece as one gigantic audio file to my email inbox, and then from there I sent it to a Bay Area journalist, who sent it to a voice authentication expert, who sent it back to the journalist, who sent it to law enforcement while simultaneously posting a downloadable version to her outlet's website so that the content reached the public and could never be controlled by authorities.

The forty-eight hours, two minutes, and seventeen seconds of his spoken word autobiography provided all that anyone could wish for either to support or to damn Copeland Cane V. Those who shared his vision of the world and those who wanted him shoveled underneath the prison's foundation celebrated equally the mysterious appearance of the lengthy confessional in equal measure, believing it would bring about the legal result that they desired. More important, law enforcement took notice of the recording as well, which led to Keisha Manigault and Ayesha "Free" Ali having all charges against them dropped. Meanwhile, the investigation into the murder of Officer Bergen narrowed to just two figures: DeMichael Bradley, who remained in police custody, and Copeland, who remained at large.

While it is true that police found both DeMichael's and Copeland's DNA—trace amounts of blood, specifically—on several screws and on the barrel and the trigger itself, a fact which the Alert Desk was only too eager to report in the lead-up to trial, it was also revealed at trial that the fingerprints of two other people were found on the gun as well, those being DeMichael's granny and another unidentified person. With that evidence entered into the record, DeMichael's very ownership of the firearm and his access to it on the day of the shooting came under some question.

At trial, a lot of things came under question. The testimony of Copeland Cane never made it into evidence, but that fact didn't really matter. By the time of the trial, every prospective jury member had already plucked the Cane testimony out of the cloud. Even though Copeland had maintained fantastically that he was a victim of Treasure Island radiation, even though he had been a juvenile delinquent with the priors to prove it, even though he was nearly expelled from high school for violations of athletic department rules, even though he said he didn't see shit on the day of the shooting when in reality he probably did, there was a larger truth that his testimony pointed toward. Copeland's words made people question the objectivity of his and his friends' opponents. It didn't help the prosecution's case that they flew in a whore from Denver who gave ballistics testimony that inexplicably contradicted the coroner's findings. It didn't help that they leaked sealed juvenile records to the press in an attempt to bias the nation before the trial even got under way, or that they announced only half the forensic findings until they were under oath and had to tell the whole truth. I guess our recording wasn't exactly objective either, but given what we were up against, it only served to balance the scales of justice.

Two separate juries hung.

Over the course of those two trials, many in the public, myself included, concluded that neither Cope nor DeMichael but the still unidentified figure who taught DeMichael to shoot actually killed the cop. Possibly a member of law enforcement who sought to break up the protest or settle a score or both: sabotage by sacrifice. Few find the idea implausible since, of course, it's not exactly a secret that they can get away with murder—see Miguel, as just one example: that murder case, which by chronology should have gone to trial before DeMichael's case, was instead never even charged, and as a result it never made it to trial. The body cam footage, if it even existed, was never made public. The police union, the Fraternal Order of Police, Soclear Security, and a social media-generated defense fund claiming more than one hundred donors from California to Australia all backed Officer Enriquez. With his friends neck-deep in their own legal problems and his family too broke for a proper funeral, nobody backed that dead boy. And no, there was no protest movement made out of his murder. Nothing was made out of it but some flower arrangements, a preacher who misquoted Scripture, and an East Oakland burial. It isn't 2020 anymore. Law enforcement knows what it's doing. Cops know what they're doing. The whole apparatus is better organized, better funded, and, as a result, more willing to fight in the courts and the streets and everywhere in between than ever before.

Cope's street protest died almost before it was born, but his testimony lives on. The complete recording in its unedited entirety, I should say, is much, much longer than what's been published. There was a lot more of me in the original. I talk about myself, Copeland talks about me; it was our story, not just his. But all that extra didn't make it through edits—I made sure of that. I wasn't trying to go from a journalism major to jail, after all.

I will confess that Copeland required a lot of editing. Raw and uncut, he's such a mess of digressions and contradictions and hallucinations and obscenities and obscurities that I had to cut away the excess just to make him understandable. This is the Copeland Cane that I believe the public needed to hear. Of course, he simply couldn't be contained—not by me, not by a murder, not by the ways that the media imagined him. Cope was his own creation, way beyond anyone's identifiers.

As for me, I'm as invisible as ever, a disembodied female voice placed upon a made-up male sobriquet. Upon investigation into me, authorities uncovered that there was more than one black girl at our elite prep school. Imagine that. There are, in fact, a select few such girls in my graduating class, meaning that I could be any one of us, or all of us, in composite sketch. Maybe I'm not exactly the girl who's been described in these memories. Maybe I'm not tall and thin and light-skinned, maybe I never went to school in the Ivy League, maybe I'm not quite the girl you've been encouraged to conceive. For now,

I'd like to keep it that way—deus ex machina, until I'm safe enough to tell my story.

The story, Walter Benjamin writes, "does not aim to convey the pure essence of the thing, like information or a report. It sinks the thing into the life of the storyteller, in order to bring it out of him again. Thus traces of the storyteller cling to the story the way the handprints of the potter cling to the clay vessel." I tried to preserve his handprints even though Copeland had surrendered himself to me as clay to do with what I would. I presented him cracks and all, but not uncut, not unedited. I took care in shaping Copeland's narrative so that it conveyed that which I believe he most wanted the listener to hear. I took pleasure in each rambling, unnecessary digression that I deleted and each epiphany that my editing emphasized. Yes, I was his editor and his author in that sense, even if, in the end, I can't say that I know exactly who he was or what he wanted other than to disappear.

I know he wanted justice, then he didn't, then he did again. I know he wanted to bury his father inside himself. I know he loved us all and I know he left us to ourselves. I know he's promised me that he'll return if America can look itself in the mirror and I know that it cannot. I want to believe that America can change and I know that all change finds its opponent in fear. And I know that fear—faceless, blind fear—is really all that keeps Copeland at large—thank you, Soclear.

Actually, thank God that Soclear and law enforcement haven't reunited with the Stolz Jungs movement and re-formed into a Mega-MAGA much worse than what we've already lived through, but even remaining as they are, even if they magically never move another tick toward takeover, they are already a horror show—multiple horror shows, in fact. It's strange how we've simply gotten used to so much horror in America. These are the horror shows that we know, I suppose. Meanwhile, people like Cope, people who see these traditions of terror for what they are and somehow can't make amends and just live like normal, they're the ones who are called crazy.

After editing and releasing the recording, I took note of its reception. I listened to the discussions and roundtables and cross-examinations and closing arguments. I even read the study out of Clemson University authored by two tenure-hunting criminology professors, who advanced the idea that Copeland and Miguel were lovers and that Copeland killed Officer Bergen to avenge his lover's murder, which might be a thing because I definitely do think they loved each other—except for the fact that it was not Copeland, not DeMichael, who murdered Officer Bergen, not to mention the disturbingly homophobic overtones of the professors' analysis. Unlike the professors, I don't want to speculate on the unspoken spectrum that is a boy's sexuality. Leave love out of it, for the moment, at least.

I graduated from college and moved back to California and worked and fucked and ate and slept. Being a gentrifier is a strange thing. You don't even realize that the job you take at the tech company and the rent you pay for your loft apartment and the money you spend at restaurants and rooftop bars are part of something you once criticized. It's especially true when you're of color and you're used to color-coding the crimes of capital, and then suddenly you no longer can—you are amongst the criminals. Your university education in the humanity of white people has somehow resulted in a six-figure income and the right to expel another working-class black family from their neighborhood. People of color had obviously never been one people no matter how much the Democratic Party told us we were. But even black people were so obviously divided by our different wants and needs.

I always wanted to have a great mind, to understand my world in large and encompassing ways, but the more I lived, the more granular everything became, most of all my understanding of myself. I understood that I was a complicated woman. The contradictions that had so irritated me when I found them in other people I now saw in myself. I had adult relationships where sex, companionship, love, and betrayal made their imprint upon me. I began to see my own faults and shortcomings in the failings of others. The feelings that I had held for and against black boys and black men like Copeland eased in that self-reflecting prism, and I started to see him specifically as less epic and less catastrophic and more human in his impacts.

I found myself engaged to be married to a black man, but it fell apart for reasons that I won't get into here, reasons that don't make black men any easier to love. Anyway, I ran away from that reality and went to law school. I ran away to and from a lot of things. In those years studying in graduate school, I thought I had left behind not just the mystery of the murder but the whole idea of whoever Copeland was. I guess in relegating him to my past I was mimicking, however faintly, what the world around me had done with him. Like the discarded things that make up the landfill that packs the Bay Area's islands, Copeland was buried alive by the news cycle, which moved on to other events, and by the processes of the justice system, which classified his case cold and moved on to other murders. Officially, he remains a fugitive. But the Insurgency Alert Desk that serves as America's public record of crimes against itself rarely reports on him. New threats have emerged amongst us; new wars have been declared against ourselves.

During my 1L year in law school, word reached me that Copeland Cane IV, Cope's father, had passed away in Antioch in the apartment—they could not afford to keep the house—that he shared with Sherelle Rowland, Cope's mother. I did not attend old man Cane's funeral and do not know if a young man who knew everybody, yet who nobody knew, watched quietly from the back row, but I do know that when I got the news on social media I exploded in tears for the father, for Ms. Sherelle, for their son, for the tragedies that bind us more tightly than love. I saw Tulsa in my tears. I saw a neighborhood a hundred years older than ours burnt to the ground, boys born guilty and men shot and women widowed and wounded, and trauma encoded in our blood. I saw that community breaking apart into the pieces that put Copeland on the run and put me, well, here, where I can write all this. I decided not to mourn but instead to do something easy with myself. I cleaned, or I read something trashy, or I called up a friend. But behind the mop and bucket and bleach, behind the novel, behind the man inside of me, I saw the helical ghosts turning loose inside our bodies, I saw our bodies unbound from one another by history, brought back together in deception and infiltration and incarceration in a new world where the Greenwoods and Rockwoods are not even a memory anymore. I want love, I want marriage, I want children. But I want a world to love them where whatever we have is not under investigation, or at risk, or subject to sanction; where life's death sentence is an abstraction, not your naked hand on a hot coal burning.

I applied to doctorate programs in Europe and Australia only to find, like my ancestors, that America would not let me go—a job offer came along that was too good to sensibly refuse. I work in fin-tech or entertainment law or something like that, something with a salary that would allow me to house and feed three families in Kansas if I lived in Kansas. I live on the East Coast somewhere, in a big city full of people and money and power, and nobody cares where I came from or why I'm here.

Even though I live far from the Bay Area, I keep tabs. Social media, like death, is inescapable, so I am well aware that Douglas Deadrich is now the principal at Piedmontagne Prep, Kennedy having been ousted after revelations about his multiple sexual affairs with teachers directly under his supervision. Deadrich has also gone into business with Michael Guzzo; ironically, and unwittingly, it was Copeland himself who brought them together. And now, together, the two of them have built hundreds of units of low-income, government-subsidized housing on Treasure Island. The apartment complexes have social justice–themed names, which is kind of cool, I guess. Perhaps Deadrich and Guzzo see this as the last best means to alleviate the Bay Area's housing crisis, and they are simply unwilling to allow the perfect and unpolluted to be the enemy of necessity. Maybe Cope and his father were wrong, maybe no lasting harm will come to the residents of that island. But I have to side with Cope on this one: something about that place just is not right. At any rate, I hear rental units on the island are in constant demand. Business is booming.

In his time in our common world, Cope faced an array of authorities who thought they knew him better than they did: Principal Morgan, Judge Khan, that warden woman, whatever her name was, and Mrs. Greenberg and Principal Kennedy and others. Most of these people must be either retired or at least eyeing their pensions by now. Maybe at such a stage in life no news is the best news. Even the notorious Sarina Jayachandra Campbell-Zayas managed to land on her feet after the demolition of Rockwood, the closure of its high school, and the termination of her visiting lecturer position at the university. Ingeniously, Campbell-Zayas has enacted a move down the colleges and up the ranks, recasting herself as a community college president in one of those California desert towns where there are more prisons than schools and anyone smart enough to lie about having a college degree probably deserves to preside over the education of others.

But I don't think all of Copeland's acquaintances and associates have fared so well as these privileged few. I've heard rumors for years that Ms. McDonald's father, he being the businessman who owned and then sold Rockwood to the developers who razed it, actually wrote his daughter out of his will because of her participation in the protest rally where the policeman was shot. I believe she teaches English overseas now, or something like that.

Meanwhile, Rockwood's former residents and the boys of the Youth Control have even more totally disappeared from my radar, either because they're dead and I don't know it or because we simply move in such dissimilar circles that there's no way my informational path will cross with theirs. I have no idea what's happened to Vista and Trey and Keisha's crazy people and the barber who climbed out of an Oakland pothole to cut a frightened child's hair one afternoon. "Time," Georg Lukács writes, "can become constitutive only when connection with the transcendental home has been lost." Or, as Copeland himself said, the world that he's from and that I came to know long enough to know him doesn't exist anymore. That is true and I feel its death like a ghost flying inside of me.

I have this dream—it recurs whenever I begin to forget it. I'm in my last year in law school. I sit at a coffee shop downtown, textbook in my hands. I am studying for a law and ethics course. And then two shadows appear before me, darkening the text. I look up and I recognize the masked shadows. "Keisha and Ayesha?" I ask, even though Cope's descriptions of both of them are etched so permanently in my mind that despite their masks the question is unnecessary. "I thought you were dead." They look at me silently; of course they are not dead. "Is he dead?" I ask in a rush, but of course he is not dead. "He's here, isn't he?" I whisper.

They do not answer.

I scan the square that surrounds the shop for his face, or a mask with which he might disguise himself. I see the students who scatter the square, their heads drawn down into their texts. I look to the bootleggers, the can collectors, the panhandlers, the drug merchants. So many marginal people. Cope could be any one of them, man or woman, black or blacker, legally or illegally involved. *Boy,* I think, *boy, boy, boy, you are here.*

I turn back to the two women. I want to ask them if America's changed enough for the rabbit to reveal himself, but as I begin to speak, Keisha raises her hand, signaling for my silence. I hold my question. She and Ayesha turn and walk away, and I can do nothing but watch them go. They move quickly across the square and disappear around a corner or into a crowd, and then I see at my feet a folded piece of paper that I pick up. It is folded incredibly complicatedly. I fumble with it, trying to figure out its design. I pull it apart at its edges and tease it out a little at a time. Unraveling it takes a lifetime and I can never quite get it all the way open, but in the preliminary interior folds, I read like scattered truths the words "love" and "Cope" and "rabbit."

The dream ends.

What does it mean, Dr. Freud?

Well, I guess it means not a thing since I can never unravel the whole complicated message. Perhaps Copeland Cane V is the rabbit, the African trickster god who came with us to the islands and then to America, showing us how to survive. Or perhaps he's the rabbit in the track race that leads the pack and dies by preordained decree. Take your pick.

But it's my dream, so maybe I should be the one to do what I want with it. I'll refuse to interpret it. I'll leave it there as is, a statement of the mind, that part of the mind that holds itself against interpretation. That's all. Cope gave me his story, so I can do whatever I want with it, remember: I can destroy it or ignore it or forget it. But of course I couldn't do those things even if I wished to. My heart tells me not to forget but to place him upon the public square and to leave him there for the people. That's what he wanted: to put his words out to the people, even if they refuse to listen, even if all they'll have him as is a dead man and maybe a murderer.

It's too painful, all this old shit from years ago, I swear—but I will say this one last little thing about the dream. My thought on it is simple: love. Simple love sent from Copeland Cane to me and to all his people, all the good and bad and suffering people on this rock that spins and spins in darkness carrying us upon it. It is love I reciprocate, however distantly, however difficultly. It was part of my destiny to love and to free that innocent boy, and I confess that that is exactly what I did in my quiet way. When I dream around him to this day, I confess that it is still that boy that I see. It is that boy that I knew. Enter that into my record—àṣẹ.*

---

*Insurgency Alert Desk, Third Bureau: Copeland Cane V remains a fugitive from justice. It is unfortunate that he has become a symbol of sorts for a new wave of radicals, anti-state anarchists, black identity extremists, etcetera.

Keenan Norris is a novelist, essayist and short story writer. He holds an M.F.A. from Mills College and a Ph.D. from the University of California, Riverside. Keenan was a 2017 Marin Headlands Artist-in-Residence and has garnered a Public Voices fellowship (2020), a Callaloo fellowship (2016) and two Yerba Buena Center for the Arts fellowships (2017, 2015). He teaches American Literature and Creative Writing at San Jose State University and serves as a guest editor for the Oxford African-American Studies Center. He is the editor of the seminal *Street Lit: Representing the Urban Landscape*. Keenan's short work has appeared in numerous forums, including the *Los Angeles Review of Books, Los Angeles Times, Alta*, popmatters.com, *BOOM: A Journal of California* and several anthologies of California literature.

@unnamedpress

facebook.com/theunnamedpress

unnamedpress.tumblr.com

www.unnamedpress.com

@unnamedpress